Mary Angela Dickens

A Mere Cypher

A novel. Vol. 1

Mary Angela Dickens

A Mere Cypher
A novel. Vol. 1

ISBN/EAN: 9783337066932

Printed in Europe, USA, Canada, Australia, Japan

Cover: Foto ©Andreas Hilbeck / pixelio.de

More available books at **www.hansebooks.com**

A MERE CYPHER

𝔄 𝔑𝔬𝔳𝔢𝔩

BY

MARY ANGELA DICKENS

AUTHOR OF "CROSS CURRENTS."

" Nor are those empty-hearted whose low sound
Reverbs no hollowness."

IN THREE VOLUMES

Vol. I.

London

MACMILLAN & CO.

AND NEW YORK

1893

CHARLES DICKENS AND EVANS,
CRYSTAL PALACE PRESS.

This Story has been published in Serial form under the title "A MODERN JUDITH." It is now republished under the title originally intended for it by the Author.

A MERE CYPHER

CHAPTER I.

ALL day long, from heavy February skies, drizzling rain had fallen, and now that evening was closing in it was falling faster than ever. There was no break to be seen anywhere in the grey clouds, and daylight was giving place at least an hour before its time to that most dreary twilight which is, in part, the coming on of evening and, in part, the darkness of a rainy day.

It was only four o'clock, and to the station - master of the little station at Thornsdyke—an official whose conclusions

were adhered to with a tenacity worthy of
the length of time occupied in their formation—unseemly vagaries on the part of the
weather formed no good reason for any
such variation in the station routine as
would have been involved in the lighting
of the lamps half an hour earlier than usual.

No conceivable quantity of gas, not
even the brightest sunlight, could have
made of the station a cheerful spot at any
time; and now, in the depressing half
light, it presented a most prosaic and
unpicturesque picture of dreariness and
desolation. It was a very small station,
and it seemed to have been dropped into
the midst of the surrounding country with
no particular end in view—that is to say,
there were no houses, not even a cottage,
near at hand to suggest inhabitants to
whom it might be a convenience. The

surrounding country was rather flat and bare. And the uninterrupted stretch of dripping landscape fading away in the distance into a grey blur of rain; the un-interrupted stretch of grey cloud above, which seemed to be settling lower and lower over the earth as though to shut out such light as remained, seemed to emphasize at once the insignificance and the dreariness of the poor little forlorn station with its two wet platforms, its two diminutive buildings, and its dripping signal-box.

There was not a human being to be seen. The wet platforms were deserted, the wet road which led to them was deserted too. Nor was there any one in the waiting-rooms — which were very moist inside as though their constitutions were not cal-culated, as indeed they were not, to withstand so persistent a downpour. The porter had sought refuge and companionship in the signal-box, and the station-master was revolving abstruse problems before the fire in the little den behind the ticket office. His eyes were shut.

The rain outside fell steadily and drearily, and a cold, gusty wind rose and howled round the station, and by-and-by the down train signal fell with a dull clash. The porter emerged slowly and reluctantly from the signal-box, pulling up the collar of his coat as he came, the station-master opened his eyes and appeared in the doorway, and a few minutes later the train, wet and dreary-looking like everything else, steamed slowly up.

Nobody had arrived along the road prepared to get in, and for a moment—as the porter, standing as well under cover as might be, called out the name of the station as though he were well aware that the remark interested no one—it seemed as though there were no one to get out. Then the door of one of the first-class carriages opened, far down the train, and a young man got out.

The porter was exchanging comments on the weather—not of a benedictory nature—with the guard at the other end of the platform; and for a minute or two the solitary arrival stood still, his tall figure in its dark overcoat sharply outlined against the dreary grey background of rainy landscape behind him, looking along the platform in the gloomy light to where the grey landscape opened out again, as though uncertain what to do. Then he shifted the rug he had flung over his arm into a more manageable position and began to walk up the platform, hailing the porter as he moved.

"Portmanteau in the front van; brown; name, Strange," he said laconically, as that functionary, having covered the space between them in so short a space of time as was only to be accounted for by his intense astonishment at the sudden appearance of so unexpected a phenomenon as a first-class passenger, stood touching his cap before him. And the lad turned away in search of the luggage thus described, with a mental comment drawn forth by something indescribable in the solitary traveller's voice and manner.

"A real gentleman, too! Had ought to have been met, I reckon."

He turned his head, partly to take another look at the real gentleman, and partly to look along the deserted road for

the carriage which, as he expressed it,
"had ought" to have met him, and added
to himself: "Why don't he go under cover,
instead o' standing there? Seems like as
though he didn't know it was raining!"
Then with a grin at his own pleasantry,
Tom Wilson, commonly known in the village
as "Tom-at-the-station," dived energetically
into the luggage van.

But, indeed, his last comment on the
new-comer was by no means unreasonable.
A few yards from where the latter stood
the open door of the waiting-room offered
a certain amount of shelter, at least, from
the rain, but the traveller remained where
the porter had left him, his rug still over
his arm, his hat pulled rather forward over
his forehead, as if quite unconscious of his
own discomfort. He had not even looked
round to see if shelter was within reach,

and he was still standing motionless, his dark overcoat shining with the fast-falling raindrops, when "Tom-at-the-station," with the brown portmanteau over his shoulder, returned to him with increased alacrity.

"There comes the carriage, sir!" he announced cheerily, indicating the road along which a dogcart, still at some distance, was advancing rapidly. "You're for the Castle, sir, o' course? It's the Castle dogcart, sir!"

The traveller started and turned instinctively, apparently to look in the direction indicated.

"The Castle!" he said quickly, almost roughly. "No, no! I'm not for the Castle." He paused, and then as though movement and speech had waked him to full consciousness, he said: "There is no one here to meet me then, I suppose? No one from Dr. Custance?"

There was something rather strange about the manner in which the last words were spoken. The traveller's voice, which was young and pleasant, became a trifle hard and constrained as he spoke them with a somewhat overdone assumption of unconcern, and the effect of the words themselves upon the porter was no less perceptible. "Tom-at-the-station" withdrew his eyes suddenly from the advancing dog-cart and fixed them on the figure by his side with as much change of expression as his face was capable of.

"Dr. Custance?" he said. "Oh, you're for Dr. Custance's, sir?"

"I said so, didn't I?" was the response, given with a sudden flash of anger as hot as it was apparently unprovoked. "Now, what's my best way to get there? I don't want to stay here all night! I suppose there's no way of getting a conveyance in this confounded hole ?"

By this time Tom had become aware that his superior was watching the colloquy with a slow curiosity from the door of the waiting-room, and motives of policy urged him to share the interest of the position. His expression showed that it was a keen interest.

"You'd better speak to the station-master, sir," he said, with a glance at the portly form in the narrow doorway. "Mr. Moore, he'll know what you'd ought to do."

The young man turned as though to put the suggestion into effect, and then he stopped suddenly and, turning away from both porter and station - master, stooped down to turn up his trousers. "You can ask him," he said, and Tom, without waiting for a second bidding, moved hastily away with the alacrity of one who has news to impart.

He had just made his communication in a gruff whisper, as though some motive of delicacy made him desirous that it should not reach the ears of the traveller, when the advancing dogcart was pulled up suddenly at the station gate, and putting the brown portmanteau hastily down in the waiting-room he hurried out to meet it, leaving the traveller and the station-master alone together. There was a moment's pause. The young man, to whose ears two words of " Tom-at-the-station's " whisper had penetrated—" the doctor's "—was standing, again apparently with no consciousness of the rain which was being dashed against him now by a sudden gust of wind, his back to the

waiting-room door, and as much as could
be seen of his face between the coat
collar he had pulled up and the hat he
had pulled down, white and set. The
station-master, a man of mind, according
to his fellow-villagers, was also a man of
deliberation, and a minute or two elapsed
before he said, as though he were advancing an incontrovertible discovery of his
own :

"You're for the doctor's ? "

"Yes."

"They ain't met you ? "

"No."

The monosyllabic answers were given
in a restrained tone which seemed to in-
dicate that the temper which had flashed
out upon Tom Wilson was only under
temporary control; and the negative was
followed by a silence. The silence was

broken by "Tom-at-the-station," returned as hastily as he had departed.

"It's Mr. Edward!" he said, addressing his superior, with a backward glance to where a good-looking young man on the box - seat of the dogcart was restraining the impatience of the horse whilst the groom made some arrangements behind. "He's driven down for that there box from London. How'd it be to tell him as how they haven't met the gentleman? He'll pass the doctor's on his way, and I reckon he'd save the gentleman the five miles' walk, such a night as this."

Tom had lowered his voice and put up a rough hand as a shield to his words, with a side - glance at the straight back of the traveller, as he made the suggestion tentatively enough; but before he could receive from the station-master the rebuke

he evidently half expected, the young man
had turned suddenly upon him.

"You will do no such thing!" he said,
almost fiercely. "I prefer to walk." He
looked for an instant toward the cheery
young fellow on the dogcart, and then
drew suddenly back out of the line of
sight as though anxious to avoid any
possibility of such an invitation as Tom
Wilson had suggested for him.

Station - master and porter alike con-
templated him with open-mouthed astonishment, broken in upon the next instant by
sounds of departure from the dogcart, and,
that interlude over, they were free once
more to concentrate upon him their un-
divided attention. The train which had
brought the stranger had steamed slowly
on its way some minutes earlier, the dogcart, taking a sharp turn, disappeared from

sight, and the little station resumed its previous appearance of dreary, dripping quiet, but for the little group of men that now stood on the platform. The station-master and his assistant did not apparently find themselves prepared to offer any further suggestions or to do anything but gaze curiously at the young man in the dark overcoat, and after a moment's pause the silence was broken by the latter.

"Which is my best way?" he enquired tersely.

"You'll find it a good step, sir."

"Which is the best way?"

"Well," began the station-master impressively, and then, apparently considering that the directions he was prepared to give would be too weighty for the mental capacity of the recipient, he turned to his subordinate and said: "Tom, you just take the gentleman to the gate and put him in the way to the doctor's."

Almost before the last word was uttered the traveller had turned and was walking down the platform to the little wicket-gate, and Tom, with another tug at the collar of his coat for some protection against the rain, followed him hastily. The directions as given by him were neither long nor complicated.

"It's pretty straight nigh all the way, your road, sir," he finished. "But it's a bad road an' no mistake—particular towards the end."

The young man laughed—a low, harsh laugh.

"So I've heard," he said, and "Tom-at-the-station" wished that his face was not so invisible between the dim light, his coat collar, and his hat. "So I've heard. Thanks ; good evening!" And he was striding out on to the muddy apology for a path when Tom Wilson stopped him.

"Beg pardon, sir," he said, "but won't you leave your rug and have it sent up with the luggage ?"

Pulling up suddenly and glancing down at his arm, the young man seemed to become aware for the first time that he still carried his heavy rug.

"Thanks!" he said, as he gave it into Tom Wilson's hands, and then his hand went into his waistcoat pocket and out again towards Tom. "Good night, my man," he said, in the pleasant tone in which he had first spoken, and which had elicited the porter's first approving comment.

"Thank ye, sir. Good night to you!"

responded "Tom - at - the - station." He
lingered a minute or two, in spite of the
rain, watching the receding figure, and
then he turned and ran back to where
the station-master still stood in the waiting-
room doorway. He did not return to his
refuge in the signal-box. Apparently a
common subject of interest had arisen
between him and his superior, for they
disappeared together into the warm little
fire-lighted den behind the ticket office,
and the little wet platforms lay once more
wet and deserted in the fast-falling rain
and the fading light.

CHAPTER II.

THE rain was blown in his face by the wind, the puddles through which he passed splashed up round him as the quick drops pattered in them, but the young man kept on his way with no more apparent consciousness of the active discomforts of his present position than he had shown in his passivity on the platform. Out in the open with the straight road stretching in front, and a rain-blurred expanse of country on either side; with a cold wind howling and shuddering in the few creaking, swaying trees; with twilight closing in with every moment—the dreariness was indescribable.

C 2

But the young man strode along, never
varying his heavy, regular movement, never
moving his hands from the pockets into
which he had thrust them, looking neither
to the right nor to the left.   He had
covered three miles in the same heavy
absorption, when the road before him
suddenly branched off to right and left,
and he pulled up abruptly.

"Right or left?" he said to himself.
"Which did the fellow say?   Wasn't I
attending, or—memory going, I suppose."

By this time it was nearly dusk, and
though, as he stood there looking keenly
along each of the roads before him, certain
words spoken by "Tom - at - the - station"
concerning landmarks came back to him,
it was impossible to distinguish any object
that was not in the immediate foreground.

"Confound it all!" he said to himself,

as he gazed at the two roads before him,
and back at the one along which he had
come, in a perplexity which their appearance
in no way helped to lighten. "What am
I to do? The village must be somewhere
near. I suppose I must go on till I meet
some one or come to a cottage. Hullo!"

He was moving slowly forward with a
backward glance over his shoulder when
he uttered his concluding exclamation and
stood still again. Coming towards him
through the dusk, slouching through the
mud and rain with heavy, tired footsteps,
was a man with a carpenter's basket slung
over his shoulder, and turning towards
him the traveller stood waiting, evidently
intending to ask his way. Nearer and
nearer came the footsteps; the man came
up to him, cast on him the dull, uninterested
glance of the unintelligent countryman, and

passed on; passed on unquestioned. The question the traveller had waited to put found no utterance when the time for words came, and the slouching footsteps dying away in the distance left him once more alone with his perplexity. They had quite died away before he moved, and, pushing his hat from his forehead for a moment with a strangely despairing gesture, only to pull it further over his forehead again, he strode suddenly forward, choosing his road evidently at random and taking that to the right.

Half an hour more passed and he was still striding along an apparently endless road, by this time in nearly total darkness, when he stopped again and turned his head as if to listen. "What a fool I was!" he said to himself bitterly. "Why couldn't I ask the fellow?" He listened again. "Wheels!" he said to himself. "Now, Norman Strange, no more confounded humbug!"

He drew back to the side of the road and stood there, with his hands thrust once more into his pockets, as the lamp of what seemed to be a spring-cart appeared round a turn of the road and came nearer and nearer at a good round pace, the wheels and the tread of the horse making a swishing sound in the mud. It was still some yards distant from him when he called out:

"Hullo, there! Is this the road to Thornsdyke village?"

There was no answer. The lights came on until they were close to him; then they stopped, and a clear, strong girl's voice called back as a gust of wind caught the trees near and howled wildly through them:

"What part of the village do you want?"

It was a light spring-cart, and the young man could see, now that they were close to him, that its only occupants were two women. They were cloaked and waterproofed until it was impossible to judge of their figures, but as the young man, lifting his hat, stepped forward hastily, the light from the lamp fell on the face of the one who was driving. It was the face of a singularly handsome girl, so brilliant in colouring, with its bright complexion, luxuriant, reddish brown hair, and large, brilliant dark eyes as to be almost startling, set in such sombre surroundings.

"Where are you going to?" she demanded peremptorily, and her accent and tone, like her beauty, were essentially of the people.

" Pardon me for stopping you ! " he said. " I have walked from the station, and I must have missed my way, I think. Can you tell me the way to Dr. Custance's house ? "

Again, evidently in spite of himself, his tone altered as he spoke the last words, and as it had come to the porter's face and manner, so a change came to the face and manner of the girl whose flashing black eyes were fixed now upon the figure before her —soaked by this time through and through.

" Dr. Custance ! " she repeated. " Oh ! " She paused and looked him curiously up and down as though she would have liked, as the porter would have liked, to see the face so obstinately concealed. " You're not far," she continued. " Take the first turning to your right and you'll come to the house in a few minutes. It's about a mile."

" Thank you."

Not raising his face to her as he did it, the young man stepped back to let the cart go on its way. But the girl had caught a glimpse of a white, good-looking young face. With a slight glance at her companion — a much older woman — she said quickly :

" Won't you have a lift ? We're passing the house, and it's a poor night for walking."

" Thanks, no. I prefer to walk."

He lifted his hat again and turned to proceed on his way as the girl, with an injured toss at once of her head and the reins she held, put the pony she drove into its former sober trot. The young man did not hear her comment to her companion as the cart passed him, nor did he hear the response :

" Just come down !"

" Poor young fellow !"

He fell once more into his heavy, regular stride, and ten minutes later he had groped his way through a garden gate that seemed as it swung back to do so on but one hinge, had passed between dripping, sighing trees up to a house with a light in one of the lower windows only, and was ringing the bell.

There was no response to his first peal. He heard the sound of the bell reverberate apparently in empty premises and die away into silence ; he waited a minute or two and then he rang again. This time sounds in the house followed, and a moment later the door was opened by a rather untidy maid-servant.

" I am Mr. Strange," said the young man, in a hard, constrained tone, moving past her as he spoke into the dimly-lighted little hall. " Is Dr. Custance in ? "

Apparently the house was not remarkable for the thickness of its walls for, as he asked the question, a door at the end of the hall opened quickly, and a tall, fair man came out hastily.

" Mr. Strange ! " he exclaimed. " I had no expectation of seeing you to-night. I am delighted ! My dear fellow," he added, as he shook hands with his visitor with a warmth which found no response in the young man's hand-clasp, " my dear fellow, you are wet through ! Is it possible that you have walked from the station ? Come to the fire in my smoking-room and let me understand how such a wretched misunderstanding has come about. I am more sorry than I can say ! "

" The fault was mine, no doubt ! " returned

the young man courteously, though his voice was hard and constrained. "Thanks, if you don't mind I think I will go to my room at once and get rid of these wet things."

Dr. Custance turned to the servant who was still standing by.

"Is Mr. Strange's room ready, Ellen?" he said. "You know, the one at the end of the passage—next to Mr. Caton's."

"There ain't no bed made up," was the response given, with a mixture of confusion and alacrity. "Nor no water, nor nothing, but——"

"Take up what is wanted at once," returned her master; "and bring a lamp, quickly. Or, stay, I will take this," lifting an oil lamp from the hall table as he spoke. "This way, Mr. Strange, please."

He led the way up a staircase, as dimly lighted as was the hall, and the young man

followed him along a passage until he opened
a door.

"This is your room," he said. "I am
so sorry it is not more comfortably prepared
to receive you. I suppose the post office is
at the bottom of the mistake?"

"My letter must have missed the post,"
answered the young man in the same constrained tone—a tone that contrasted
strangely with the easy pleasantness of his
host. "I wrote to you yesterday, but "—he
paused a moment—"I was late, I know, in
posting it."

Dr. Custance received the explanation
with a smile.

"Well, the only thing to be done is
to make you as comfortable as possible
now that you are here," he said. "What
can I lend you? We are much of a size,
are we not?"

They faced one another on the words,
and, as though glad, each in a different
way, to take advantage of the opportunity,
looked one another over; the elder man
with keen curiosity, the younger with a
heavy, almost painful, momentary interest.
They were, as Dr. Custance had said, almost
exactly the same height, but the differences
between them in breadth and build were
very marked. Dr. Custance was a man
apparently of about five-and-forty, rather
broad in build, and with a certain
looseness and absence of sharp outline
about him that suggested an inactive life.
His face was very handsome; long in
shape, with admirably cut features and
rather indolent grey eyes. The mouth was
hidden by a long, fair moustache. The
younger man, now that he was divested
of his dark overcoat, was an active, well-

made figure, with a capital carriage, but rather too thin. The hands, too — strong, nervous-looking hands—were thinner than a young man's hands should be, and his face was absolutely haggard. His hair was dark, and the contrast seemed to heighten his extreme pallor; his eyes, sunken now, and with heavy shadows beneath them, were dark, too. He wore neither beard nor moustache, and his features were rather irregular. It was a good face, however, in spite of the expression of heavy, almost sullen, stiffness and self-restraint. It sat oddly and most unnaturally upon it, and seemed to battle all the time with something in his eyes which was, or might have been if he had allowed himself expression, something strangely pitiful.

The battle of expression went on in the new-comer's face during all his host's offers of dry clothes, during all the little stir and movement attending the production by the agitated maid of the various toilet necessaries, and it was going on still when Dr. Custance, telling him that supper would be ready at half-past eight, finally shut the door and left him.

He stood for a moment motionless, looking towards the door as though realising the fact that he was alone; and then his eyes wandered slowly round the room—a bare and rather dingy room which the servant's hurried efforts had failed to make either comfortable or attractive. His glance rested for a moment on the dreary paper, the worn carpet, the shabby, scanty furniture, the empty grate, without apparently taking in anything that he saw. Then he walked in a mechanical, preoccupied way across the room, as though to lay something down on the table there. He stood

still and put out his hand, and then quite
suddenly he dropped heavily into a chair
that stood by, and, laying his arms on the
table, let his head fall forward on them
with a low, despairing groan. Time passed
on, and still he sat there motionless, his
face buried in his arms. Nearly an hour
had gone by when the sound of a bell
ringing downstairs startled him suddenly
to his feet, and, as he moved, the expression
of misery, which softened his face and made
it most pathetic and attractive, changed
suddenly into a hard, fierce recklessness,
which altered the whole man indescribably
for the worse. Such changes in his dress
as were absolutely necessary he made hastily
and roughly, but he did nothing further,
and his whole appearance as he laid his
hand on the door was strangely uncared
for and disorderly. He caught sight of

himself in the looking-glass as he turned to leave the room, and his mouth grew harder and more bitterly reckless.

"What does it matter?" he muttered to himself. "What does anything matter, now?"

He opened the door and went rapidly downstairs, pausing as he reached the bottom as if in uncertainty. Then he caught sight of an open door leading into a lighted room and went towards it. He passed across the threshold and stopped short.

It was a drawing-room, small and not particularly well or tastefully furnished, but looking in the warm light of a bright little fire and shaded lamp very pretty and comfortable. There was a piano at the further end, several little feminine odds and ends were strewn about, and on a low chair near the fire, her back towards the young man as he stood in the doorway, sat a lady.

For a second or two the young man hesitated, and the reckless hardness of his face was touched by a mixed expression of astonishment and annoyance. Then he came slowly into the room, and at the sound of his footstep the lady turned with a nervous start and rose hastily.

"How do you do?" she said, holding out her hand nervously.

With the ready, deferential courtesy of a well-bred man, which sat oddly upon his disorderly figure, the young man shook hands with her and made the conventional response in a manner in which the natural instinct of the man seemed to break through the hard, almost sullen constraint which had grown upon him with every moment that had passed since his arrival.

The lady before him was a little woman, dressed in an old black silk dress that was neither fashionable nor becoming. She had a small, worn, faded face, which might once have been pretty, but which in losing its girlishness had gained nothing in character or intelligence. There was no trace of youthfulness about it, but neither were there any of the usual signs of age—no wrinkles, no crowsfeet, no grey in the smooth brown hair which was drawn plainly off her face and knotted behind with scrupulous neat-ness, but after a fashion that suggested a total absence of consideration of any other effect in the wearer's mind. Her figure, though the dress she wore effectually dis-guised the fact, was slight and undeveloped as that of a young girl. The blue eyes which she lifted to the young man's face as he spoke to her were so ill-assured as to be almost frightened, and her manner was equally ill-assured as she continued :

" My husband will be back directly. He was here a moment ago. Won't you—won't you sit down ? "

" I am hardly fit to sit down in a lady's drawing room, Mrs. Custance,", answered the young man, regarding himself with frank disapprobation.   He spoke very pleasantly and courteously, and with a smile, as though he was altogether surprised out of the mood in which he had left his bedroom ; and any one who had seen him in both phases would have realised that this was the man in his normal condition.   The sullenness and the recklessness had alike disappeared completely, displaced, apparently, by the impulse of courtesy to a lady, obviously innate, and so suddenly and apparently unexpectedly called upon ; and his face was very attractive under its present aspect.   The last words were evidently spoken at a venture, and he con-

tinued quickly : "I do hope you will excuse
me. I had no idea—I mean I did not
know—Dr. Custance has always taken it for
granted that I knew he was married. I am
afraid I have kept you waiting in the first
place, and in the second, I am not fit to be
seen."

Mrs. Custance was apparently not prepared for such an apology. The blue eyes,
which were neither quick-looking nor intelli-
gent, glanced at the young man with a slow
surprise, and she murmured something incoherent as she subsided into her chair.

"I hope my unannounced arrival this
evening is not inconvenient?" went on the
young man, as he followed her example and
sat down.

"Not at all," she responded hastily and
deprecatingly. "I—I am sorry I was out."
There was a moment's pause, during which

the blue eyes furtively scanned the face before them, and then she spoke again, evidently with a nervous consciousness that she ought to say something, and a nervous incapacity for thinking of the right thing to say.

"I am so sorry you have to wait for supper," she faltered; "Dr. Custance will be here in a moment. He—Mr. Caton is not well, I believe."

She coloured very faintly as she spoke, and the young man suddenly flushed to the roots of his thick, dark hair a deep, painful scarlet. There was another pause—an awkward one this time apparently—and then the silence was broken by the voice of Dr. Custance as he came quickly into the room.

"So sorry to keep you waiting!" he said. "Shall we go in to supper?"

His wife rose hurriedly and moved towards the door in silence ; and the young man, with the natural, easy impulse of a gentleman, held it for her to pass out. As she did so she lifted her eyes to him again with the same vague surprise with which she had received his apology.

CHAPTER III.

THE house which was known in Thornsdyke village as " the doctor's," was a large and rambling building which might possibly, from its appearance, have started in life as a cottage, and developed by degrees to its present dimensions, or which might have been originally the substantial farmhouse of well-to-do farmers. It did not look particularly substantial now, nor did it look as though its present tenants were particularly well-to-do. Its white plaster surface was much discoloured, in many places in actual need of repair; and there was a pervading air of dilapidation of which the details were slight enough in themselves, while the whole effect was singularly depressing.

The best-kept of country houses could hardly have looked anything but depressing on the morning following the unexpected arrival of "the doctor's" guest. The rain had stopped indeed, but only recently, and nature seemed to be in a momentarily quiescent state ; pausing, as it were, all dripping and heavy, before passing into another and brighter state of activity. The dull grey clouds still hung over the earth, and beneath them everything had a watery, almost sodden appearance.

The garden surrounding the doctor's house, as neglected as the house itself, looked particularly dreary under these circumstances. Its principal feature was an uncared-for lawn, surrounded on two sides by untidy flower-beds, and on the other two by an equally untidy gravel path.

At the end of this path, at about nine o'clock on the morning after his arrival, stood the doctor's guest.

It was nearly an hour since he had come out of the house to wander restlessly about, and he had come to a standstill at last, his face expressing perfect fellowship with the dreariness, atmospheric and actual, before him. His eyes passed slowly from the barren landscape to the neglected garden; from thence to the dilapidated house; and there, in the window of the dining-room, a long window on a level with the path, he saw his hostess, a small, ungraceful figure, no inharmonious element in the picture, in its dull drab gown. No such change as the unexpected presence of a lady had brought to his face on the previous evening came to it now, but he made an obvious effort, unsuccessful enough, to lighten its expression as he lifted his hat to her courteously. The bow with which she returned his acknowledgment of her presence in the window was hurried and nervous, as though she had not been prepared for such a necessity as she stood there watching him. She was evidently waiting breakfast for him, and he moved quickly, though with none of the elasticity that the step of so young a man should have possessed, towards the house.

Three years before Norman Strange had taken a good degree and left the University one of the most popular men of his college; a cheery, impulsive, generous-hearted young fellow. He had had his full share of the wide and somewhat quixotic views of life, the fixed, and — to their originators—unalterable opinions, the ambition at once high-minded and impracticable, which should characterise youth. He had numbers of friends, with all of whom he was on the same genial terms of good-fellowship to the exclusion of any one intimate friendship ; but he was singularly poor in relations. He had neither brother nor sister, his father and mother had died in his boyhood, and his guardian during his minority had been his mother's only brother. Of his father's relations, the only two remaining were elderly unmarried ladies, possessed of considerable wealth, and living very quietly in the Lake district. Between these ladies and his guardian there was a feud of long standing, and Norman Strange in consequence knew little of his aunts. His uncle, Mr. Kingdon, was a bachelor and a prominent Q.C., a man with few sympathies, on whose original hard and narrow severity, an extended professional

acquaintance with the weakness and wicked-
ness of human nature had had no softening
effect. He had seen little of his nephew and
ward during his boyhood, and when the latter
finally came to London to start in life there
was no affection between the two, hardly even
familiarity; nothing but respect, and a chilly
sense of distance on the young man's part,
and a certain cold interest on that of his
uncle.

More by reason of his uncle's tacit
assumption that such was his obvious destiny,
than through any natural aptitude of his own,
Norman Strange was entered at the Temple.
The law seemed to him as good a field as
any other; a distinguished Q.C. or a learned
judge having apparently as many opportunities as most men for benefiting his fellow-
men. If he could not candidly assert that the
entire bar and bench took advantage of these

opportunities, of course there was no doubt in his mind that he himself would do so. He established himself in very desirable bachelor quarters and applied himself with enthusiasm to the study of the law.

He was a very good-looking young man in those days, far better-looking than the thin, haggard Norman Strange who arrived at Thornsdyke on that February evening. There was a dash and fire about him that was even more attractive than regularity of feature. His manner was excellent. His uncle had taken care that his social as well as his intellectual education should be of the best kind, and the result on a temperament naturally chivalrous and refined was the production of a very finished gentleman in the best sense of the word. Such introductions as his University connection left still to be desired, his uncle, a man of the world himself, and keenly appreciative of the advantages to a young man of a footing in society, supplied to him. He was universally popular, and went about a great deal, combining work and play with inexhaustible energy.

Nearly two years passed, and then Norman Strange developed a fit of excessive studiousness. He refused all invitations, shut himself up in his chambers, and worked at his profession with feverish energy. The attack was the first visible effect upon his ardent and uncompromising youth of a gradual realisation of the heavy drudgery involved in legal study for a mind with no special aptitude for it; and it was followed by the inevitable reaction. Having overworked himself considerably he took a complete holiday, and he took it in the wrong company. There was a set of young men

with whom he had just kept in touch after
a slight college acquaintance, but whose
gaieties he had rather avoided as being "too
rapid for a working man," as he explained.
During a holiday, however, with the general
slackening of moral tension involved in such
a proceeding, and the vague desire to forget
his distaste to the work to which he must
eventually return, he saw no reason against
accepting any invitation he received.   In the
set into which he went thus as part of the
general change and relaxation of his holiday,
it was "the thing" to drink a great deal
more champagne and a great deal more
whisky than had ever been the custom with
Norman Strange, and the latter, doing at
Rome as the Romans did, found the effect
very satisfactory in its stimulus of spirits and
energies really rather jaded by overwork,
and in the freedom it involved from that

constant worrying doubt as to his suitability to his profession. He grew to look forward to and to count upon the exhilaration common in a greater or less degree to all the members of his new set after a dinner or supper. He had been excited, quarrelsome, incoherent again and again—phases to which his present companions were well accustomed in one another—when at last the climax came.

A dinner was given, by one of the set, from which Norman Strange rose something more than excited. He had an engagement for a dance, at which he expected to meet a girl a little flirtation with whom had formed another feature of his holiday, and in spite of the laughing advice of a friend more self-possessed than himself, he insisted on departing forthwith in a hansom to keep it. The drive or an instinctive sense of absolute necessity

steadied him to some extent, and he presented himself to his hostess to all outward
appearances his usual self. He found the
girl he had come to meet, exchanged
greetings with her, asked and was promised
a dance, and was holding out his hand for
her programme when she suddenly drew it
back.

"I — I'm afraid my card is full," she
faltered, and then as a partner came up to
claim her, she turned away hastily without
another word or glance.

With the half-stupid consciousness that
she had "noticed something," ashamed
without knowing why, there came to
Norman Strange the instinct to pull himself together, and he went down to the
supper-room. Half an hour later and he
was still there, but by that time he was
drunk, noisily, horribly drunk, and the

men - servants of the house were doing their best to get him quietly out of the room.

The house was one to which his uncle had introduced him, one of the most popular centres of a good "set." When Norman Strange woke from his drunken sleep next day, he woke to the consciousness that his fall was known to, at least, half his acquaintance, and upon his agony of despair and self-loathing came a peremptory summons from his uncle. He obeyed it mechanically, to hear from that gentleman, who had himself been one of the witnesses of the scene of the previous evening, a short, stern speech delivered without the faintest touch of pity or tenderness, to the effect that he had disgraced himself beyond retrieval, and that nothing remained for him but to go abroad for a time immediately, previously sending an abject apology to his insulted hostess. The early part of the speech was as the voice of doom itself to the wretched young fellow, who listened, standing with his head bent, his face ashen, trembling from head to foot. It formulated his own conviction. The latter part he hardly seemed to hear. He turned away, on a dry contemptuous dismissal, without a word and went back to his chambers.

He had tried his strength severely by his course of overwork, and his subsequent course of dissipation had not tended to restore it. Physical weakness reacted upon his mental force, and he was utterly powerless to bear up against the intolerable sense of shame that crushed him to the earth.

During the two months that followed

he hardly left his rooms; he saw nobody,
he did no work.   Humiliated and degraded
already in his own eyes beyond all hope
of redemption, it mattered nothing to him
in his despair how much farther he fell.
He had even a kind of bitter satisfaction
in each fresh proof of his own worthless-
ness.   He drank, not wildly or desperately,
but with a heavy carelessness of consequences and a miserable longing for
forgetfulness—the only good life any longer
held for him.

After rather more than two months had
passed, his uncle, who had taken it for
granted that his advice as to the advisability
of leaving the country, had been followed,
found out his mistake.   He heard through
a servant a highly-coloured account of his
nephew's present life in all its vice and
none of its misery.   It was an account which,

to a man of his temperament — cold and irreproachable—was inexpressibly disgusting; as given of a young man for whom he was to some extent responsible, it was a keen humiliation.

He went to his nephew's chambers, and what he found there—Norman at his very worst—was not calculated to soften his cold anger and contempt. " The boy " had "gone to the devil," he told himself, and there was nothing to be done but to keep the disgraceful fact as quiet as possible. Accordingly, a day or two later he had another interview with his nephew—the latter sober this time, but silent with the sullenness of absolute despair—in which he half proposed, half commanded, that he should leave London and live " for the present," as he put it drily, in the house of a certain Dr. Custance, of whom Mr. Kingdon had heard through a client. Little was said about this Dr. Custance by Mr. Kingdon, except that his references and terms were satisfactory, and that he was in the habit of receiving dipsomaniacs. It was tacitly understood by both uncle and nephew that the idea of cure or reformation—whichever word might be most applicable—was nominal only, and that the words used by Mr. Kingdon—"you will put yourself under the care of Dr. Custance"—were a mere phrase; and Norman Strange had assented heavily to the proposal, as though nothing was any longer of consequence. Six months before his life had been all before him, bright and full of promise. Now it was as though a heavy pall had descended upon· it. Energy was dead, hope was dead, self-respect was dead, and with these had gone all that made life worth living.

As he stood in Dr. Custance's garden
on that February morning his only hope
was that that life itself might soon be taken
from him.

CHAPTER IV.

THERE was the same heavy restraint on his face, and it was little less white than it had been the night before, when he entered the dining-room where breakfast was waiting.

"I am afraid I have kept you waiting again," he said to Mrs. Custance, as she turned hastily from the window on his entrance.

There was none of that reversion to his old self which had been produced by his surprise at his first meeting with his hostess on the previous evening, but his grave, toneless voice and reserved manner

were perfectly courteous. Then, as Mrs.
Custance, deprecating his apology to herself
with a nervous murmur, glanced towards her
husband as he stood before the fire, he added
to the latter a formal "Good morning."

The making of small talk was no slight
effort to Norman in his present state, and
he was heavily conscious of something wrong
in the breakfast-table conversation that
followed — something that suggested that
the trio who should have been engaged
in it were entirely unable to strike a common
chord. His remarks to his hostess seemed
to embarrass her. She replied in mono-
syllables only, with nervous glances at her
husband. Dr. Custance was ready enough
to talk, but Norman's instincts of courtesy
forbade the total ignoring of the wife apparently involved in conversation with the
husband. Dr. and Mrs. Custance and

Norman Strange completed the party. The other inmate—the resources of the White House enabled Dr. Custance to receive only two—the Mr. Caton, to whose indisposition Mrs. Custance had alluded on the previous evening, was, presumably, not sufficiently recovered to appear at breakfast.

It was a relief to Norman when breakfast was over and Dr. Custance rose. The next moment he was wondering wearily what he should do, when that gentleman looked round from a cursory inspection of the weather, and said easily :

"We must have a little interview by-and-by, Mr. Strange. If you would like a cigar will you go to the smoking-room now ? —you know the way—and I'll come to you there in a few minutes."

Norman Strange flushed hotly—the deep, painful scarlet of the night before—and he glanced instinctively towards Mrs. Custance, who had just risen from her chair. He could not see her face, and he answered evidently at random in a low, hurried voice, in which there was a tone that was almost reproof, and, turning away, left the room.

In the hall outside, with the door closed behind him, he paused for a moment irresolute. He had nowhere definite to go, nothing definite to do. He might as well smoke, he told himself, as anything else.

He moved listlessly along the winding, uneven passage that led to the smoking-room, opened the door, and went in. Dr. Custance had shown him the room with the rest of the house on the night before, but he had hardly looked at it then. Now, glancing round it, he saw that it was a small room, comfortable looking, though everything in it was more or less shabby. There was a long wicker chair, plentifully supplied with shabby cushions, at right angles with the fireplace, in which a bright fire was burning. There were several other luxurious-looking chairs, and Norman Strange let himself sink into one of these and slowly took out his cigar-case. He lit his cigar and began to smoke, letting his head fall back against the cushions of his chair.

His most prominent sensation; during the first reposeful moments following on the painful strain of breakfast, was one of physical lassitude. On the previous night, almost for the first time for two months, he had gone to bed sober, and he was missing in every fibre the stimulant to which he was accustomed. But after a few moments, from his sense of physical discomfort and his realisation of its cause, his thoughts, vague and indefinite enough, and becoming not less so as he smoked and they drifted, passed to what had induced that cause.

He had been inexpressibly taken by surprise by the presence of a lady in Dr. Custance's house. For two months he had not spoken to a lady; he had come down to Thornsdyke prepared to shut himself up in a bachelor household, where in the society of the fellow " patient " he should find company for which he was fit, as he told himself bitterly ; where no depths of degradation to which he might sink would cause surprise or disgust ; and where the end might come to him when and how fate would. The presence of Dr. Custance's wife was a factor on which he had not calculated, and the current of his reckless self-abandonment had been, for the moment, arrested on the night before by the unexpectedness of the circumstances in which he found himself. Short as had

been the evening before he went to his room
—perhaps because it had been so short, and
the first impression of a womanly atmosphere
was still so strong upon him—its influence
had held him fast. He could not drink—he
could not " make a beast of himself so soon,"
he had muttered to himself ; there was a lady
under the same roof ; how near him she might
be he could not tell, and he could not do it.

He sat on now smoking, and his thoughts,
from a vague, indefinite consideration of the
night before, gradually narrowed and focussed
themselves round the actual woman in
question. He had no definite impressions
with regard to Mrs. Custance. Even her
personal appearance was not very distinct to
him. Considering her now, carelessly enough,
he decided that she was a very nervous little
woman, and perhaps not particularly intelli-
gent.

"It must be a dull enough life down here to stupefy any one," he said to himself, thinking for the first time for weeks of something unconnected with himself; and then remembering certain little significant signs and tokens in her manner of receiving his attention which seemed to imply that Mrs. Custance was not used to such courteous respect as came naturally from him to a lady and his hostess, he thought to himself how soon men living out of the world grow careless with women; and suddenly his face flamed again as it had done on Dr. Custance's speech about their interview after breakfast.

"Before his wife!" he muttered to himself. "How could he?"

The thought recalled him indirectly to himself and his own affairs, and his mind turned to the interview before him. He had finished his cigar, and his expression, which had softened slightly under the influence of physical weariness and impersonal meditation, grew harder and heavier moment by moment. A touch on the handle of the door made him lift to it a pair of eyes that were at once sullen and desperate, and the next moment he had risen to his feet with a face which he rendered suddenly, by a strong effort of self-control, perfectly impassive. Mrs. Custance was standing hesitating in the doorway.

"I beg your pardon," she said, "my husband wishes me to say how sorry he is that he can't see you just now. He is obliged to—to go out. He will see you when he comes in, he says."

She said the rather unnecessary last words evidently with the irresistible impulse natural to some people to repeat words that are painful or difficult to utter. She had coloured faintly, and she was painfully embarrassed by her obvious consciousness of the object of the postponed interview. It was evidently no want of consideration but sheer nervousness that made her, after letting her eyes wander round the room as she spoke, finally fix them on his face.

"Thank you," he said, "it is most kind of you to take this trouble!"

She made no direct response, though she paused a moment, uncertainly, as though feeling that she ought to do or say something. Then she said hurriedly:

"My husband told me to take you to see the village—if you would care to go. He may not be in until late this afternoon, and he thought you might be dull. If you would care to go with me——"

She stopped. There had been something curiously humble and self-depreciating in her shy tone which turned the polite refusal with which Norman Strange had instinctively prepared to reply into the words :

" It is very kind of you, Mrs. Custance It will give me great pleasure."

" Then would you mind coming soon— I mean in about half an hour ?" she said. " I have to go down to the shop then, and, besides, it may be raining later on."

With a heavy sense that all times were alike to him, Norman Strange assured her that he was entirely at her service, and the slight, drab figure disappeared. Twenty minutes later he stood in the hall waiting for her as she came downstairs.

" You've been waiting," she said, lifting her eyes to him as she reached him, almost as if deprecating his annoyance.

"Why not?" he answered lightly. "May I not carry your basket?" he added, holding out his hand as he spoke for the little covered basket she held.

She let him take it without a word, nor did she speak as they crossed the garden and went out on to the road. The silence was broken at last by Norman Strange.

"Thornsdyke is an old village, is it not?" he said.

He had spoken solely from a sense that civility demanded conversation of some sort, but Mrs. Custance lifted her eyes and answered eagerly:

"Oh, yes," she said. "I believe it is quite old; at least, the houses are dreadfully miserable and tumbledown, some of them. But it's rather pretty in the summer, bits of it. The people think a great deal of their gardens. I'm afraid it won't look very pretty this morning, though."

She was so obviously anxious that he should be pleased and interested, that his answer was given with more warmth of manner than he would have believed possible of himself where his new surroundings, with their terrible weight of significance, were concerned. And as they turned a corner of the muddy lane down which they were walking, he exclaimed:

"What a remarkably fine old church! What is the date, Mrs. Custance?"

"The date," she answered rather vaguely, "the date when it was built? I'm afraid I don't know. Do you think it's a pretty church? It's rather—rather dreary-looking, don't you think?"

Norman Strange had noticed the church more with a view to helping her than from any other reason, but architecture had been a hobby of his at one time, and as they drew nearer he was roused to something very like enthusiasm.

"It's magnificent," he said. "Can we get in, Mrs. Custance? I should very much like to see the interior. I never saw anything more perfect than that Early English work."

That Mrs. Custance was ignorant of the very simplest architectural terms, that her knowledge, historical or artistic, was as slight as was her capacity—or indeed her desire — to conceal her ignorance, was very evident to Norman Strange before he had finished his exploration of the exterior of the church—the interior was inaccessible. And there was something in her wistful consciousness and deprecation of her own shortcomings, and in her unconsciously betrayed admiration of his learning, that touched his youthful tendency to instruct.

"I could soon show you," he said at last, referring to the first principles of architecture, and speaking quite eagerly. "It is not a bit difficult, and you really ought to understand how fine this is."

He was still discoursing on the subject, when a few minutes later another turn in the lane brought them into the village street, and a woman passing wished the doctor's wife good morning, and favoured her companion with a prolonged stare. Instantly conscious of it as he was, the inspection seemed to recall him to his present self. He finished his sentence in a different tone, and his face hardened into the impassive whiteness which was the mask his sullen misery considered due to the companionship of a lady.

"I am afraid I must go in here," said Mrs. Custance as he finished speaking, stopping at the door of a little nondescript village shop. "I shan't be a minute. Will you—will you come in with me?"

Norman Strange glanced through the half-open door into the interior of the shop where two or three figures were to be seen.

"Thank you," he said, "I will wait here, I think." And he turned, as Mrs. Custance disappeared, and leant against a post, one of a series of five or six connected by an iron chain which faced the little shop on the opposite side of the pathway, and were, apparently, the remains of a continuous paling. He had waited about five minutes when a voice from the interior of the shop caught his ear, and he lifted his head mechanically as he wondered where he had heard it before. Nearly the whole of the little shop was visible to him as he stood, and by the counter, leaning back upon it on her elbow, stood the driver of the cart he had stopped the night before. Her wonderful red-gold hair was uncovered, and she was evidently at home. She was listening now to Mrs. Custance, who was holding a baby in her arms as she talked to the woman from whom she had apparently taken it. Norman saw her bend her own faded face over the child, kiss it gently, and then return it to its mother with a gesture that made him wonder vaguely that he had thought her ill-assured. Then she turned to the handsome girl.

"I will come up now, Alice," she said, "only——" She hesitated and glanced out towards Norman Strange. He hardly caught her next words, but he saw the girl glance quickly in his direction, and he understood that she took in the position instantly. She followed Mrs. Custance as the latter walked to the shop door and said to Norman Strange—all the assurance with which she had touched the child gone from her manner—" Would you mind walking on a little way and coming back to me? There is a woman ill here, and I should like just to see her."

" Please don't think of me," returned Norman Strange quickly. He raised his hat slightly as he spoke in acknowledgment of the recognition in the flashing black eyes which were fixed on him from behind Mrs. Custance, who turned nervously.

" You found the house, then," said the

girl carelessly. She spoke with an ease of manner which contrasted as curiously with Mrs. Custance's diffidence as did their physical presences as they stood together in the doorway.

"Thanks to your direction," he replied. Then, as Mrs. Custance made a hesitating sound of enquiry, he waited while the girl explained, and after another word of thanks for her directions, he said simply to Mrs. Custance: "Please don't think of hurrying on my account. I will walk on and come back," and turned away.

He had walked nearly the length of the village street, his eyes bent on the ground, when he became aware that he was monopolising the narrow, cobblestone pavement, and that a man coming towards him was intimating his right to a share. Norman Strange lifted his head suddenly.

and was moving aside with a word of
apology, when the other man said:

"Mr. Strange, I infer?"

Norman Strange stopped and looked at
his questioner, who stood in the middle of
the footpath with a large cigar in his mouth.
He was a young man of about middle height,
rather large in figure, with a face that was
handsome enough but for a certain indescribable coarseness about it. He was
dressed in an old tweed suit, and there was
something slovenly about his whole appearance. His eyes, which were slightly
bloodshot, were fixed on Norman with an
inquisitive stare.

"Strange is my name," returned Norman
distantly.

"Thought as much," continued the
other. "Spotted you in a moment, and
thought I'd introduce myself. My name is

Caton—Robert Caton. You've heard it, of course ?"

There was an instant's dead silence as Norman Strange's haggard, dark eyes met the bloodshot ones before him. This was his fellow patient; his most suitable associate; the man with whom he must stand henceforth on an equality. Then he said in a voice that came from between set teeth :

" I have had that pleasure—yes !"

"That's all right, then ; we know each other !" answered the other carelessly. "Taking a look at the place, eh ? I was sorry not to meet you last night, but I was in need of a little repose."

He had turned as he began to speak and Norman Strange was retracing his steps, perforce beside him, but he made no reply either to the words or to the coarse laugh with which his companion ended, and the latter continued :

" Feel a bit out of sorts this morning still, and thought I'd get a breath of air and look into the shop. Been into the shop ? Come in with me, and I'll show the finest woman you've ever seen. Don't frighten yourself, old man, that's not the lady !"

The last sentence was uttered in a lower tone, half sneer, half "chaff," and he finished with another laugh. Mrs. Custance had come to the threshold of the shop alone. Seeing the two men she moved hurriedly and came towards them.

Without a glance at the man beside him, his face very white and set, Norman Strange went hastily forward to meet her.

" I hope you have not been waiting for me," he said. " Shall we go on ?"

He turned as he spoke and stood at her

side, waiting almost grimly as she said timidly :

"Good morning, Mr. Caton!"

And as he saw the small hand she held out touched carelessly by the shaking hand of the man they faced, his own hand thrust into his pocket was fiercely clenched.

"Shall we go on, Mrs. Custance?" he repeated.

CHAPTER V.

" A CAPITAL day's sport altogether ! "

The speaker was Robert Caton, and the words concluded an account of a ratting expedition in which he had spent the afternoon. It was about eight o'clock in the evening. The drawing-room of the White House had long been lighted up, and the surface appearance of the room and its occupants—two men talking together while a woman sat by at work—was one of comfort and domesticity. Robert Caton was lounging in a large armchair with his feet on the fender as though he had recently come in, cold. His dress was negligent in the extreme, and smoking

jacket and slippers alike might have been
said to have done their work. Opposite to
him with his easy-chair pushed back, as
though he had been comfortably established
there for so long that a nearer neighbourhood to the fire was no longer desirable,
sat Dr. Custance, with a newspaper across
his knee. He, too, wore a smoking jacket,
but his was in very much better condition
than Robert Caton's, and in its first freshness had evidently been very handsome.

"You must have found it cold," he com-
mented, as Robert Caton brought his speech
to a close. "The east wind is abominable!"

He glanced over his shoulder as he
spoke, shifting his attitude carelessly as he
did so into another and easier variety of
cross-legged negligence, and his wife rose
silently, with a simple matter-of-course movement, rearranged the thick curtain over the

window behind him, and returned to her seat. It was a stiff little chair, placed nearly in the middle of the room, convenient doubtless for the light obtained from the hanging lamp, but rather cold and isolated in consequence of the two large chairs that shut in so much of the hearth. Mrs. Custance was rather pale; the recent ratting conversation had been slightly brutal in detail. Her face had not sufficient capacity of expression to show the anxiety with which she listened lest it should be resumed, or her relief at the short silence which ensued.

" Where's Strange ? "

The question was asked by Robert Caton, and he struck his foot idly against the fender as he spoke, with a frown.

" Strange ! " returned the doctor carelessly. " I haven't an idea. Leila, do you know where Strange is ? "

He did not turn his head as he addressed his wife—repeating the whole question as though the previous words exchanged between himself and Caton had been inaudible to her; but Mrs. Custance turned towards him as she answered at once quickly and timidly.

"I don't know, I'm sure. Isn't he in his own room?"

"If I could say that, I should hardly ask where he was," returned her husband. His careless tone was hard with sarcasm; and Mrs. Custance took up her work again hurriedly and nervously, without speaking.

"What do you make of him, Custance, eh?"

The questioner was again Robert Caton, and the fender received another kick as the words were spoken. Dr. Custance glanced at him for a moment with eyes which looked as though they would have been keen had their owner taken sufficient trouble.

"I don't know that I have made anything of him as yet," he answered placidly. "He has only been here three days."

"Three hours is enough for me to tell whether a fellow is my sort or not. Strange isn't, and that's the fact."

Neither of the men saw the face of the woman behind them, as she lifted it from her work for a moment. Nor would they have read much in it had they done so, for only in her eyes as she fixed them on Caton there struggled feebly an expression which strove to become disgust. Quite unconscious of the faded blue eyes, Robert Caton continued :

"He's such an unsociable brute! I've done the civil to him as hard as I can, and he isn't up to anything. Asked him to come out ratting to-day, and he barely thanked me."

" Perhaps he's not much of a sportsman," suggested Dr. Custance absently.

" Confound it all, he must be something! I don't know whether he's opened out to you at all, but I've not seen him show a sign of interest in any blessed thing."

Robert Caton paused, but Dr. Custance's only reply was an inarticulate and indefinite sound, and he began again with a laugh :

" Perhaps we shall chum up by-and-by, eh, doctor? He's a better fellow drunk than sober, very likely, if he'd only give us the chance to see. It's time he did, in my opinion, instead of keeping so jolly dark."

Light as was the tone there was an undercurrent of brutal earnest in it, as though the confirmed and hopelessly de-

graded drunkard resented the three days'
sobriety of the man in whom he expected to
find a comrade. Robert Caton was nine-
and-twenty, and his days of sobriety since
he had been nineteen had been few. How
far his vices were the result of heredity, how
far of education, no one could have said.
He had been a good-looking, self-indulgent
boy, he had been a self-indulgent, vicious
youth, and he was now well content to pay
the fee required by Dr. Custance, that he
might go his own way comparatively shielded
from social consequences by that gentleman's
protective and pity-compelling medical dictum
—"incurable."

Dr. Custance smiled at him now, half
indulgently, half reprovingly; but in the
spare fingers of the little ungainly figure
behind him the needle snapped suddenly.
Mrs. Custance rose abruptly and as abruptly

sat down again. As though glad to effect
a diversion, her husband glanced over his
shoulder and said, in the tone of nonchalant
sarcasm that he had used to her before:

"You don't find your chair comfortable,
Leila, apparently. Suppose you take another
and fidget less upon it."

He had turned his eyes away before
she could lift hers, confused and bewildered,
to his face, and his lips were parted to speak
to Caton when the bell rang for supper.
At the same moment the door opened, and
Norman Strange came into the room.

The semblance of his old self, which had
shown in him more or less distinctly during
the day following his arrival at the White
House, had disappeared almost completely,
and the whole man seemed to be enveloped
in some sort of heavy, intangible cloud.
His eyes were hard and fierce, and his

mouth was set with a dogged expression at once of suffering and of indifference.

He did not look towards Mrs. Custance, and her eyes were fixed on him for an instant with a miserable, wistful questioning. Then she passed hurriedly out of the door as he held it open for her mechanically, listening at the same moment to Caton's self-assertive announcement of the capital sport he had had. His reply was civil in its interest and no more, and would have done nothing to uphold the conversation if Dr. Custance had not neatly grafted on to it a comment which led to an animated dissertation on sport generally from Caton. If it was aimed indirectly at Norman Strange, the latter was quite unconscious of the fact. He made no attempt to join in the conversation, but sat with his eyes fixed moodily on the tablecloth, eating nothing.

"Don't you care about killing things, Mr. Strange?"

The voice was very low, frightened at its own sound apparently, and Caton's loud tones drowned it before it reached either himself or Dr. Custance; but Norman Strange started violently as he heard it. He did not turn to her, and he poured some water into the glass beside him as he said briefly:

"Not much, Mrs. Custance."

The words did not invite further conversation, and Mrs. Custance's supper lay untouched upon her plate as her hands stole nervously into her lap and there clasped and twisted one another painfully. Her eyes were almost bright with the effort she was making, as she continued:

"Gentlemen always — it seems to me there is always something to be said between them about things like that. I have always wondered why it is so interesting."

The interesting topic in question had reached a point between Robert Caton and Dr. Custance at which the details were not pleasant hearing; and glancing towards her, Norman Strange thought that her heightened colour and the nervous twitch about her mouth were due to physical repulsion. He could not tell that not one word that Robert Caton was saying was heard by her, and he took up her words quickly, though with an obvious effort, anxious to distract her attention.

"Half the world is always wondering at the amusements of the other half," he said. "That is a truism, I'm afraid, Mrs. Custance, but really I think there is no subject on which we are so intolerant of tastes that differ from our own individual taste. It isn't only that we can't get on with a man whose amusements are different to our own—that's not so unnatural perhaps —but we do look down upon him so!"

He finished with the smile that his words demanded. She smiled vaguely in return, evidently hardly understanding him. But she answered, with a brave effort to keep his attention, if somewhat irrelevantly:

"Are you fond of boating? We used to boat on the Dart a great deal before— when I was at home."

The boating anecdotes into which he plunged lasted until supper was nearly over, and were interrupted by a domestic enquiry addressed by Dr. Custance to his wife. The sporting discussion being by that time disposed of and the necessity for a second conversation removed, Norman Strange relapsed once more into silence, and Mrs.

Custance, though her eyes had wandered
wistfully towards him more than once, had
made no further attempt to make him break
that silence when her husband rose from
the table.

"Will you smoke, Strange?" he said.

"Thanks!" was the brief answer.
"No!"

"Then you would rather go back to the
drawing-room than come to the smoking-
room, no doubt?"

There was a moment's pause, and then
Norman Strange answered, in a tone and
manner full of heavy constraint:

"I have some letters to write, and I
will go upstairs at once, I think. Good
night."

He was turning away with a slight bow
to her, when Mrs. Custance held out her
hand, timidly and awkwardly enough.

"Good night, Mr. Strange," she said.

He barely touched her fingers with his own, and went slowly and heavily out of the room.

A few minutes later Mrs. Custance returned to her needlework in the empty drawing-room, going back to the little uncomfortable seat in the middle of the room as if from force of habit. But there was something about her face to-night that was not habitual. It was not definitely unhappy; it was one of those faces in which an expression of great distress or of great joy is alike inconceivable—a face in which every emotion is reflected subdued and faint in tone. But to-night the faint, wistful distress which had struggled to life in her eyes on Norman Strange's entrance before supper did not die out. She lifted her head now and again as though to listen

for a sound in the room above—Norman
Strange's room—and though she went on
with her work mechanically after each pause,
the stitches she set were far less even than
usual.

There was the same look in her eyes
the next morning, and they were rather
heavy, too, when she lifted them to Norman
Strange's face when he came down to
breakfast. This time he did not seem to
see the hand she offered him — perhaps
because the little gesture was made so
timidly. At any rate he did not take it,
nor did he meet her eyes. The dark
shadow that had hung about him on the
evening before brooded about him now
more heavily than ever. His replies to
Dr. Custance's suave words as to his dis-
posal of the day before him were as curt
as was consistent with courtesy. He was

going to take a long walk, he said, and
he might not be back until the evening.
There was a certain covert defiance in his
tone as though he thought it possible that
the man under whose charge he was—
nominally at least—might offer some objec-
tion.   But Dr. Custance never objected
unless to something that interfered with his
own comfort, and as he uttered his easy
assent his "patient" left the room.

It was a bright morning—the first of
March—and spring seemed to be asserting
itself with exuberant freshness and gaiety.
But Mrs. Custance coming towards the
White House at about four o'clock in the
afternoon after her solitary country walk,
seemed to be in no wise touched by the
bright influences about her.   On the contrary, it was not only her little lonely, sombrely-
dressed figure that seemed out of harmony

with the surrounding light and life. Her
step was dull and tired, and there was a
faintly oppressed look on her face as though
the brightness was almost painful to her in
its contrast with a care that would not be
forgotten.

She opened the door of the White
House, and stood a moment in the hall,
hesitating. Then, awkwardly and hurriedly,
almost furtively, she opened the door first
of the drawing-room, then of the dining-
room, and looked in. Each room was empty.
She stood for a moment on the threshold of
the dining-room and then went suddenly along
the passage to the smoking-room. The door
was shut and she paused a moment, her
faded face quite white with the rapid beating
of her heart. Then she opened it as she
had opened the other two.

" Mrs. Custance! I hope I may flatter

myself you were looking for me? Is there anything I can do for you? Won't you come and sit down in this delightful chair and have a chat?"

Norman Strange was alone in the room and he had apparently sprung out of the long chair on her appearance. He stood before her now catching unsteadily at its tall back, his breath coming irregularly, his face flushed, his eyes bright and watery. His words had come thickly and indistinctly in that far-away, unreal voice which is characteristic of these strange absences of the mind —drunkenness or delirium—with an expansive exuberant flow as unlike the natural man as could be.

Without a word, but with a little catch in her quick breath, Mrs. Custance had stopped short in the doorway; she stood there looking full at him, with a terrible suggestion

in her direct gaze and absolute absence of
self-consciousness that the soul of the man
before her was not there, that she was, and
felt herself to be, alone with its empty shell.
Perhaps it was its whiteness, perhaps it was
because she was indeed drawn completely out
of herself, but her face for the moment was
absolutely expressive ; expressive of that
pitiful misery which women can feel for a
fallen and degraded man. She did not
speak, and her silence seemed to affect him
somehow, for he laughed foolishly.

"I'm afraid I've offended you, Mrs. Custance," he began, in the same exaggeratedly
open and ingenuous manner. "Perhaps you
think it's not the thing to have brandy bottles
behind that sofa ? Well, you're right, no
doubt—no doubt ; but it was just a joke, and
you can make allowances for a joke, I
know ?"

He paused as if for her answer, and repeated more urgently :

"You'll make allowance for a joke, won't you ?"

He fixed his eyes on hers as he spoke, and with the necessity for speech an agony of confusion seemed to fall on her. She stammered something incoherent, and he interrupted her with another laugh ; a noisy one this time.

"It's my belief you think I've been drinking that brandy—think I'm drunk— drunk! I don't want to be rude to a lady, but really, you know! Why, just look here!"

He took his hand from the chair to which he had been clinging as if to demonstrate to her the fact that he could stand alone, and attempting to make a step towards her, reeled heavily back and fell helplessly upon the cushions behind him.

With an inarticulate sound of inexpressible pity and pain, Mrs. Custance shut the door suddenly, and clasping her hands for a moment over her face, she hurried away down the passage. As she passed the hall door it opened ; her husband came in and she stopped suddenly.

"Arnold," she said, " Mr. Strange is in the smoking-room."

She was trembling from head to foot, and her hands were tightly squeezed together, but her voice was its low, subdued self.

"Well," answered her husband. " Is that all ? "

" He—he——"

" He's drunk, I suppose ? "

" Yes ! "

The word was hardly audible, and as she uttered it Mrs. Custance turned away and went upstairs.

CHAPTER VI.

ANOTHER bright March morning had come and gone; this one, in spite of its brightness, piercingly cold. Into the dining-room of the White House no sunshine came, and the small face and figure of Mrs. Custance as she sat sewing by the table looked grey and pinched. The fire had sunk low in the grate with those depressing sounds a dying fire makes, but she had not noticed it. All the morning she had hardly moved, except when a need for something from the work-basket at her hand caused her to lift for an instant a wan, dull face.

One o'clock struck from the little clock

on the mantelpiece unheeded by her, and then the door was opened and she started violently. It was the youth from the village who did duty in the doctor's house as page, and he had come to lay the table for lunch. Mrs. Custance rose hurriedly and glanced from his tray to the clock as she hastily collected her work materials.

"I — I didn't know it was so late, William!" she said nervously; and then she shivered a little, and going to the fire-place she knelt down on the rug and began to put the embers together, warming her small blue hands. She turned her head as she did so to watch the boy as he laid the table, and there was something in her attitude which was strangely girlish, and at variance with the worn, subdued face, and the sombre matronliness of her dress. The boy was setting places for two only, and with another little shiver she turned once more to the fire. The boy finished his work, left the room, and returned with the lunch itself, and still she did not move. Then he withdrew and rang the dinner-bell, and she started to her feet and stood with her eyes on the floor, her fingers working nervously at a fold of her dress. Quite five minutes passed, and then a man's step came slowly along the hall, and Norman Strange came into the room.

White as his face had been when he opened the door, his very lips lost their colour as his eyes fell upon the solitary occupant of the room. He stopped short and his eyes dropped. He did not speak or move, nor did the little, trembling woman at the other end of the room so much as raise her eyes, and there was a moment's dead silence. Then Mrs. Custance said in a low voice, which all her efforts could not render steady :

"My husband told me to say that he was very sorry to be obliged to go and see about a horse to-day. Mr. Caton has gone with him."

Having made the necessary statement she stopped, as though not trusting herself to do more than control her nervousness. She had moved to her place at the head of the table as she spoke, and without a word Norman Strange took the other place. Such words as are almost indispensable to the commencement of a meal passed between them—low murmurs on her part, monosyllabic responses on his part—and then silence fell between them again ; silence in which the whole meal passed. Mrs. Custance sat with her eyes fixed upon the knife and fork with which she merely played, afraid ap-

parently to look up. Norman Strange sat
intrenched, as far as his shaken nerves and
miserable physical condition would allow, in
dogged endurance; hardly even pretending
to eat. No sooner did Mrs. Custance,
having folded her table napkin with fingers
that would hardly be controlled, rise
nervously and mechanically from her chair
than he rose too, and left the room, as he
had entered it, in silence.

Almost for the first time since the bell
for luncheon had sounded, Mrs. Custance
raised her eyes as he turned away and
followed him with them to the door. He
shut it behind him, and she walked vaguely
to the window and stood there for a minute
or two with her forehead leaning against the
pane. Then she moved with a little breath,
which would have been a long sigh had she
been a woman given to expression, and

prepared to resume the monotonous needlework in which her solitary afternoon as well
as her long morning was generally spent.

It was not until nearly an hour later that
she remembered suddenly some wishes of
her husband with regard to the alteration
of some pictures in the drawing-room. He
had wished it made that day, and she rose
from her seat with nervous haste as she
realised how nearly she had forgotten it. It
signified an anxious sense of her own negligence that there was apparently no room in
her mind for the thought of summoning help,
or for the thought of a possible caller. She
fetched the steps herself and took down the
two smaller pictures that were to be moved.
Then she moved the steps—dragging them
with some difficulty this time, as though her
stock of strength had been small enough to
be considerably affected by her previous

demands on it—and mounted them again. The picture now to be moved was a very large engraving in a heavy frame ; the nail was high above her head, and some minutes of painful effort were necessary before she succeeded in jerking the wire from it, to be herself nearly overbalanced by the weight thus suddenly thrown upon her arms. She did not fall, but her nerves were shaken by the shock; and she was standing clutching the picture, unable to descend the steps with her burden, and unable to get rid of it by any other means, when a low voice from the door-way said suddenly :

"Let me take it from you, Mrs. Custance," and Norman Strange crossed the room quickly, and reaching up, took the picture from her, even then not lifting his eyes to her face. Then, seeing that she was clinging tremulously to the steps, he gave her his hand and helped her carefully down.

"Where is it to go?" he said. "It is too heavy for you!"

She explained to him in a few confused words, and gravely bowing his head in acquiescence, he fetched the smaller pictures, put them up, and then moved the steps and hung the larger one, all with the same ready helpfulness and in the same silence. Having finished, he was leaving the room again when Mrs. Custance, who had watched him in a silence like his own, made an agitated, uncertain step towards him.

"Mr. Strange," she faltered, "won't you—won't you—if you would help me—there is the book-case!"

He stopped, his hand on the door, not turning towards her and speaking apparently through clenched teeth.

"Get one of the servants to help you, Mrs. Custance," he said. "They are fitter company for you than I."

"If you would help me!" She stopped, clasping her hands tightly as though her inability to express herself, to do more than reiterate words already used, was absolute distress to her. Something in her low, stifled voice seemed to touch him. He turned abruptly.

"Mrs. Custance," he said, "there is one thing I should like to say. I beg you earnestly to believe that if I had had any idea that there was a lady here I should never have come. For yesterday —if words of apology from such a brute as I am were of any worth at all——" His voice had sunk to a hoarse murmur and he turned away with a gesture of humiliation and despair terrible to see. "It can't last long!" he muttered brokenly, "it can't last long!"

Whether she heard the last words or no she made no answer to them, only her eyes dilated, and she pressed her hands together until the pressure must have been absolute pain.

"It isn't that you need say anything to me," she began in a voice so low that he could hardly catch the words. "It isn't for me it matters! But — but — oh, why?"

The last word came from her the merest frightened whisper, but in its pitiful, forlorn enquiry, its speechless appeal for allowance for her own audacity in making that enquiry, it was indescribably eloquent. Her eyes, full of a dumb struggle, were fixed full upon him; her face was all quivering with nervousness and distress.

No eloquent harangue, no adjuration, could have appealed to Norman Strange as did that mute beseeching for an answer. He paused a moment looking at her, and a sharp spasm passed across his face. Then he said, with a self-restrained gentleness about which there was a reassurance and protection for her which made the situation inexpressibly curious, his words themselves inexpressibly terrible :

"It's done, Mrs. Custance. Nothing can alter it or help me now. I have degraded myself. I'm not fit to speak to a lady, I am not fit to work, I am not fit to live. There is no hope and no future for such a brute as I am. Do you think it possible to get over such shame as I have brought upon myself?"

In his morbid despair he had asked the question with a half-smile, as though the answer were only too self-evident. But Mrs. Custance, to whom his previous words in their contrast with the manner in which they were uttered, had conveyed little but confusion, seized upon the straightforward question and answered it in all simplicity.

"Yes," she said.

It was the first syllable of hope that had come to him, and he staggered under it for an instant as though it had been a blow. Then he recovered himself and smiled again.

"I am afraid you don't quite understand," he said. "Every one who knows me knows me now as—a drunkard! I know myself as—that. You are pitiful, Mrs. Custance! Except out of pity you could not speak to me at all. You don't respect me. I don't respect myself. It's all over with me!"

As he reiterated the words their full

significance seemed to rise up within. him and he turned away abruptly. He walked to the window and stood with his back to her. But it was only for a moment, and then he dropped into a chair and his head fell forward upon his hands with a groan.

There was an interval of perfect stillness —an interval in which the only movement in the room was the movement of her nervous hands—and then Mrs. Custance, with a faint, pink flush of intense effort in her sallow face, crossed the room and stood beside him.

" Don't be angry with me for speaking of what I dare say I don't understand!" she began in a low, hurried, and uneven voice. " Perhaps I've made a mistake, but it seems to me as if you were going on because you think you can never get back. Oh," her voice rose to a little stifled cry, "oh! what can I say to make you see how dreadfully mistaken that is? I'm so stupid and I say things so badly, but I know—I know that it is never too late to get back if one really wants to. If one repents one can always be forgiven."

She paused, stopped apparently by a sense of the utter inadequacy of the conventional phrase to which she had been driven by the narrow limitation of her power of expression, and Norman Strange moved wearily and lifted his head.

"That is a good woman's argument," he said, gently. "But the world is not like that, Mrs. Custance."

"But what do people think of but the present?" she answered rapidly and incoherently. "Who thinks of anything in anybody's life beyond what they can see? Get better and go back to your life, and who will remember anything that is past? Who will remember enough even to know what you have done in getting back? Ah! how badly, how badly I say it!"

She stopped abruptly, looking into his face with an unconscious reliance on his power to understand her, an unconscious appeal to him to do so; and he waited a moment looking at her with strange eyes which he had lifted to her as she spoke, and which had grown stranger as he listened.

"You said I didn't respect you, Mr. Strange," she went on, and though her tone grew only more stifled and suppressed as her earnestness increased, the faint flush was a burning spot of colour now, on either cheek. "Oh, won't you try and think that all the things you've said to me are as much mistakes as that? I feel so sure that you are too—too clever and—and everything, not to be able to save yourself if you will only try! Oh, don't you see that you are only making bad worse? Don't you see that it is throwing your life away of your own accord to say it's hopeless? It's wicked——" she stopped herself suddenly, as though realising what she was saying. "I beg your pardon," she faltered. "I beg your pardon!"

"My own accord!" he repeated slowly, not noticing her last words. He was still sitting, as though his mind was too fully occupied for physical consciousness, and as she stood looking down at him he looked away from her into space as he repeated the words: "My own accord. And what do you think I ought to do, Mrs. Custance?"

But the unusual excitement that had carried her so far had died out in that moment of realisation, and Mrs. Custance turned away to the window behind them, her hand working at the window curtain, her eyes full of tears.

"I don't—I didn't mean that I could—that I had any right to speak to you," she murmured. "It is only that—if you would only try!"

The tears were running fast down the face she kept turned to the window, and the last word came with a hard little sob.

Norman Strange rose and turned sharply towards her.

"It is too late," he cried, the pain in his voice making it harsh and intense as he seemed to thrust from him the hope her words presented. "It is too late! If it were not—perhaps—perhaps I might!"

CHAPTER VII.

A QUIET girlhood passed in a country village;
an early marriage followed by eight years of
married life, unmarked by any more striking
incident than two changes of residence, from
London to a north country town, and from
thence to the village of Thornsdyke; cannot
be said to constitute an eventful life. Mental
experiences, passionate mental life, are of
course compatible with the most peaceful outward circumstances. But though the former
is indeed an inseparable adjunct of all human
life, the share of it that had fallen to Mrs. Custance had been transmuted, by the temperament on which it acted, into something so

matter-of-fact in its dreariness that only a very sympathetic onlooker, and one who should have known her infinitely better than she knew herself, could have understood that anything so spiritual in its associations had indeed formed a feature in her colourless life.

Having neither home nor parents of her own, she had grown up with her only sister in the house of an uncle in Devonshire. The uncle was rich; the atmosphere of the house was practical and matter-of-fact. The dependence of the two sisters was cheerily accepted and ignored, but there was an unexpressed understanding that the present state of things would only last until they were of marriageable age, and that they would then provide for themselves. The elder sister was a very pretty, bright girl, and the younger one, Leila, was a faint copy of her; pretty but not very pretty, a little stupid and weak in character, but sweeter-natured than her sister, behind whom she sheltered.

At nineteen the elder girl did what was expected of her in the most satisfactory way ; she became engaged to a rich man in the Indian Civil Service. The pleased excitement of the household took the form of constant hopeful auguries for the younger sister; and it seemed a dispensation of Providence into which it would have been impertinent to enquire too closely when a doctor from one of the neighbouring villages, who was vaguely understood to have recently come into some money, and to have bought a practice in London, proposed to Leila. She accepted him, as a matter of course. He was fifteen years her senior, but he was very handsome and very pleasant ; she liked him very much, and if anything more was

necessary she did not know it. Her girlhood had been quite happy in its colourless
contentment, and in the same colourless
contentment she went away with her husband into her new life, a girl of eighteen,
with all her character and her future to be
moulded by his hands.

If the Mrs. Custance who was accepted
by Norman Strange as the middle-aged wife
of a middle-aged man, had had imagination
enough to conjure up before her present
self a picture of the eighteen-year-old girl
who had left her uncle's house only eight
years before, she would not have recognised
the picture ; she would have been unable to
realise that she had ever been other than she
now was. There had been no shock of
disappointment, for she had expected nothing ; no sharp suffering, for it had all come
about so naturally, and keen pain was as

foreign to her nature as keen pleasure. Her husband had grown tired of her; she had subsided from bride to wife—as such a man as she had married understands the word. The faint liking she had had for him died gradually away, and as gradually a faint fear of him rose in her and became the only sentiment with which he inspired her. They had been very poor, and life had been dull and grey and very lonely, though she hardly realised it. Her sister had gone to India, and after her marriage she had never revisited her Devonshire home. The friends of her girlhood had passed out of her life with girlhood itself; she had indeed no friends, properly so called. Such slight acquaintances as she made found her dull and uninteresting; and she, shy and ill-assured, had been unable to pass beyond the stiffest stage of conventionality. There

had only once been a time when she had
been conscious of unhappiness, when her
desire for the touch of baby hands—a desire
never to be satisfied—had been a dull in-
cessant ache. But that was long ago now,
and it had died away, numbed by the passing
of monotonous years. When she had come
to Thornsdyke with her husband, a year
before the coming of Norman Strange, her
youth was past at twenty-six, as though it
had never been, and she had been unhesi-
tatingly accepted by the neighbourhood as a
rather stupid and shy little middle-aged
woman.

Nervous and uncertain as her manner
always was, there was something about her
subdued and absolutely crushed throughout
the evening that followed upon her
frightened and apparently fruitless appeal to
Norman Strange. Dr. Custance returned

from his horse-dealing expedition in a decidedly unpleasant frame of mind, but even his sarcasm could add little to her shrinking, unobtrusive, evidently entirely unconscious depression. Her face was very small and white, and there were red rims round her eyes.

There was a dumb misery in those blue eyes, and with it a forlorn, inarticulate appeal, as she lifted them momentarily to his face as she and Norman Strange met at supper. They rested on a white, set face with haggard eyes, which looked to them, if possible, more desperate than before, and then they fell, the misery in them stronger than ever. She did not look at him again, even when she wished him an inaudible good night, and she did not offer him her hand. Something in her tone and manner suggested that she dared not.

Throughout the next day she saw him
only at supper, when he came into the room
looking very tired. He had been walking
all day, he explained briefly, in answer to
Robert Caton's comments. The explanation was apparently by no means satisfactory
to Caton, and with a covert sneer he
plunged into an ostentatiously intimate discussion with Dr. Custance, to the complete
exclusion of any third person.

No sooner had Norman disappeared,
however—and he did so directly supper
was over—than Caton, who was accustomed
to ignore Mrs. Custance's presence with as
little ceremony as did her husband, broke
into a coarse tirade against him. To his
fellow "patient" Norman's reserve and the
heavy shadow of despair that hung about
him was neither more nor less than "confounded humbug and unsociableness"; and

he proceeded to dilate upon the subject with great energy and force of language, while Dr. Custance threw in here and there a remark of as soothing a nature as possible. Neither of them noticed that when the torrent of abuse was at its highest, Mrs. Custance rose, shaking from head to foot, and left the room with her blue eyes quite bright.

She was in the dining-room on the morning following, spending the hours between breakfast and lunch, as she generally did spend them, in dreary solitude, her fingers occupied with the monotonous needle-work which was her only occupation ; her little figure in the dull, silent room, looking dreary enough against its background of rain-blurred window-panes. It was a wet morning, wet enough, at present, to keep indoors any one whose duty did not call him out, and she had heard, as she moved about the house on her household duties, the voices of Robert Caton and her husband as they established themselves in the smoking-room to spend an idle morning. She had been sitting alone for nearly an hour, when the door opened, and lifting her eyes with a start, she met those of Norman Strange, who was standing in the doorway.

"Mrs. Custance," he said, "may I come and sit in here? Shall I be in your way? I am rather tired of smoke."

There was an instant's pause, and Mrs. Custance sat, her needle resting in her hand, her face lifted to him, with the lips a little parted, as though in some sudden shock of surprise. Then she answered quickly, and rather incoherently:

"Not at all! Oh, no! I mean I shall be very glad if you will come."

He had brought with him no book—no occupation of any kind, and for some minutes he sat motionless, with his arms folded on the table, and his eyes fixed on the thin hands of his hostess, moving again now, but moving rapidly and awkwardly under his unseeing gaze. Then he said absently:

"It is very good of you to have me here."

The quiet of the room and the gentle womanly presence were very pleasant to him, though he did not trace his sense of rest to that, or, indeed, to any definite source.

She did not answer, except in a faint, hardly articulate murmur of deprecation; but she lifted her eyes hurriedly to his face and dropped them instantly again. There was another pause, and then he said slowly and ponderingly:

"Mrs. Custance, do you really think there would be any chance for me?"

Her fingers tightened suddenly on the piece of work she held, and she turned her face to him mutely as though quite unable to find any words in the sudden surprise and hope which quivered for an instant in her face. But he had apparently asked the question more for the sake of giving it words than with any wish for her opinion, and he went on unanswered:

"I wonder whether you know how it's been with me?" and hardly waiting for her sympathetic murmur, he told her all the story. He was evidently telling it more to himself than to her, and he made it as black as the plain facts could be made. But there were the plain facts only, with none of the morbidness which had given them their hopelessness, and as he finished,

K 2

terrible as it was, the end was not final.
It was obviously not a story of irretrievable
disgrace.

And not even the wholly new significance
about the end of the story stood out in
stronger contrast to the tone of the man of
thirty-six hours before than did the manner
of the telling—grave and stern, but desperate
and reckless no longer, The whole personality of the man was altered. His face
was haggard still, but it was haggard with
long strain of thought, and not with hopeless
misery. The hard constraint was gone from
his voice.

Over the dull despair of Norman
Strange's life a change had come indeed, and
it had not come lightly. As there are
physical diseases for which the cure must be
sought in pain, so the first stirring in him of
desire and hope of redemption had tortured

him as his hopelessness itself had never
done. When and how the thought of
possible salvation had dawned in him he
never knew. The stress of the struggle
with himself and with his morbid despair
into which it slowly ripened obscured altogether its dim beginnings, and the words in
which it had in truth originated—words
uttered by the little woman to whom he
hardly gave a thought—were almost forgotten
by him. He had come to Mrs. Custance
this morning with a hazy remembrance only
of their interview of two days before; come
to her, indeed, with a vague sense that
between them the ice was already broken;
but mainly because she was a woman, and
his nature was one craving that expression
that only a woman would allow him.

Having spoken he paused—paused so
long that the quivering lips of the woman

who had listened to him were parted, as
though with a tremendous effort, to falter
out words which would have been a poor
reflection of her confused feelings, when he
said slowly—and in the words the change in
him seemed to touch its consummation :

"Perhaps, after all, I'm nothing but a
coward! Perhaps I might do something
with my life, even now! The man who
hasn't courage to show fight——" The last
word came from him with an unmistakable
ring and he broke off, rose suddenly, and
turned to the window.

"You will! Oh, you will!"

Vaguely as she had understood him, far
above the level of her stunted spiritual
understanding as was the long-dormant impulse which was stirring in him once again,
the main fact at its simplest was clear to her.
The words she spoke were stifled, suppressed,

hopelessly inadequate, but she was shaking from head to foot, her eyes were full of tears, and her lips trembled. He turned his head as she spoke and as his eyes fell on her face, and on the hands clasped tightly together as though in self-repression, something in them touched him.

"Poor little woman!" he said to himself vaguely. "Poor little woman!"

She was not pretty; there was no youth about her to affect him; she had none of that confidence in the power of her sex which is a woman's weapon. She had no confidence at all. He was not conscious of her influence as he must have been had it been exercised in any of the ordinary womanly ways; but about her very weakness, her ungainly fadedness, in the deprecating appeal which strove to declare itself on her dull face, there was a power which swayed

him, unrecognised as it was, and swayed him
for his good. He looked at her for a
moment and then answered her gently and
quickly, speaking even protectingly and reassuringly.

"I will, Mrs. Custance," he said. "Yes,
indeed I will!"

And in those words, almost without
consciousness of what he was doing, he took
his first definite step back to his lost self-
respect; for as he uttered them they became
a pledge with himself.

"I am so glad!"

She spoke the words in a low, jerky
tone, which did not serve to lessen their
futility, but by this time it had become
natural to Norman Strange to make allowances for her. The painful tension that
must, under any other circumstances, have
attended the resolution at which he had just

arrived was hardly felt by him in the instinct to put her at her ease ; the deeper issues of the moment seemed to stand aside, and he smiled as he said :

" And I may think of you as my friend ? "

" If—if you care to," she faltered. " I'm afraid——"

She did not finish her sentence. It was a habit of hers to leave sentences unfinished as though she had realised half-way through that they could be of no interest to any one. But the self-depreciation of her tone was not unpleasant to him ; on the contrary, it fell gratefully on his broken self-esteem, and seemed to throw his humiliation further into the background. With the stirring of his self-respect something of the superiority of clever young manhood touched him again, and it made his tone very pleasant as he said :

" You are only too good to me ! "

The words seemed to recall him to the
present, and he turned to the window again
with a sudden shadow on his face, and a
short, sharp sigh.

The rain, which earlier in the morning
had threatened to last all day, had ceased,
and a watery gleam of sunshine was
struggling for existence with the clouds.
The garden over which the window looked
was separated by a hedge from the road to
the village, and at the bottom of the garden
Norman Strange's eyes fell upon a figure,
the sight of which deepened the shadow
in them—the figure of Robert Caton. He
was leaning over the hedge, evidently talking
to some one in the road, and the next instant
Norman Strange saw that that some one was
the handsome girl at the village post office.

Two days before, Norman Strange, in

his heavy disregard of everything about him, would have noticed nothing; would have looked at Robert Caton with only a shuddering sense of their fellowship. But to-day in his newly-roused condition he was struck by something significant about the picture made by the man and the girl as she lingered in the road with her handsome face turned towards him as he leant over the hedge.

There was something in the outline of Caton's pose, something coarse and familiar in his gesture as he talked to her, which made the man who watched glance with a sudden youthful indignation at the face of the listening girl. He was wishing vaguely that he could see its expression, when he heard Mrs. Custance say:

"Ah, there is Alice! Is she coming for a lesson, I wonder?" She paused a moment she had come up to him, and was looking past him out of the window. "I wish she would not talk so much to Mr. Caton!" she murmured uneasily.

With a chivalrous instinct against watching the girl, Norman Strange turned from the window, speaking lightly and easily as though he had seen nothing.

"Miss Alice, whoever she may be, doesn't look as though she were likely to be a very docile pupil. What do you teach her, may I ask, Mrs. Custance?"

"Oh, I teach her—it's nothing. Alice is much cleverer than I am. I only show her about needlework. She is such a good girl at the bottom, only she is not like other girls."

"She isn't like most other girls to look at, certainly. Who is she, Mrs. Custance?"

"She's — oh, she's one of the village girls; her grandmother, who brought her up, is the post-mistress. She brought her up very badly, I'm afraid, for she's dreadfully—dreadfully headstrong. I'm teaching her needlework, because when her grandmother dies she must keep herself somehow —I don't believe she'll ever marry; she's dreadful to all the young men about—and she says she won't ever be a servant. And, indeed, I don't think she would ever get a place."

Mrs. Custance stopped abruptly as though self-convicted of having made a very long speech; her subject had evidently been very near her heart, and Norman Strange said interestedly:

"And so you teach her needlework? That is very good of you, isn't it?"

"Oh, no," she answered with some

surprise in her tone. "It is good of her to let me try and help her."

She was looking uneasily out of the window as she spoke, and Norman Strange knew that the pair on either side of the hedge were still there, even before she interrupted herself suddenly, and said in an undertone with a slight sigh of relief:

"Ah, here she comes!" The words had been merely a parenthesis, and Mrs. Custance turned away from the window as she went on: "I am very fond of her, and I know — there was a little baby in the village, the child of the woman in the next cottage to the Eades, and its mother died." She stopped as if too little used to being listened to to tell the story she had evidently begun upon. "The baby died," she said, "and I've known Alice ever since."

"And she knows you?" he suggested lightly and courteously.

"She is fond of me," she answered simply. "They say—she says—" she paused and finished—"I am very fond of her."

Mrs. Custance turned to the table and took up her work again, and Norman Strange said:

"The lesson comes off here, no doubt, Mrs. Custance, and I should be in the way, I'm afraid. It is fairly fine now, you see, and I will go for a walk."

She murmured something hesitating and inaudible, and taking the murmur to signify assent he responded pleasantly and moved down the room with a smile of farewell. He did not see her eyes, as they followed him with mute distress and uncertainty in their glance; but turning, with his hand on the door, the solitariness of the figure he was leaving struck him forcibly. He paused.

"Are you generally at work in here in the morning, Mrs. Custance?" he said. "May I come and read to you sometimes, or would it bore you?"

"Oh, no! I should—it would be so nice —only—it's very kind. Wouldn't it be a trouble to you?"

There was such genuine eagerness, astonishment, and self-depreciation in her tone, it put him into the position of conferring so great a favour, that no good-natured young man who had once had his fair share of pleasure in that position, and a fair sense of his own value, could fail to be touched by it. Norman Strange had never thought to find himself looked up to, to find himself an object for gratitude again; his self-respect revived still further, and something of his old enthusiasm stirred in him again as he responded eagerly, unconsciously accepting, in the very graciousness of his tone and manner, the position she allotted to him.

" It would be a pleasure, on the contrary." He paused, and then remembering their first walk together and her ignorance on the subject of Thornsdyke church, he added, in the same tone: " Perhaps you might like to get up some architecture, Mrs. Custance? It would be the greatest pleasure to me to help you, if you would care about it. I'll see about some books."

His hand was still upon the door-handle, but as he spoke the last words he drew back as a sharp tap fell upon the other side of the door.

" Thank you! Oh, come in! It's very kind!" said Mrs. Custance confusedly, and then the door opened and Alice Eade came in.

"Did you expect me, Mrs. Custance?" she said. "I couldn't remember what we arranged."

Her face was flushed, and she spoke rather hurriedly, taking no notice of Norman.

"I think we arranged for this afternoon, Alice," returned Mrs. Custance; "but it doesn't matter in the least—not in the least," she repeated, as the girl uttered a quick exclamation of regret. "This will suit me quite as well; I've—I've nothing to do."

She glanced at Norman as she spoke, and Alice Eade turned to him.

"Good morning," she said.

"Good morning," he returned pleasantly, looking at her with eyes quite other than the haggard, uninterested ones with which he had seen her on the occasion of their two previous meetings. "Well, Mrs. Custance, I won't interrupt," and with another

"Good morning" to the girl, he left the room.

"Why does she let that fellow speak to her?" he said to himself. He did not know how strong a token of returning mental health lay in the fact that his thoughts as he went towards the front door did not revert immediately to himself. And the youthful chivalrous indignation for the girl was not a more significant sign of his reversion to his old self than was the fact that Caton figured in his thoughts as "that fellow," with none of that bitter sense of his own equality with his fellow - patient which had made every thought of the latter a hideous humiliation to him. "Why does she let him speak to her? They looked from that window—— What's he doing?"

More than once — with increasing frequency, indeed — during the days that

followed, Norman Strange asked himself
the same uneasy question. It seemed to
him that he never met or heard of Alice
Eade without a suggestion of Caton in the
background. And it so happened that he
saw a good deal of her. She was often
at the White House, and he chanced to
meet her frequently about the village and
in his country walks.

The interest in her, which had been
stirred by the merest accident, almost simultaneously with the renewal of his old force;
an interest quickened by the vague uneasiness
for her created in his mind by the picture
she had made with Caton as he looked at
them from the window; seemed to develope
as that force developed, and to belong
naturally and as a matter of course to his
new life.

CHAPTER VIII.

For to all intents and purposes it was a new life that Norman Strange led as the windy March days followed one upon another; or rather, it was a renewal of the life that had seemed to have completely passed away. The struggle involved was fierce, at times agonising. Half-hearted action, gradual or tentative measures were impossible to him; what he did he must needs do hotly. Having decided with himself that his position might indeed yet be retrieved he threw himself into the contest with a certain ardour of self-conquest, a certain fierce exultation in the thought of riding rough-shod over weakness and faint-heartedness. He anticipated only the mental difficulty of sustaining his new faith in the possibility of such retrieval. He fortified himself mainly to do battle with his own despair, and he overlooked altogether the awful power of the master whose slave he had become. The shock of finding that despair and faint-heartedness were not the only forces arrayed against him; the self-loathing and contempt induced in him by the physical suffering which he could only endure and by no means prevent; almost threw him once more off his balance when he first realised the truth. The check had come only just in time. A little later and the physical difficulties might have been insuperable, except with years of treatment, and even as it was he suffered terribly. There came hours when the horrible craving—by which at the same time he felt himself unspeakably

degraded—was almost more than he could
bear, when he could hardly force himself to
speak or move without some hideous out-
break, when to meet his own eyes in the looking-glass was to meet incarnate temptation.

He never thought of reading the
frightened blue eyes that watched him at
such times with such a misery of impotent
sorrow and longing. But often and often—
and even in his worst moments this would
happen—he was faintly conscious of an
appeal in them; an appeal which stirred his
gentleness and his consideration; an appeal
which—though he only thought vaguely of not
distressing Mrs. Custance, as he would have
thought it brutal to frighten a child—stood
between him and the demon he had fostered

Everything that external temptation
could add to internal craving was supplied to
the situation by Robert Caton, by whom the

line taken by the man in whom he had
expected to find a boon companion was
regarded as neither more nor less than a
personal insult. He tried good fellowship;
he tried coarse laughter. He even en-
deavoured to enlist Dr. Custance by jeering
at him as to his probable loss of a portion of
his income, but Dr. Custance smiled in-
dolently and took the whole affair as a jest.
And as the days passed Norman Strange
saw less and less of either of the other two
men. He drifted gradually into spending
the greater part of his time with Mrs. Custance. In the intervals between his darkest
hours—intervals, each one of which saw him
more nearly his old self—she was at once a
rest and an occupation to him. His readings to her diverged rapidly in all directions.
There was hardly any point on which they
touched on which she did not lack informa-

tion, and to his youthful energy in impart-
ing knowledge the fact that his pupil was
rather dull was hardly a drawback. She was
apparently never tired of listening, and the
ardour of youth was never tired of laying
down the law. She evidently looked up
with timid admiration to his learning, and
his intellect generally, and an instinct of
kindly superiority towards her developed in
him rapidly. He had been conscious now
and then, even from the very first, of being
rather sorry for her, and this feeling, too,
developed with time, though he hardly knew
why. No one seemed to consider her, and
her life seemed to him on the whole a grey
affair.

And still as the weeks went on; as the
struggle grew less painful, and he became
more and more himself; as his old chivalry,
his old enthusiasm for truth and justice and

right revived in him again ; an uneasy sense
of some as yet undefined demand made on
his manhood by Alice Eade grew upon him.
It would not have been like him to reflect
that, after all, the wrongs—even if she should
have wrongs—of a stray young woman in
the village could be no concern of his. He
thought vaguely that she was a protégée of
Mrs. Custance's ; that the dreadful fellowship he himself had acknowledged with
Caton constituted some kind of indefinite
claim on him, but probably his desire to
protect her if she should need protection
went deeper than either of these fanciful
causes, and had its root in inbred quixotism.
He knew that the girl met Caton constantly.
Once, knowing that Caton was waiting for
her, he had walked with her himself down to
the village under pretext of a necessity for
stamps.

"She doesn't thank me," he said to himself on that occasion. "If she only knew
what a brute he is!"

But he did not see his way to en-
lightening her on the subject either then or
at any of their subsequent meetings, though,
as has been said, these were frequent. He
thought of speaking to Mrs. Custance on the
subject, but not being, as he said to himself,
"either an old woman or a cad," he found
this course also closed to him. Then there
grew upon him a conviction that the only
thing to be done was for him to "have it
out" with Robert Caton.

Nearly two months had passed since his
coming to the White House, and it was on
an April afternoon that he finally put his
characteristically straightforward but somewhat desperate resolution into effect. It
was a desperate resolution because he had

absolutely nothing to go upon; all the significance of the situation lay in such subtleties as would not be expressed in words; and the interview was as futile as it could not fail to be. Caton laughed insolently at him, and if his manner intensified Norman's distrust, it gave him no more tangible ground for it. Caton was master of the situation, and with a coarse jest and laugh in his ears Norman left him abruptly, conscious of having put himself hopelessly in the wrong, and burning with impotent indignation. He took his hat and burst out of the house, thinking that a walk would cool him and settle his disturbed thoughts. He took a short cut down a lane to the highroad—a lane little used except by the inmates of the White House—and turning a corner sharply he came upon a sight that tended little to compose him. Alice Eade was sauntering to and fro evidently waiting for some one. Norman Strange pulled up short.

" Good evening," he said.

" Good evening, Mr. Strange," she answered carelessly, though her colour had heightened considerably. They were very close together in the narrow lane, and at the moment, from the opposite direction to that in which Norman had come, an old man appeared. They drew back to let him pass, and as Norman recognised the acknowledged scandal-monger of the village he turned away with an irrepressible gesture of an-noyance, and cut at the weeds in the hedge-row with his stick. It seemed to him that the old man must inevitably put upon Alice Eade's presence in the little-used lane the construction that he himself had put upon it.

If any other possibility occurred to the

girl it seemed to amuse her rather than
otherwise, for as the old man passed she
turned to Norman with a mischievous toss of
her head, and a sparkle of roguery in her
eyes, and said lightly :

"It's a splendid evening for a walk, isn't
it, Mr. Strange ?"

Norman did not answer her. He
watched the old man out of sight and then
turned quickly towards her.

"Miss Eade," he said, quickly and
impulsively, "hadn't you better go home ?"

And then he coloured like a girl, lifted
his hat hurriedly, and disappeared round the
turn of the lane.

CHAPTER IX.

"THERE, Mrs. Custance! That's as fine a bit of descriptive writing as you can meet anywhere! There is another bit here, now!" Norman Strange took up the book, which he had laid down as he spoke in a tone full of fire and animation, and began to turn the leaves eagerly over.

He was sitting by the table in the dining-room, his chair pushed back from it, his legs stretched out under it, his folded arms resting upon it in an attitude of concentrated mental energy and physical unconsciousness that was characteristic of him. He was surrounded by a confusion of books of all

descriptions. Opposite him, with her needlework in her hand, sat Mrs. Custance. She
had been listening to his spirited reading
with her head bent over the work, in and out
of which her needle moved rather slowly;
and as he stopped speaking she lifted her
head, either as though in expectation of the
coming extract or as though the sudden ces-
sation of sound had interrupted some train of
thought in her mind, and looked across the
table at him as he sat engrossed in his search.

The searching sunlight of a bright May
day fell full upon his face as he faced the
open window, lighting up unsparingly every
line of it; and it fell upon a face so different
from the haggard, miserable mask that
Norman Strange had worn on his first
coming to the White House, that the very
features were hardly recognisable as the
same. The constraint was gone from it;

the bitterness was gone from it ; the despair
was gone from it. It was still pale, but no
longer with the pallor of ill-health ; it was
still thin, but it was the thinness of an
intellectual man in excellent physical training.
The eyes were bright and clear, and the
whole face was alight and aglow with
interest, energy, and life.

It was nearly three months now since
Norman Strange had determined to retrieve
the past, and he had never wavered. To all
intents and purposes he was now his old self
again ; on the surface, indeed, strangely his
own self ; youthful, confident, eager as ever ;
unaltered, apparently, by all that he had
suffered. The developements and changes
brought about by his bitter experience and
his valiant self-conquest, lay in the depths of
his nature ; in an added strength ; in a purity
and steadiness of principle having its root

now in the deliberate choice of manhood
rather than in the unstable enthusiasm of
youth; in a germ which life had yet to
develope of that peculiar sympathy and
tenderness for humanity which only sin and
repentance can produce.

He turned the pages of his book impetuously, and Mrs. Custance watched him
quietly.   Their two faces were a curious
contrast.   His so alert, intellectual and expressive; hers so wanting in life, so utterly
without that glow and colour that comes
from within, so subdued and insignificant.
And yet as she watched him there seemed
to pass from his face to hers a strange, faint,
ghostly reflection of his brightness.   Exactly
what it was or in which of her pale, dull
features it lay, it would have been impossible
to say; but it was there and her whole face
was changed by it.

"Here it is, Mrs. Custance!" exclaimed Norman at last. "I think you'll like this!" He was very careful to adapt his selections to her capacity, taking a kindly, lofty pride in not "going over the poor little woman's head," as he had said to himself once. "Just listen to this!"

But Mrs. Custance was not destined to listen after all, though she took up her work again and prepared obediently to do so. Norman Strange's first sentence was cut short by the entrance of the servant with a note for her mistress, and as Mrs. Custance took it her face changed very slightly and was its subdued self again.

"I'm very sorry," she said apologetically to Norman as the servant left the room. "I won't read it yet. Please go on, if you don't mind."

"There's no hurry, Mrs. Custance," he

returned, with a certain gracious con-
descension that was too frankly youthful
to be unpleasant. "We've been very hard
at work. Let us take a rest. I don't
know how you can suggest keeping that
important - looking document waiting," he
added with a laugh.

"It's from the Warrens at Sletton,"
she answered ; " Kathleen Warren's writing
is so large. I wonder what it can be
about ? "

She took up the envelope hesitatingly
and opened it as he said :

"That's the young lady we pulled out
of a ditch the other day, isn't it ? "

"Yes," she answered. "It is an invitation for a tennis - party on Friday."
She read it through with a certain careful
precision — an invitation was a rare circumstance and one of rather overwhelming

importance to her—and then with a faint, nervous flush in her cheeks she said very tentatively: "They will be so pleased if you will go over there with us for the tennis - party. They want us all to go. Will you"—she hesitated—" will you care about it ?"

She handed the letter timidly to him and took up her work again. During his first weeks at the White House, Norman Strange had given it to be understood that he would go nowhere. All invitations extended to him out of the mixture of curiosity and compassion felt by the country round for Dr. Custance's "patients" were, indeed, abhorrent to him in his morbid misery, and even since his recovery he had avoided introductions. He had made the acquaintance of the Miss Warren in question, however — the pretty daughter of some rich people living about three miles away — in an unconventional manner, by helping her in a difficulty with an obstinate pony, and he answered Mrs. Custance cheerily as he glanced over the letter.

" I will go with pleasure, Mrs. Custance, if you think of going. Rather jolly sort of affair, I should think ? "

" They know every one for miles round," returned Mrs. Custance with a faint sigh, as if the prospect before her were terrible to her shyness. " Yes, we shall go, I expect. Mr. Caton is asked. I wonder whether he will be well enough to go ? "

She spoke the last words in her ordinary hesitating voice, but in the most matter-of-fact way. Her own intense distaste to going out with Robert Caton had never been of the faintest consequence to any one, and it never occurred to her to complain. Norman glanced at her now with a quick flash of pity, which the thought of her in connection with Caton always stirred in him, and said rather constrainedly :

" Dr. Custance considers him almost recovered, I believe."

A sudden suspension of Norman's anxieties for Alice Eade had been brought about the very day after his meeting with her in the lane by an accident to Robert Caton, which, trivial to another man, threatened serious results to him.   He broke his arm and was laid up for a fortnight with sufficient fever to give Dr. Custance a great deal of trouble.   And before he was about again another event occurred that made it unlikely that he would have any further opportunities of rousing Norman's ire as

far as Mrs. Custance's handsome protégée
was concerned. Alice Eade's grandmother,
and only relation, an old woman who had
long been ailing, died suddenly, and left her
alone. She had no means of supporting herself in Thornsdyke, and Mrs. Custance
arranged for her going without delay to a
small dressmaking firm in Newcastle, as
apprentice. It had seemed probable at first
that she would have left the village before
Robert Caton was downstairs again, and
Norman had dismissed all perturbation on
her behalf from his mind. Her departure
had been delayed for one reason and another
more than once ; Robert Caton had been
about now for more than a fortnight, and she
was still alone in the cottage that had been
her grandmother's ; but to Norman the latter
arrangement was so temporary a state of
things, he looked upon the whole affair as

so completely and necessarily over, that no
return of his former vague uneasiness was
possible to him. He no more thought her
choice of a subject a curious coincidence than
did Mrs. Custance herself, when the latter,
after the short silence that followed his last
words, said, with the mixture of timidity and
confidence which was the outcome of her
constant intercourse with Norman, and which
made her manner to him when they were
alone together quite different from her
manner to the rest of her world :

"I hoped Alice would have gone to
Newcastle on Friday, but they have put her
off again this morning."

"You will miss her very much, I'm afraid,
Mrs. Custance."

At the same moment there came the tap
at the door that Norman Strange knew now
as well as Mrs. Custance did, and in answer

to the latter's rather surprised " Come in!"
Alice Eade in person opened the door. She
was dressed in a plain black dress, and
perhaps it was because neither of them was
used to its new setting, that her beauty
struck both Norman Strange and Mrs.
Custance — though their respective impressions differed considerably in distinctness
of outline—as being absolutely startling.

" I know you didn't expect me this
morning," she said to Mrs. Custance, and
her vigorous, self-confident tone was a little
quicker and more resonant than usual. " But
I thought perhaps——" She left her sentence unfinished, a very unusual thing with
her, and glancing at Norman said carelessly :
" Good morning, Mr. Strange."

His first meeting with her after their
brief interview in the lane had been somewhat embarrassing to Norman, though he

had carried it off with himself with a high hand. Perhaps it was fortunate that it did not occur until after her grandmother's death had necessarily thrown their last parting to some extent into the background of her thoughts ; at any rate the slightest possible undercurrent in her manner to him, half mocking, half scornful, constituted all the notice she apparently cared to give it, and on the few subsequent occasions of their meeting her manner to him had been simply careless. Now, however, as he returned her greeting, Norman wondered idly whether he had done anything to offend her, or whether she was simply annoyed at not finding Mrs. Custance alone, for though her tone was carelessness itself, her eyes, as she looked towards him from Mrs. Custance, changed to a look of hardness that was almost defiance.

Acting on his last supposition he said easily :

" Well, Mrs. Custance, I ought to do an hour's work before dinner, and I will go and do it. You are going to plunge into the mysteries of needlework with Miss Eade, no doubt, and I am very grateful to her for bringing me up to the point."

And with a smile and a pleasant parting word he left the room. He was working steadily now at his old law work ; and he was quite unconscious that he owed his first impetus towards renewed study, not as he believed, to his own energy, but to a few timid incoherent words uttered in a low, uncertain voice, in a pause in one of his monologues to Mrs. Custance.

No sooner was the dining-room door shut upon him than Alice Eade crossed the room quickly and stood close to Mrs. Custance, looking down at her as she sat. The handsome face with its bold, decided outlines and its great black eyes, was no more capable of delicate shades of expression than the nature behind was capable of delicate shades of feeling. But the broader, stronger passions with which that nature was aglow were always distinctly legible upon her features, and as one impulse gave swift place to another in her undisciplined heart the change was as swiftly reflected upon her face. It had changed now, curiously and completely, since Norman Strange's departure.

"You don't mind my coming?" she said abruptly.

"Mind!" repeated Mrs. Custance with gentle wonder. "Of course not, Alice! Is it something you want to ask me about that dress? Sit down, my dear."

But Alice did not sit down. She moved

with a vigorous, restless movement to the window, and stood with her back to Mrs. Custance as she answered : " No—I mean yes ! "

She asked a trivial question on the subject of the dress in question, and listened to the simple answer, still standing with her face turned away, and apparently without paying much attention, for after Mrs. Custance finished her explanation there was a pause. Then the girl turned suddenly and looked down at her again.

" What a lot of trouble you've taken about me, Mrs. Custance ! " she said in an odd brusque tone, which harmonised strangely with the rough affection on her face. " What do you do it for ? "

Mrs. Custance smiled faintly. She thought Alice was odd to-day, but she was used to vigorous unconventionality from her.

"I'm very fond of you, Alice," she said simply.

"It's very foolish of you!" said the girl with sudden energy. "Yes, it is, Mrs. Custance. Oh, I know! You think because I'm not the vixen they make me out down in Thornsdyke that I'm all right, but I'm not, and that's flat. P'raps you'll be sorry one day!"

"I don't think so, Alice."

"I know you don't!" was the quick, vehement response. "That's because you're like what you are, Mrs. Custance. You think you've seen something good in me, I tell you, and you think that it must be all through the same. You wouldn't ever see anything wrong if it wasn't as plain as print." The girl paused a moment, and the affection in her face was tempered by what in a more refined nature would have been pity, but

which became in her coarser physique contempt, for the simplicity of the small worn
face raised to hers. "Why don't you see
how bad everybody is?" she said vehemently.
"Then you'd know how much better you are
than everybody, and you wouldn't let yourself be so put upon all round. Why, there
isn't any one in the place but me knows what
you're like—how kind you are, and how
patient, and how you put up with one."

The face on which her eyes were fixed
with a kind of angry excitement was patient
enough, in truth, but it was also exceedingly
bewildered. Mrs. Custance, indeed, had
hardly taken in the actual words addressed
to her in her surprise at their general
drift.

"Alice!" she said remonstratingly,
"Alice! my dear!'

"You ought to think more of yourself,

Mrs. Custance. That's what you ought.
What's the use of letting every one look
down on you?" She stopped abruptly,
touched apparently by something in the blue
eyes to which no touch of offended dignity
had come. Quite suddenly all the coarse
contempt and aggression passed from her
flushed face to be succeeded by a passionate
self-loathing. With a sharp stamp of her
foot, the awkward, impotent gesture of an
unemotional class where a girl of another
class would have flung herself upon her knees
beside the woman to whom she spoke, Alice
cried passionately: "I ought to be ashamed
of myself! I ought to be ashamed! When
I know how good you are! Mrs. Custance,
Mrs. Custance, you know I'm grateful, you
do know I'm grateful?"

There was a passionate appeal, a passionate
self-reproach in her voice, and Mrs. Custance

rose hurriedly and took one of the strong hot hands into both her own small pale ones.

"Of course I know, Alice," she said; "don't be so excited. I don't know what you've been talking about, or what you mean, and I don't think you know either, but you know that I am always your friend."

Good and bad, high and low, black and white, the inevitable elements brought to the making of every human being from everlasting to everlasting; in what proportion these are found combined by nature or by developement at certain moments of a man's life, of which no other human being can say, "It was then" or "then"; it. is on this that the subsequent turn of every individual life upwards or downwards depends. Unknown to either Alice Eade's moment came to her as she stood there with her hand in Mrs. Custance's hand, and she

followed her strongest bent. Mrs. Custance's words brought back her self-con-
fidence, and it came back hard and coarse
and slightly contemptuous of the gentleness,
the want of quickness, in a mind as slow
to apprehend as to resent. Her affection
remained, but it was her affection at its
lowest, its least perceptive and appreciative.

"You've always been kind to me, Mrs.
Custance," she said, and her tone now,
compared to that in which she had spoken
before, was almost careless; "I'm sure I
ask your pardon if I've said anything I
shouldn't. There've been so many changes,
you see, and what with one thing and
another I'm upset, I expect, and talk nonsense. I must go home now."

The brilliancy and glow had come back
to her face as she spoke, and as she said
good-bye her beauty struck Mrs. Custance

N 2

again with the vague shock of realisation
she had felt on her entrance. She was
hardly conscious of any surprise when the
beautiful face, in what seemed to her at the
moment the natural conscious pride of its
beauty, bent suddenly and kissed her.

"Good-bye, Mrs. Custance," said the
girl, "Good-bye." And then she was gone.

There was a vague sense of shock, of
bewilderment, and perplexity, in Mrs. Custance's mind when she was left alone, and
its traces were still visible in her manner
when luncheon-time came. Alice's visit had
caused her to forget some trifling order she
had had to give with regard to Robert
Caton's room, and the faltering apology
with which she met her husband's sarcastic
comments was uttered with eyes that were
unusually frightened and deprecating. Dr.
Custance himself, indeed, was unusually

severe, but Robert Caton, who still looked weak and shattered and wore a sling, took the affair very lightly, and was altogether in boisterous spirits.

"It's no matter," he said carelessly, when Mrs. Custance apologised to him. "It's no matter. You'll soon be rid of me altogether. A good riddance, too, eh, Mrs. Custance? There's one fellow here who thinks so, I know," and he turned with a rough laugh to Norman. "Heard the good news, Strange? I'm going to relieve you of my company for six months at least. Off in a day or two."

CHAPTER X

"By-the-bye, Mrs. Custance, I hear that Mr. Caton is going away immediately. I suppose he is incurable, poor man. Dear, dear, a nice-looking young man, too, and very agreeable except for that unfortunate failing. It does seem very sad. When is he going?"

"I think—that is—he is going to-morrow morning. Dr. Custance — Mr. Caton — he has been ill, you know, and he thinks a thorough change——"

It was a lovely May afternoon, hot with the breath of coming summer, fresh and gracious with the breath of passing spring. The large gardens of Sletton Court, the

home of the young lady extricated by
Norman Strange from a ditch, were looking
their very best, and to the shy eyes of Mrs.
Custance the lawns presented a bewildering
confusion of people; all constantly moving
to and fro, all talking and laughing; all, as
far as the female contingent was concerned,
in bright summer frocks, which made her
look more insignificant and dowdy than ever.

She was sitting under a tree on a seat
which she had instinctively chosen as being
rather out of the way, but not sufficiently so
to be conspicuous, talking to, or rather being
talked to by, a stout, elderly lady of considerable presence and apparently unlimited
curiosity. Mrs. Custance had in all innocent
unconsciousness, through sheer nervous inability to carry on a conversation, foiled
several attempts on the part of her interlocutor to find out the nature and extent of

Dr. Custance's income, and a short pause had ensued, during which Mrs. Custance's eyes had wandered towards the tennis-courts, which lay to the left on a lower lawn. She had started and turned her eyes rather hurriedly to her companion, apparently self-convicted of wandering attention, as that lady resumed the conversation with the question as to Robert Caton's proceedings.

A thorough change after his illness was in fact the reason given by Robert Caton for his departure, and, as Mrs. Custance had said, he was to leave Thornsdyke on the following morning. The three days which had elapsed between his announcement of his intention and Mrs. Warren's tennis-party had seen all his arrangements made and his very train fixed, and these facts had had a strong influence on the atmosphere of the White House for those three days. The personal

contentment that Mrs. Custance felt in them
was as nothing against the access of nervousness and hesitating timidity produced in her
by the increase of sarcasm and cold contempt
towards her which was the outcome of the
effect upon her husband's temper of the
anticipated loss of his "patient." Her eyes
grew frightened now, and she hoped vaguely
that her companion would not speak to him
of Robert Caton as she saw her husband
coming towards them as they sat together
under the trees.

Dr. Custance came commissioned by
his hostess, he said, to see if the lady
who was sitting by his wife would take
some tea. The lady in question proving
more than willing, and his wife hurriedly
declining his careless invitation to herself,
the two moved away together. Left alone,
Mrs. Custance's eyes wandered back again

instinctively to the tennis-courts, and as they did so up from the lower lawn came Norman Strange and the master of the house, a young man of about his own age, Mrs. Warren's son. The former saw her, made her a little gesture of greeting with his racquet, and passed on laughing and talking with the other and disappeared into the house.

It was many months since Norman had enjoyed himself with the simple exhilaration of young animal spirits that he was feeling this afternoon. In the old days he had delighted in society, and it was significant of the thoroughly healthy tone which his mind had regained, that no sooner had he found himself on Mrs. Warren's lawn in the midst of a crowd of young and apparently happy people than his spirits had begun to rise. He gave

not a thought to his position, it never
occurred to him in his renewed self-
confidence and zest of life that he was
there as Dr. Custance's "patient," and he
threw himself into the spirit of the thing
with even more than his old enjoyment
and animation. He had talked and laughed
and made himself agreeable and useful by
handing tea and ices with unfailing readiness
and ease; and, as a well-bred young man
of the world was rather a novelty in that
quiet country place, he had attracted a
good deal of attention. Finally he had
accepted from the young master of the
house the loan of the necessary shoes, etc.,
and had played tennis with considerable
energy and science and immense enjoyment, until young Warren came up to
him as he stood, hot, eager, and triumphant
after a long set, and said with a laugh:

"You've worked like a horse, and I'm sure you must be done up. Come in with me and have a drink." And Norman, excited, pleased, and responsive, answered lightly:

"Thanks. A drink would suit me capitally."

Young Warren had, of course, heard earlier in the afternoon that Norman Strange had come with the Custances, but seeing him so bright, popular, and pleasant it had never entered his head to identify him as one of the doctor's patients. He supposed Norman to be a visitor at the White House, and he had taken a great fancy to him. The talk between them was quick and interested as they passed up the garden, and as they entered the house the young host interrupted himself in a brisk hunting anecdote to say:

"I'm taking you to my smoking-room, by-the-bye. I always make it a point with my mother on these occasions to have some drinks put there that a fellow may have a chance of cooling down quietly. Who's here, I wonder?"

He opened a door as he spoke and disclosed a room in which there were about half-a-dozen men. He introduced Norman to two or three of those near the door, pressed him to help himself from the trays on the table, and departed with cheery zeal to do his duty elsewhere.

"You've been playing a hard set!" observed one of the men, a tall, muscular young fellow to whom his host had particularly commended the new-comer, as Norman's countenance became temporarily eclipsed by a large tumbler of lemon and soda. "Take a cigarette and a chair."

"Thanks!" returned Norman readily.
It was delightful to him to find himself
once more in a smoking-room with "the
right sort of fellow," as he mentally
designated his present companions as he
glanced round him. He had seen on
his first entrance that Robert Caton was
one of a group at the far end of the
room; but in his elation of spirits he was
prepared to ignore, and if necessary to
tolerate him on this, the last day on which
they would be even nominally associated.
And in the ardour of the conversation that
followed—a conversation on a neighbouring election, which had been interrupted by
his entrance and in which he was immediately given a footing — he entirely for-
got his fellow "patient's" vicinity until an
opinion advanced by him was suddenly com-
mented on from the other end of the room

in the coarse voice and manner he knew so well.

"You don't believe in wholesale pledges, eh, Strange? That's something new from you!"

Robert Caton sauntered up as he spoke and stood by the table, looking down at Norman with an indescribably evil shadow on his face as the latter leant back in his chair, one leg thrown carelessly over the other, cigarette in hand, animated, and enthusiastic. All the scores that had accumulated in his unwholesome mind against the man who had done what he had not even wished to do had summed themselves together as he sat at the other end of the room watching and listening.

"You believe in the blue ribbon, I take it!" he continued with a sneer, as Norman, apparently occupied with the ashes of his

cigarette, did not answer for the moment.
"Come, now, Strange, you believe in the
blue ribbon ?"

A silence had perforce fallen on the other
men in the group on Caton's interruption, a
silence tinged with a perceptible chill. But
in spite of themselves there was a little stir
of interest among them on his last words.
Only one or two, as it happened, knew Caton
and not one knew anything of his relations with Norman Strange. Norman had
spent the last quarter of an hour arguing
brilliantly in a youthful, theoretical way
against pledges, written or unwritten, as
destructive to a man's strength of will, and
the men who had noticed his adherence to
lemon and soda were curious as to what he
would say. There was a moment's pause
and then he looked Caton full in the face and
said quietly :

"No! I don't believe in the blue ribbon."

Caton laughed.

"Don't like the name, eh? Well, blue ribbon, taking the pledge, total abstinence, call it what you like, you believe in the thing itself?"

"No!" Norman spoke slowly and still more quietly as if with something of an effort. "I don't!"

They were looking one another full in the face; Caton with an evil, insolent, sneering challenge; Norman with his expression indescribably alert behind his temporary quiet; and the other men remained instinctively silent as if watching a duel. There was another laugh from Caton, a laugh the ring of which seemed to release some of the youthful spirit which Norman was apparently holding in check, and the former said:

"You don't believe in total abstinence!

Why, man, you're a total abstainer yourself!
Stand to your colours."

There was another movement among the
men round as Norman made a spirited movement, as if to speak. Without in the least
understanding what was going on they began
to feel the position strained, and one young
fellow stretched out his hand for the whisky
bottle.

" What nonsense!" he said. " Here, Mr.
Strange, let me put some whisky into that
squash of yours and make him feel small."

With a quick instinctive movement
Norman moved his glass to avoid the
proffered whisky, and Caton exclaimed:

"Not he! His will's so strong, I tell
you, that he's afraid it wouldn't get exercise
enough if he once began upon whisky!"

His sneering eyes were full upon
Norman's as he spoke, and under the

intolerable taunt in them a boyish flash of indignation leapt into Norman's face, breaking down on the instant all his forced reserve, and he stretched out his glass impetuously to the man who held the whisky.

"That's a lie!" he cried impetuously, answering the eyes with which the other taunted him with being afraid. "Here, let's have some whisky!"

The quick splash of the liquid and another laugh followed, and simultaneously with these and most incongruously there came a low, hurried woman's voice from the door.

"I beg your pardon!" it said; "I was looking for Mr. Strange."

Mrs. Custance stood in the doorway, her small face white to the very lips, her hands clasping her sunshade in an intense grip. She did not seem to be aware that every man in the room had turned at the sound

of her voice; she fixed her eyes full upon
Norman Strange as he sprang up, setting
his tumbler of whisky on the table, and
came quickly towards her; and she went
on in the same low, hurried, but quite un-
hesitating voice:

"I came to see if you are ready, Mr.
Strange. Mrs. Ward has offered to take
back two of our party, and I thought perhaps
you would not mind going with me now!"

The next moment with a few rapid words
of farewell, and without a glance at Caton,
he had followed her through the doorway
and out of the house with a rather pale face.

The kindly old lady who had been rather
surprised at Mrs. Custance's ready accep-
tance of her offer of two seats in her carriage,
was no less surprised to find both her companions equally silent. Mrs. Custance was
even more painfully confused and embar-

rassed than was usual with her, and Norman
Strange hardly spoke.   Mrs. Custance had
by no means recovered herself, even when
they reached home, and as they walked in
silence up the garden, though Norman was
too preoccupied to notice it, she was trembling from head to foot.

" Please, ma'am, Mrs. Johnson is in the
kitchen and wants to speak to you very
particular," said the servant to her as she
opened the door, and Norman passed upstairs to his room as she went into the
dining-room, telling the girl to bring Mrs.
Johnson in.

Half an hour later he came downstairs
again, his face grave still, but no longer
painfully so.   He had forgotten Mrs. Johnson
apparently, or had concluded that she was
gone, for he opened the dining-room door
and then prepared to retreat again hastily as

he became aware of a homely figure in a shawl standing with Mrs. Custance by the window. But at the sound of his voice as he apologised, Mrs. Custance turned quickly to him, her blue eyes shocked and pitiful, her lips trembling.

"Oh, Mr. Strange!" she exclaimed, "what can I do? What can I do? Alice is gone!"

"Gone!" he repeated enquiringly, thinking of the girl's apprenticeship in Newcastle. "You did not expect that she would go so soon, Mrs. Custance?"

"I did not expect her to go at all!" she answered, her voice so shaken as to be hardly audible. "I mean, it's not to Newcastle she's gone! She's gone away from me—away from all of us, and I don't know where she is! Oh, Mr. Strange, don't you understand? Don't you understand?"

CHAPTER XI.

A SHORT, sharp exclamation broke from
Norman Strange as Mrs. Custance's shaken,
incoherent words stopped suddenly, and it
was followed by a moment's dead silence.
The woman from the village had turned
quickly towards Norman on his entrance,
and was looking at him with a pair of sharp
curious eyes. Mrs. Custance had turned
away her quivering face, and one hand was
working nervously at the window curtain,
by which she stood, as though she tried
instinctively even then to suppress herself
and her own emotion. Norman stood just
as her first words—startled from her ap-

parently by her irrepressible distress—had arrested him, almost in the doorway. Then Norman shut the door, and coming further into the room, said in a tone that was very low and grave :

" Is it not possible that there may be some mistake, Mrs. Custance? Will you tell me what is known ? "

Apparently the sympathetic voice let loose the current of her great distress, for the tears fell fast down her cheeks, and she tried in vain to answer him. Mrs. Johnson, who was by no means incapacitated from speech, in whose frame of mind, indeed, excitement and interest seemed to predominate, answered for her. She was the woman who had been with Alice Eade in the cart which Norman had stopped in the lane on the night of his arrival at Thornsdyke.

"It's very little as is known, sir, and
that's the fact!" she began; "but that
little's certain, and there's only one way
it points.   It's something to be thankful
for, I'm sure, that it's come to light when
it has!"—the reason for Mrs. Johnson's
thankfulness was somewhat obscure—"and
it was all along of my going by accident
into Wellborough this morning, by train."
Wellborough was the market-town.   "I
was going by the ten o'clock train," continued Mrs. Johnson, embarking on her
story with a certain enjoyment of it, "and
I got up to the station early, and while I
was waiting, Tom-at-the-station, he comes
up to me and says, 'So Miss Eade's gone to
stay for a bit in Wellborough!' Tom, he's
had a hankering after Alice this long time,
for all she never give him so much as a
look, and he's always got something to say

to me about her, thinking as she and me's
been more on terms, in a way of speaking,
than her and other Thornsdyke folks. So
I says to him, 'Oh, has she ? ' I says. 'It's
the first I've heard of it.'   I did think
then as it was rather strange like, that I
should never have heard of her havin'
friends in Wellborough, but I didn't give
it no more than a passing thought, and
I shouldn't have again as likely as not ; but
as I was a-going out of the Wellborough
station, who should I happen to meet but
Mrs. Williams, which is my master's cousin,
sir, and just as I was a-givin' her good day,
and goin' on, she says to me, 'Alice Eade's
gone to her place, then, Mrs. Johnson, and
a good riddance for Thornsdyke.'   Mrs.
Williams she never could see anything
in Alice. 'I see her settin' off for London
yesterday mornin', and it would have been

more becomin' in her, to my way o' thinkin',
to been seen off by some friend as wasn't
a young gentleman.' 'Setting off for
London, Mrs. Williams!' I says. 'Alice's
place ain't in London at all, nor she isn't
going to it yet awhile, either. You must
a' been mistook.' 'Mistook, Mrs. Johnson,'
says she. 'Now, I ask you only, is Alice
Eade the kind of girl to be mistook in?'
And the long and short of it is, sir, Mrs.
Williams was as positive as she was of
her own name that she'd seen Alice Eade
see'd off to London yesterday mornin' by a
gentleman. She couldn't say that she'd know
the gentleman again—for I thought it right,
as you'll believe, by that time, sir, to ask
her very particular. He had on a kind of
flapping coat thing. But she was sure he
was a gentleman, and a young gentleman,
sir."

Mrs. Johnson had spoken the last sentence in a peculiar tone that was at once lofty and confidential, and the eyes which she had fastened more intently than ever on Norman's face as she spoke were quite preternaturally keen and inquisitive. Neither of her auditors, however, noticed either tone or look, and directly she had taken breath she went on again.

"The mistakes I made with my shoppin' at Wellborough, sir, is past believin', I was that put about and upset, and the very first thing as I did when I got back home was to go round to Alice's place. My heart, I do assure you, sir, was in my mouth as I knocked at the door. I knocked, and I shook it, and I tapped at the window, and it was as quiet as a graveyard. She was gone, sure enough!"

Mrs. Johnson drew a long breath, as

one who has reached the climax of her story, and paused. There was a moment's silence, and then Norman said gently to Mrs. Custance:

"When did you see her last?"

"I've not seen her for three or four days," she answered brokenly. "Not since that morning when she came unexpectedly— you know! She sent me a message to say she couldn't come the next day. Oh, poor girl! What can we do?"

There was nothing immediate to be done, as Norman told her gently. He volunteered to go to Wellborough to make further enquiries, an offer which, as throwing doubt on her evidence, caused Mrs. Johnson to toss her head; he even volunteered to go to London and see if anything could be discovered at the terminus there, an offer which produced a still more pronounced toss of the head and a sniff of much emphasis from the same quarter.

Mrs. Custance's only thought, apparently, was the girl herself, and it was not until the interview was perforce drawn to a close by her uneasy sense of the approaching advent of supper-time and her husband, that the thought which occupied the minds of the other two of this oddly constituted trio was put into words with a kind of hesitating daring by Mrs. Johnson, as she darted another keen glance at Norman Strange:

" It's all very well to say where can she be ? " she said. " But there's a shorter question than that, Mrs. Custance, if I may take the liberty, that would tell us a deal. Who's the gentleman ? "

Mrs. Custance's grieving blue eyes were fixed on her for a moment with a startled expression as though the importance of the suggested question had only just occurred to her, and as she turned them helplessly on Norman as though appealing to him to answer it, he said to her, speaking gravely, almost sternly :

"You have no idea, Mrs. Custance ? "

"No!" she answered. "None at all! I can't think !"

Mrs. Johnson pursed up her lips into an expression in which were blended importance, mystery, and a certain unconcealed contempt for Mrs. Custance's want of penetration, and finally, moved by her burning desire to discuss the question in more responsive circles, she took her leave.

Meals at the White House, with the incongruous elements they brought together, could never be said to be either genial or sociable occasions. But over the supper which ensued half an hour later there seemed

to hang a strange unusual shadow. The
only one of the party whose spirits were un-
impaired was Robert Caton, and he was
even more than ordinarily boisterous and
insolent in manner. Dr. Custance was out
of temper; he had a summons to one of his
few patients which obliged him to go out
before supper was over; and while he was in
the room he hardly spoke, except to visit his
annoyance on his wife in the cutting sarcasm
from which she always shrank. Norman
was very silent, very stern, utterly unlike
himself; to Caton he spoke not a word.

That Mrs. Custance's voice should be
hardly heard was by no means an unusual
circumstance; but her face, her eyes red-
dened with her recent tears, was confused
and bewildered with distress. After the
departure of Dr. Custance she seemed to
notice Norman's tacit refusal to address

Caton, and that distress deepened. Perhaps
the remembrance of what she must have
seen and heard as she stood in the doorway
of the smoking-room at Sletton Court
suggested to her the thought that Norman
was resenting Caton's conduct on that
occasion, and inspired her with a vague
dread lest that resentment should develope
further, for apparently she found it almost
impossible to bring herself to leave them
alone together. As long as it was possible,
much longer than was usual with her, she
sat at the table, her pale face growing paler
and her hands trembling, and when at last
she rose, it was with the sudden, hasty movements of desperation. At the very door she
turned and looked back again as though
hesitating—looked at Caton leaning back in
his chair, careless, satisfied, hilarious; at
Norman, standing holding the door for her

in stern silence. The next moment she had moved on mechanically, and the door had closed behind her.

It was very still and peaceful in the drawing-room, and either that or the sudden relaxation of the strain with which the mental atmosphere of the dining-room had been charged had its effect on her. She was trembling less, and the colour was returning to her lips, when it was suddenly startled away again, and she rose abruptly from her chair, as the silence was broken by an angry voice from the dining-room. The passage that separated the rooms was narrow, the walls thin, and though she could hear no words she could distinctly distinguish that the first voice was answered by a second, insolent and sneering, and that it replied again more hotly than before. White as ashes, and trembling from head to foot, she

stood as though absolutely unable to move,
as the voices rose and fell in quick succession,
getting always higher and higher, until at last
as a violent retort brought almost the very
words to her ears, she suddenly crossed the
room and opened the drawing-room door just
as the hall door close to her right hand was
opened by her husband, who stopped short
on seeing her. She did not hear his question
to her. She was wholly absorbed in the
sudden silence in the dining-room that had
succeeded the last passionate words; a
silence which had arrested her in the drawing-room doorway, and in which she seemed
to hear the quick, hot breath of two angry
men standing face to face. It lasted for an
instant only, and then she and her husband
alike heard Norman Strange's voice ring out,
full and passionate :

"Tell me where she is ?"

There was a reply, an insolent, sneering reply, of which the words were inaudible. Then, before Dr. Custance could take the few steps between the hall door and the dining-room, there was a fierce exclamation :

"You scoundrel!" the sudden sound of a blow, a heavy thud, and the dining-room door was dashed open by Norman Strange, his face white, his eyes flashing, apparently beside himself with passion.

"You'd better go to him," he cried to Dr. Custance, apparently not even seeing the shrinking figure in the drawing-room doorway. "I've knocked him down, and I'll do it again whenever he's ready!" And before Dr. Custance had well taken in his words the front door shut behind him with a violent bang.

He dashed down the garden and started up the road at a pace of which he was no more conscious than he was of any destination for his hasty footsteps. Every pulse was leaping and throbbing, every nerve was strained and tense, he was conscious of nothing but such passion as perhaps only early manhood knows ; the hot, hardly controllable passion of youth combined with a man's fury of contempt for something unutterably base and degraded. For more than half an hour he walked at the top of his speed with no coherent thought, with no conscious volition, simply because the rapid movement supplied some outlet for the surging force within him ; the surging force which rose and shook him again and again until at last time and the physical exertion began to take effect. Very slowly and gradually the power of thought and consideration came back to him. Out of the red-hot glow of passion facts began to stand forth, he began to recollect and to reflect in detail, with a calmness which grew always sterner and sterner as his excitement subsided.

On the instant, as Mrs. Johnson spoke of a gentleman in connection with Alice Eade's disappearance, the thought of Caton had leapt into his mind, and the conviction that he was indeed the man had grown with every breath he drew. The temporary suspension of his original doubts and fears as to the flirtation carried on by Caton with the girl gave them double distinctness in the retrospect, and endued his present suspicion with a sense of absolute certainty that seemed to carry it out of the bounds of conjecture and to make it knowledge. And at the same time the thought that his fears should have been so lightly suspended, that he should have been so careless, so easily blinded, complicated the situation by adding to it for him the bitterness of self-reproach. It was characteristic of his boyish, impulsive chivalry that he should feel himself thus additionally responsible, additionally called upon to make some stand for womanhood in the person of the missing girl.

Exactly what his intentions had been when he found himself alone with Caton after supper he tried in vain to recall now as he walked along the country road, with the quiet summer darkness all about him and the fierce heat of passion subsiding in his heart. Had he himself begun, or had some covert sneer of Caton's given him an opening, he asked himself? One word had led to another, Caton's answers kindling in him an ever strengthening fire of indignation until at last, Caton, not perfectly sober, had avowed the truth, and avowed it with a brutal boast and an allusion to the girl which had destroyed

Norman's last remnant of self-control.   His
passionate demand as to her present where-
abouts had been met by a coarse taunt, and
on the instant a sudden, well-directed blow had
stretched the other man on the floor at his
feet.   Much more than this Norman was
unable to remember.   He was conscious of
having rushed out of the room, and he was
vaguely aware of having found himself face
to face with Dr. Custance in the hall; but of
what he had said or done since then he had
very little consciousness, until he found
himself about two hours later standing once
more outside the White House, having made
a round of nearly ten miles.

He was quite quiet now; his passion had
spent itself, and in its place was a steady,
implacable sternness.   He had made no plan
of future action; he knew that Caton was a
coward, and that there was little chance of

their meeting again that night, and for the morrow time and circumstances would develope his course of action. There was no regret in his mind for what had passed, but for the present he was quiescent. He stood a moment before entering the house, and looked up at the quiet night sky and round at the peaceful darkness of the landscape. The wind was sighing gently in the trees, and coming on the fierce excitement through which he had passed, the stillness and peace of the night seemed to suggest a sleeping earth, on which all the inhabitants slept also. Then he opened the hall door softly, lest Mrs. Custance should have gone to bed, and went in.

It was very quiet in the house. The stillness outside, with its calm suggestion of sleep, seemed to be intensified until it was almost oppressive. Its suggestiveness seemed in some indefinable way to intensify also, and it was no longer of the sleep of a night that it spoke. Norman paused a moment in the hall, vaguely conscious of a change in the atmosphere. All the doors were shut, and he thought that every one must be gone to bed. Then, seeing a light under the dining-room door, he determined to get some water before going upstairs, and crossed the hall with that intent. He opened the dining-room door and stood still suddenly.

Never while he lived could Norman Strange account for, or even define, the awful sense of chill horror that fell upon him in that moment. The room was perfectly quiet and orderly, perhaps even more orderly than usual, the gas was turned down. There was nothing out of the common to be seen, except that on the table there was something long and narrow, covered with a

white sheet.   Without knowing why or how
he did it, impelled by the horror that had
fallen on him as he opened the door, Norman
Strange walked mechanically up to the table
and lifted the sheet.   Beneath it lay Robert
Caton—dead.

CHAPTER XII.

" BUT hadn't they used to be pretty good friends, Drew ?"

The man addressed, a little wiry, sharp-faced man, suspended his proceedings with a plane—proceedings which had been merely nominal in the interest of the discussion going on around him, and answered confidentially :

"Well, Mr. Snowdon," he said, "that's according as how you take it. There's no one as can say as they ever saw them thick like, and my boy William, he's said times and again to his mother and me as he didn't believe Mr. Strange and Mr. Caton—poor

gentleman—could abide one another. An'
he says, too," he added parenthetically, " as
I've told you, sir, he says as the words
between 'em before it came to blows that
night was something enough to wake the dead.
He heard them, and Mrs. Scott's Emma, as
is cook at the White House, she heard 'em
too, as they was a-sittin' in the kitchen at
supper ! "

The scene was quaint and picturesque
enough. A long, low carpenter's shed, with
an odd cross-light from the wide opening
into the yard of which its creeper-grown
wall formed one side, and a small haphazard
pane of glass through which there streamed
a ray of light straight from the setting sun.
The carpenter himself stood at his bench,
and his interlocutor was leaning up against the
entrance, a stout, prosperous-looking figure,
of the small farmer class, with a stupid, good-

natured face. Farther into the shed, sitting
on a pile of newly-sawn wood which gave
its peculiar odour to the air, was a white-
bearded old man with a bright scarlet waistcoat, and outside, clustering together round
the doorway, were three or four women.

The workshop of Joshua Drew, the
Thornsdyke carpenter, was the head-quarters
of the village as far as gossip was concerned;
any one anxious for information as to their
neighbours' affairs invariably went to consult
its master, and seldom went in vain. On
the tragedy which had formed one of the
two subjects of excited discussion in Thornsdyke for the last three days, the death of
Robert Caton, his information was practically inexhaustible, and had all the majesty
of derivation from the fountain-head, since
his eldest son officiated in Dr. Custance's
house as pageboy. And to his own intense

satisfaction, Joshua Drew had hardly spent a moment alone in his workshop since the news was first known.

"There's some says one thing and some another," he resumed now with an impartial air. "There's some as 'as seen her with one and some with another. Here's Mr. Rogers, now," turning to the old man behind him; he was the old man who had come down the lane when Norman had found Alice Eade waiting, as he believed, for Robert Caton; "here's Mr. Rogers says he's seen her and Mr. Strange as thick as you please in Five-acre Lane."

"Ah!" interrupted a woman by the door, as Mr. Rogers prepared to endorse the carpenter's statement in a quavery treble, "an' I've seen her times out o' mind with Mr. Caton! A shameless hussy!"

"An' that's how it stands, Mr. Snowdon,"

continued Joshua Drew, presenting the woman's words to the farmer with confidential politeness; "some says one thing and some another; but one thing as there ain't no doubt on is as Mr. Strange knocked Mr. Caton down and killed him on the nail."

"I'm sorry to disturb that comfortable conviction, Drew, but such is not the fact!"

There was a sudden start and simultaneous turn of every member of the group in the direction of the indolent, sarcastic voice they all knew well. Unnoticed by any one, Dr. Custance had come down the yard in time to hear the last words, and he stood now confronting the talkers, as they acknowledged his presence in their various ways, with an expression which was by no means pleasant to them.

"I am very glad to have this opportunity of telling you, and I hope — I have no doubt, indeed—that you will each of you go and tell it to somebody else : that Dr. Harding finds that Mr. Caton's death was caused by heart disease. The interesting episode, of which you all seem to know a great deal more than I do, had, he says, nothing in the world to do with it."

There was a moment's dead silence, and then Joshua Drew made a valiant effort to retrieve his position in the eyes of the believers who had witnessed his fall by accepting Dr. Custance's words as a private and confidential communication addressed to himself.

"I'm very glad, indeed, to hear you say so, sir, I'm sure," he said. "Disease of the heart! Well, now, and to think that one never would have thought it! And the

blow had nothing to do with it — it all
happened simultaneous like ?   Well, now !"

"The blow, if there was a blow, had
nothing to do with it," returned Dr.
Custance, with a look under which a
woman on the outskirts of the group hastily
and unobtrusively departed.

"Nothing to do with it!   To be sure !"
responded Joshua Drew.   "Well, that
makes a wonderful deal o' difference, don't
it, now ? "

"I don't know so much about that !"
The words came in a slow and ruminating
voice from the farmer at the door, who was
collecting information for the edification of
his wife; and his social status bringing him a
degree nearer to Dr. Custance than were the
other members of the party, made it possible
to him to say what they ventured only to
think.   "It makes a difference in a way,

certainly ; but I don't see that it throws much light on which of 'em has done for the girl."

Dr. Custance turned on him quickly, a look of surprise on his face. He knew, of course, of the disappearance of Alice Eade, and he had arrived at a pretty clear estimate of the truth ; but he was ignorant of the confusion of mind existing in the village on the subject.

"What do you mean ?" he said.

"Well, which of 'em was it, doctor, you see ? No offence, I'm sure!" added the man awkwardly.

There was a moment's pause, and then Dr. Custance said callously :

"There is no particular reason, as far as I can see, to suppose that either of my patients had a hand in the affair. The girl, as you all know, was as likely as not to have

plenty of strings to her bow. Anyway,
Mr. Caton, poor fellow, is dead, and Mr.
Strange leaves Thornsdyke in two days'
time; and least said soonest mended."

He turned on his heel as he spoke and
left the yard. In Dr. Custance's opinion
the non-committal was the only policy that
could be relied upon for keeping a man out
of situations demanding exertion.

Robert Caton had died of aneurism
of the heart. Dr. Custance, going, on
Norman's hasty exit, to the prostrate figure
visible within the dining-room had found
him dead, had guessed the truth, though he
had never troubled to acquaint himself ac-
curately with the organic condition of his
" patient," and had himself summoned a
brother practitioner with an energy and
promptitude which only his desire to
minimise his own trouble and responsi-

bility could have induced in him. The colleague thus summoned was naturally the one nearest at hand; a very old gentleman whose services were somewhat at a discount in the neighbourhood, and whose easy-going amiability would have rendered him in any case ready to cover a scandal in the house of a brother doctor. But in this case his amiability was in no way taxed. Less medical skill than he possessed would have found no difficulty in ascribing, on examination, a perfectly natural cause for Robert Caton's death; and he announced it as an undoubted fact that the blow and the subsequent fall had been practically without results, since the action of the heart had in all probability failed in the very instant in which the blow fell. The certificate signed by him had assigned as the cause of death a more technical version of the simple statement made by Dr. Custance in Joshua Drew's workshop.

And as Dr. Custance had said, Norman Strange was leaving Thornsdyke immediately. Free as he was from any shadow of blame, the painful interest which must have attached itself to him in the neighbourhood, the painful associations which his present surroundings must hold for him for the future, made it impossible that he should remain. Circumstances made it necessary that he should go, the bare outline of his conduct was determined for him; but behind them, filling them in with life and glow, underlying all the painful solemnity of the original cause, all the self-reproach of which he could not quite divest himself, was an impulse which grew hourly more potent and all-dominating. In the agony of the hour when he believed that he had killed the man he hated, and in the reaction of relief when he found himself completely exonerated, the last traces of those remains of physical and mental weakness which had made it natural and advantageous to him to stay on at the White House had been finally scorched away. He found himself suddenly ready to face the world again, eager to be at work.

He seemed to himself to be living a strange mental life during the week that elapsed between his consciousness of the necessity for his departure, and that departure as an accomplished fact; a life in which the present was nothing but the meeting-ground of the past and future. The past was past for him now, indeed, as it had never been before. He seemed to stand aloof from it and look at it; he went through all its phases over and over again with unshrinking steadiness and courage, with a sense of its blackness, which time would only deepen in him. But it was to him as something done and over, of which only the painful memory remained; while before him, glowing and beating with vigorous life, his own to use and work in, lay the future. With every day, almost with every hour, that future became to him more real, more tangible; his plans became more definite, his zest in them grew keener. All his thoughts, like all his hopes, were centred in it, he was already living in it in anticipation. The course of life at the White House in which he had lived for the last three months, during which so much had gradually changed for him, and which he was so soon to leave behind, had no more substance, no more reality for him, now, than the merest shadow of a dream.

One present interest connected solely
with the past, and one only, still had
vigorous life for him. Of Alice Eade
nothing had been heard in Thornsdyke
since she left it. Norman knew from the
dead man's own lips—and Norman only—
why she had left Thornsdyke, and that
she was waiting now for Caton somewhere.
Where she was he did not know; and the
thought of that terrible waiting, of the sick
suspense that could only end in despair,
of the girl's probable future if she should
not be found, haunted him. It was on
his own impulse quite as much as in his
pity for Mrs. Custance's distress that he
left no stone unturned to trace her.

Norman believed that Mrs. Custance
knew the whole truth. No words had
passed between them on the subject except
as to the means employed in vain to find

the missing girl, but as each day that brought
his going nearer and found him more confident, hopeful, and courageous, found her
quieter, paler, and more nervous, he
ascribed such change in her as he was
carelessly conscious of to that mental picture
of Alice Eade by which he himself was
haunted. He did not know that in the
fearful shock of finding Caton dead all sense
of the words she had heard in that listening
moment at the drawing-room door had been
confused for her beyond the possibility of
application; he did not know that she never
once connected the dead man and the
missing girl; that Alice's disappearance was,
in fact, only a background of dull pain to
her in the days on which, for him, it formed
the only shadow.

One by one those days went by until
that morning came which was to be

Norman's last at the White House. It
was a wet morning, and as he stood alone
at the dining-room window waiting for
breakfast, he looked out over the dreary
garden and recalled the night of his arrival;
recalled it with a bright, confident flash
in his eyes, as the thought seemed to lead
whither all his thoughts now led—to the
future. How little chance there had been
then of any future but one for him!

The light was still in his face, his whole
personality was instinct with hope and confidence as he turned quickly from the
window. Mrs. Custance had come into the
room, and was wishing him a scarcely audible
good morning. He did not notice that her
voice was very low, nor did he notice that
the hand he touched was as cold as ice.
Her face, to his eyes, showed little change
at any time. If, this morning, it was more

wan than usual; if the blue eyes were duller,
the manner more uncertain, he did not see
the difference. A certain blunted, dull
expression which gave her face a look that
was almost apathetic, would have been
detected only by a very keen observer.

It was so usual with her to say very
little that it escaped notice that during breakfast she said absolutely nothing. Norman
was to leave almost immediately after; he
had made all his arrangements before
coming down, and as Dr. Custance left
the room to give some orders, he rose
cheerily and turned to Mrs. Custance.

"I shall always think kindly of this room,
Mrs. Custance," he said. "We have had
some pleasant mornings here, haven't we?
I hope you'll miss our readings a little bit."
He spoke with a good-natured sense of her
very slight intellectual appreciation of the

readings, and he strolled to the window as
he spoke. He did not see the blue eyes
change for one instant with a flash of
absolute terror, which left them, as it
instantly subsided, duller than before. She
was standing awkwardly by her chair facing
him as he glanced round for her answer,
and her appearance was as far removed
from any touch of emotion as were her
hesitating words.

" It has been very nice."

There was a moment's pause. Norman
Strange's boot was apparently engaging
his attention, and she stood still facing him,
with the same apathetic face and fingers
closely pressed together. The silence was
suddenly broken, as he said abruptly,
drawing nearer to her, and speaking rather
low and quickly :

" Mrs. Custance, I want to speak to

you about that day at Sletton. I don't know, of course, what you heard when you came to the smoking-room, but I think you may have heard me take that whisky, and I should just like to put myself right with you as to the future. It's just as well, I believe, that I did not drink it, but as things turned out as they did I am very glad to have made the mistake then. It has shown me where to distrust myself, and forewarned is forearmed, you know. It won't occur again."

"You will — you will!' The words seemed to come from her under a resistless pressure of inward necessity, but she did not finish her sentence. Only the sudden intensity of appeal with which her face—from which all the dulness had passed as he spoke—was quivering as she raised it to his, spoke for her. As it had always done, her wistful incoherence revived in him a sense of superiority and protection, and his tone changed from its gravity of explanation.

"Indeed I will!" he said reassuringly, almost lightly. There was another moment's pause, and then he changed the subject. "Mrs. Custance," he said gently, "I heard this morning from Scotland Yard. They have no news for us!"

The life died out of her face, and she paused a moment, as though she followed him with some difficulty, groping her way for the definite subject presented to her where all was vague distress.

"No news!" she said, "no news! Oh, poor Alice!"

"I will do all that can be done, Mrs. Custance," he said quickly, "and I will write to you. I shall go to Scotland Yard this afternoon. I——" He was interrupted.

"Strange!" called Dr. Custance from the hall. "We must be off at once!"

Norman turned to Mrs. Custance and held out his hand.

"Good-bye!" he said, the future even then holding all his thoughts. "Good-bye! I will find her if it is to be done. Don't be distressed!"

"Good-bye!" she answered him, in a strange, mechanical, far-away voice. "Good-bye, Mr. Strange."

The next moment he was gone, taking with him nothing from the old life to the new but the thought of Alice Eade.

END OF VOL. I.

CHARLES DICKENS AND EVANS, CRYSTAL PALACE PRESS.

A CLASSIFIED
CATALOGUE OF BOOKS
IN GENERAL LITERATURE
PUBLISHED BY
MACMILLAN AND CO.
BEDFORD STREET, STRAND, LONDON, W.C.

For purely Educational Works see MACMILLAN AND CO.'S *Educational Catalogue.*

AGRICULTURE.

(*See also* BOTANY; GARDENING.)

FRANKLAND (Prof. P. F.).—A HANDBOOK OF AGRICULTURAL CHEMICAL ANALYSIS. Cr. 8vo. 7s. 6d.

TANNER (Henry).—ELEMENTARY LESSONS IN THE SCIENCE OF AGRICULTURAL PRACTICE. Fcp. 8vo. 3s. 6d.
—— FIRST PRINCIPLES OF AGRICULTURE. 18mo. 1s.
—— THE PRINCIPLES OF AGRICULTURE. For Use in Elementary Schools. Ext. fcp. 8vo.—THE ALPHABET OF THE PRINCIPLES OF AGRICULTURE. 6d.—FURTHER STEPS IN THE PRINCIPLES OF AGRICULTURE. 1s.—ELEMENTARY SCHOOL READINGS ON THE PRINCIPLES OF AGRICULTURE FOR THE THIRD STAGE. 1s.
—— THE ABBOT'S FARM; or, Practice with Science. Cr. 8vo. 3s. 6d.

ANATOMY, Human. (*See* PHYSIOLOGY.)

ANTHROPOLOGY.

BROWN (J. Allen).—PALÆOLITHIC MAN IN NORTH-WEST MIDDLESEX. 8vo. 7s. 6d.

DAWKINS (Prof. W. Boyd).—EARLY MAN IN BRITAIN AND HIS PLACE IN THE TERTIARY PERIOD. Med. 8vo. 25s.

DAWSON (James). — AUSTRALIAN ABORIGINES. Small 4to. 14s.

FINCK (Henry T.).—ROMANTIC LOVE AND PERSONAL BEAUTY. 2 vols. Cr. 8vo. 18s.

FISON (L.) and HOWITT (A. W.).—KAMILAROI AND KURNAI GROUP. Group-Marriage and Relationship, and Marriage by Elopement. 8vo. 15s.

FRAZER (J. G.).—THE GOLDEN BOUGH: A Study in Comparative Religion. 2 vols. 8vo. 28s.

GALTON (Francis).—ENGLISH MEN OF SCIENCE: THEIR NATURE AND NURTURE. 8vo. 8s. 6d.
—— INQUIRIES INTO HUMAN FACULTY AND ITS DEVELOPMENT. 8vo. 16s.
—— RECORD OF FAMILY FACULTIES. Consisting of Tabular Forms and Directions for Entering Data. 4to. 2s. 6d.
—— LIFE-HISTORY ALBUM: Being a Personal Note-book, combining Diary, Photograph Album, a Register of Height, Weight, and other Anthropometrical Observations, and a Record of Illnesses. 4to. 3s.6d.—Or with Cards of Wool for Testing Colour Vision. 4s. 6d.

GALTON (Francis).—NATURAL INHERITANCE. 8vo. 9s.
—— HEREDITARY GENIUS: An Enquiry into its Laws and Consequences. Ext. cr 8vo. 7s. net.
—— FINGER PRINTS. 8vo. 6s. net.

M'LENNAN (J. F.).—THE PATRIARCHAL THEORY. Edited and completed by DONALD M'LENNAN, M.A. 8vo. 14s.
—— STUDIES IN ANCIENT HISTORY. Comprising "Primitive Marriage." 8vo. 16s.

MONTELIUS—WOODS. — THE CIVILISATION OF SWEDEN IN HEATHEN TIMES. By Prof. OSCAR MONTELIUS. Translated by Rev. F. H. WOODS. Illustr. 8vo. 14s.

TURNER (Rev Geo.).—SAMOA, A HUNDRED YEARS AGO AND LONG BEFORE. Cr. 8vo. 9s.

TYLOR (E. B.).—ANTHROPOLOGY. With Illustrations. Cr. 8vo. 7s. 6d.

WESTERMARCK (Dr. Edward).—THE HISTORY OF HUMAN MARRIAGE. With Preface by Dr. A. R. WALLACE. 8vo. 14s. net.

WILSON (Sir Daniel).—PREHISTORIC ANNALS OF SCOTLAND. Illustrated. 2 vols. 8vo. 36s.
—— PREHISTORIC MAN: Researches into the Origin of Civilisation in the Old and New World. Illustrated. 2 vols. 8vo. 36s.
—— THE RIGHT HAND: LEFT HANDEDNESS. Cr. 8vo. 4s. 6d.

ANTIQUITIES.

(*See also* ANTHROPOLOGY.)

ATKINSON (Rev. J. C.).—FORTY YEARS IN A MOORLAND PARISH. Ext. cr. 8vo. 8s. 6d. net.—*Illustrated Edition.* 12s. net.

BURN (Robert).—ROMAN LITERATURE IN RELATION TO ROMAN ART. With Illustrations. Ext. cr. 8vo. 14s.

DILETTANTI SOCIETY'S PUBLICATIONS.
ANTIQUITIES OF IONIA. Vols. I.—III. 2l. 2s. each, or 5l. 5s. the set, net.—Vol. IV. Folio, half morocco, 3l. 13s. 6d. net.
AN INVESTIGATION OF THE PRINCIPLES OF ATHENIAN ARCHITECTURE. By F. C. PENROSE. Illustrated. Folio. 7l. 7s. net.
SPECIMENS OF ANCIENT SCULPTURE: EGYPTIAN, ETRUSCAN, GREEK, AND ROMAN. Vol. II. Folio. 5l. 5s. net.

DYER (Louis).—STUDIES OF THE GODS IN GREECE AT CERTAIN SANCTUARIES RECENTLY EXCAVATED. Ext. cr. 8vo. 8s.6d. net.

ANTIQUITIES—continued.

GARDNER (Percy).—SAMOS AND SAMIAN COINS: An Essay. 8vo. 7s. 6d.

GOW (J., Litt.D.).—A COMPANION TO SCHOOL CLASSICS. Illustrated. 3rd Ed. Cr. 8vo. 6s.

HARRISON (Miss Jane) and VERRALL (Mrs.).—MYTHOLOGY AND MONUMENTS OF ANCIENT ATHENS. Illustrated. Cr. 8vo. 16s.

LANCIANI (Prof. R.).—ANCIENT ROME IN THE LIGHT OF RECENT DISCOVERIES. 4to. 24s.

MAHAFFY (Prof. J. P.).—A PRIMER OF GREEK ANTIQUITIES. 18mo. 1s.
— SOCIAL LIFE IN GREECE FROM HOMER TO MENANDER. 6th Edit. Cr. 8vo. 9s.
— RAMBLES AND STUDIES IN GREECE. Illustrated. 3rd Edit. Cr. 8vo. 10s. 6d.
(See also HISTORY, p. 11.)

NEWTON (Sir C. T.).—ESSAYS ON ART AND ARCHÆOLOGY. 8vo. 12s. 6d.

SHUCHHARDT (Carl).—DR. SCHLIEMANN'S EXCAVATIONS AT TROY, TIRYNS, MYCENAE, ORCHOMENOS, ITHACA, IN THE LIGHT OF RECENT KNOWLEDGE. Trans. by EUGENIE SELLERS. Preface by WALTER LEAF, Litt. D. Illustrated. 8vo. 18s. net.

STRANGFORD. (See VOYAGES & TRAVELS.)

WALDSTEIN (C.).—CATALOGUE OF CASTS IN THE MUSEUM OF CLASSICAL ARCHÆOLOGY, CAMBRIDGE. Crown 8vo. 1s. 6d.— Large Paper Edition. Small 4to. 5s.

WHITE (Gilbert). (See NATURAL HISTORY.)

WILKINS (Prof. A. S.).—A PRIMER OF ROMAN ANTIQUITIES. 18mo. 1s.

ARCHÆOLOGY. (See ANTIQUITIES.)

ARCHITECTURE.

FREEMAN (Prof. E. A.).—HISTORY OF THE CATHEDRAL CHURCH OF WELLS. Cr. 8vo. 3s. 6d.
— HISTORICAL AND ARCHITECTURAL SKETCHES, CHIEFLY ITALIAN. Illustrated by the Author. Cr. 8vo. 10s. 6d.

HULL (E.).—A TREATISE ON ORNAMENTAL AND BUILDING STONES OF GREAT BRITAIN AND FOREIGN COUNTRIES. 8vo. 12s.

MOORE (Prof. C. H.).—THE DEVELOPMENT AND CHARACTER OF GOTHIC ARCHITECTURE. Illustrated. Med. 8vo. 18s.

PENROSE (F. C.). (See ANTIQUITIES.)

STEVENSON (J. J.).—HOUSE ARCHITECTURE. With Illustrations. 2 vols. Roy. 8vo. 18s. each.—Vol. I. ARCHITECTURE; Vol. II. HOUSE PLANNING.

ART.

(See also MUSIC.)

ART AT HOME SERIES. Edited by W. J. LOFTIE, B.A. Cr. 8vo.
THE BEDROOM AND BOUDOIR. By Lady BARKER. 2s. 6d.
NEEDLEWORK. By ELIZABETH GLAISTER. Illustrated. 2s. 6d.
MUSIC IN THE HOUSE. By JOHN HULLAH. 4th edit. 2s. 6d.

ART AT HOME SERIES—continued.

THE DINING-ROOM. By Mrs. LOFTIE. With Illustrations. 2nd Edit. 2s. 6d.
AMATEUR THEATRICALS. By WALTER H. POLLOCK and LADY POLLOCK. Illustrated by KATE GREENAWAY. 2s. 6d.

ATKINSON (J. B.).—AN ART TOUR TO NORTHERN CAPITALS OF EUROPE. 8vo. 12s.

BURN (Robert). (See ANTIQUITIES.)

CARR (J. Comyns).—PAPERS ON ART. Cr. 8vo. 8s. 6d.

COLLIER (Hon. John).—A PRIMER OF ART. 18mo. 1s.

COOK (E. T.).—A POPULAR HANDBOOK TO THE NATIONAL GALLERY. Including Notes collected from the Works of Mr. RUSKIN. 3rd Edit. Cr. 8vo, half morocco. 14s.— Large paper Edition, 250 copies. 2 vols. 8vo.

CRANE (Lucy).—LECTURES ON ART AND THE FORMATION OF TASTE. Cr. 8vo. 6s.

DELAMOTTE (Prof. P. H.).—A BEGINNER'S DRAWING-BOOK. Cr. 8vo. 3s. 6d.

ELLIS (Tristram).—SKETCHING FROM NATURE. Illustr. by H. STACY MARKS, R.A., and the Author. 2nd Edit. Cr. 8vo. 3s. 6d.

HAMERTON (P. G.).—THOUGHTS ABOUT ART. New Edit. Cr. 8vo. 8s. 6d.

HERKOMER (H.).—ETCHING AND MEZZOTINT ENGRAVING. 4to. 42s. net.

HOOPER (W. H.) and PHILLIPS (W. C.).—A MANUAL OF MARKS ON POTTERY AND PORCELAIN. 16mo. 4s. 6d.

HUNT (W.).—TALKS ABOUT ART. With a Letter from Sir J. E. MILLAIS, Bart., R.A. Cr. 8vo. 3s. 6d.

LECTURES ON ART By REGD. STUART POOLE, Professor W. B. RICHMOND, E. J. POYNTER, R.A., J. T. MICKLETHWAITE, and WILLIAM MORRIS. Cr. 8vo. 4s. 6d.

NEWTON (Sir C. T.).—(See ANTIQUITIES.)

PALGRAVE (Prof. F. T.).—ESSAYS ON ART. Ext. fcp. 8vo. 6s.

PATER (W.).—THE RENAISSANCE: Studies in Art and Poetry. 4th Edit. Cr. 8vo. 10s. 6d.

PENNELL (Joseph).—PEN DRAWING AND PEN DRAUGHTSMEN. With 158 Illustrations. 4to. 3l. 13s. 6d. net.

PROPERT (J. Lumsden).—A HISTORY OF MINIATURE ART. Illustrated. Super roy. 4to. 3l. 13s. 6d.—Bound in vellum. 4l. 14s. 6d.

TURNER'S LIBER STUDIORUM: A DESCRIPTION AND A CATALOGUE. By W. G. RAWLINSON. Med. 8vo. 12s. 6d.

TYRWHITT (Rev. R. St. John).—OUR SKETCHING CLUB. 5th Edit. Cr. 8vo. 7s. 6d.

WYATT (Sir M. Digby).—FINE ART: A Sketch of its History, Theory, Practice, and Application to Industry. 8vo. 5s.

ASTRONOMY.

AIRY (Sir G. B.).—POPULAR ASTRONOMY. Illustrated. 7th Edit. Fcp. 8vo. 4s. 6d.
— GRAVITATION. An Elementary Explanation of the Principal Perturbations in the Solar System. 2nd Edit. Cr. 8vo. 7s. 6d.

BLAKE (J. F.).—Astronomical Myths. With Illustrations. Cr. 8vo. 9s.

CHEYNE (C. H. H.).—An Elementary Treatise on the Planetary Theory. Cr. 8vo. 7s. 6d.

CLARK (L.) and SADLER (H.).—The Star Guide. Roy. 8vo. 5s.

CROSSLEY (E.), GLEDHILL (J.), and WILSON (J. M.).—A Handbook of Double Stars. 8vo. 21s.

—— Corrections to the Handbook of Double Stars. 8vo. 1s.

FORBES (Prof. George).—The Transit of Venus. Illustrated. Cr. 8vo. 3s. 6d.

GODFRAY (Hugh).—An Elementary Treatise on the Lunar Theory. 2nd Edit. Cr. 8vo. 5s. 6d.

—— A Treatise on Astronomy, for the use of Colleges and Schools. 8vo. 12s. 6d.

LOCKYER (J. Norman, F.R.S.).—A Primer of Astronomy. Illustrated. 18mo. 1s.

—— Elementary Lessons in Astronomy. Illustr. New Edition. Fcp. 8vo. 5s. 6d.

—— Questions on the same. By J. Forbes Robertson. Fcp. 8vo. 1s. 6d.

—— The Chemistry of the Sun. Illustrated. 8vo. 14s.

—— The Meteoritic Hypothesis of the Origin of Cosmical Systems. Illustrated. 8vo. 17s. net.

—— The Evolution of the Heavens and the Earth. Illustrated. Cr. 8vo.

—— Star-Gazing Past and Present. Expanded from Notes with the assistance of G. M. Seabroke. Roy. 8vo. 21s.

MILLER (R. Kalley).—The Romance of Astronomy. 2nd Edit. Cr. 8vo. 4s. 6d.

NEWCOMB (Prof. Simon).—Popular Astronomy. Engravings and Maps. 8vo. 18s.

PENROSE (Francis).—On a Method of Predicting, by Graphical Construction, Occultations of Stars by the Moon and Solar Eclipses for any given place. 4to. 12s.

RADCLIFFE (Charles B.).—Behind the Tides. 8vo. 4s. 6d.

ROSCOE—SCHUSTER. (See Chemistry.)

ATLASES.

(See also Geography).

BARTHOLOMEW (J. G.).—Elementary School Atlas. 4to. 1s.

—— Physical and Political School Atlas. 80 maps. 4to. 8s. 6d.; half mor. 10s. 6d.

—— Library Reference Atlas of the World. With Index to 100,000 places. Folio. 52s. 6d. net.—Also in 7 parts. 5s. net; Geographical Index. 7s. 6d. net.

LABBERTON (R. H.).—New Historical Atlas and General History. 4to. 15s.

BIBLE. (See under Theology, p. 32.)

BIBLIOGRAPHY.

A BIBLIOGRAPHICAL CATALOGUE OF MACMILLAN AND CO.'S PUBLICATIONS, 1843—89. Med. 8vo. 10s. net.

MAYOR (Prof. John E. B.).—A Bibliographical Clue to Latin Literature. Cr. 8vo. 10s. 6d.

RYLAND (F.).—Chronological Outlines of English Literature. Cr. 8vo. 6s.

BIOGRAPHY.

(See also History.)

For other subjects of Biography, *see* English Men of Letters, English Men of Action, Twelve English Statesmen.

ABBOTT (E. A.).—The Anglican Career of Cardinal Newman. 2 vols. 8vo. 25s. net.

AGASSIZ (Louis): His Life and Correspondence. Edited by Elizabeth Cary Agassiz. 2 vols. Cr. 8vo. 18s.

ALBEMARLE (Earl of).—Fifty Years of My Life. 3rd Edit., revised. Cr. 8vo. 7s. 6d.

ALFRED THE GREAT. By Thomas Hughes. Cr. 8vo. 6s.

AMIEL (Henri Fréderic).—The Journal Intime. Translated by Mrs. Humphry Ward. 2nd Edit. Cr. 8vo. 6s.

ANDREWS (Dr. Thomas). (See Physics.)

ARNAULD, ANGELIQUE. By Frances Martin. Cr. 8vo. 4s. 6d.

ARTEVELDE. James and Philip van Artevelde. By W. J. Ashley. Cr. 8vo. 6s.

BACON (Francis): An Account of his Life and Works. By E. A. Abbott. 8vo. 14s.

BARNES. Life of William Barnes, Poet and Philologist. By his Daughter, Lucy Baxter ("Leader Scott"). Cr. 8vo. 7s. 6d.

BERLIOZ (Hector): Autobiography of. Trns. by R. & E. Holmes. 2 vols. Cr. 8vo. 21s.

BERNARD (St.). The Life and Times of St. Bernard, Abbot of Clairvaux. By J. C. Morison, M.A. Cr. 8vo. 6s.

BLACKBURNE. Life of the Right Hon. Francis Blackburne, late Lord Chancellor of Ireland, by his Son, Edward Blackburne. With Portrait. 8vo. 12s.

BLAKE. Life of William Blake. With Selections from his Poems, etc. Illustr. from Blake's own Works. By Alexander Gilchrist. 2 vols. Med. 8vo. 42s.

BOLEYN (Anne): A Chapter of English History, 1527—36. By Paul Friedmann. 2 vols. 8vo. 28s.

BROOKE (Sir Jas.), The Raja of Sarawak (Life of). By Gertrude L. Jacob. 2 vols. 8vo. 25s.

BURKE. By John Morley. Globe 8vo. 5s.

CALVIN. (See Select Biography, p. 6.)

CARLYLE (Thomas). Edited by Charles E. Norton. Cr. 8vo.

—— Reminiscences. 2 vols. 12s.

—— Early Letters, 1814—26. 2 vols. 18s.

—— Letters, 1826—36. 2 vols. 18s.

—— Correspondence between Goethe and Carlyle. 9s.

BIOGRAPHY—*continued*.

CARSTARES (Wm.): A CHARACTER AND CAREER OF THE REVOLUTIONARY EPOCH (1649—1715). By R. H. STORY. 8vo. 12s.

CAVOUR. (*See* SELECT BIOGRAPHY, p. 6.)

CHATTERTON: A STORY OF THE YEAR 1770. By Prof. DAVID MASSON. Cr. 8vo. 5s.
—— A BIOGRAPHICAL STUDY. By Sir DANIEL WILSON. Cr 8vo. 6s. 6d.

CLARK. MEMORIALS FROM JOURNALS AND LETTERS OF SAMUEL CLARK, M.A. Edited by HIS WIFE. Cr. 8vo. 7s. 6d.

CLOUGH (A. H.). (*See* LITERATURE, p. 20.)

COMBE. LIFE OF GEORGE COMBE. By CHARLES GIBBON. 2 vols. 8vo. 32s.

CROMWELL. (*See* SELECT BIOGRAPHY, p. 6.)

DAMIEN (Father): A JOURNEY FROM CASHMERE TO HIS HOME IN HAWAII. By EDWARD CLIFFORD. Portrait. Cr. 8vo. 2s. 6d.

DANTE: AND OTHER ESSAYS. By Dean CHURCH. Globe 8vo. 5s.

DARWIN (Charles): MEMORIAL NOTICES. By T. H. HUXLEY, G. J. ROMANES, Sir ARCH. GEIKIE, and W. THISELTON DYER. With Portrait. Cr. 8vo. 2s. 6d.

DEÁK (Francis): HUNGARIAN STATESMAN. A Memoir. 8vo. 12s. 6d.

DRUMMOND OF HAWTHORNDEN. By Prof. D. MASSON. Cr. 8vo. 10s. 6d.

EADIE. LIFE OF JOHN EADIE, D.D. By JAMES BROWN, D.D. Cr. 8vo. 7s. 6d.

ELLIOTT. LIFE OF H. V. ELLIOTT, OF BRIGHTON. By J. BATEMAN. Cr. 8vo. 6s.

EMERSON. LIFE OF RALPH WALDO EMERSON. By J. L. CABOT. 2 vols. Cr. 8vo. 18s.

ENGLISH MEN OF ACTION. Cr. 8vo. With Portraits. 2s. 6d. each.
CLIVE. By Colonel Sir CHARLES WILSON.
COOK (CAPTAIN). By WALTER BESANT.
DAMPIER. By W. CLARK RUSSELL.
DRAKE. By JULIAN CORBETT.
GORDON (GENERAL). By Col. Sir W. BUTLER.
HASTINGS (WARREN). By Sir A. LYALL.
HAVELOCK (Sir HENRY). By A. FORBES.
HENRY V. By the Rev. A. J. CHURCH.
LAWRENCE (LORD). By Sir RICH. TEMPLE.
LIVINGSTONE. By THOMAS HUGHES.
MONK. By JULIAN CORBETT.
MONTROSE. By MOWBRAY MORRIS.
MOORE (Sir JOHN). By Col. MAURICE. [*In prep.*
NAPIER (Sir CHARLES). By Colonel Sir WM. BUTLER.
PETERBOROUGH. By W. STEBBING.
RODNEY. By DAVID HANNAY.
SIMON DE MONTFORT. By G. W. PROTHERO. [*In prep.*
STRAFFORD. By H. D. TRAILL.
WARWICK, THE KING-MAKER. By C. W. OMAN.
WELLINGTON. By GEORGE HOOPER.

ENGLISH MEN OF LETTERS. Edited by JOHN MORLEY. Cr. 8vo. 2s. 6d. each. Cheap Edition, 1s. 6d.; sewed, 1s.
ADDISON. By W. J. COURTHOPE.
BACON. By Dean CHURCH.
BENTLEY. By Prof. JEBB.

ENGLISH MEN OF LETTERS—*contd.*

BUNYAN. By J. A. FROUDE.
BURKE. By JOHN MORLEY.
BURNS. By Principal SHAIRP.
BYRON. By JOHN NICHOL.
CARLYLE. By JOHN NICHOL.
CHAUCER. By Prof. A. W. WARD.
COLERIDGE. By H. D. TRAILL.
COWPER. By GOLDWIN SMITH.
DEFOE. By W. MINTO.
DE QUINCEY. By Prof. MASSON.
DICKENS. By A. W. WARD.
DRYDEN. By G. SAINTSBURY.
FIELDING. By AUSTIN DOBSON.
GIBBON. By J. COTTER MORISON.
GOLDSMITH. By WILLIAM BLACK.
GRAY. By EDMUND GOSSE.
HAWTHORNE. By HENRY JAMES.
HUME. By T. H. HUXLEY.
JOHNSON. By LESLIE STEPHEN.
KEATS. By SIDNEY COLVIN.
LAMB. By Rev. ALFRED AINGER.
LANDOR. By SIDNEY COLVIN.
LOCKE. By Prof. FOWLER.
MACAULAY. By J. COTTER MORISON.
MILTON. By MARK PATTISON.
POPE. By LESLIE STEPHEN.
SCOTT. By R. H. HUTTON.
SHELLEY. By J. A. SYMONDS.
SHERIDAN. By Mrs. OLIPHANT.
SIDNEY. By J. A. SYMONDS.
SOUTHEY. By Prof. DOWDEN.
SPENSER. By Dean CHURCH.
STERNE. By H. D. TRAILL.
SWIFT. By LESLIE STEPHEN.
THACKERAY. By ANTHONY TROLLOPE.
WORDSWORTH. By F. W. H. MYERS.

ENGLISH STATESMEN, TWELVE Cr. 8vo. 2s. 6d. each.
WILLIAM THE CONQUEROR. By EDWARD A. FREEMAN, D.C.L., LL.D.
HENRY II. By Mrs. J. R. GREEN.
EDWARD I. By T. F. TOUT, M.A. [*In prep.*
HENRY VII. By JAMES GAIRDNER.
CARDINAL WOLSEY. By Bp. CREIGHTON.
ELIZABETH. By E. S. BEESLY.
OLIVER CROMWELL. By F. HARRISON.
WILLIAM III. By H. D. TRAILL.
WALPOLE. By JOHN MORLEY.
CHATHAM. By JOHN MORLEY. [*In the Press.*
PITT. By LORD ROSEBERY.
PEEL. By J. R. THURSFIELD.

EPICTETUS. (*See* SELECT BIOGRAPHY, p. 6.)

FAIRFAX. LIFE OF ROBERT FAIRFAX OF STEETON, Vice-Admiral, Alderman, and Member for York, A.D. 1666-1725. By CLEMENTS R. MARKHAM, C.B. 8vo. 12s. 6d.

FITZGERALD (Edward). (*See* LITERATURE, p. 21.)

FORBES (Edward): MEMOIR OF. By GEORGE WILSON, M.P., and Sir ARCHIBALD GEIKIE, F.R.S., etc. Demy 8vo. 14s.

FRANCIS OF ASSISI. By Mrs. OLIPHANT. Cr. 8vo. 6s.

FRASER. JAMES FRASER, SECOND BISHOP OF MANCHESTER: A Memoir. By T. HUGHES. Cr. 8vo. 6s.

GARIBALDI. (*See* SELECT BIOGRAPHY, p. 6.)

GOETHE: LIFE OF. By Prof. HEINRICH DÜNTZER. Translated by T. W. LYSTER. 2 vols. Cr. 8vo. 21s.

GOETHE AND CARLYLE. (*See* CARLYLE.)

GORDON (General): A SKETCH. By REGINALD H. BARNES. Cr. 8vo. 1s.
—— LETTERS OF GENERAL C. G. GORDON TO HIS SISTER, M. A. GORDON. 4th Edit. Cr. 8vo. 3s. 6d.

HANDEL: LIFE OF. By W. S. ROCKSTRO. Cr. 8vo. 10s. 6d.

HOBART. (*See* COLLECTED WORKS, p. 22.)

HODGSON. MEMOIR OF REV. FRANCIS HODGSON, B.D. By his Son, Rev. JAMES T. HODGSON, M.A. 2 vols. Cr. 8vo. 18s.

JEVONS (W. Stanley).—LETTERS AND JOURNAL. Edited by HIS WIFE. 8vo. 14s.

KAVANAGH (Rt. Hon. A. McMurrough): A BIOGRAPHY. From papers chiefly unpublished, compiled by his Cousin, SARAH L. STEELE. With Portrait. 8vo. 14s. net.

KINGSLEY: HIS LETTERS, AND MEMORIES OF HIS LIFE. Edited by HIS WIFE. 2 vols. Cr. 8vo. 12s.—Cheap Edition. 1 vol. 6s.

LAMB. THE LIFE OF CHARLES LAMB. By Rev. ALFRED AINGER, M.A. Globe 8vo. 5s.

LOUIS (St.). (*See* SELECT BIOGRAPHY, p 6.)

MACMILLAN (D.). MEMOIR OF DANIEL MACMILLAN. By THOMAS HUGHES, Q.C. With Portrait. Cr. 8vo. 4s. 6d.—Cheap Edition. Cr. 8vo, sewed. 1s.

MALTHUS AND HIS WORK. By JAMES BONAR. 8vo. 12s. 6d.

MARCUS AURELIUS. (*See* SELECT BIOGRAPHY, p. 6.)

MATHEWS. THE LIFE OF CHARLES J. MATHEWS. Edited by CHARLES DICKENS. With Portraits. 2 vols. 8vo. 25s.

MAURICE. LIFE OF FREDERICK DENISON MAURICE. By his Son, FREDERICK MAURICE, Two Portraits. 2 vols. 8vo. 36s.—Popular Edit. (4th Thousand). 2 vols. Cr. 8vo. 16s.

MAXWELL. PROFESSOR CLERK MAXWELL, A LIFE OF. By Prof. L. CAMPBELL, M.A., and W. GARNETT, M.A. Cr. 8vo. 7s. 6d.

MAZZINI. (*See* SELECT BIOGRAPHY, p. 6.)

MELBOURNE. MEMOIRS OF VISCOUNT MELBOURNE. By W. M. TORRENS. With Portrait. 2nd Edit. 2 vols. 8vo. 32s.

MILTON. THE LIFE OF JOHN MILTON. By Prof. DAVID MASSON. Vol. I., 21s.; Vol. III., 18s.; Vols. IV. and V., 32s.; Vol. VI., with Portrait, 21s. (*See also* p. 16.)

MILTON, JOHNSON'S LIFE OF. With Introduction and Notes by K. DEIGHTON. Globe 8vo. 1s. 9d.

NAPOLEON I., HISTORY OF. By P. LANFREY. 4 vols. Cr. 8vo. 30s.

NELSON. SOUTHEY'S LIFE OF NELSON. With Introduction and Notes by MICHAEL MACMILLAN, B.A. Globe 8vo. 3s. 6d.

NORTH (M.).—RECOLLECTIONS OF A HAPPY LIFE. Being the Autobiography of MARIANNE NORTH. Ed. by Mrs. J. A. SYMONDS. 2nd Edit. 2 vols. Ex. cr. 8vo. 17s. net.

OXFORD MOVEMENT, THE, 1833—45. By Dean CHURCH. Gl. 8vo. 5s.

PATTESON. LIFE AND LETTERS OF JOHN COLERIDGE PATTESON, D.D., MISSIONARY BISHOP. By C. M. YONGE. 2 vols. Cr. 8vo. 12s. (*See also* BOOKS FOR THE YOUNG, p. 41.)

PATTISON (M.).—MEMOIRS. Cr. 8vo. 8s. 6d.

PITT. (*See* SELECT BIOGRAPHY, p. 6.)

POLLOCK (Sir Frdk., 2nd Bart.).—PERSONAL REMEMBRANCES. 2 vols. Cr. 8vo. 16s.

POOLE, THOS., AND HIS FRIENDS. By Mrs. SANDFORD. 2nd edit. Cr. 8vo. 6s.

RITCHIE (Mrs.).—RECORDS OF TENNYSON, RUSKIN, AND BROWNING. Globe 8vo. 5s.

ROBINSON (Matthew): AUTOBIOGRAPHY OF. Edited by J. E. B. MAYOR. Fcp. 8vo. 5s.

ROSSETTI (Dante Gabriel): A RECORD AND A STUDY. By W. SHARP. Cr. 8vo. 10s. 6d.

RUMFORD. (*See* COLLECTED WORKS, p. 23.)

SCHILLER, LIFE OF. By Prof. H. DÜNTZER. Trans. by P. E. PINKERTON. Cr. 8vo. 10s. 6d.

SHELBURNE. LIFE OF WILLIAM, EARL OF SHELBURNE. By Lord EDMOND FITZMAURICE. In 3 vols.—Vol. I. 8vo. 12s.—Vol. II. 8vo. 12s.—Vol. III. 8vo. 16s.

SIBSON. (*See* MEDICINE.)

SMETHAM (Jas.).: LETTERS OF. Ed. by SARAH SMETHAM and W. DAVIES. Portrait. Globe 8vo. 5s.

SPINOZA: A STUDY OF. By JAMES MARTINEAU. LL.D. 2nd Edit. Cr. 8vo. 6s.

TAIT. THE LIFE OF ARCHIBALD CAMPBELL TAIT, ARCHBISHOP OF CANTERBURY. By the BISHOP OF ROCHESTER and Rev. W. BENHAM, B.D. 2 vols. Cr. 8vo. 10s. net.
—— CATHARINE AND CRAWFURD TAIT, WIFE AND SON OF ARCHIBALD CAMPBELL, ARCHBISHOP OF CANTERBURY: A Memoir. Ed. by Rev. W. BENHAM, B.D. Cr. 8vo. 6s. —Popular Edit., abridged. Cr. 8vo. 2s. 6d.

THRING (Edward): A MEMORY OF. By J. H. SKRINE. Cr. 8vo. 6s.

VICTOR EMMANUEL II., FIRST KING OF ITALY. By G. S. GODKIN. Cr. 8vo. 6s.

WARD. WILLIAM GEORGE WARD AND THE OXFORD MOVEMENT. By his Son, WILFRID WARD. With Portrait. 8vo. 14s.

WATSON. A RECORD OF ELLEN WATSON. By ANNA BUCKLAND. Cr. 8vo. 6s.

WHEWELL. DR. WILLIAM WHEWELL, late Master of Trinity College, Cambridge. An Account of his Writings, with Selections from his Literary and Scientific Correspondence. By I. TODHUNTER, M.A. 2 vols. 8vo. 25s.

WILLIAMS (Montagu).—LEAVES OF A LIFE. Cr. 8vo. 3s. 6d.
—— LATER LEAVES. Being further Reminiscences. With Portrait. Cr. 8vo. 3s. 6d.
—— ROUND LONDON, DOWN EAST AND UP WEST. 8vo. 15s.

WILSON. MEMOIR OF PROF. GEORGE WILSON, M.D. By HIS SISTER. With Portrait. 2nd Edit. Cr. 8vo. 6s.

WORDSWORTH. DOVE COTTAGE, WORDSWORTH'S HOME, 1800—8. Gl. 8vo, swd. 1s

Select Biography.

BIOGRAPHIES OF EMINENT PERSONS. Reprinted from the *Times*. Vol. I. Cr. 8vo. 3s. 6d.

FARRAR (Archdeacon).—SEEKERS AFTER GOD. Cr. 8vo. 3s. 6d.

FAWCETT (Mrs. H.). — SOME EMINENT WOMEN OF OUR TIMES. Cr. 8vo 2s. 6d.

GUIZOT.—GREAT CHRISTIANS OF FRANCE: ST. LOUIS AND CALVIN. Cr. 8vo. 6s.

HARRISON (Frederic).—THE NEW CALENDAR OF GREAT MEN. Ex.cr. 8vo. 7s.6d. net.

MARRIOTT (J. A. R.).—THE MAKERS OF MODERN ITALY: MAZZINI, CAVOUR, GARIBALDI. Cr 8vo. 1s. 6d.

MARTINEAU (Harriet). — BIOGRAPHICAL SKETCHES, 1852—75. Cr. 8vo. 6s.

NEW HOUSE OF COMMONS, JULY, 1892. Reprinted from the *Times*. 16mo 1s.

SMITH (Goldwin).—THREE ENGLISH STATESMEN: CROMWELL, PYM, PITT. Cr. 8vo. 5s.

WINKWORTH (Catharine). — CHRISTIAN SINGERS OF GERMANY. Cr. 8vo. 4s. 6d.

YONGE (Charlotte M.).—THE PUPILS OF ST. JOHN. Illustrated. Cr. 8vo. 6s.
— PIONEERS AND FOUNDERS; or, Recent Workers in the Mission Field. Cr. 8vo. 6s.
— A BOOK OF WORTHIES. 18mo. 2s. 6d. net
— A BOOK OF GOLDEN DEEDS. 18mo. 2s.6d. net --*Globe Readings Edition*. Gl. 8vo. 2s. *Abridged Edition*. Pott 8vo. 1s.

BIOLOGY.

(*See also* BOTANY; NATURAL HISTORY; PHYSIOLOGY; ZOOLOGY.)

BALFOUR (F. M.).—COMPARATIVE EMBRYOLOGY. Illustrated. 2 vols. 8vo. Vol. I. 18s. Vol. II. 21s.

BALL (W. P.).—ARE THE EFFECTS OF USE AND DISUSE INHERITED? Cr. 8vo. 3s. 6d.

BASTIAN (H. Charlton).—THE BEGINNINGS OF LIFE. 2 vols. Crown 8vo. 28s.
— EVOLUTION AND THE ORIGIN OF LIFE. Cr. 8vo. 6s. 6d.

BATESON (W.).—MATERIALS FOR THE STUDY OF VARIATION IN ANIMALS. Part I. DISCONTINUOUS VARIATION. Illustr. 8vo.

BERNARD (H. M.).—THE APODIDAE. Cr. 8vo. 7s. 6d.

BIRKS (T. R.).—MODERN PHYSICAL FATALISM, AND THE DOCTRINE OF EVOLUTION. Including an Examination of Mr. Herbert Spencer's "First Principles." Cr. 8vo. 6s.

DE VARIGNY (H.).—EXPERIMENTAL EVOLUTION. Cr. 8vo. 5s.

EIMER (G. H. T.).—ORGANIC EVOLUTION AS THE RESULT OF THE INHERITANCE OF ACQUIRED CHARACTERS ACCORDING TO THE LAWS OF ORGANIC GROWTH. Translated by J. T. CUNNINGHAM, M.A. 8vo. 12s. 6d.

FISKE (John).—OUTLINES OF COSMIC PHILOSOPHY, BASED ON THE DOCTRINE OF EVOLUTION. 2 vols. 8vo. 25s.
— MAN'S DESTINY VIEWED IN THE LIGHT OF HIS ORIGIN. Cr. 8vo. 3s. 6d.

FOSTER (Prof. M.) and BALFOUR (F. M.). —THE ELEMENTS OF EMBRYOLOGY. Ed. A. SEDGWICK, and WALTER HEAPE. Illus. 3rd Edit., revised and enlarged. Cr. 8vo. 10s. 6d.

HUXLEY (T. H.) and MARTIN (H. N.).— (*See under* ZOOLOGY, p. 43.)

KLEIN (Dr. E.).—MICRO-ORGANISMS AND DISEASE. With 121 Engravings. 3rd Edit. Cr. 8vo. 6s.

LANKESTER (Prof. E. Ray).—COMPARATIVE LONGEVITY IN MAN AND THE LOWER ANIMALS. Cr. 8vo. 4s. 6d.

LUBBOCK (Sir John, Bart.). — SCIENTIFIC LECTURES. Illustrated. 2nd Edit. 8vo. 8s. 6d.

PARKER (T. Jeffery).—LESSONS IN ELEMENTARY BIOLOGY. Illustr. Cr. 8vo. 10s.6d.

ROMANES (G. J.).—SCIENTIFIC EVIDENCES OF ORGANIC EVOLUTION. Cr. 8vo. 2s. 6d.

WALLACE (Alfred R.).—DARWINISM: An Exposition of the Theory of Natural Selection. Illustrated. 3rd Edit. Cr. 8vo. 9s.
— CONTRIBUTIONS TO THE THEORY OF NATURAL SELECTION, AND TROPICAL NATURE; and other Essays. New Ed. Cr.8vo. 6s.
— THE GEOGRAPHICAL DISTRIBUTION OF ANIMALS. Illustrated. 2 vols, 8vo. 42s.
— ISLAND LIFE. Illustr. Ext. Cr. 8vo. 6s.

BIRDS. (*See* ZOOLOGY; ORNITHOLOGY.)

BOOK-KEEPING.

THORNTON (J.).—FIRST LESSONS IN BOOKKEEPING. New Edition. Cr. 8vo. 2s. 6d.
— KEY. Oblong 4to. 10s. 6d.
— PRIMER OF BOOK-KEEPING. 18mo. 1s.
— KEY. Demy 8vo. 2s. 6d.
— EXERCISES IN BOOK-KEEPING. 18mo. 1s.

BOTANY.

(*See also* AGRICULTURE; GARDENING.)

ALLEN (Grant). — ON THE COLOURS OF FLOWERS. Illustrated. Cr. 8vo. 3s. 6d.

BALFOUR (Prof. J B.) and WARD (Prof. H. M.).—A GENERAL TEXT-BOOK OF BOTANY. 8vo. *[In preparation.*

BETTANY (G. T.).—FIRST LESSONS IN PRACTICAL BOTANY. 18mo. 1s.

BOWER (Prof. F. O.).—A COURSE OF PRACTICAL INSTRUCTION IN BOTANY. Cr. 8vo. 10s. 6d.—Abridged Edition. *[In preparation.*

CHURCH (Prof. A. H.) and SCOTT (D. H.). —MANUAL OF VEGETABLE PHYSIOLOGY. Illustrated. Crown 8vo. *[In preparation.*

GOODALE (Prof. G. L.).—PHYSIOLOGICAL BOTANY.—1. OUTLINES OF THE HISTOLOGY OF PHÆNOGAMOUS PLANTS; 2. VEGETABLE PHYSIOLOGY. 8vo. 10s. 6d.

GRAY (Prof. Asa).—STRUCTURAL BOTANY; or, Organography on the Basis of Morphology. 8vo. 10s. 6d.
— THE SCIENTIFIC PAPERS OF ASA GRAY. Selected by C. S. SARGENT. 2 vols. 8vo. 21s.

HANBURY (Daniel). — SCIENCE PAPERS, CHIEFLY PHARMACOLOGICAL AND BOTANICAL. Med. 8vo. 14s.

HARTIG (Dr. Robert).—TEXT-BOOK OF THE DISEASES OF TREES. Transl. by Prof. WM. SOMERVILLE, B.Sc. With Introduction by Prof. H. MARSHALL WARD. 8vo.

HOOKER (Sir Joseph D.).—THE STUDENT'S FLORA OF THE BRITISH ISLANDS. 3rd Edit. Globe 8vo. 10s. 6d.
—— A PRIMER OF BOTANY. 18mo. 1s.

LASLETT (Thomas).—TIMBER AND TIMBER TREES, NATIVE AND FOREIGN. Cr. 8vo. 8s. 6d.

LUBBOCK (Sir John, Bart.).—ON BRITISH WILD FLOWERS CONSIDERED IN RELATION TO INSECTS. Illustrated. Cr. 8vo. 4s. 6d.
—— FLOWERS, FRUITS, AND LEAVES. With Illustrations. Cr. 8vo. 4s. 6d.

MÜLLER—THOMPSON.— THE FERTILISATION OF FLOWERS. By Prof. H. MÜLLER. Transl. by D'ARCY W. THOMPSON. Preface by CHARLES DARWIN, F.R.S. 8vo. 21s.

OLIVER (Prof. Daniel).—LESSONS IN ELEMENTARY BOTANY. Illustr. Fcp. 8vo. 4s. 6d.
—— FIRST BOOK OF INDIAN BOTANY. Illustrated. Ext. fcp. 8vo. 6s. 6d.

ORCHIDS: BEING THE REPORT ON THE ORCHID CONFERENCE HELD AT SOUTH KENSINGTON, 1885. 8vo. 2s. net.

PETTIGREW (J. Bell).—THE PHYSIOLOGY OF THE CIRCULATION IN PLANTS, IN THE LOWER ANIMALS, AND IN MAN. 8vo. 12s.

SMITH (J.).—ECONOMIC PLANTS, DICTIONARY OF POPULAR NAMES OF; THEIR HISTORY, PRODUCTS, AND USES. 8vo. 14s.

SMITH (W. G.).—DISEASES OF FIELD AND GARDEN CROPS, CHIEFLY SUCH AS ARE CAUSED BY FUNGI. Illust. Fcp. 8vo. 4s. 6d.

STEWART (S. A.) and CORRY (T. H.).— A FLORA OF THE NORTH-EAST OF IRELAND. Cr. 8vo. 5s. 6d.

WARD (Prof. H. M.).—TIMBER AND SOME OF ITS DISEASES. Illustrated. Cr. 8vo. 6s.

YONGE (C. M.).—THE HERB OF THE FIELD. New Edition, revised. Cr. 8vo. 5s.

BREWING AND WINE.

PASTEUR—FAULKNER. — STUDIES ON FERMENTATION: THE DISEASES OF BEER, THEIR CAUSES, AND THE MEANS OF PREVENTING THEM. By L. PASTEUR. Translated by FRANK FAULKNER. 8vo. 21s.

THUDICHUM (J. L. W.) and DUPRÉ (A.) —TREATISE ON THE ORIGIN, NATURE, AND VARIETIES OF WINE. Med. 8vo. 25s.

CHEMISTRY.

(*See also* METALLURGY.)

BRODIE (Sir Benjamin).—IDEAL CHEMISTRY. Cr 8vo. 2s.

COHEN (J. B.). — THE OWENS COLLEGE COURSE OF PRACTICAL ORGANIC CHEMISTRY. Fcp. 8vo. 2s. 6d.

COOKE (Prof. J. P., jun.).—PRINCIPLES OF CHEMICAL PHILOSOPHY. New Ed. 8vo. 19s.

DOBBIN (L.) and WALKER (Jas.)—CHEMICAL THEORY FOR BEGINNERS. 18mo. 2s. 6d.

FLEISCHER (Emil).—A SYSTEM OF VOLUMETRIC ANALYSIS. Transl. with Additions, by M. M. P. MUIR, F.R.S.E. Cr.8vo. 7s.6d.

FRANKLAND (Prof. P. F.). (*See* AGRICULTURE.)

GLADSTONE (J. H.) and TRIBE (A.).— THE CHEMISTRY OF THE SECONDARY BATTERIES OF PLANTÉ AND FAURE. Cr.8vo. 2s.6d.

HARTLEY (Prof. W. N.).—A COURSE OF QUANTITATIVE ANALYSIS FOR STUDENTS. Globe 8vo. 5s.

HEMPEL (Dr. W.). — METHODS OF GAS ANALYSIS. Translated by L. M. DENNIS. Cr. 8vo. 7s. 6d.

HOFMANN (Prof. A. W.).—THE LIFE WORK OF LIEBIG IN EXPERIMENTAL AND PHILOSOPHIC CHEMISTRY. 8vo. 5s.

JONES (Francis).—THE OWENS COLLEGE JUNIOR COURSE OF PRACTICAL CHEMISTRY. Illustrated. Fcp. 8vo. 2s. 6d.
—— QUESTIONS ON CHEMISTRY. Fcp.8vo. 3s.

LANDAUER (J.). — BLOWPIPE ANALYSIS. Translated by J. TAYLOR. Gl. 8vo. 4s. 6d.

LOCKYER (J. Norman, F.R.S.). — THE CHEMISTRY OF THE SUN. Illustr. 8vo. 14s.

LUPTON (S.). — CHEMICAL ARITHMETIC, With 1200 Problems. Fcp. 8vo. 4s. 6d.

MANSFIELD (C. B.).—A THEORY OF SALTS. Cr. 8vo. 14s.

MELDOLA (Prof. R.).—THE CHEMISTRY OF PHOTOGRAPHY. Illustrated. Cr. 8vo. 6s.

MEYER (E. von).—HISTORY OF CHEMISTRY FROM EARLIEST TIMES TO THE PRESENT DAY. Trans. G. McGOWAN. 8vo. 14s. net.

MIXTER (Prof. W. G.).—AN ELEMENTARY TEXT-BOOK OF CHEMISTRY. Cr. 8vo. 7s. 6d.

MUIR (M. M. P.).—PRACTICAL CHEMISTRY FOR MEDICAL STUDENTS (First M. B. Course). Fcp. 8vo. 1s. 6d.

MUIR (M. M. P.) and WILSON (D. M.).— ELEMENTS OF THERMAL CHEMISTRY. 12s.6d.

OSTWALD (Prof.).—OUTLINES OF GENERAL CHEMISTRY. Trans. Dr. J. WALKER. 10s. net.

RAMSAY (Prof. William).—EXPERIMENTAL PROOFS OF CHEMICAL THEORY FOR BEGINNERS. 18mo. 2s. 6d.

REMSEN (Prof. Ira).—THE ELEMENTS OF CHEMISTRY. Fcp. 8vo. 2s. 6d.
—— AN INTRODUCTION TO THE STUDY OF CHEMISTRY (INORGANIC CHEMISTRY). Cr 8vo. 6s. 6d.
—— A TEXT-BOOK OF INORGANIC CHEMISTRY. 8vo. 16s.
—— COMPOUNDS OF CARBON; or, An Introduction to the Study of Organic Chemistry. Cr. 8vo. 6s. 6d.

ROSCOE (Sir Henry E., F.R.S.).—A PRIMER OF CHEMISTRY. Illustrated. 18mo. 1s.
—— LESSONS IN ELEMENTARY CHEMISTRY, INORGANIC AND ORGANIC. Fcp. 8vo. 4s. 6d.

ROSCOE (Sir H. E.) and SCHORLEMMER (Prof. C.).—A COMPLETE TREATISE ON INORGANIC AND ORGANIC CHEMISTRY. Illustr. 8vo.—Vols. I. and II. INORGANIC CHEMISTRY: Vol. I. THE NON-METALLIC ELEMENTS, 2nd Edit., 21s. Vol. II. Parts I. and II. METALS, 18s. each.—Vol. III. ORGANIC CHEMISTRY: THE CHEMISTRY OF THE HYDRO-CARBONS AND THEIR DERIVATIVES. Parts I. II. IV. and VI. 21s.; Parts III. and V. 18s. each.

ROSCOE (Sir H. E.) and SCHUSTER (A.).
—SPECTRUM ANALYSIS. By Sir HENRY E.
ROSCOE. 4th Edit., revised by the Author
and A. SCHUSTER, F.R.S. With Coloured
Plates. 8vo. 21s.

THORPE (Prof. T. E.) and TATE (W.).—
A SERIES OF CHEMICAL PROBLEMS. With
KEY. Fcp. 8vo. 2s.

THORPE (Prof. T. E.) and RÜCKER (Prof
A. W.).—A TREATISE ON CHEMICAL PHY-
SICS. Illustrated. 8vo. [In preparation.

WURTZ (Ad.).—A HISTORY OF CHEMICAL
THEORY. Transl. by H. WATTS. Cr. 8vo. 6s.

CHRISTIAN CHURCH, History of the.
(See under THEOLOGY, p. 34.)

CHURCH OF ENGLAND, The.
(See under THEOLOGY, p. 34.)

COLLECTED WORKS.
(See under LITERATURE, p. 20.)

COMPARATIVE ANATOMY.
(See under ZOOLOGY, p. 42.)

COOKERY.
(See under DOMESTIC ECONOMY, below.)

DEVOTIONAL BOOKS.
(See under THEOLOGY, p. 35)

DICTIONARIES AND GLOSSARIES.
AUTENRIETH (Dr. G.).—AN HOMERIC
DICTIONARY. Translated from the German,
by R. P. KEEP, Ph.D. Cr. 8vo. 6s.

BARTLETT (J.).—FAMILIAR QUOTATIONS.
Cr. 8vo. 12s. 6d.
—— A SHAKESPEARE GLOSSARY. Cr. 8vo
12s. 6d.

GROVE (Sir George).—A DICTIONARY OF
MUSIC AND MUSICIANS. (See MUSIC.)

HOLE (Rev. C.).—A BRIEF BIOGRAPHICAL
DICTIONARY. 2nd Edit. 18mo. 4s. 6d.

MASSON (Gustave).—A COMPENDIOUS DIC-
TIONARY OF THE FRENCH LANGUAGE.
Cr. 8vo. 3s. 6d.

PALGRAVE (R. H. I.).—A DICTIONARY OF
POLITICAL ECONOMY. (See POLITICAL
ECONOMY.)

WHITNEY (Prof. W. D.).—A COMPENDIOUS
GERMAN AND ENGLISH DICTIONARY. Cr.
8vo. 5s.—German-English Part separately.
3s. 6d.

WRIGHT (W. Aldis).—THE BIBLE WORD-
BOOK. 2nd Edit. Cr. 8vo. 7s. 6d.

YONGE (Charlotte M.).—HISTORY OF CHRIS-
TIAN NAMES. Cr. 8vo. 7s. 6d.

DOMESTIC ECONOMY.
Cookery—Nursing—Needlework.
Cookery.
BARKER (Lady).—FIRST LESSONS IN THE
PRINCIPLES OF COOKING. 3rd Ed. 18mo. 1s.

BARNETT (E. A.) and O'NEILL (H. C.).—
PRIMER OF DOMESTIC ECONOMY. 18mo. 1s.

FREDERICK (Mrs.).—HINTS TO HOUSE-
WIVES ON SEVERAL POINTS, PARTICULARLY
ON THE PREPARATION OF ECONOMICAL AND
TASTEFUL DISHES. Cr. 8vo. 1s.

MIDDLE-CLASS COOKERY BOOK, THE.
Compiled for the Manchester School of
Cookery. Fcp. 8vo. 1s. 6d.

TEGETMEIER (W. B.).—HOUSEHOLD MAN-
AGEMENT AND COOKERY. 18mo. 1s.

WRIGHT (Miss Guthrie). — THE SCHOOL
COOKERY-BOOK. 18mo. 1s.

Nursing.
CRAVEN (Mrs. Dacre).—A GUIDE TO DIS-
TRICT NURSES. Cr 8vo. 2s. 6d.

FOTHERGILL (Dr. J. M.).—FOOD FOR THE
INVALID, THE CONVALESCENT, THE DYSPEP-
TIC, AND THE GOUTY. Cr. 8vo. 3s. 6d.

JEX-BLAKE (Dr. Sophia).—THE CARE OF
INFANTS. 18mo. 1s.

RATHBONE (Wm.).—THE HISTORY AND
PROGRESS OF DISTRICT NURSING, FROM 1859
TO THE PRESENT DATE. Cr 8vo. 2s. 6d.

RECOLLECTIONS OF A NURSE. By
E. D. Cr. 8vo. 2s.

STEPHEN (Caroline E.).—THE SERVICE OF
THE POOR. Cr. 8vo. 6s. 6d.

Needlework.
GLAISTER (Elizabeth).—NEEDLEWORK. Cr.
8vo. 2s. 6d.

GRAND'HOMME. — CUTTING OUT AND
DRESSMAKING. From the French of Mdlle.
E. Grand'homme. 18mo. 1s.

GRENFELL (Mrs.)-DRESSMAKING. 18mo. 1s.

DRAMA, The.
(See under LITERATURE, p. 14.)

ELECTRICITY.
(See under PHYSICS, p. 28.)

EDUCATION.
ARNOLD (Matthew).—HIGHER SCHOOLS AND
UNIVERSITIES IN GERMANY. Cr. 8vo. 6s.
—— REPORTS ON ELEMENTARY SCHOOLS,
1852-82. Ed. by Lord SANDFORD. 8vo. 3s. 6d.
—— A FRENCH ETON: OR MIDDLE CLASS
EDUCATION AND THE STATE. Cr. 8vo. 6s.

BLAKISTON (J R.).—THE TEACHER: HINTS
ON SCHOOL MANAGEMENT. Cr. 8vo. 2s. 6d.

CALDERWOOD (Prof. H.).—ON TEACH-
ING. 4th Edit. Ext. fcp. 8vo. 2s. 6d.

COMBE (George).—EDUCATION: ITS PRIN-
CIPLES AND PRACTICE AS DEVELOPED BY
GEORGE COMBE. Ed. by W. JOLLY. 8vo. 15s.

CRAIK (Henry).—THE STATE IN ITS RELA-
TION TO EDUCATION. Cr 8vo. 3s. 6d.

FEARON (D. R.).—SCHOOL INSPECTION.
6th Edit. Cr. 8vo. 2s. 6d.

FITCH (J. G.).—NOTES ON AMERICAN
SCHOOLS AND TRAINING COLLEGES. Reprinted by permission. Globe 8vo. 2s. 6d.

GLADSTONE (J. H.).—SPELLING REFORM
FROM AN EDUCATIONAL POINT OF VIEW.
3rd Edit. Cr. 8vo. 1s. 6d.

HERTEL (Dr.).—OVERPRESSURE IN HIGH SCHOOLS IN DENMARK. With Introduction by Sir J. CRICHTON-BROWNE. Cr. 8vo. 3s. 6d.

KINGSLEY (Charles).—HEALTH AND EDUCATION. Cr. 8vo. 6s.

LUBBOCK (Sir John, Bart.).—POLITICAL AND EDUCATIONAL ADDRESSES. 8vo. 8s. 6d.

MAURICE (F. D.).—LEARNING AND WORKING. Cr. 8vo. 4s. 6d.

RECORD OF TECHNICAL AND SECONDARY EDUCATION. Crown 8vo. Sewed, 2s. net. No. I. Nov 1891.

THRING (Rev. Edward).—EDUCATION AND SCHOOL. 2nd Edit. Cr. 8vo. 6s.

ENGINEERING.

ALEXANDER (T.) and THOMSON (A.W.)—ELEMENTARY APPLIED MECHANICS. Part II. TRANSVERSE STRESS. Cr. 8vo. 10s. 6d.

CHALMERS (J B.).—GRAPHICAL DETERMINATION OF FORCES IN ENGINEERING STRUCTURES. Illustrated. 8vo. 24s.

COTTERILL (Prof. J. H.).—APPLIED MECHANICS: An Elementary General Introduction to the Theory of Structures and Machines. 3rd Edit. 8vo. 18s.

COTTERILL (Prof. J. H.) and SLADE (J. H.).—LESSONS IN APPLIED MECHANICS. Fcp. 8vo. 5s. 6d.

KENNEDY (Prof. A. B. W.).—THE MECHANICS OF MACHINERY. Cr. 8vo. 12s. 6d.

PEABODY (Prof. C. H.).—THERMODYNAMICS OF THE STEAM ENGINE AND OTHER HEAT-ENGINES. 8vo. 21s.

SHANN (G.).—AN ELEMENTARY TREATISE ON HEAT IN RELATION TO STEAM AND THE STEAM-ENGINE. Illustrated. Cr. 8vo. 4s. 6d.

WHITHAM (Prof. J. M.).—STEAM-ENGINE DESIGN. For the use of Mechanical Engineers, Students, and Draughtsmen. Illustrated. 8vo. 25s.

WOODWARD (C. M.).—A HISTORY OF THE ST. LOUIS BRIDGE. 4to. 2l. 2s. net.

YOUNG (E. W.).—SIMPLE PRACTICAL METHODS OF CALCULATING STRAINS ON GIRDERS, ARCHES, AND TRUSSES. 8vo. 7s. 6d.

ENGLISH CITIZEN SERIES.
(See POLITICS.)

ENGLISH MEN OF ACTION.
(See BIOGRAPHY.)

ENGLISH MEN OF LETTERS.
(See BIOGRAPHY.)

ENGLISH STATESMEN, Twelve.
(See BIOGRAPHY.)

ENGRAVING. (See ART.)
ESSAYS. (See under LITERATURE, p. 20.)

ETCHING. (See ART.)
ETHICS. (See under PHILOSOPHY, p. 27.)

FATHERS, The.
(See under THEOLOGY, p. 35.)

FICTION, Prose.
(See under LITERATURE, p. 18.)

GARDENING.
(See also AGRICULTURE; BOTANY.)

BLOMFIELD (R.) and THOMAS (F. I.).—THE FORMAL GARDEN IN ENGLAND. Illustrated. Ex. cr. 8vo. 7s. 6d. net.—Large-Paper Edition. 8vo. 21s. net.

BRIGHT (H. A.).—THE ENGLISH FLOWER GARDEN. Cr. 8vo. 3s. 6d.
—— A YEAR IN A LANCASHIRE GARDEN. Cr. 8vo. 3s. 6d.

HOBDAY (E.). — VILLA GARDENING. A Handbook for Amateur and Practical Gardeners. Ext. cr. 8vo. 6s.

HOPE (Frances J.).—NOTES AND THOUGHTS ON GARDENS AND WOODLANDS. Cr. 8vo. 6s.

GEOGRAPHY.
(See also ATLASES.)

BLANFORD (H. F.).—ELEMENTARY GEOGRAPHY OF INDIA, BURMA, AND CEYLON. Globe 8vo. 2s. 6d.

CLARKE (C. B.).—A GEOGRAPHICAL READER AND COMPANION TO THE ATLAS. Cr. 8vo. 2s.
—— A CLASS-BOOK OF GEOGRAPHY. With 18 Coloured Maps. Fcp. 8vo. 3s.; swd., 2s. 6d.

DAWSON (G. M.) and SUTHERLAND (A.).—ELEMENTARY GEOGRAPHY OF THE BRITISH COLONIES. Globe 8vo. 3s

ELDERTON (W. A.).—MAPS AND MAP-DRAWING. Pott 8vo. 1s.

GEIKIE (Sir Archibald).—THE TEACHING OF GEOGRAPHY. A Practical Handbook for the use of Teachers. Globe 8vo. 2s.
—— GEOGRAPHY OF THE BRITISH ISLES. 18mo. 1s.

GREEN (J. R. and A. S.).—A SHORT GEOGRAPHY OF THE BRITISH ISLANDS. Fcp. 8vo. 3s. 6d.

GROVE (Sir George).—A PRIMER OF GEOGRAPHY. Maps. 18mo. 1s.

KIEPERT (H.).—MANUAL OF ANCIENT GEOGRAPHY. Cr. 8vo. 5s.

MILL (H. R.).—ELEMENTARY CLASS-BOOK OF GENERAL GEOGRAPHY. Cr. 8vo. 3s. 6d.

SIME (James).—GEOGRAPHY OF EUROPE. With Illustrations. Globe 8vo. 3s.

STRACHEY (Lieut.-Gen. R.).—LECTURES ON GEOGRAPHY. Cr. 8vo. 4s. 6d.

TOZER (H. F.).—A PRIMER OF CLASSICAL GEOGRAPHY. 18mo. 1s.

GEOLOGY AND MINERALOGY.

BLANFORD (W. T.). — GEOLOGY AND ZOOLOGY OF ABYSSINIA. 8vo. 21s.

COAL: ITS HISTORY AND ITS USES. By Profs. GREEN, MIALL, THORPE, RÜCKER, and MARSHALL. 8vo. 12s. 6d.

DAWSON (Sir J. W.).—THE GEOLOGY OF NOVA SCOTIA, NEW BRUNSWICK, AND PRINCE EDWARD ISLAND; or, Acadian Geology. 4th Edit. 8vo. 21s.

GEIKIE (Sir Archibald).—A PRIMER OF GEOLOGY. Illustrated. 18mo. 1s.
—— CLASS-BOOK OF GEOLOGY. Illustrated. Cr 8vo. 4s. 6d.

GEOLOGY AND MINERALOGY—*contd.*

GEIKIE (Sir A.).—GEOLOGICAL SKETCHES AT HOME AND ABROAD. Illus. 8vo. 10s.6d.
—— OUTLINES OF FIELD GEOLOGY. With numerous Illustrations. Gl. 8vo. 3s. 6d.
—— TEXT-BOOK OF GEOLOGY. Illustrated. 2nd Edit. 7th Thousand. Med. 8vo. 28s.
—— THE SCENERY OF SCOTLAND. Viewed in connection with its Physical Geology. 2nd Edit. Cr. 8vo. 12s. 6d.

HULL (E.).—A TREATISE ON ORNAMENTAL AND BUILDING STONES OF GREAT BRITAIN AND FOREIGN COUNTRIES. 8vo. 12s.

PENNINGTON (Rooke).—NOTES ON THE BARROWS AND BONE CAVES OF DERBYSHIRE. 8vo. 6s.

RENDU—WILLS.—THE THEORY OF THE GLACIERS OF SAVOY. By M. LE CHANOINE RENDU. Trans. by A. WILLS, Q.C. 8vo. 7s.6d.

ROSENBUSCH—IDDINGS.— MICROSCOPICAL PHYSIOGRAPHY OF THE ROCK-MAKING MINERALS. By Prof. H. ROSENBUSCH. Transl. by J. P. IDDINGS. Illustr. 8vo. 24s.

WILLIAMS (G. H.).—ELEMENTS OF CRYSTALLOGRAPHY. Cr. 8vo. 6s.

GLOBE LIBRARY. (*See* LITERATURE, p. 21.)

GLOSSARIES. (*See* DICTIONARIES.)

GOLDEN TREASURY SERIES. (*See* LITERATURE, p. 21.)

GRAMMAR. (*See* PHILOLOGY.)

HEALTH. (*See* HYGIENE.)

HEAT. (*See under* PHYSICS, p. 29.)

HISTOLOGY. (*See* PHYSIOLOGY.)

HISTORY.
(*See also* BIOGRAPHY.)

ANNALS OF OUR TIME. A Diurnal of Events, Social and Political, Home and Foreign. By JOSEPH IRVING. 8vo.—Vol. I June 20th, 1837, to Feb. 28th, 1871, 18s.; Vol. II. Feb. 24th, 1871, to June 24th, 1887, 18s. Also Vol. II. in 3 parts: Part I. Feb. 24th, 1871, to March 19th, 1874, 4s. 6d.; Part II. March 20th, 1874, to July 22nd, 1878, 4s. 6d.; Part III. July 23rd, 1878, to June 24th, 1887, 9s. Vol. III. By H. H. FYFE. Part I. June 25th, 1887, to Dec. 30th, 1890. 4s. 6d.; sewed, 3s. 6d. Part II. 1891, 1s. 6d.; sewed, 1s.

ARNOLD (T.).—THE SECOND PUNIC WAR. By THOMAS ARNOLD, D.D. Ed. by W. T. ARNOLD, M.A. With 8 Maps. Cr. 8vo. 5s.

ARNOLD (W. T.).—A HISTORY OF THE EARLY ROMAN EMPIRE. Cr. 8vo. [*In prep.*]

BEESLY (Mrs.).—STORIES FROM THE HISTORY OF ROME. Fcp. 8vo. 2s. 6d.

BLACKIE (Prof. John Stuart).—WHAT DOES HISTORY TEACH? Globe 8vo. 2s. 6d.

BRETT (R. B.)—FOOTPRINTS OF STATESMEN DURING THE EIGHTEENTH CENTURY IN ENGLAND. Cr. 8vo. 6s.

BRYCE (James, M.P.).—THE HOLY ROMAN EMPIRE. 8th Edit. Cr. 8vo. 7s. 6d.— *Library Edition.* 8vo. 14s.

BUCKLEY (Arabella).—HISTORY OF ENGLAND FOR BEGINNERS. Globe 8vo. 3s.
—— PRIMER OF ENGLISH HISTORY. 18mo. 1s.

BURKE (Edmund). (*See* POLITICS.)

BURY (J. B.).—A HISTORY OF THE LATER ROMAN EMPIRE FROM ARCADIUS TO IRENE, A.D. 390—800. 2 vols. 8vo. 32s.

CASSEL (Dr. D.).—MANUAL OF JEWISH HISTORY AND LITERATURE. Translated by Mrs. HENRY LUCAS. Fcp. 8vo. 2s. 6d.

COX (G. V.).—RECOLLECTIONS OF OXFORD. 2nd Edit. Cr. 8vo. 6s.

ENGLISH STATESMEN, TWELVE. (*See* BIOGRAPHY, p. 4.)

FISKE (John).—THE CRITICAL PERIOD IN AMERICAN HISTORY, 1783—89. Ext. cr 8vo. 10s. 6d.
—— THE BEGINNINGS OF NEW ENGLAND; or, The Puritan Theocracy in its Relations to Civil and Religious Liberty. Cr. 8vo. 7s. 6d.
—— THE AMERICAN REVOLUTION. 2 vols. Cr. 8vo. 18s.
—— THE DISCOVERY OF AMERICA. 2 vols. Cr. 8vo. 18s.

FRAMJI (Dosabhai). — HISTORY OF THE PARSIS, INCLUDING THEIR MANNERS, CUSTOMS, RELIGION, AND PRESENT POSITION. With Illustrations. 2 vols. Med. 8vo. 36s.

FREEMAN (Prof. E. A.).—HISTORY OF THE CATHEDRAL CHURCH OF WELLS. Cr. 8vo. 3s. 6d.
—— OLD ENGLISH HISTORY. With 3 Coloured Maps. 9th Edit., revised. Ext. fcp. 8vo. 6s.
—— HISTORICAL ESSAYS. First Series. 4th Edit. 8vo. 10s. 6d.
—— —— Second Series. 3rd Edit., with Additional Essays. 8vo. 10s. 6d.
—— —— Third Series. 8vo. 12s.
—— —— Fourth Series. 8vo. 12s. 6d.
—— THE GROWTH OF THE ENGLISH CONSTITUTION FROM THE EARLIEST TIMES. 5th Edit. Cr. 8vo. 5s.
—— COMPARATIVE POLITICS. Lectures at the Royal Institution. To which is added "The Unity of History." 8vo. 14s.
—— SUBJECT AND NEIGHBOUR LANDS OF VENICE. Illustrated. Cr. 8vo. 10s. 6d.
—— ENGLISH TOWNS AND DISTRICTS. A Series of Addresses and Essays. 8vo. 14s.
—— THE OFFICE OF THE HISTORICAL PROFESSOR. Cr. 8vo. 2s.
—— DISESTABLISHMENT AND DISENDOWMENT; WHAT ARE THEY? Cr. 8vo. 2s.
—— GREATER GREECE AND GREATER BRITAIN: GEORGE WASHINGTON THE EXPANDER OF ENGLAND. With an Appendix on IMPERIAL FEDERATION. Cr. 8vo. 3s. 6d.
—— THE METHODS OF HISTORICAL STUDY. Eight Lectures at Oxford. 8vo. 10s. 6d.
—— THE CHIEF PERIODS OF EUROPEAN HISTORY. With Essay on "Greek Cities under Roman Rule." 8vo. 10s. 6d.
—— FOUR OXFORD LECTURES, 1887; FIFTY YEARS OF EUROPEAN HISTORY; TEUTONIC CONQUEST IN GAUL AND BRITAIN. 8vo. 5s.

FRIEDMANN (Paul). (*See* BIOGRAPHY.)

GIBBINS (H. de B.).—HISTORY OF COMMERCE IN EUROPE. Globe 8vo. 3s. 6d.

GREEN (John Richard).—A Short History of the English People. New Edit., revised. 159th Thousand. Cr. 8vo. 8s. 6d.—Also in Parts, with Analysis. 3s. each.—Part I. 607—1265; II. 1204—1553; III. 1540—1689; IV. 1660—1873.—*Illustrated Edition*, in Parts. Super roy. 8vo. 1s. each net.—Part I. Oct. 1891. Vols. I. and II. 12s. each net.
—— History of the English People. In 4 vols. 8vo. 16s. each.
—— The Making of England. 8vo. 16s.
—— The Conquest of England. With Maps and Portrait. 8vo. 18s.
—— Readings in English History. In 3 Parts. Fcp. 8vo. 1s. 6d. each.

GREEN (Alice S.).—The English Town in the 15th Century. 2 vols. 8vo.

GUEST (Dr. E.).—Origines Celticæ. Maps. 2 vols. 8vo. 32s.

GUEST (M. J.)—Lectures on the History of England. Cr. 8vo. 6s.

HISTORY PRIMERS. Edited by John Richard Green. 18mo. 1s. each.
Europe. By E. A. Freeman, M.A.
Greece. By C. A. Fyffe, M.A.
Rome. By Bishop Creighton.
France. By Charlotte M. Yonge.
English History. By A. B. Buckley.

HISTORICAL COURSE FOR SCHOOLS. Ed. by Edw. A. Freeman, D.C.L. 18mo.
General Sketch of European History. By E. A. Freeman. Maps. 3s. 6d.
History of England. By Edith Thompson. Coloured Maps. 2s. 6d.
History of Scotland. By Margaret Macarthur. 2s.
History of Italy. By the Rev. W. Hunt, M.A. With Coloured Maps. 3s. 6d.
History of Germany. By James Sime, M.A. 3s.
History of America. By J. A. Doyle. With Maps. 4s. 6d.
History of European Colonies. By E. J. Payne, M.A. Maps. 4s. 6d.
History of France. By Charlotte M. Yonge. Maps. 3s. 6d.

HOLE (Rev. C.).—Genealogical Stemma of the Kings of England and France. On a Sheet. 1s.

INGRAM (T. Dunbar).—A History of the Legislative Union of Great Britain and Ireland. 8vo. 10s. 6d.
—— Two Chapters of Irish History: 1. The Irish Parliament of James II.; 2. The Alleged Violation of the Treaty of Limerick. 8vo. 6s.

JEBB (Prof. R. C.).—Modern Greece. Two Lectures. Crown 8vo. 5s.

JENNINGS (A. C.).—Chronological Tables of Ancient History. 8vo. 5s.

KEARY (Annie).—The Nations Around. Cr. 8vo. 4s. 6d.

KINGSLEY (Charles).—The Roman and the Teuton. Cr. 8vo. 3s. 6d.
—— Historical Lectures and Essays. Cr. 8vo. 3s. 6d.

LABBERTON (R. H.). (*See* Atlases.)

LEGGE (Alfred O.).—The Growth of the Temporal Power of the Papacy. Cr. 8vo. 8s. 6d.

LETHBRIDGE (Sir Roper).—A Short Manual of the History of India. Cr. 8vo. 5s.
—— The World's History. Cr. 8vo, swd. 1s.
—— Easy Introduction to the History of India. Cr. 8vo, sewed. 1s. 6d.
—— History of England. Cr. 8vo, swd. 1s. 6d.
—— Easy Introduction to the History and Geography of Bengal. Cr. 8vo. 1s. 6d.

LYTE (H. C. Maxwell).—A History of Eton College, 1440—1884. Illustrated. 8vo. 21s.
—— A History of the University of Oxford, from the Earliest Times to the Year 1530. 8vo. 16s.

MAHAFFY (Prof. J. P.).—Greek Life and Thought, from the Age of Alexander to the Roman Conquest. Cr. 8vo. 12s. 6d.
—— Social Life in Greece, from Homer to Menander. 6th Edit. Cr. 8vo. 9s.
—— The Greek World under Roman Sway, from Polybius to Plutarch. Cr. 8vo. 10s. 6d.
—— Problems in Greek History. Crown 8vo. 7s. 6d.

MARRIOTT (J. A. R.). (*See* Select Biography, p. 6.)

MICHELET (M.).—A Summary of Modern History. Translated by M. C. M. Simpson. Globe 8vo. 4s. 6d.

MULLINGER (J. B.).—Cambridge Characteristics in the Seventeenth Century. Cr. 8vo. 4s. 6d.

NORGATE (Kate).—England under the Angevin Kings. In 2 vols. 8vo. 32s.

OLIPHANT (Mrs. M. O. W.).—The Makers of Florence: Dante, Giotto, Savonarola, and their City. Illustr. Cr. 8vo. 10s. 6d.—*Edition de Luxe*. 8vo. 21s. net.
—— The Makers of Venice: Doges, Conquerors, Painters, and Men of Letters. Illustrated. Cr. 8vo. 10s. 6d.
—— Royal Edinburgh: Her Saints, Kings, Prophets, and Poets. Illustrated by G. Reid, R.S.A. Cr. 8vo. 10s. 6d.
—— Jerusalem, its History and Hope. Illust. 8vo. 21s.—Large Paper Edit. 50s. net.

OTTÉ (E. C.).—Scandinavian History. With Maps. Globe 8vo. 6s.

PALGRAVE (Sir F.).—History of Normandy and of England. 4 vols. 8vo. 4l.4s.

PARKMAN (Francis).—Montcalm and Wolfe. Library Edition. Illustrated with Portraits and Maps. 2 vols. 8vo. 12s. 6d. each.
—— The Collected Works of Francis Parkman. Popular Edition. In 10 vols. Cr. 8vo. 7s. 6d. each; or complete, 3l. 13s. 6d.—Pioneers of France in the New World, 1 vol.; The Jesuits in North America, 1 vol.; La Salle and the Discovery of the Great West, 1 vol.; The Oregon Trail, 1 vol.; The Old Régime in Canada under Louis XIV., 1 vol.; Count Frontenac and New France under Louis XIV., 1 vol.; Montcalm and Wolfe, 2 vols.; The Conspiracy of Pontiac, 2 vols.
—— A Half Century of Conflict. 2 vols. 8vo. 25s.
—— The Oregon Trail. Illustrated. Med. 8vo. 21s.

PERKINS (J. B).—France under the Regency. Cr. 8vo. 8s. 6d.

HISTORY—*continued.*

POOLE (R. L.).—A HISTORY OF THE HUGUE-NOTS OF THE DISPERSION AT THE RECALL OF THE EDICT OF NANTES. Cr. 8vo. 6s.

RHODES (J. F.).—HISTORY OF THE UNITED STATES FROM THE COMPROMISE OF 1850 TO 1880. 2 vols. 8vo. 24s.

ROGERS (Prof. J. E. Thorold).—HISTORICAL GLEANINGS. Cr. 8vo.—1st Series. 4s. 6d.—2nd Series. 6s.

SAYCE (Prof. A. H.).—THE ANCIENT EM-PIRES OF THE EAST. Cr. 8vo. 6s.

SEELEY (Prof. J R.). — LECTURES AND ESSAYS. 8vo. 10s. 6d.
—— THE EXPANSION OF ENGLAND. Two Courses of Lectures. Cr. 8vo. 4s. 6d.
—— OUR COLONIAL EXPANSION. Extracts from the above. Cr. 8vo. 1s.

SEWELL (E. M.) and **YONGE** (C. M.).—EUROPEAN HISTORY, NARRATED IN A SERIES OF HISTORICAL SELECTIONS FROM THE BEST AUTHORITIES. 2 vols. 3rd Edit. Cr. 8vo. 6s. each.

SHUCKBURGH (E. S.).—A SCHOOL HIS-TORY OF ROME. Cr. 8vo. [In preparation.

STEPHEN (Sir J. Fitzjames, Bart.).—THE STORY OF NUNCOMAR AND THE IMPEACH-MENT OF SIR ELIJAH IMPEY. 2 vols. Cr. 8vo. 15s.

TAIT (C. W. A.).—ANALYSIS OF ENGLISH HISTORY, BASED ON GREEN'S "SHORT HIS-TORY OF THE ENGLISH PEOPLE." Cr. 8vo. 4s. 6d.

TOUT (T. F.).—ANALYSIS OF ENGLISH HIS-TORY. 18mo. 1s.

TREVELYAN (Sir Geo. Otto).—CAWNPORE. Cr. 8vo. 6s.

WHEELER (J. Talboys).—PRIMER OF IN-DIAN HISTORY, ASIATIC AND EUROPEAN. 18mo. 1s.
—— COLLEGE HISTORY OF INDIA, ASIATIC AND EUROPEAN. Cr. 8vo. 3s.; swd. 2s. 6d.
—— A SHORT HISTORY OF INDIA. With Maps. Cr. 8vo. 12s.
—— INDIA UNDER BRITISH RULE. 8vo. 12s. 6d.

WOOD (Rev. E. G.).—THE REGAL POWER OF THE CHURCH. 8vo. 4s. 6d.

YONGE (Charlotte).—CAMEOS FROM ENGLISH HISTORY. Ext. fcp. 8vo. 5s. each.—Vol. 1. FROM ROLLO TO EDWARD II.; Vol. 2. THE WARS IN FRANCE; Vol. 3. THE WARS OF THE ROSES; Vol. 4. REFORMATION TIMES; Vol. 5. ENGLAND AND SPAIN; Vol. 6. FORTY YEARS OF STEWART RULE (1603–43); Vol. 7 THE REBELLION AND RESTORATION (1642–1678).
—— THE VICTORIAN HALF-CENTURY. Cr. 8vo. 1s. 6d.; sewed, 1s.
—— THE STORY OF THE CHRISTIANS AND MOORS IN SPAIN. 18mo. 4s. 6d.

HORTICULTURE. (*See* GARDENING.)

HYGIENE.

BERNERS (J.)—FIRST LESSONS ON HEALTH. 18mo. 1s.

BLYTH (A. Wynter).—A MANUAL OF PUBLIC HEALTH. 8vo. 17s. net.

BROWNE (J. H. Balfour).—WATER SUPPLY. Cr. 8vo. 2s. 6d.

CORFIELD (Dr W. H.).—THE TREATMENT AND UTILISATION OF SEWAGE. 3rd Edit. Revised by the Author, and by LOUIS C. PARKES, M.D. 8vo. 16s.

GOODFELLOW (J.).—THE DIETETIC VALUE OF BREAD. Cr. 8vo. 6s.

KINGSLEY (Charles).—SANITARY AND SO-CIAL LECTURES. Cr. 8vo. 3s. 6d.
—— HEALTH AND EDUCATION. Cr. 8vo. 6s.

REYNOLDS (Prof. Osborne).—SEWER GAS, AND HOW TO KEEP IT OUT OF HOUSES. 3rd Edit. Cr. 8vo. 1s. 6d.

RICHARDSON (Dr. B. W.).—HYGEIA: A CITY OF HEALTH. Cr. 8vo. 1s.
—— THE FUTURE OF SANITARY SCIENCE. Cr. 8vo. 1s.
—— ON ALCOHOL. Cr. 8vo. 1s.

HYMNOLOGY.

(*See under* THEOLOGY, p. 35.)

ILLUSTRATED BOOKS.

BALCH (Elizabeth). — GLIMPSES OF OLD ENGLISH HOMES. Gl. 4to. 14s.

BLAKE. (*See* BIOGRAPHY, p. 3.)

BOUGHTON (G. H.) and **ABBEY** (E. A.). (*See* VOYAGES AND TRAVELS.)

CHRISTMAS CAROL (A). Printed in Colours, with Illuminated Borders. 4to. 21s.

DAYS WITH SIR ROGER DE COVER-LEY. From the *Spectator.* Illustrated by HUGH THOMSON. Cr. 8vo. 6s.—Also with uncut edges, paper label. 6s.

DELL (E. C.).—PICTURES FROM SHELLEY. Engraved by J. D. COOPER. Folio. 21s. net.

GASKELL (Mrs.).—CRANFORD. Illustrated by HUGH THOMSON. Cr. 8vo. 6s.—Also with uncut edges paper label. 6s.

GOLDSMITH (Oliver). — THE VICAR OF WAKEFIELD. New Edition, with 182 Illus-trations by HUGH THOMSON. Preface by AUSTIN DOBSON. Cr. 8vo. 6s.—Also with Uncut Edges, paper label. 6s.

GREEN (John Richard). — ILLUSTRATED EDITION OF THE SHORT HISTORY OF THE ENGLISH PEOPLE. In Parts. Sup. roy. 8vo. 1s. each net. Part I. Oct. 1891. Vols. I. and II. 12s. each net.

GRIMM. (*See* BOOKS FOR THE YOUNG.)

HALLWARD (R. F.).—FLOWERS OF PARA-DISE. Music, Verse, Design, Illustration. 6s.

HAMERTON (P. G.).—MAN IN ART. With Etchings and Photogravures. 3l. 13s. 6d. net. —Large Paper Edition. 10l. 10s. net.

IRVING (Washington).—OLD CHRISTMAS. From the Sketch Book. Illustr. by RANDOLPH CALDECOTT. Gilt edges. Cr. 8vo. 6s.—Also with uncut edges, paper label. 6s.—Large Paper Edition. 30s. net.
—— BRACEBRIDGE HALL. Illustr. by RAN-DOLPH CALDECOTT. Gilt edges. Cr. 8vo. 6s.—Also with uncut edges, paper label. 6s.
—— OLD CHRISTMAS AND BRACEBRIDGE HALL. *Edition de Luxe.* Roy. 8vo. 21s.

KINGSLEY (Charles).—The Water Babies. (*See* Books for the Young.)
—— The Heroes. (*See* Books for the Young.)
—— Glaucus. (*See* Natural History.)

LANG (Andrew).—The Library. With a Chapter on Modern English Illustrated Books, by Austin Dobson. Cr. 8vo. 4s. 6d.
—Large Paper Edition. 21s. net.

LYTE (H. C. Maxwell). (*See* History.)

MAHAFFY (Rev. Prof. J. P.) and ROGERS (J. E.). (*See* Voyages and Travels.)

MEREDITH (L. A.).—Bush Friends in Tasmania. Native Flowers, Fruits, and Insects, with Prose and Verse Descriptions. Folio. 52s. 6d. net.

OLD SONGS. With Drawings by E. A. Abbey and A. Parsons. 4to, mor. gilt. 31s. 6d.

PROPERT (J. L.). (*See* Art.)

STUART, RELICS OF THE ROYAL HOUSE OF. Illustrated by 40 Plates in Colours drawn from Relics of the Stuarts by William Gibb. With an Introduction by John Skelton, C.B., LL.D., and Descriptive Notes by W. St. John Hope. Folio, half morocco, gilt edges. 10l. 10s. net.

TENNYSON (Lord H.).—Jack and the Bean-Stalk. English Hexameters. Illustrated by R. Caldecott. Fcp. 4to. 3s. 6d.

TRISTRAM (W. O.).—Coaching Days and Coaching Ways. Illust. H. Railton and Hugh Thomson. Ext. cr. 4to. 31s. 6d.

TURNER'S LIBER STUDIORUM: A Description and a Catalogue. By W. G. Rawlinson. Med. 8vo. 12s. 6d.

WALTON and COTTON—LOWELL.—The Complete Angler. With Introduction by Jas. Russell Lowell. 2 vols. Ext. cr. 8vo. 52s. 6d. net.

LANGUAGE. (*See* Philology.)

LAW.

BERNARD (M.).—Four Lectures on Subjects connected with Diplomacy. 8vo. 9s.

BIGELOW (M. M.).—History of Procedure in England from the Norman Conquest, 1066-1204. 8vo. 16s.

BOUTMY (E.).—Studies in Constitutional Law. Transl. by Mrs. Dicey. Preface by Prof. A. V. Dicey. Cr. 8vo. 6s.
—— The English Constitution. Transl. by Mrs. Eaden. Introduction by Sir F. Pollock, Bart. Cr. 8vo. 6s.

CHERRY (R. R.).—Lectures on the Growth of Criminal Law in Ancient Communities. 8vo. 5s. net.

DICEY (Prof. A. V.).—Lectures Introductory to the Study of the Law of the Constitution. 3rd Edit. 8vo. 12s. 6d.

ENGLISH CITIZEN SERIES, THE. (*See* Politics.)

HOLLAND (Prof. T. E.).—The Treaty Relations of Russia and Turkey, from 1774 to 1853. Cr. 8vo. 2s.

HOLMES (O. W., jun.).—The Common Law. 8vo. 12s.

LIGHTWOOD (J. M.).—The Nature of Positive Law. 8vo. 12s. 6d.

MAITLAND (F. W.).—Pleas of the Crown for the County of Gloucester, A.D. 1221. 8vo. 7s. 6d.
—— Justice and Police. Cr. 8vo. 3s. 6d.

MONAHAN (James H.).—The Method of Law. Cr. 8vo. 6s.

PATERSON (James).—Commentaries on the Liberty of the Subject, and the Laws of England relating to the Security of the Person. 2 vols. Cr. 8vo. 21s.
—— The Liberty of the Press, Speech, and Public Worship. Cr. 8vo. 12s.

PHILLIMORE (John G.).—Private Law among the Romans. 8vo. 6s.

POLLOCK (Sir F., Bart.).—Essays in Jurisprudence and Ethics. 8vo. 10s. 6d.
—— The Land Laws. Cr. 8vo. 3s. 6d.
—— Leading Cases done into English. Cr. 8vo. 3s. 6d.

RICHEY (Alex. G.).—The Irish Land Laws. Cr. 8vo. 3s. 6d.

SELBORNE (Earl of).—Judicial Procedure in the Privy Council. 8vo. 1s. net.

STEPHEN (Sir J. Fitzjames, Bart.).—A Digest of the Law of Evidence. Cr. 8vo. 6s.
—— A Digest of the Criminal Law: Crimes and Punishments. 4th Ed. 8vo. 16s.
—— A Digest of the Law of Criminal Procedure in Indictable Offences. By Sir J. F., Bart., and Herbert Stephen, LL.M. 8vo. 12s. 6d.
—— A History of the Criminal Law of England. 3 vols. 8vo. 48s.
—— A General View of the Criminal Law of England. 2nd Edit. 8vo. 14s.

STEPHEN (J. K.).—International Law and International Relations. Cr. 8vo. 6s.

WILLIAMS (S. E.).—Forensic Facts and Fallacies. Globe 8vo. 4s. 6d.

LETTERS. (*See under* Literature, p. 20.)

LIFE-BOAT.

GILMORE (Rev. John).—Storm Warriors; or, Life-Boat Work on the Goodwin Sands. Cr. 8vo. 3s. 6d.

LEWIS (Richard).—History of the Life-Boat and its Work. Cr. 8vo. 5s.

LIGHT. (*See under* Physics, p. 29.)

LITERATURE.

History and Criticism of—Commentaries, etc.—Poetry and the Drama—Poetical Collections and Selections—Prose Fiction—Collected Works, Essays, Lectures, Letters, Miscellaneous Works.

History and Criticism of.
(*See also* Essays, p. 20.)

ARNOLD (M.). (*See* Essays, p. 20.)

BROOKE (Stopford A.).—A Primer of English Literature. 18mo. 1s. — Large Paper Edition. 8vo. 7s. 6d.
—— A History of Early English Literature. 2 vols. 8vo. 20s. net.

LITERATURE.
History and Criticism of—*continued.*

CLASSICAL WRITERS. Edited by JOHN RICHARD GREEN. Fcp. 8vo. 1s. 6d. each.
DEMOSTHENES. By Prof. BUTCHER, M.A.
EURIPIDES. By Prof. MAHAFFY.
LIVY. By the Rev. W W CAPES, M.A.
MILTON. By STOPFORD A. BROOKE.
SOPHOCLES. By Prof. L. CAMPBELL, M.A.
TACITUS. By Messrs. CHURCH and BRODRIBB.
VERGIL. By Prof. NETTLESHIP, M.A.

ENGLISH MEN OF LETTERS. (*See* BIOGRAPHY, p. 4.)

HISTORY OF ENGLISH LITERATURE. In 4 vols. Cr. 8vo.
EARLY ENGLISH LITERATURE. By STOPFORD BROOKE, M.A. [*In preparation.*
ELIZABETHAN LITERATURE (1560—1665). By GEORGE SAINTSBURY. 7s. 6d.
EIGHTEENTH CENTURY LITERATURE (1660 —1780). By EDMUND GOSSE, M.A. 7s. 6d.
THE MODERN PERIOD. By Prof. DOWDEN. [*In preparation.*

JEBB (Prof. R. C.).—A PRIMER OF GREEK LITERATURE. 18mo. 1s.
—— THE ATTIC ORATORS, FROM ANTIPHON TO ISAEOS. 2 vols 8vo. 25s.

JOHNSON'S LIVES OF THE POETS. MILTON, DRYDEN, POPE, ADDISON, SWIFT, AND GRAY. With Macaulay's "Life of Johnson" Ed. by M. ARNOLD. Cr.8vo. 4s.6d.

KINGSLEY (Charles). — LITERARY AND GENERAL LECTURES. Cr. 8vo. 3s. 6d.

MAHAFFY (Prof. J. P.).—A HISTORY OF CLASSICAL GREEK LITERATURE. 2 vols. Cr. 8vo.—Vol. 1. THE POETS. With an Appendix on Homer by Prof. SAYCE. In 2 Parts.—Vol. 2. THE PROSE WRITERS. In 2 Parts. 4s. 6d. each.

MORLEY (John). (*See* COLLECTED WORKS, p. 23.)

NICHOL (Prof. J.) and McCORMICK (Prof (W. S.).—A SHORT HISTORY OF ENGLISH LITERATURE. Globe 8vo. [*In preparation.*

OLIPHANT (Mrs. M. O. W.).—THE LITERARY HISTORY OF ENGLAND IN THE END OF THE 18TH AND BEGINNING OF THE 19TH CENTURY. 3 vols. 8vo. 21s.

RYLAND (F.).—CHRONOLOGICAL OUTLINES OF ENGLISH LITERATURE. Cr. 8vo. 6s.

WARD (Prof. A. W.).—A HISTORY OF ENGLISH DRAMATIC LITERATURE, TO THE DEATH OF QUEEN ANNE. 2 vols. 8vo. 32s.

WILKINS (Prof. A. S.).—A PRIMER OF ROMAN LITERATURE. 18mo. 1s.

Commentaries, etc.

BROWNING.
A PRIMER ON BROWNING. By MARY WILSON. Cr. 8vo. 2s. 6d.
DANTE.
READINGS ON THE PURGATORIO OF DANTE. Chiefly based on the Commentary of Benvenuto da Imola. By the Hon. W. W. VERNON, M.A. With an Introduction by Dean CHURCH. 2 vols. Cr. 8vo. 24s.

HOMER.
HOMERIC DICTIONARY. (*See* DICTIONARIES.)
THE PROBLEM OF THE HOMERIC POEMS By Prof. W. D. GEDDES. 8vo. 14s.
HOMERIC SYNCHRONISM. An Inquiry into the Time and Place of Homer. By the Rt. Hon. W. E. GLADSTONE. Cr. 8vo. 6s.
PRIMER OF HOMER. By the same. 18mo. 1s.
LANDMARKS OF HOMERIC STUDY, TOGETHER WITH AN ESSAY ON THE POINTS OF CONTACT BETWEEN THE ASSYRIAN TABLETS AND THE HOMERIC TEXT. By the same. Cr. 8vo. 2s. 6d.
COMPANION TO THE ILIAD FOR ENGLISH READERS. By W. LEAF, Litt. D. Crown 8vo. 7s. 6d.

HORACE.
STUDIES, LITERARY AND HISTORICAL, IN THE ODES OF HORACE. By A. W. VERRALL, Litt. D. 8vo. 8s. 6d.

SHAKESPEARE.
SHAKESPEARE GLOSSARY. *See* DICTIONARIES.
A PRIMER OF SHAKSPERE. By Prof. DOWDEN. 18mo. 1s.
A SHAKESPEARIAN GRAMMAR. By Rev. E. A. ABBOTT. Ext. fcp. 8vo. 6s.
SHAKESPEAREANA GENEALOGICA. By G. R. FRENCH. 8vo. 15s.
A SELECTION FROM THE LIVES IN NORTH'S PLUTARCH WHICH ILLUSTRATE SHAKESPEARE'S PLAYS. Edited by Rev. W. W. SKEAT, M.A. Cr. 8vo. 6s.
SHORT STUDIES OF SHAKESPEARE'S PLOTS. By Prof. CYRIL RANSOME. Cr. 8vo. 3s. 6d. —Also separately: HAMLET, 9d.; MACBETH, 9d.; TEMPEST, 9d.
CALIBAN: A Critique on "The Tempest" and "A Midsummer Night's Dream." By Sir DANIEL WILSON. 8vo. 10s. 6d.

TENNYSON.
A COMPANION TO "IN MEMORIAM." By ELIZABETH R. CHAPMAN. Globe 8vo. 2s.

WORDSWORTH.
WORDSWORTHIANA: A Selection of Papers read to the Wordsworth Society. Edited by W. KNIGHT. Cr. 8vo. 7s. 6d.

Poetry and the Drama.

ALDRICH (T. Bailey).—THE SISTERS' TRAGEDY: with other Poems, Lyrical and Dramatic. Fcp. 8vo. 3s. 6d. net.

AN ANCIENT CITY: AND OTHER POEMS. Ext. fcp. 8vo. 6s.

ANDERSON (A.).—BALLADS AND SONNETS. Cr. 8vo. 5s.

ARNOLD (Matthew). — THE COMPLETE POETICAL WORKS. New Edition. 3 vols. Cr. 8vo. 7s. 6d. each.
Vol. 1. EARLY POEMS, NARRATIVE POEMS AND SONNETS.
Vol. 2. LYRIC AND ELEGIAC POEMS.
Vol. 3. DRAMATIC AND LATER POEMS.
—— COMPLETE POETICAL WORKS. 1 vol. Cr. 8vo. 7s. 6d.
—— SELECTED POEMS. 18mo. 4s. 6d.

AUSTIN (Alfred).—POETICAL WORKS. New Collected Edition. 6 vols. Cr. 8vo. 5s. each.
Vol. 1. THE TOWER OF BABEL.
Vol. 2. SAVONAROLA, etc.
Vol. 3. PRINCE LUCIFER.
Vol. 4. THE HUMAN TRAGEDY.
Vol. 5. LYRICAL POEMS.
Vol. 6. NARRATIVE POEMS.
—— SOLILOQUIES IN SONG. Cr. 8vo. 6s.
—— AT THE GATE OF THE CONVENT : and other Poems. Cr. 8vo. 6s.
—— MADONNA'S CHILD. Cr. 4to. 3s. 6d.
—— ROME OR DEATH. Cr. 4to. 9s.
—— THE GOLDEN AGE. Cr. 8vo. 5s.
—— THE SEASON. Cr. 8vo. 5s.
—— LOVE'S WIDOWHOOD. Cr. 8vo. 6s.
—— ENGLISH LYRICS. Cr. 8vo. 3s. 6d.
—— FORTUNATUS THE PESSIMIST. Cr.8vo. 6s.

BETSY LEE : A FO'C'S'LE YARN. Ext. fcp. 8vo. 3s. 6d.

BLACKIE (John Stuart).—MESSIS VITAE : Gleanings of Song from a Happy Life. Cr. 8vo. 4s. 6d.
—— THE WISE MEN OF GREECE. In a Series of Dramatic Dialogues. Cr. 8vo. 9s.
—— GOETHE'S FAUST. Translated into English Verse. 2nd Edit. Cr. 8vo. 9s.

BLAKE. (See BIOGRAPHY, p. 3.)

BROOKE (Stopford A.).—RIQUET OF THE TUFT : A Love Drama. Ext. cr. 8vo. 6s.
—— POEMS. Globe 8vo. 6s.

BROWN (T. E.).—THE MANX WITCH : and other Poems. Cr. 8vo. 7s. 6d.

BURGON (Dean).—POEMS. Ex.fcp.8vo. 4s.6d.

BURNS. THE POETICAL WORKS. With a Biographical Memoir by ALEXANDER SMITH. In 2 vols. Fcp. 8vo. 10s. (See also GLOBE LIBRARY, p. 21.)

BUTLER (Samuel).—HUDIBRAS. Edit. by ALFRED MILNES. Fcp. 8vo.—Part I. 3s. 6d.; Parts II. and III. 4s. 6d.

BYRON. (See GOLDEN TREASURY SERIES, p. 21.)

CALDERON.—SELECT PLAYS. Edited by NORMAN MACCOLL. Cr. 8vo. 14s.

CAUTLEY (G. S.).—A CENTURY OF EMBLEMS. With Illustrations by Lady MARION ALFORD. Small 4to. 10s. 6d.

CLOUGH (A. H.).—POEMS. Cr. 8vo. 7s.6d.

COLERIDGE : POETICAL AND DRAMATIC WORKS. 4 vols. Fcp. 8vo. 31s. 6d.—Also an Edition on Large Paper, 2l. 12s. 6d.

COLQUHOUN.—RHYMES AND CHIMES. By F. S. COLQUHOUN (née F. S. FULLER MAITLAND). Ext. fcp. 8vo. 2s. 6d.

COWPER. (See GLOBE LIBRARY, p. 21; GOLDEN TREASURY SERIES, p. 21.)

CRAIK (Mrs.).—POEMS. Ext. fcp. 8vo. 6s.

DOYLE (Sir F. H.).—THE RETURN OF THE GUARDS : and other Poems. Cr. 8vo. 7s. 6d.

DRYDEN. (See GLOBE LIBRARY, p. 21.)

EMERSON. (See COLLECTED WORKS, p. 21.)

EVANS (Sebastian). — BROTHER FABIAN'S MANUSCRIPT : and other Poems. Fcp. 8vo. 6s.
—— IN THE STUDIO : A Decade of Poems. Ext. fcp. 8vo. 5s.

FITZ GERALD (Caroline).—VENETIA VICTRIX : and other Poems. Ext. fcp. 8vo. 3s. 6d.

FITZGERALD (Edward).—THE RUBÁIYÁT OF OMAR KHÁYYÁM. Ext. cr. 8vo. 10s. 6d.

FO'C'SLE YARNS, including "Betsy Lee," and other Poems. Cr. 8vo. 7s. 6d.

FRASER-TYTLER. — SONGS IN MINOR KEYS. By C. C. FRASER-TYTLER (Mrs. EDWARD LIDDELL). 2nd Edit. 18mo. 6s.

FURNIVALL (F. J.).—LE MORTE ARTHUR. Edited from the Harleian MSS. 2252, in the British Museum. Fcp. 8vo. 7s. 6d.

GARNETT (R.).—IDYLLS AND EPIGRAMS. Chiefly from the Greek Anthology. Fcp. 8vo. 2s. 6d.

GOETHE.—FAUST. (See BLACKIE.)
—— REYNARD THE FOX. Transl. into English Verse by A. D. AINSLIE. Cr. 8vo. 7s. 6d.

GOLDSMITH.—THE TRAVELLER AND THE DESERTED VILLAGE. With Introduction and Notes, by ARTHUR BARRETT, B.A. 1s. 9d.; sewed, 1s.6d.—THE TRAVELLER (separately), sewed, 1s.—By J. W. HALES. Cr. 8vo. 6d. (See also GLOBE LIBRARY, p. 21.)

GRAHAM (David).—KING JAMES I. An Historical Tragedy. Globe 8vo. 7s.

GRAY.—POEMS. With Introduction and Notes, by J. BRADSHAW, LL.D. Gl. 8vo. 1s. 9d.; sewed, 1s. 6d. (See also COLLECTED WORKS, p. 22.)

HALLWARD. (See ILLUSTRATED BOOKS.)

HAYES (A.).—THE MARCH OF MAN : and other Poems. Fcp. 8vo. 3s. 6d. net.

HERRICK. (See GOLDEN TREASURY SERIES, p. 21.)

HOPKINS (Ellice).—AUTUMN SWALLOWS : A Book of Lyrics. Ext. fcp. 8vo. 6s.

HOSKEN (J. D.).—PHAON AND SAPPHO, AND NIMROD. Fcp. 8vo. 5s.

JONES (H. A.).—SAINTS AND SINNERS. Ext. fcp. 8vo. 3s. 6d.

KEATS. (See GOLDEN TREASURY SERIES, p. 21.)

KINGSLEY (Charles).—POEMS. Cr. 8vo. 3s. 6d.—Pocket Edition. 18mo. 1s. 6d.—Eversley Edition. 2 vols. Cr. 8vo. 10s.

LAMB. (See COLLECTED WORKS, p. 22.)

LANDOR. (See GOLDEN TREASURY SERIES, p. 22.)

LONGFELLOW. (See GOLDEN TREASURY SERIES, p. 22.)

LOWELL (Jas. Russell).—COMPLETE POETICAL WORKS. 18mo. 4s. 6d.
—— With Introduction by THOMAS HUGHES, and Portrait. Cr. 8vo. 7s. 6d.
—— HEARTSEASE AND RUE. Cr. 8vo. 5s.
—— OLD ENGLISH DRAMATISTS. Cr. 8vo. 5s. (See also COLLECTED WORKS, p. 23.)

LUCAS (F.).—SKETCHES OF RURAL LIFE. Poems. Globe 8vo. 5s.

LITERATURE.

Poetry and the Drama—*continued.*

MEREDITH (George). — A READING OF EARTH. Ext. fcp. 8vo. 5s.
—— POEMS AND LYRICS OF THE JOY OF EARTH. Ext. fcp. 8vo. 6s.
—— BALLADS AND POEMS OF TRAGIC LIFE. Cr. 8vo. 6s.
—— MODERN LOVE. Ex. fcap. 8vo. 5s.
—— THE EMPTY PURSE. Fcp. 8vo. 5s.

MILTON. — POETICAL WORKS. Edited, with Introductions and Notes, by Prof. DAVID MASSON, M.A. 3 vols. 8vo. 2l. 2s.—[Uniform with the Cambridge Shakespeare.]
—— —— Edited by Prof MASSON. 3 vols. Fcp. 8vo. 15s.
—— —— *Globe Edition.* Edited by Prof. MASSON. Globe 8vo. 3s. 6d.
—— PARADISE LOST, BOOKS 1 and 2. Edited by MICHAEL MACMILLAN, B.A. 1s. 9d.; sewed, 1s. 6d.—BOOKS 1 and 2 (separately), 1s. 3d. each; sewed, 1s. each.
—— L'ALLEGRO, IL PENSEROSO, LYCIDAS, ARCADES, SONNETS, ETC. Edited by WM. BELL, M.A. 1s. 9d.; sewed, 1s. 6d.
—— COMUS. By the same. 1s. 3d.; swd. 1s.
—— SAMSON AGONISTES. Edited by H. M. PERCIVAL, M.A. 2s.; sewed, 1s. 6d.

MOULTON (Louise Chandler). — IN THE GARDEN OF DREAMS: Lyrics and Sonnets. Cr. 8vo. 6s.
—— SWALLOW FLIGHTS. Cr. 8vo. 6s.

MUDIE (C. E.). — STRAY LEAVES: Poems. 4th Edit. Ext. fcp. 8vo. 3s. 6d.

MYERS (E.). — THE PURITANS: A Poem. Ext. fcp. 8vo. 2s. 6d.
—— POEMS. Ext. fcp. 8vo. 4s. 6d.
—— THE DEFENCE OF ROME: and other Poems. Ext. fcp. 8vo. 5s.
—— THE JUDGMENT OF PROMETHEUS: and other Poems. Ext. fcp. 8vo. 3s. 6d.

MYERS (F. W. H.). — THE RENEWAL OF YOUTH: and other Poems. Cr. 8vo. 7s. 6d.
—— ST. PAUL: A Poem. Ext. fcp. 8vo. 2s.6d.

NORTON (Hon. Mrs.). — THE LADY OF LA GARAYE. 9th Edit. Fcp. 8vo. 4s. 6d.

PALGRAVE(Prof.F.T.). — ORIGINAL HYMNS. 3rd Edit. 18mo. 1s. 6d.
—— LYRICAL POEMS. Ext. fcp. 8vo. 6s.
—— VISIONS OF ENGLAND. Cr. 8vo. 7s. 6d.
—— AMENOPHIS. 18mo. 4s. 6d.

PALGRAVE (W G.). — A VISION OF LIFE: SEMBLANCE AND REALITY. Cr. 8vo. 7s. net.

PEEL (Edmund). — ECHOES FROM HOREB: and other Poems. Cr. 8vo. 3s. 6d

POPE. (*See* GLOBE LIBRARY, p. 21.)

RAWNSLEY (H. D.). — POEMS, BALLADS, AND BUCOLICS. Fcp. 8vo. 5s.

ROSCOE (W. C.). — POEMS. Edit. by E. M. ROSCOE. Cr. 8vo. 7s. net.

ROSSETTI (Christina). — POEMS. New Collected Edition. Globe 8vo. 7s. 6d.
—— A PAGEANT: and other Poems. Ext. fcp. 8vo. 6s.

SCOTT. — THE LAY OF THE LAST MINSTREL, and THE LADY OF THE LAKE. Edited by Prof. F. T. PALGRAVE. 1s.
—— THE LAY OF THE LAST MINSTREL. By G. H. STUART, M.A., and E. H. ELLIOT, B.A. Globe 8vo. 2s.; sewed, 1s. 9d.—Canto I 9d.—Cantos I.–III, and IV.–VI. 1s. 3d. each; sewed, 1s. each.
—— MARMION. Edited by MICHAEL MACMILLAN, B.A. 3s.; sewed, 2s. 6d.
—— MARMION, and THE LORD OF THE ISLES. By Prof. F. T. PALGRAVE. 1s.
—— THE LADY OF THE LAKE. By G. H. STUART, M.A. Gl. 8vo. 2s. 6d.; swd. 2s.
—— ROKEBY. By MICHAEL MACMILLAN, B.A. 3s.; sewed, 2s. 6d.

(*See also* GLOBE LIBRARY, p. 21.)

SHAIRP (John Campbell). — GLEN DESSERAY: and other Poems, Lyrical and Elegiac. Ed. by F. T. PALGRAVE. Cr. 8vo. 6s.

SHAKESPEARE. — THE WORKS OF WILLIAM SHAKESPEARE. *Cambridge Edition.* New and Revised Edition, by W. ALDIS WRIGHT, M.A. 9 vols. 8vo. 10s. 6d. each.
—— *Victoria Edition.* In 3 vols.—COMEDIES; HISTORIES; TRAGEDIES. Cr. 8vo. 6s. each.
—— THE TEMPEST. With Introduction and Notes, by K. DEIGHTON.. Gl. 8vo. 1s. 9d.; sewed, 1s. 6d.
—— MUCH ADO ABOUT NOTHING. 2s.; sewed, 1s. 9d.
—— A MIDSUMMER NIGHT'S DREAM. 1s. 9d.; sewed, 1s. 6d.
—— THE MERCHANT OF VENICE. 1s. 9d.; sewed, 1s. 6d.
—— AS YOU LIKE IT. 1s. 9d.; sewed, 1s. 6d.
—— TWELFTH NIGHT. 1s. 9d.; sewed, 1s. 6d.
—— THE WINTER'S TALE. 2s.; sewed, 1s. 9d.
—— KING JOHN. 1s. 9d.; sewed, 1s. 6d.
—— RICHARD II. 1s. 9d.; sewed, 1s. 6d.
—— HENRY V. 1s. 9d.; sewed, 1s. 6d.
—— RICHARD III. By C. H. TAWNEY, M.A. 2s. 6d.; sewed, 2s.
—— CORIOLANUS. By K. DEIGHTON. 2s. 6d.; sewed, 2s.
—— JULIUS CÆSAR. 1s. 9d.; sewed, 1s. 6d.
—— MACBETH. 1s. 9d.; sewed, 1s. 6d.
—— HAMLET. 2s. 6d.; sewed, 2s.
—— KING LEAR. 1s. 9d.; sewed, 1s. 6d.
—— OTHELLO. 2s.; sewed, 1s. 9d.
—— ANTONY AND CLEOPATRA. 2s.6d.; swd. 2s.
—— CYMBELINE. 2s. 6d.; sewed, 2s.

(*See also* GLOBE LIBRARY, p. 21; GOLDEN TREASURY SERIES, p. 21.)

SHELLEY. — COMPLETE POETICAL WORKS Edited by Prof. DOWDEN. Portrait. Cr. 8vo. 7s.6d. (*See* GOLDEN TREASURY SERIES, p. 21.)

SMITH (C. Barnard). — POEMS. Fcp. 8vo. 5s.

SMITH (Horace). — POEMS. Globe 8vo. 5s.
—— INTERLUDES. Cr. 8vo. 5s.

SPENSER. (*See* GLOBE LIBRARY, p. 21.)

STEPHENS (J. B.). — CONVICT ONCE: and other Poems. Cr. 8vo. 7s. 6d.

STRETTELL (Alma). — SPANISH AND ITALIAN FOLK SONGS. Illustr. Roy.16mo. 12s.6d.

SYMONS (Arthur). — DAYS AND NIGHTS. Globe 8vo. 6s.

TENNYSON (Lord).—COMPLETE WORKS. New and Enlarged Edition, with Portrait. Cr. 8vo. 7s. 6d.—*School Edition.* In Four Parts. Cr. 8vo. 2s. 6d. each.
—— POETICAL WORKS. *Pocket Edition.* 18mo, morocco, gilt edges. 7s 6d. net.
—— WORKS. *Library Edition.* In 8 vols. Globe 8vo. 5s. each. [Each volume may be had separately.]—POEMS, 2 vols.—IDYLLS OF THE KING.—THE PRINCESS, and MAUD.—ENOCH ARDEN, and IN MEMORIAM.—BALLADS, and other Poems.—QUEEN MARY, and HAROLD.—BECKET, and other Plays.
—— WORKS. *Ext. fcp. 8vo. Edition,* on Handmade Paper. In 7 vols. (supplied in sets only). 3l. 13s. 6d.—EARLY POEMS.—LUCRETIUS, and other Poems.—IDYLLS OF THE KING.—THE PRINCESS, and MAUD.—ENOCH ARDEN, and IN MEMORIAM.—QUEEN MARY, and HAROLD.—BALLADS, and other Poems.
—— WORKS. *Miniature Edition,* in 16 vols., viz. THE POETICAL WORKS. 12 vols. in a box. 25s.—THE DRAMATIC WORKS. 4 vols. in a box. 10s. 6d.
—— WORKS. *Miniature Edition on India Paper.* POETICAL AND DRAMATIC WORKS. 8 vols. in a box. 40s. net.
—— *The Original Editions.* Fcp. 8vo.
POEMS. 6s.
MAUD: and other Poems. 3s. 6d.
THE PRINCESS. 3s. 6d.
THE HOLY GRAIL: and other Poems. 4s.6d.
BALLADS: and other Poems. 5s.
HAROLD: A Drama. 6s.
QUEEN MARY: A Drama. 6s.
THE CUP, and THE FALCON. 5s.
BECKET. 6s.
TIRESIAS: and other Poems. 6s.
LOCKSLEY HALL SIXTY YEARS AFTER, etc. 6s.
DEMETER: and other Poems. 6s.
THE FORESTERS: ROBIN HOOD AND MAID MARIAN. 6s.
THE DEATH OF OENONE, AKBAR'S DREAM, AND OTHER POEMS. 6s.
—— *The Royal Edition.* 1 vol. 8vo. 16s.
—— THE TENNYSON BIRTHDAY BOOK. Edit. by EMILY SHAKESPEAR. 18mo. 2s. 6d.
—— THE BROOK. With 20 Illustrations by A. WOODRUFF. 32mo. 2s. 6d.
—— SONGS FROM TENNYSON'S WRITINGS. Square 8vo. 2s. 6d.
—— SELECTIONS FROM TENNYSON. With Introduction and Notes, by F. J. ROWE, M.A., and W. T. WEBB, M.A. Globe 8vo. 3s. 6d.
—— ENOCH ARDEN. By W. T. WEBB, M.A. Globe 8vo. 2s. 6d.
—— AYLMER'S FIELD. By W. T. WEBB, M.A. Globe 8vo. 2s. 6d.
—— THE COMING OF ARTHUR, and THE PASSING OF ARTHUR. By F. J. ROWE. Gl. 8vo. 2s.6d.
—— THE PRINCESS. By P. M. WALLACE, M.A. Globe 8vo. 3s. 6d.
—— GARETH AND LYNETTE. By G. C. MACAULAY, M.A. 2s. 6d.
—— GERAINT AND ENID. By G. C. MACAULAY, M.A. 2s. 6d.
—— TENNYSON FOR THE YOUNG. By Canon AINGER. 18mo. 1s. net.—Large Paper, uncut, 3s. 6d.; gilt edges, 4s. 6d.

TENNYSON (Frederick).—THE ISLES OF GREECE: SAPPHO AND ALCAEUS. Cr. 8vo. 7s. 6d.
—— DAPHNE: and other Poems. Cr. 8vo. 7s.6d.

TENNYSON (Lord H). (*See* ILLUSTRATED BOOKS.)

TRUMAN (Jos.).—AFTER-THOUGHTS: Poems. Cr. 8vo. 3s. 6d.

TURNER (Charles Tennyson).—COLLECTED SONNETS, OLD AND NEW. Ext. fcp. 8vo. 7s.6d.

TYRWHITT (R. St. John).—FREE FIELD. Lyrics, chiefly Descriptive. Gl. 8vo. 3s. 6d.
—— BATTLE AND AFTER, concerning SERGEANT THOMAS ATKINS, GRENADIER GUARDS: and other Verses. Gl. 8vo. 3s.6d.

WARD (Samuel).—LYRICAL RECREATIONS. Fcp. 8vo. 6s.

WATSON (W.).—POEMS. Fcap. 8vo. 5s.
—— LACHRYMAE MUSARUM. Fcp. 8vo. 4s.5d.
(*See also* GOLDEN TREASURY SERIES, p. 22.)

WHITTIER.—COMPLETE POETICAL WORKS OF JOHN GREENLEAF WHITTIER. With Portrait. 18mo. 4s. 6d. (*See also* COLLECTED WORKS, p. 23.)

WILLS (W. G.).—MELCHIOR. Cr. 8vo. 9s.

WOOD (Andrew Goldie).—THE ISLES OF THE BLEST: and other Poems. Globe 8vo. 5s.

WOOLNER (Thomas). — MY BEAUTIFUL LADY. 3rd Edit. Fcp. 8vo. 5s.
—— PYGMALION. Cr. 8vo. 7s. 6d.
—— SILENUS. Cr. 8vo. 6s.

WORDSWORTH. — COMPLETE POETICAL WORKS. Copyright Edition. With an Introduction by JOHN MORLEY, and Portrait. Cr. 8vo. 7s. 6d.
—— THE RECLUSE. Fcp. 8vo. 2s. 6d.—Large Paper Edition. 8vo. 10s. 6d.
(*See also* GOLDEN TREASURY SERIES, p. 21.)

Poetical Collections and Selections.

(*See also* GOLDEN TREASURY SERIES, p. 21; BOOKS FOR THE YOUNG, p. 41.)

HALES (Prof. J. W.).—LONGER ENGLISH POEMS. With Notes, Philological and Explanatory, and an Introduction on the Teaching of English. Ext. fcp. 8vo. 4s. 6d.

MACDONALD (George).—ENGLAND'S ANTIPHON. Cr. 8vo. 4s. 6d.

MARTIN (F.). (*See* BOOKS FOR THE YOUNG, p. 41.)

MASSON (R. O. and D.).—THREE CENTURIES OF ENGLISH POETRY. Being Selections from Chaucer to Herrick. Globe 8vo. 3s. 6d.

PALGRAVE (Prof. F. T.).—THE GOLDEN TREASURY OF THE BEST SONGS AND LYRICAL POEMS IN THE ENGLISH LANGUAGE. Large Type. Cr. 8vo. 10s. 6d. (*See also* GOLDEN TREASURY SERIES, p. 21; BOOKS FOR THE YOUNG, p. 41.)

WARD (T. H.).—ENGLISH POETS. Selections, with Critical Introductions by various Writers, and a General Introduction by MATTHEW ARNOLD. Edited by T. H. WARD, M.A. 4 vols. 2nd Edit. Cr. 8vo. 7s. 6d. each.— Vol. I. CHAUCER TO DONNE; II. BEN JONSON TO DRYDEN; III. ADDISON TO BLAKE; IV WORDSWORTH TO ROSSETTI.

LITERATURE.

WOODS (M. A.).—A First Poetry Book. Fcp. 8vo. 2s. 6d.
—— A Second Poetry Book. 2 Parts. Fcp. 8vo. 2s. 6d. each.—Complete, 4s. 6d.
—— A Third Poetry Book. Fcp. 8vo. 4s. 6d.

WORDS FROM THE POETS. With a Vignette and Frontispiece. 12th Edit. 18mo. 1s.

Prose Fiction.

BIKELAS (D.).—Loukis Laras; or, The Reminiscences of a Chiote Merchant during the Greek War of Independence. Translated by J. Gennadius. Cr. 8vo. 7s. 6d.

BJÖRNSON (B.).—Synnövë Solbakken. Translated by Julie Sutter. Cr. 8vo. 6s.

BOLDREWOOD (Rolf).—*Uniform Edition.* Cr. 8vo. 3s. 6d. each.
Robbery Under Arms.
The Miner's Right.
The Squatter's Dream.
A Sydney-Side Saxon.
A Colonial Reformer.
Nevermore.

BURNETT(F. H.).—Haworth's. Gl. 8vo. 2s.
—— Louisiana, and That Lass o' Lowrie's. Illustrated. Cr. 8vo. 3s. 6d.

CALMIRE. 2 vols. Cr. 8vo. 21s.

CARMARTHEN (Marchioness of). — A Lover of the Beautiful. Cr. 8vo. 6s.

CONWAY (Hugh). — A Family Affair. Cr. 8vo. 3s. 6d.
—— Living or Dead. Cr. 8vo. 3s. 6d.

CORBETT (Julian).—The Fall of Asgard: A Tale of St. Olaf's Day. 2 vols. Gl. 8vo. 12s.
—— For God and Gold. Cr. 8vo. 6s.
—— Kophetua the Thirteenth. 2 vols. Globe 8vo. 12s.

CRAIK (Mrs.).—*Uniform Edition.* Cr. 8vo. 3s. 6d. each.
Olive.
The Ogilvies. Also Globe 8vo, 2s.
Agatha's Husband. Also Globe 8vo, 2s.
The Head of the Family.
Two Marriages. Also Globe 8vo, 2s.
The Laurel Bush.
My Mother and I.
Miss Tommy: A Mediæval Romance.
King Arthur: Not a Love Story.

CRAWFORD(F. Marion).—*Uniform Edition.* Cr. 8vo. 3s. 6d. each.
Mr. Isaacs: A Tale of Modern India.
Dr. Claudius.
A Roman Singer.
Zoroaster.
A Tale of a Lonely Parish.
Marzio's Crucifix.
Paul Patoff.
With the Immortals.
Greifenstein.
Sant' Ilario.
A Cigarette Maker's Romance.
Khaled: A Tale of Arabia.
—— The Witch of Prague. Cr. 8vo. 6s.
—— The Three Fates. Cr. 8vo. 6s.
—— Don Orsino. 3 vols. Cr. 8vo. 31s. 6d.
—— Children of the King. 2 vols. Globe 8vo. 12s.

CUNNINGHAM (Sir H. S.).—The Cœruleans: A Vacation Idyll. Cr. 8vo. 3s. 6d.
—— The Heriots. Cr. 8vo. 3s. 6d.
—— Wheat and Tares. Cr. 8vo. 3s. 6d.

DAGONET THE JESTER. Cr. 8vo. 4s. 6d.

DAHN (Felix).—Felicitas. Translated by M. A. C. E. Cr. 8vo. 4s. 6d.

DAY (Rev. Lal Behari).—Bengal Peasant Life. Cr. 8vo. 6s.
—— Folk Tales of Bengal. Cr. 8vo. 4s. 6d.

DEFOE (D.). (*See* Globe Library, p. 21: Golden Treasury Series, p. 22.)

DEMOCRACY: An American Novel. Cr. 8vo. 4s. 6d.

DICKENS (Charles). — *Uniform Edition.* Cr. 8vo. 3s. 6d. each.
The Pickwick Papers.
Oliver Twist.
Nicholas Nickleby.
Martin Chuzzlewit.
The Old Curiosity Shop.
Barnaby Rudge.
Dombey and Son.
Christmas Books.
Sketches by Boz.
David Copperfield.
American Notes, and Pictures from Italy.
—— The Posthumous Papers of the Pickwick Club. Illust. Edit. by C. Dickens, Jun. 2 vols. Ext. cr. 8vo. 21s.

DILLWYN (E. A.).—Jill. Cr. 8vo. 6s.
—— Jill and Jack. 2 vols. Globe 8vo. 12s.

DUNSMUIR (Amy).—Vida: Study of a Girl. 3rd Edit. Cr. 8vo. 6s.

EBERS (Dr. George).—The Burgomaster's Wife. Transl. by C. Bell. Cr. 8vo. 4s. 6d.
—— Only a Word. Translated by Clara Bell. Cr. 8vo. 4s. 6d.

"ESTELLE RUSSELL" (The Author of).— Harmonia. 3 vols. Cr. 8vo. 31s. 6d.

FALCONER (Lanoe).—Cecilia de Noël. Cr. 8vo. 3s. 6d.

FLEMING(G.).—A Nile Novel. Gl. 8vo. 2s.
—— Mirage: A Novel. Globe 8vo. 2s.
—— The Head of Medusa. Globe 8vo. 2s.
—— Vestigia. Globe 8vo. 2s.

FRATERNITY: A Romance. 2 vols. Cr. 8vo. 21s.

"FRIENDS IN COUNCIL" (The Author of).—Realmah. Cr. 8vo. 6s.

GRAHAM (John W.).—Neæra: A Tale of Ancient Rome. Cr. 8vo. 6s.

HARBOUR BAR, THE. Cr. 8vo. 6s.

HARDY (Arthur Sherburne).—But yet a Woman: A Novel. Cr. 8vo. 4s. 6d.
—— The Wind of Destiny. 2 vols. Gl. 8vo. 12s.

HARDY (Thomas). — The Woodlanders. Cr. 8vo. 3s. 6d.
—— Wessex Tales. Cr. 8vo. 3s. 6d.

HARTE (Bret).—Cressy. Cr. 8vo. 3s. 6d.
—— The Heritage of Dedlow Marsh; and other Tales. Cr. 8vo. 3s. 6d.
—— A First Family of Tasajara. Cr. 8vo. 3s. 6d.

"HOGAN, M.P." (The Author of).—HOGAN, M.P. Cr. 8vo. 3s. 6d. Globe 8vo. 2s.

—— THE HON. MISS FERRARD. Gl. 8vo. 2s.

—— FLITTERS, TATTERS, AND THE COUNSELLOR, ETC. Globe 8vo. 2s.

—— CHRISTY CAREW. Globe 8vo. 2s.

—— ISMAY'S CHILDREN. Globe 8vo. 2s.

HOPPUS (Mary).—A GREAT TREASON: A Story of the War of Independence. 2 vols. Cr. 8vo. 9s.

HUGHES (Thomas).—TOM BROWN'S SCHOOL DAYS. By AN OLD BOY.—Golden Treasury Edition. 2s. 6d. net.—Uniform Edit. 3s. 6d. —People's Edition. 2s.—People's Sixpenny Edition. Illustr. Med. 4to. 6d.—Uniform with Sixpenny Kingsley. Med. 8vo. 6d.

—— TOM BROWN AT OXFORD. Cr. 8vo. 3s. 6d.

—— THE SCOURING OF THE WHITE HORSE, and THE ASHEN FAGGOT. Cr. 8vo. 3s. 6d.

IRVING (Washington). (See ILLUSTRATED BOOKS, p. 12.)

JACKSON (Helen).—RAMONA. Gl. 8vo. 2s.

JAMES (Henry).—THE EUROPEANS: A Novel. Cr. 8vo. 6s.; 18mo, 2s.

—— DAISY MILLER: and other Stories. Cr. 8vo. 6s.; Globe 8vo, 2s.

—— THE AMERICAN. Cr. 8vo. 6s.—18mo, 2 vols. 4s.

—— RODERICK HUDSON. Cr. 8vo. 6s.; Gl. 8vo, 2s.; 18mo, 2 vols. 4s.

—— THE MADONNA OF THE FUTURE: and other Tales. Cr. 8vo. 6s.; Globe 8vo, 2s.

—— WASHINGTON SQUARE, THE PENSION BEAUREPAS. Globe 8vo. 2s.

—— THE PORTRAIT OF A LADY. Cr. 8vo. 6s.; 18mo, 3 vols. 6s.

—— STORIES REVIVED. In Two Series. Cr. 8vo. 6s. each.

—— THE BOSTONIANS. Cr. 8vo. 6s.

—— NOVELS AND TALES. Pocket Edition. 18mo. 2s. each volume.
CONFIDENCE. 1 vol.
THE SIEGE OF LONDON; MADAME DE MAUVES. 1 vol.
AN INTERNATIONAL EPISODE; THE PENSION BEAUREPAS; THE POINT OF VIEW. 1 vol.
DAISY MILLER, a Study; FOUR MEETINGS; LONGSTAFF'S MARRIAGE; BENVOLIO. 1 vol.
THE MADONNA OF THE FUTURE; A BUNDLE OF LETTERS; THE DIARY OF A MAN OF FIFTY; EUGENE PICKERING. 1 vol.

—— TALES OF THREE CITIES. Cr. 8vo. 4s. 6d.

—— THE PRINCESS CASAMASSIMA. Cr. 8vo. 6s.; Globe 8vo, 2s.

—— THE REVERBERATOR. Cr. 8vo. 6s.

—— THE ASPERN PAPERS; LOUISA PALLANT; THE MODERN WARNING. Cr. 8vo. 3s. 6d.

—— A LONDON LIFE. Cr. 8vo. 3s. 6d.

—— THE TRAGIC MUSE. Cr. 8vo. 3s. 6d.

—— THE LESSON OF THE MASTER, AND OTHER STORIES. Cr. 8vo. 6s.

KEARY (Annie).—JANET'S HOME. Cr. 8vo. 3s. 6d.

—— CLEMENCY FRANKLYN. Globe 8vo. 2s.

—— OLDBURY. Cr. 8vo. 3s. 6d.

—— A YORK AND A LANCASTER ROSE. Cr. 8vo. 3s. 6d.

—— CASTLE DALY. Cr. 8vo. 3s. 6d.

—— A DOUBTING HEART. Cr. 8vo. 3s. 6d.

KENNEDY (P.).—LEGENDARY FICTIONS OF THE IRISH CELTS. Cr. 8vo. 3s. 6d.

KINGSLEY (Charles).—Eversley Edition. 13 vols. Globe 8vo. 5s. each.—WESTWARD HO! 2 vols.—TWO YEARS AGO. 2 vols.—HYPATIA. 2 vols.—YEAST. 1 vol.—ALTON LOCKE. 2 vols.—HEREWARD THE WAKE. 2 vols.

—— Complete Edition. Cr. 8vo. 3s. 6d. each. —WESTWARD HO! With a Portrait.— HYPATIA.—YEAST.—ALTON LOCKE.—TWO YEARS AGO.—HEREWARD THE WAKE.

—— Sixpenny Edition. Med. 8vo. 6d. each. — WESTWARD HO! — HYPATIA. — YEAST.—ALTON LOCKE.—TWO YEARS AGO. — HEREWARD THE WAKE.

KIPLING (Rudyard).—PLAIN TALES FROM THE HILLS. Cr. 8vo. 6s.

—— THE LIGHT THAT FAILED. Cr. 8vo. 6s.

—— LIFE'S HANDICAP: Being Stories of mine own People. Cr. 8vo. 6s.

LAFARGUE (Philip).—THE NEW JUDGMENT OF PARIS. 2 vols. Globe 8vo. 12s.

LEE (Margaret).—FAITHFUL AND UNFAITHFUL. Cr. 8vo 3s. 6d.

LEVY (A.).—REUBEN SACHS. Cr. 8vo. 3s. 6d.

LITTLE PILGRIM IN THE UNSEEN, A. 24th Thousand. Cr. 8vo. 2s. 6d.

"LITTLE PILGRIM IN THE UNSEEN, A" (Author of).—THE LAND OF DARKNESS. Cr. 8vo. 5s.

LYTTON (Earl of).—THE RING OF AMASIS: A Romance. Cr. 8vo. 3s. 6d.

McLENNAN (Malcolm).—MUCKLE JOCK; and other Stories of Peasant Life in the North. Cr. 8vo. 3s. 6d.

MACQUOID (K. S.).—PATTY. Gl. 8vo. 2s.

MADOC (Fayr).—THE STORY OF MELICENT. Cr. 8vo. 4s. 6d.

MALET (Lucas).—MRS. LORIMER: A Sketch in Black and White. Cr. 8vo. 3s. 6d.

MALORY (Sir Thos.). (See GLOBE LIBRARY, p. 21.)

MINTO (W.).—THE MEDIATION OF RALPH HARDELOT. 3 vols. Cr. 8vo. 31s. 6d.

MITFORD (A. B.).—TALES OF OLD JAPAN. With Illustrations. Cr. 8vo. 3s. 6d.

MIZ MAZE (THE); OR, THE WINKWORTH PUZZLE. A Story in Letters by Nine Authors. Cr. 8vo. 4s. 6d.

MURRAY (D. Christie). — AUNT RACHEL. Cr. 8vo. 3s. 6d.

—— SCHWARTZ. Cr. 8vo. 3s. 6d.

—— THE WEAKER VESSEL. Cr. 8vo. 3s. 6d.

—— JOHN VALE'S GUARDIAN. Cr. 8vo. 3s. 6d.

LITERATURE.

Prose Fiction—*continued.*

MURRAY (D. Christie) and **HERMAN** (H.). —He Fell among Thieves. Cr.8vo. 3s.6d.

NEW ANTIGONE, THE: A Romance. Cr. 8vo. 3s. 6d.

NOEL (Lady Augusta).—Hithersea Mere. 3 vols. Cr. 8vo. 31s. 6d.

NORRIS (W. E.).—My Friend Jim. Globe 8vo. 2s.
—— Chris. Globe 8vo. 2s.

NORTON (Hon. Mrs.).—Old Sir Douglas. Cr. 8vo. 6s.

OLIPHANT (Mrs. M. O. W.).—A Son of the Soil. Globe 8vo. 2s.
—— The Curate in Charge. Globe 8vo. 2s.
—— Young Musgrave. Globe 8vo. 2s.
—— He that will not when He may. Cr. 8vo. 3s. 6d.—Globe 8vo. 2s.
—— Sir Tom. Globe 8vo. 2s.
—— Hester. Cr. 8vo. 3s. 6d.
—— The Wizard's Son. Globe 8vo. 2s.
—— The Country Gentleman and his Family. Globe 8vo. 2s.
—— The Second Son. Globe 8vo. 2s.
—— Neighbours on the Green. Cr. 8vo. 3s. 6d.
—— Joyce. Cr. 8vo. 3s. 6d.
—— A Beleaguered City. Cr. 8vo. 3s. 6d.
—— Kirsteen. Cr. 8vo. 3s. 6d.
—— The Railway Man and his Children. Cr. 8vo. 3s. 6d.
—— The Marriage of Elinor. Cr.8vo. 3s.6d.
—— The Heir-Presumptive and the Heir-Apparent. 3 vols. Cr. 8vo. 31s. 6d

PALMER (Lady Sophia).—Mrs. Penicott's Lodger: and other Stories. Cr. 8vo. 2s. 6d.

PARRY (Gambier). —The Story of Dick. Cr. 8vo. 6s.

PATER (Walter).—Marius the Epicurean: His Sensations and Ideas. 3rd Edit. 2 vols. 8vo. 12s.

ROSS (Percy).—A Misguidit Lassie. Cr. 8vo. 4s. 6d.

ROY (J.).—Helen Treveryan: or, the Ruling Race. 3 vols. Cr. 8vo. 31s. 6d.

RUSSELL (W. Clark).—Marooned. Cr. 8vo. 3s. 6d.
—— A Strange Elopement. Cr. 8vo. 3s.6d.

ST. JOHNSTON (A.).—A South Sea Lover: A Romance. Cr. 8vo. 6s.

SHORTHOUSE (J. Henry).—*Uniform Edition.* Cr. 8vo. 3s. 6d. each.
John Inglesant: A Romance.
Sir Percival: A Story of the Past and of the Present.
The Little Schoolmaster Mark: A Spiritual Romance.
The Countess Eve.
A Teacher of the Violin: and other Tales.
—— Blanche, Lady Falaise. Cr. 8vo. 6s.

SLIP IN THE FENS, A. Globe 8vo. 2s.

THEODOLI (Marchesa)—Under Pressure. 2 vols. Globe 8vo. 12s.

TIM. Cr. 8vo. 6s.

TOURGÉNIEF.—Virgin Soil. Translated by Ashton W. Dilke. Cr. 8vo. 6s.

VELEY (Margaret).—A Garden of Memories; Mrs. Austin, Lizzie's Bargain. Three Stories. 2 vols. Globe 8vo. 12s.

VICTOR (H.).—Mariam: or Twenty One Days. Cr. 8vo. 6s.

VOICES CRYING IN THE WILDERNESS: A Novel. Cr. 8vo. 7s. 6d.

WARD (Mrs. T. Humphry).—Miss Bretherton. Cr. 8vo. 3s. 6d.

WORTHEY (Mrs.).—The New Continent: A Novel. 2 vols. Globe 8vo. 12s.

YONGE (C. M.). (*See* p. 23.)

Collected Works; Essays; Lectures; Letters; Miscellaneous Works.

ADDISON.—Selections from the "Spectator." With Introduction and Notes by K. Deighton. Globe 8vo. 2s. 6d.

AN AUTHOR'S LOVE. Being the Unpublished Letters of Prosper Mérimée's "Inconnue." 2 vols. Ext. cr. 8vo. 12s.

ARNOLD (Matthew).—Essays in Criticism. 6th Edit. Cr. 8vo. 9s.
—— Essays in Criticism. Second Series. Cr. 8vo. 7s. 6d.
—— Discourses in America. Cr. 8vo. 4s.6d.

BACON. With Introduction and Notes, by F. G. Selby, M.A. Gl. 8vo. 3s.; swd. 2s.6d. (*See also* Golden Treasury Series, p. 21.)

BLACKIE (J. S.).—Lay Sermons. Cr. 8vo. 6s.

BRIDGES (John A.).—Idylls of a Lost Village. Cr. 8vo. 7s. 6d.

BRIMLEY (George).—Essays. Globe 8vo. 5s.

BUNYAN (John).—The Pilgrim's Progress from this World to that which is to Come. 18mo. 2s. 6d. net.

BUTCHER (Prof. S. H.).—Some Aspects of the Greek Genius. Cr. 8vo. 7s. 6d. net.

CARLYLE (Thomas). (*See* Biography.)

CHURCH (Dean).—Miscellaneous Writings. Collected Edition. 6 vols. Globe 8vo. 5s. each.—Vol. I Miscellaneous Essays.—II. Dante: and other Essays.—III. St. Anselm.—IV Spenser.—V. Bacon.—VI. The Oxford Movement, 1833–45.

CLIFFORD (Prof. W. K.). Lectures and Essays. Edited by Leslie Stephen and Sir F Pollock. Cr. 8vo. 8s. 6d.

CLOUGH (A. H.).—Prose Remains. With a Selection from his Letters, and a Memoir by His Wife. Cr. 8vo. 7s. 6d.

COLLINS (J. Churton).—The Study of English Literature. Cr. 8vo. 4s. 6d.

CRAIK (Mrs.). —Concerning Men: and other Papers. Cr. 8vo. 4s. 6d.
—— About Money: and other Things. Cr. 8vo. 6s.
—— Sermons out of Church. Cr. 8vo. 3s.6d.

DE VERE (Aubrey).—Essays Chiefly on Poetry. 2 vols. Globe 8vo. 12s.
—— Essays, Chiefly Literary and Ethical. Globe 8vo. 6s.

DICKENS.—LETTERS OF CHARLES DICKENS. Ed. by GEORGINA HOGARTH and MARY DICKENS. Cr. 8vo.

DRYDEN, ESSAYS OF. Edited by Prof. C. D. YONGE. Fcp. 8vo. 2s. 6d. (See also GLOBE LIBRARY, below.)

DUFF (Rt. Hon. Sir M. E. Grant).—MISCELLANIES, Political and Literary. 8vo. 10s. 6d.

EMERSON (Ralph Waldo).—THE COLLECTED WORKS. 6 vols. Globe 8vo. 5s. each.—I. MISCELLANIES. With an Introductory Essay by JOHN MORLEY.—II. ESSAYS.—III POEMS.—IV. ENGLISH TRAITS; REPRESENTATIVE MEN.—V. CONDUCT OF LIFE; SOCIETY AND SOLITUDE.—VI. LETTERS; SOCIAL AIMS, ETC.

FITZGERALD (Edward): LETTERS AND LITERARY REMAINS OF. Ed. by W. ALDIS WRIGHT, M.A. 3 vols. Cr. 8vo. 31s. 6d.

GLOBE LIBRARY. Gl. 8vo. 3s. 6d. each:

BURNS.—COMPLETE POETICAL WORKS AND LETTERS. Edited, with Life and Glossarial Index, by ALEXANDER SMITH.

COWPER.—POETICAL WORKS. Edited by the Rev. W. BENHAM, B.D.

DEFOE.—THE ADVENTURES OF ROBINSON CRUSOE. Introduction by H. KINGSLEY.

DRYDEN.—POETICAL WORKS. A Revised Text and Notes. By W. D. CHRISTIE, M.A.

GOLDSMITH. — MISCELLANEOUS WORKS. Edited by Prof. MASSON.

HORACE.—WORKS. Rendered into English Prose by JAMES LONSDALE and S. LEE.

MALORY.—LE MORTE D'ARTHUR. Sir Thos. Malory's Book of King Arthur and of his Noble Knights of the Round Table. The Edition of Caxton, revised for modern use. By Sir E. STRACHEY, Bart.

MILTON.—POETICAL WORKS. Edited, with Introductions, by Prof. MASSON.

POPE.—POETICAL WORKS. Edited, with Memoir and Notes, by Prof. WARD.

SCOTT.—POETICAL WORKS. With Essay by Prof. PALGRAVE.

SHAKESPEARE.—COMPLETE WORKS. Edit. by W. G. CLARK and W. ALDIS WRIGHT *India Paper Edition*. Cr. 8vo, cloth extra, gilt edges. 10s. 6d. net.

SPENSER.—COMPLETE WORKS Edited by R. MORRIS. Memoir by J. W. HALES, M.A.

VIRGIL.—WORKS. Rendered into English Prose by JAMES LONSDALE and S. LEE.

GOLDEN TREASURY SERIES.—Uniformly printed in 18mo, with Vignette Titles by Sir J. E. MILLAIS, Sir NOEL PATON, T. WOOLNER, W. HOLMAN HUNT, ARTHUR HUGHES, etc. 4s. 6d. each.—Also a re-issue in fortnightly vols. 2s. 6d. net, from June, 1891.

THE GOLDEN TREASURY OF THE BEST SONGS AND LYRICAL POEMS IN THE ENGLISH LANGUAGE. Selected and arranged, with Notes, by Prof. F. T. PALGRAVE.—Large Paper Edition. 8vo. 10s. 6d. net.

THE CHILDREN'S GARLAND FROM THE BEST POETS. Selected by COVENTRY PATMORE.

GOLDEN TREASURY SERIES—*contd.*

BUNYAN.—THE PILGRIM'S PROGRESS FROM THIS WORLD TO THAT WHICH IS TO COME.—Large Paper Edition. 8vo. 10s. 6d. net.

BACON.—ESSAYS, and COLOURS OF GOOD AND EVIL. With Notes and Glossarial Index by W. ALDIS WRIGHT, M.A.—Large Paper Edition. 8vo. 10s. 6d net.

THE BOOK OF PRAISE. From the Best English Hymn Writers. Selected by ROUNDELL, EARL OF SELBORNE.

SHELLEY.—POEMS. Edited by STOPFORD A. BROOKE.—Large Paper Edit. 12s. 6d.

THE FAIRY BOOK: THE BEST POPULAR FAIRY STORIES. Selected by Mrs. CRAIK, Author of "John Halifax, Gentleman."

WORDSWORTH.—POEMS. Chosen and Edited by M. ARNOLD.—Large Paper Edition. 10s. 6d net.

PLATO.—THE TRIAL AND DEATH OF SOCRATES. Being the Euthyphron, Apology, Crito and Phaedo of Plato. Trans. F. J. CHURCH.

THE JEST BOOK. The Choicest Anecdotes and Sayings. Arranged by MARK LEMON.

HERRICK.—CHRYSOMELA. Edited by Prof. F. T. PALGRAVE.

THE BALLAD BOOK. A Selection of the Choicest British Ballads. Edited by WILLIAM ALLINGHAM.

THE SUNDAY BOOK OF POETRY FOR THE YOUNG. Selected by C. F. ALEXANDER.

A BOOK OF GOLDEN DEEDS. By C. M. YONGE.

A BOOK OF WORTHIES. By C M. YONGE.

KEATS.—THE POETICAL WORKS. Edited by Prof. F. T. PALGRAVE.

PLATO.—THE REPUBLIC. Translated by J. LL. DAVIES, M.A., and D. J. VAUGHAN.—Large Paper Edition. 8vo 10s. 6d. net.

ADDISON.—ESSAYS. Chosen and Edited by JOHN RICHARD GREEN.

DEUTSCHE LYRIK. The Golden Treasury of the best German Lyrical Poems. Selected by Dr. BUCHHEIM.

SIR THOMAS BROWNE.—RELIGIO MEDICI, LETTER TO A FRIEND, &c., AND CHRISTIAN MORALS. Ed. W. A. GREENHILL.

LAMB.—TALES FROM SHAKSPEARE. Edited by Rev. ALFRED AINGER, M.A.

THE SONG BOOK. Words and Tunes selected and arranged by JOHN HULLAH.

SCOTTISH SONG. Compiled by MARY CARLYLE AITKEN.

LA LYRE FRANÇAISE. Selected and arranged, with Notes, by G. MASSON.

BALLADEN UND ROMANZEN. Being a Selection of the best German Ballads and Romances. Edited, with Introduction and Notes, by Dr. BUCHHEIM.

A BOOK OF GOLDEN THOUGHTS. By HENRY ATTWELL.

MATTHEW ARNOLD.—SELECTED POEMS.

BYRON.—POETRY. Chosen and arranged by M. ARNOLD.—Large Paper Edit. 9s.

COWPER.—SELECTIONS FROM POEMS. With an Introduction by Mrs. OLIPHANT.

LITERATURE.

Collected Works; Essays; Lectures; Letters; Miscellaneous Works—*contd.*

GOLDEN TREASURY SERIES—*contd.*

COWPER.—LETTERS. Edited, with Introduction, by Rev. W. BENHAM.

DEFOE.—THE ADVENTURES OF ROBINSON CRUSOE. Edited by J. W. CLARK, M.A.

BALTHASAR GRACIAN'S ART OF WORLDLY WISDOM. Translated by J. JACOBS.

HARE.—GUESSES AT TRUTH. By Two Brothers.

HUGHES.—TOM BROWN'S SCHOOL DAYS.

LANDOR.—SELECTIONS. Ed. by S. COLVIN.

LONGFELLOW.—POEMS OF PLACES: ENGLAND AND WALES. Edited by H. W. LONGFELLOW. 2 vols.

— BALLADS, LYRICS, AND SONNETS.

MOHAMMAD.—SPEECHES AND TABLE-TALK. Translated by STANLEY LANE-POOLE.

NEWCASTLE.—THE CAVALIER AND HIS LADY. Selections from the Works of the First Duke and Duchess of Newcastle. With an Introductory Essay by E. JENKINS.

PALGRAVE.—CHILDREN'S TREASURY OF LYRICAL POETRY.

PLATO.—THE PHÆDRUS, LYSIS, AND PROTAGORAS. Translated by J. WRIGHT.

SHAKESPEARE.—SONGS AND SONNETS. Ed. with Notes, by Prof. F. T. PALGRAVE.

TENNYSON.—LYRICAL POEMS. Selected and Annotated by Prof. F. T. PALGRAVE.—Large Paper Edition. 9*s.*

— IN MEMORIAM. Large Paper Edit. 9*s.*

THEOCRITUS.—BION, AND MOSCHUS. Rendered into English Prose by ANDREW LANG.—Large Paper Edition. 9*s.*

WATSON.—LYRIC LOVE: An Anthology.

CHARLOTTE M. YONGE.—THE STORY OF THE CHRISTIANS AND MOORS IN SPAIN.

GOLDSMITH, ESSAYS OF. Edited by C. D. YONGE, M.A. Fcp. 8vo. 2*s.* 6*d.* (*See also* GLOBE LIBRARY, p. 21; ILLUSTRATED BOOKS, p. 12.)

GRAY (Thomas).—WORKS. Edited by EDMUND GOSSE. In 4 vols. Globe 8vo. 20*s.*—Vol. I. POEMS, JOURNALS, AND ESSAYS.—II. LETTERS.—III. LETTERS.—IV. NOTES ON ARISTOPHANES AND PLATO.

GREEN (J. R.).—STRAY STUDIES FROM ENGLAND AND ITALY. Globe 8vo. 5*s.*

HAMERTON (P. G.).—THE INTELLECTUAL LIFE. Cr. 8vo. 10*s.* 6*d.*

—— HUMAN INTERCOURSE. Cr. 8vo. 8*s.* 6*d.*

—— FRENCH AND ENGLISH: A Comparison. Cr. 8vo. 10*s.* 6*d.*

HARRISON (Frederic).—THE CHOICE OF BOOKS. Gl. 8vo. 6*s.*—Large Paper Ed. 15*s.*

HARWOOD (George).—FROM WITHIN. Cr. 8vo. 6*s.*

HELPS (Sir Arthur).—ESSAYS WRITTEN IN THE INTERVALS OF BUSINESS. With Introduction and Notes, by F. J. ROWE, M.A., and W. T. WEBB, M.A. 1*s.* 9*d.*; swd. 1*s.* 6*d.*

HOBART (Lord).—ESSAYS AND MISCELLANEOUS WRITINGS. With Biographical Sketch. Ed. Lady HOBART. 2 vols. 8vo. 25*s.*

HUTTON (R. H.).—ESSAYS ON SOME OF THE MODERN GUIDES OF ENGLISH THOUGHT IN MATTERS OF FAITH. Globe 8vo. 6*s.*

—— ESSAYS. 2 vols. Gl. 8vo. 6*s.* each. Vol. I. Literary; II. Theological.

HUXLEY (Prof. T. H.).—LAY SERMONS, ADDRESSES, AND REVIEWS. 8vo. 7*s.* 6*d.*

—— CRITIQUES AND ADDRESSES. 8vo. 10*s.* 6*d.*

—— AMERICAN ADDRESSES, WITH A LECTURE ON THE STUDY OF BIOLOGY. 8vo. 6*s.* 6*d.*

—— SCIENCE AND CULTURE, AND OTHER ESSAYS. 8vo. 10*s.* 6*d.*

—— INTRODUCTORY SCIENCE PRIMER. 18mo. 1*s.*

—— ESSAYS UPON SOME CONTROVERTED QUESTIONS. 8vo. 14*s.*

JAMES (Henry).—FRENCH POETS AND NOVELISTS. New Edition. Cr. 8vo. 4*s.* 6*d.*

—— PORTRAITS OF PLACES. Cr. 8vo. 7*s.* 6*d.*

—— PARTIAL PORTRAITS. Cr. 8vo. 6*s.*

KEATS.—LETTERS. Edited by SIDNEY COLVIN. Globe 8vo. 6*s.*

KINGSLEY (Charles).—COMPLETE EDITION OF THE WORKS OF CHARLES KINGSLEY. Cr. 8vo. 3*s.* 6*d.* each.
WESTWARD HO! With a Portrait.
HYPATIA.
YEAST.
ALTON LOCKE.
TWO YEARS AGO.
HEREWARD THE WAKE.
POEMS.
THE HEROES; or, Greek Fairy Tales for my Children.
THE WATER BABIES: A Fairy Tale for a Land Baby.
MADAM HOW AND LADY WHY; or, First Lesson in Earth-Lore for Children.
AT LAST A Christmas in the West Indies.
PROSE IDYLLS.
PLAYS AND PURITANS.
THE ROMAN AND THE TEUTON With Preface by Professor MAX MÜLLER.
SANITARY AND SOCIAL LECTURES.
HISTORICAL LECTURES AND ESSAYS.
SCIENTIFIC LECTURES AND ESSAYS.
LITERARY AND GENERAL LECTURES.
THE HERMITS.
GLAUCUS; or, The Wonders of the Sea-Shore. With Coloured Illustrations.
VILLAGE AND TOWN AND COUNTRY SERMONS.
THE WATER OF LIFE, AND OTHER SERMONS.
SERMONS ON NATIONAL SUBJECTS: AND THE KING OF THE EARTH.
SERMONS FOR THE TIMES.
GOOD NEWS OF GOD.
THE GOSPEL OF THE PENTATEUCH: AND DAVID.
DISCIPLINE, AND OTHER SERMONS.
WESTMINSTER SERMONS.
ALL SAINTS' DAY, AND OTHER SERMONS.

LAMB (Charles).—COLLECTED WORKS. Ed., with Introduction and Notes, by the Rev. ALFRED AINGER, M.A. Globe 8vo. 5*s.* each volume.—I. ESSAYS OF ELIA.—II. PLAYS, POEMS, AND MISCELLANEOUS ESSAYS.—III. Mrs. LEICESTER'S SCHOOL; THE ADVENTURES OF ULYSSES; AND OTHER ESSAYS.—IV. TALES FROM SHAKESPEARE.—V. and VI. LETTERS. Newly arranged, with additions.

—— TALES FROM SHAKESPEARE. 18mo. 4*s.* 6*d.*

LANKESTER(Prof. E. Ray).—The Advancement of Science. Occasional Essays and Addresses. 8vo. 10s. 6d.

LIGHTFOOT (Bishop).—Essays. 2 vols. 8vo. I. Dissertations on the Apostolic Age 14s.—II. Miscellaneous.

LODGE (Prof. Oliver).—The Pioneers of Science. Illustrated. Ext. cr. 8vo. 7s. 6d.

LOWELL (Jas. Russell).—Complete Works. 10 vols. Cr. 8vo. 6s. each.—Vols. I.—IV. Literary Essays.—V. Political Essays. —VI. Literary and Political Addresses. VII.—X. Poetical Works.
—— Political Essays. Ext. cr. 8vo. 7s. 6d.
—— Latest Literary Essays. Cr. 8vo. 6s.

LUBBOCK (Rt. Hon. Sir John, Bart.).—Scientific Lectures. Illustrated. 2nd Edit. revised. 8vo. 8s. 6d.
—— Political and Educational Addresses. 8vo. 8s. 6d.
—— Fifty Years of Science: Address to the British Association, 1881. 5th Edit. Cr. 8vo. 2s. 6d.
—— The Pleasures of Life. New Edit. 60th Thousand. Gl. 8vo. Part I. 1s. 6d.; swd. 1s.— Library Edition. 3s. 6d.—Part II. 1s. 6d.; sewed, 1s.—Library Edition. 3s. 6d.—Complete in 1 vol. 2s. 6d.
—— The Beauties of Nature. Cr. 8vo. 6s.

LYTTELTON (E.).—Mothers and Sons. Cr. 8vo. 3s. 6d.

MACMILLAN (Rev. Hugh).—Roman Mosaics, or, Studies in Rome and its Neighbourhood. Globe 8vo. 6s.

MAHAFFY (Prof. J. P.).—The Principles of the Art of Conversation. Cr. 8vo. 4s. 6d.

MASSON (David).—Wordsworth, Shelley, Keats: and other Essays. Cr. 8vo. 5s.

MAURICE (F. D.).—The Friendship of Books: and other Lectures. Cr. 8vo. 4s. 6d.

MORLEY (John).—Works. Collected Edit. In 11 vols. Globe 8vo. 5s. each.—Voltaire. 1 vol.—Rousseau. 2 vols.—Diderot and the Encyclopædists. 2 vols.—On Compromise. 1 vol.—Miscellanies. 3 vols.— Burke. 1 vol.—Studies in Literature. 1 vol.

MYERS (F. W. H.).—Essays. 2 vols. Cr. 8vo. 4s. 6d. each.—I. Classical; II. Modern.

NADAL (E. S.).—Essays at Home and Elsewhere. Cr. 8vo. 6s.

OLIPHANT (T. L. Kington).—The Duke and the Scholar: and other Essays. 8vo. 7s. 6d.

OWENS COLLEGE ESSAYS AND ADDRESSES. By Professors and Lecturers of the College. 8vo. 14s.

PATER (W.).—The Renaissance; Studies in Art and Poetry. 4th Ed. Cr. 8vo. 10s. 6d.
—— Imaginary Portraits. Cr. 8vo. 6s.
—— Appreciations. With an Essay on "Style." 2nd Edit. Cr. 8vo. 8s. 6d.
—— Marius the Epicurean. 2 vols. Cr. 8vo. 12s.

PICTON (J. A.).—The Mystery of Matter: and other Essays. Cr. 8vo. 6s.

POLLOCK (Sir F., Bart.).—Oxford Lectures: and other Discourses. 8vo. 9s.

POOLE (M. E.).—Pictures of Cottage Life in the West of England. 2nd Ed. Cr. 8vo. 3s. 6d.

POTTER (Louisa).—Lancashire Memories. Cr. 8vo. 6s.

PRICKARD (A. O.).—Aristotle on the Art of Poetry. Cr. 8vo. 3s. 6d.

RUMFORD.—Complete Works of Count Rumford. Memoir by G. Ellis. Portrait. 5 vols. 8vo. 4l. 14s. 6d.

SCIENCE LECTURES AT SOUTH KENSINGTON. Illustr. 2 vols. Cr. 8vo. 6s. each.

SMALLEY (George W.).—London Letters and some others. 2 vols. 8vo. 32s.

STEPHEN (Sir James F., Bart.).—Horae Sabbaticae. Three Series. Gl. 8vo. 5s. each.

THRING (Edward).—Thoughts on Life Science. 2nd Edit. Cr. 8vo. 7s. 6d.

WESTCOTT (Bishop). (See Theology, p. 39.)

WILSON (Dr. George).—Religio Chemici. Cr. 8vo. 8s. 6d.
—— The Five Gateways of Knowledge. 9th Edit. Ext. fcp. 8vo. 2s. 6d.

WHITTIER (John Greenleaf). The Complete Works. 7 vols. Cr. 8vo. 6s. each.— Vol. I. Narrative and Legendary Poems. —II. Poems of Nature; Poems Subjective and Reminiscent; Religious Poems. —III. Anti-Slavery Poems; Songs of Labour and Reform.—IV. Personal Poems; Occasional Poems; The Tent on the Beach; with the Poems of Elizabeth H. Whittier, and an Appendix containing Early and Uncollected Verses.—V. Margaret Smith's Journal; Tales and Sketches.—VI. Old Portraits and Modern Sketches; Personal Sketches and Tributes; Historical Papers.—VII. The Conflict with Slavery, Politics, and Reform; The Inner Life, Criticism.

YONGE (Charlotte M.).—*Uniform Edition.* Cr. 8vo. 3s. 6d. each.
The Heir of Redclyffe.
Heartsease.
Hopes and Fears.
Dynevor Terrace.
The Daisy Chain.
The Trial: More Links of the Daisy Chain.
Pillars of the House. Vol. I.
Pillars of the House. Vol. II.
The Young Stepmother.
Clever Woman of the Family.
The Three Brides.
My Young Alcides.
The Caged Lion.
The Dove in the Eagle's Nest.
The Chaplet of Pearls.
Lady Hester, and The Danvers Papers.
Magnum Bonum.
Love and Life.
Unknown to History.
Stray Pearls.
The Armourer's Prentices.
The Two Sides of the Shield.
Nuttie's Father.

LITERATURE.

Collected Works; Essays; Lectures; Letters; Miscellaneous Works—*contd.*

YONGE (Charlotte M.).—*Uniform Edition.* Cr. 8vo. 3s. 6d. each.

SCENES AND CHARACTERS.
CHANTRY HOUSE.
A MODERN TELEMACHUS.
BYE WORDS.
BEECHCROFT AT ROCKSTONE.
MORE BYWORDS.
A REPUTED CHANGELING.
THE LITTLE DUKE, RICHARD THE FEARLESS.
THE LANCES OF LYNWOOD.
THE PRINCE AND THE PAGE.
P'S AND Q'S: LITTLE LUCY'S WONDERFUL GLOBE.
THE TWO PENNILESS PRINCESSES.
THAT STICK.
AN OLD WOMAN'S OUTLOOK.

LOGIC. (*See under* PHILOSOPHY, p. 27.)

MAGAZINES. (*See* PERIODICALS, p. 26).

MAGNETISM. (*See under* PHYSICS, p. 28.)

MATHEMATICS, History of.

BALL (W. W. R.).—A SHORT ACCOUNT OF THE HISTORY OF MATHEMATICS. Cr. 8vo. 10s. 6d.
—— MATHEMATICAL RECREATIONS AND PROBLEMS. Cr. 8vo. 7s. net.

MEDICINE.

(*See also* DOMESTIC ECONOMY; NURSING; HYGIENE; PHYSIOLOGY.)

ACLAND (Sir H. W.).—THE ARMY MEDICAL SCHOOL: Address at Netley Hospital. 1s.

ALLBUTT (Dr. T. Clifford).—ON THE USE OF THE OPHTHALMOSCOPE. 8vo. 15s.

ANDERSON (Dr. McCall).—LECTURES ON CLINICAL MEDICINE. Illustr. 8vo. 10s. 6d.

BALLANCE (C. A.) and EDMUNDS (Dr. W.). LIGATION IN CONTINUITY. Illustr. Roy. 8vo. 30s. net.

BARWELL (Richard, F.R.C.S.). — THE CAUSES AND TREATMENT OF LATERAL CURVATURE OF THE SPINE. Cr. 8vo. 5s.
—— ON ANEURISM, ESPECIALLY OF THE THORAX AND ROOT OF THE NECK. 3s. 6d.

BASTIAN (H. Charlton).—ON PARALYSIS FROM BRAIN DISEASE IN ITS COMMON FORMS. Cr. 8vo. 10s. 6d.

BICKERTON (T. H.).—ON COLOUR BLINDNESS. Cr. 8vo.

BRAIN: A JOURNAL OF NEUROLOGY. Edited for the Neurological Society of London, by A. DE WATTEVILLE, Quarterly. 8vo. 3s. 6d. (Part I. in Jan. 1878.) Vols. I. to XII. 8vo. 15s. each. [Cloth covers for binding, 1s. each.]

BRUNTON (Dr. T. Lauder).—A TEXT-BOOK OF PHARMACOLOGY, THERAPEUTICS, AND MATERIA MEDICA. 3rd Edit. Med. 8vo. 21s.—Or in 2 vols. 22s. 6d.—SUPPLEMENT, 1s.

BRUNTON (Dr. T. Lauder).—DISORDERS OF DIGESTION: THEIR CONSEQUENCES AND TREATMENT. 8vo. 10s. 6d.
—— PHARMACOLOGY AND THERAPEUTICS; or, Medicine Past and Present. Cr. 8vo. 6s.
—— TABLES OF MATERIA MEDICA: A Companion to the Materia Medica Museum. 8vo. 5s.
—— AN INTRODUCTION TO MODERN THERAPEUTICS. Croonian Lectures on the Relationship between Chemical Structure and Physiological Action. 8vo. 3s. 6d net.

BUCKNILL (Dr.).—THE CARE OF THE INSANE. Cr. 8vo. 3s. 6d.

CARTER (R. Brudenell, F.C.S.).—A PRACTICAL TREATISE ON DISEASES OF THE EYE. 8vo. 16s.
—— EYESIGHT, GOOD AND BAD. Cr. 8vo. 6s.
—— MODERN OPERATIONS FOR CATARACT. 8vo. 6s.

CHRISTIE (J.).—CHOLERA EPIDEMICS IN EAST AFRICA. 8vo. 15s.

COWELL (George).—LECTURES ON CATARACT: ITS CAUSES, VARIETIES, AND TREATMENT. Cr. 8vo. 4s. 6d.

FLÜCKIGER (F. A.) and HANBURY (D.). —PHARMACOGRAPHIA. A History of the Principal Drugs of Vegetable Origin met with in Great Britain and India. 8vo. 21s.

FOTHERGILL (Dr. J. Milner).—THE PRACTITIONER'S HANDBOOK OF TREATMENT; or, The Principles of Therapeutics. 8vo. 16s.
—— THE ANTAGONISM OF THERAPEUTIC AGENTS, AND WHAT IT TEACHES. Cr. 8vo. 6s.
—— FOOD FOR THE INVALID, THE CONVALESCENT, THE DYSPEPTIC, AND THE GOUTY. 2nd Edit. Cr. 8vo. 3s. 6d.

FOX (Dr. Wilson).—ON THE ARTIFICIAL PRODUCTION OF TUBERCLE IN THE LOWER ANIMALS. With Plates. 4to. 5s. 6d.
—— ON THE TREATMENT OF HYPERPYREXIA, AS ILLUSTRATED IN ACUTE ARTICULAR RHEUMATISM BY MEANS OF THE EXTERNAL APPLICATION OF COLD. 8vo. 2s. 6d.

GRIFFITHS (W. H.).—LESSONS ON PRESCRIPTIONS AND THE ART OF PRESCRIBING. New Edition. 18mo. 3s. 6d.

HAMILTON (Prof. D. J.).—ON THE PATHOLOGY OF BRONCHITIS, CATARRHAL PNEUMONIA, TUBERCLE, AND ALLIED LESIONS OF THE HUMAN LUNG. 8vo. 8s. 6d.
—— A TEXT-BOOK OF PATHOLOGY, SYSTEMATIC AND PRACTICAL. Illustrated. Vol. I. 8vo. 25s.

HANBURY (Daniel). — SCIENCE PAPERS, CHIEFLY PHARMACOLOGICAL AND BOTANICAL. Med. 8vo. 14s.

KLEIN (Dr. E.).—MICRO-ORGANISMS AND DISEASE. An Introduction into the Study of Specific Micro-Organisms. Cr. 8vo. 6s.
—— THE BACTERIA IN ASIATIC CHOLERA. Cr. 8vo. 5s.

LEPROSY INVESTIGATION COMMITTEE, JOURNAL OF THE. Edited by P. S. ABRAHAM, M.A. Nos. 2—4. 2s. 6d. each net.

LINDSAY (Dr. J. A.). — THE CLIMATIC TREATMENT OF CONSUMPTION. Cr. 8vo. 5s.

MACLAGAN (Dr. T.).—THE GERM THEORY. 8vo. 10s. 6d.

MACLEAN (Surgeon-General W. C.).—DISEASES OF TROPICAL CLIMATES. Cr. 8vo. 10s. 6d.

MACNAMARA (C.).—A HISTORY OF ASIATIC CHOLERA. Cr. 8vo. 10s. 6d.
—— ASIATIC CHOLERA, HISTORY UP TO JULY 15, 1892 : CAUSES AND TREATMENT. 8vo. 2s. 6d.

MERCIER (Dr. C.).—THE NERVOUS SYSTEM AND THE MIND. 8vo. 12s. 6d.

PIFFARD (H. G.).—AN ELEMENTARY TREATISE ON DISEASES OF THE SKIN. 8vo. 16s.

PRACTITIONER, THE: A MONTHLY JOURNAL OF THERAPEUTICS AND PUBLIC HEALTH. Edited by T. LAUDER BRUNTON F.R.S., etc.; DONALD MACALISTER, M.A. M.D., and J. MITCHELL BRUCE, M.D 1s. 6d. monthly. Vols. I.—XLVI Half yearly vols. 10s. 6d. each. [Cloth covers for binding, 1s. each.]

REYNOLDS (J. R.).—A SYSTEM OF MEDICINE. Edited by J. RUSSELL REYNOLDS, M.D., in 5 vols. Vols. I.—III. and V 8vo. 25s. each.—Vol. IV. 21s.

RICHARDSON (Dr. B. W.).—DISEASES OF MODERN LIFE. Cr. 8vo.
—— THE FIELD OF DISEASE. A Book of Preventive Medicine. 8vo. 25s.

SEATON (Dr Edward C.).—A HANDBOOK OF VACCINATION. Ext. fcp. 8vo. 8s. 6d.

SEILER (Dr. Carl). — MICRO-PHOTOGRAPHS IN HISTOLOGY, NORMAL AND PATHOLOGICAL. 4to. 31s. 6d.

SIBSON (Dr. Francis).—COLLECTED WORKS Edited by W. M. ORD, M.D. Illustrated 4 vols. 8vo. 3l. 3s.

SPENDER (J. Kent).—THERAPEUTIC MEANS FOR THE RELIEF OF PAIN. 8vo. 8s. 6d.

SURGERY (THE INTERNATIONAL ENCYCLOPAEDIA OF). A Systematic Treatise on the Theory and Practice of Surgery by Authors of various Nations. Edited by JOHN ASHHURST, jun., M.D. 6 vols Roy. 8vo. 31s. 6d. each.

THORNE (Dr. Thorne).—DIPHTHERIA. Cr 8vo. 8s. 6d.

WHITE (Dr. W Hale).—A TEXT-BOOK OF GENERAL THERAPEUTICS. Cr. 8vo. 8s. 6d

ZIEGLER (Ernst).—A TEXT-BOOK OF PATHOLOGICAL ANATOMY AND PATHOGENESIS Translated and Edited by DONALD MAC ALISTER, M.A., M.D. Illustrated. 8vo.—Part I. GENERAL PATHOLOGICAL ANATOMY 12s. 6d.—Part II. SPECIAL PATHOLOGICAL ANATOMY. Sections I.—VIII. and IX.—XII. 8vo. 12s. 6d. each.

METALLURGY.

(*See also* CHEMISTRY.)

HIORNS (Arthur H.).—A TEXT-BOOK OF ELEMENTARY METALLURGY. Gl. 8vo. 4s
—— PRACTICAL METALLURGY AND ASSAYING Illustrated. 2nd Edit. Globe 8vo. 6s.

HIORNS (Arthur H.).—IRON AND STEEL MANUFACTURE. Illustrated. Globe 8vo. 3s. 6d.
—— MIXED METALS OR METALLIC ALLOYS. Globe 8vo. 6s.
—— METAL COLOURING AND BRONZING. Globe 8vo. 5s.

PHILLIPS (J. A.).—A TREATISE ON ORE DEPOSITS. Illustrated. Med. 8vo. 25s.

METAPHYSICS.

(*See under* PHILOSOPHY, p. 27.)

MILITARY ART AND HISTORY.

ACLAND (Sir H. W.). (*See* MEDICINE.)

AITKEN (Sir W.).—THE GROWTH OF THE RECRUIT AND YOUNG SOLDIER. Cr. 8vo. 8s. 6d

CUNYNGHAME (Gen. Sir A. T.). — MY COMMAND IN SOUTH AFRICA, 1874—78. 8vo. 12s. 6d.

DILKE (Sir C) and WILKINSON (S.).—IMPERIAL DEFENCE. Cr 8vo. 3s. 6d.

HOZIER (Lieut.-Col. H. M.).—THE SEVEN WEEKS' WAR. 3rd Edit. Cr. 8vo. 6s.
—— THE INVASIONS OF ENGLAND. 2 vols. 8vo. 28s.

MARTEL (Chas.).—MILITARY ITALY. With Map. 8vo. 12s. 6d.

MAURICE (Lt.-Col.).—WAR. 8vo. 5s. net.
—— THE NATIONAL DEFENCES. Cr. 8vo

MERCUR (Prof. J.).—ELEMENTS OF THE ART OF WAR. 8vo. 17s.

SCRATCHLEY — KINLOCH COOKE. — AUSTRALIAN DEFENCES AND NEW GUINEA. Compiled from the Papers of the late Major-General Sir PETER SCRATCHLEY, R.E., by C. KINLOCH COOKE. 8vo. 14s.

THROUGH THE RANKS TO A COMMISSION New Edition. 8vo. 2s. 6d.

WILKINSON (S.). — THE BRAIN OF AN ARMY. A Popular Account of the German General Staff. Cr. 8vo. 2s. 6d.

WINGATE (Major F R.).—MAHDIISM AND THE EGYPTIAN SUDAN. An Account of the Rise and Progress of Mahdiism, and of Subsequent Events in the Sudan to the Present Time. With 17 Maps. 8vo. 30s. net.

WOLSELEY (General Viscount).—THE SOLDIER'S POCKET-BOOK FOR FIELD SERVICE. 5th Edit. 16mo, roan. 5s.
—— FIELD POCKET-BOOK FOR THE AUXILIARY FORCES. 16mo. 1s. 6d.

MINERALOGY. (*See* GEOLOGY.)

MISCELLANEOUS WORKS.

(*See under* LITERATURE, p. 20.)

MUSIC.

FAY (Amy).—MUSIC-STUDY IN GERMANY Preface by Sir GEO. GROVE. Cr. 8vo. 4s. 6d.

MUSIC—*continued.*

GROVE (Sir George).—A DICTIONARY OF MUSIC AND MUSICIANS, A.D. 1450—1889. Edited by Sir GEORGE GROVE, D.C.L. In 4 vols. 8vo. 21*s.* each. With Illustrations in Music Type and Woodcut.—Also published in Parts. Parts I.—XIV., XIX.—XXII. 3*s.* 6*d.* each; XV. XVI. 7*s.*; XVII. XVIII. 7*s.*, XXIII.—XXV., Appendix. Edited by J. A. FULLER MAITLAND, M.A. 9*s.* [Cloth cases for binding the volumes, 1*s.* each.]

—— A COMPLETE INDEX TO THE ABOVE. By Mrs. E. WODEHOUSE. 8vo. 7*s.* 6*d.*

HULLAH (John).—MUSIC IN THE HOUSE. 4th Edit. Cr 8vo. 2*s.* 6*d.*

TAYLOR (Franklin).—A PRIMER OF PIANO-FORTE PLAYING. 18mo. 1*s.*

TAYLOR (Sedley).—SOUND AND MUSIC. 2nd Edit. Ext. cr. 8vo. 8*s.* 6*d.*

—— A SYSTEM OF SIGHT-SINGING FROM THE ESTABLISHED MUSICAL NOTATION. 8vo. 5*s.* net.

—— RECORD OF THE CAMBRIDGE CENTENARY OF W. A. MOZART. Cr. 8vo. 2*s.* 6*d.* net.

NATURAL HISTORY.

ATKINSON (J. C.). (*See* ANTIQUITIES, p. 1.)

BAKER (Sir Samuel W.). (*See* SPORT, p. 32.)

BLANFORD (W. T.).—GEOLOGY AND ZOOLOGY OF ABYSSINIA. 8vo. 21*s.*

FOWLER (W. W.).—TALES OF THE BIRDS. Illustrated. Cr. 8vo. 3*s.* 6*d.*

—— A YEAR WITH THE BIRDS.   trated. Cr. 8vo. 3*s.* 6*d.*

KINGSLEY (Charles).—MADAM HOW AND LADY WHY; or, First Lessons in Earth-Lore for Children. Cr. 8vo. 3*s.* 6*d.*

—— GLAUCUS; or, The Wonders of the Sea-Shore. With Coloured Illustrations. Cr 8vo. 3*s.* 6*d.*—*Presentation Edition.* Cr. 8vo. extra cloth. 7*s.* 6*d.*

KLEIN (E.).—ETIOLOGY AND PATHOLOGY OF GROUSE DISEASE. 8vo. 7*s.* net.

WALLACE (Alfred Russel).—THE MALAY ARCHIPELAGO: The Land of the Orang Utang and the Bird of Paradise. Maps and Illustrations. Ext. cr. 8vo. 6*s.* (*See also* BIOLOGY.)

WATERTON (Charles).— WANDERINGS IN SOUTH AMERICA, THE NORTH-WEST OF THE UNITED STATES, AND THE ANTILLES. Edited by Rev. J. G. WOOD. Illustrated. Cr. 8vo. 6*s.*—People's Edition. 4to. 6*d.*

WHITE (Gilbert).—NATURAL HISTORY AND ANTIQUITIES OF SELBORNE. Ed. by FRANK BUCKLAND. With a Chapter on Antiquities by the EARL OF SELBORNE. Cr. 8vo. 6*s.*

NATURAL PHILOSOPHY. (*See* PHYSICS.)

NAVAL SCIENCE.

KELVIN (Lord).—POPULAR LECTURES AND ADDRESSES.—Vol. III. NAVIGATION. Cr. 8vo. 7*s.* 6*d.*

ROBINSON (Rev. J. L.).—MARINE SURVEY-ING, AN ELEMENTARY TREATISE ON. For Younger Naval Officers. Illust. Cr.8vo. 7*s.*6*d.*

SHORTLAND (Admiral).—NAUTICAL SUR-VEYING. 8vo. 21*s.*

NOVELS. (*See* PROSE FICTION, p. 18.)

NURSING.

(*See under* DOMESTIC ECONOMY, p. 8.)

OPTICS (or LIGHT). (*See* PHYSICS, p. 28.)

PAINTING. (*See* ART, p. 2.)

PATHOLOGY. (*See* MEDICINE, p. 24.)

PERIODICALS.

AMERICAN JOURNAL OF PHILOLOGY, THE. (*See* PHILOLOGY.)

BRAIN. (*See* MEDICINE.)

ECONOMIC JOURNAL, THE. (*See* PO-LITICAL ECONOMY.)

ECONOMICS, THE QUARTERLY JOUR-NAL OF. (*See* POLITICAL ECONOMY.)

ENGLISH ILLUSTRATED MAGAZINE, THE.— Profusely Illustrated. Published Monthly. No. I. October, 1883. 6*d.*—Vol. I. 1884. 7*s.* 6*d.*—Vols. II.-VIII. Super royal 8vo, extra cloth, coloured edges. 8*s.* each. [Cloth Covers for binding Volumes, 1*s.* each. Reading Case, 1*s.* net.]

NATURAL SCIENCE: A MONTHLY RE-VIEW OF SCIENTIFIC PROGRESS. 8vo. 1*s.* net. No. 1   March 1892.

NATURE: A WEEKLY ILLUSTRATED JOUR-NAL OF SCIENCE. Published every Thursday. Price 6*d.*   Monthly Parts, 2*s.* and 2*s.* 6*d.*; Current Half-yearly vols., 15*s.* each. Vols. I.—XLIII. [Cases for binding vols. 1*s.* 6*d.* each.]

HELLENIC STUDIES, THE JOURNAL OF. Pub. Half-Yearly from 1880. 8vo. 30*s.*; or each Part, 15*s.* Vol. XII. Part I. 15*s.* net. The Journal will be sold at a reduced price to Libraries wishing to subscribe, but official application must in each case be made to the Council. Information on this point, and upon the conditions of Membership, may be obtained on application to the Hon. Sec., Mr. George Macmillan, 29, Bedford Street, Covent Garden.

LEPROSY INVESTIGATION COMMIT-TEE, JOURNAL OF. (*See* MEDICINE.)

MACMILLAN'S MAGAZINE. Published Monthly. 1*s.*—Vols. I.-LXV. 7*s.* 6*d.* each. [Cloth covers for binding, 1*s.* each.]

PHILOLOGY, THE JOURNAL OF. (*See* PHILOLOGY.)

PRACTITIONER, THE. (*See* MEDICINE.)

RECORD OF TECHNICAL AND SE-CONDARY EDUCATION. (*See* EDU-CATION, p. 8.)

PHILOLOGY.

AMERICAN JOURNAL OF PHILOLOGY, THE. Edited by Prof. BASIL L. GILDER-SLEEVE. 4s. 6d. each No. (quarterly).

AMERICAN PHILOLOGICAL ASSOCIATION, TRANSACTIONS OF. Vols. I.—XX. 8s. 6d. per vol. net, except Vols. XV. and XX., which are 10s. 6d. net.

CORNELL UNIVERSITY STUDIES IN CLASSICAL PHILOLOGY. Edited by I. FLAGG, W. G. HALE, and B. I. WHEELER. I. THE *CUM*-CONSTRUCTIONS: their History and Functions. Part I. Critical. 1s. 8d. net. Part II. Constructive. By W. G. HALE. 3s. 4d. net.—II. ANALOGY AND THE SCOPE OF ITS APPLICATION IN LANGUAGE. By B. I. WHEELER. 1s. 3d. net.

GILES (P.).—A SHORT MANUAL OF PHILOLOGY FOR CLASSICAL STUDENTS. Cr. 8vo.

JOURNAL OF SACRED AND CLASSICAL PHILOLOGY. 4 vols. 8vo. 12s. 6d. each.

JOURNAL OF PHILOLOGY. New Series. Edited by W. A. WRIGHT, M.A., I. BYWATER, M.A., and H. JACKSON, M.A. 4s. 6d. each No. (half-yearly).

KELLNER (Dr. L.). - HISTORICAL OUTLINES IN ENGLISH SYNTAX. Globe 8vo. 6s.

MORRIS (Rev. Richard, LL.D.).—PRIMER OF ENGLISH GRAMMAR. 18mo. 1s.
—— ELEMENTARY LESSONS IN HISTORICAL ENGLISH GRAMMAR. 18mo. 2s. 6d.
—— HISTORICAL OUTLINES OF ENGLISH ACCIDENCE. Extra fcp. 8vo. 6s.

MORRIS (R.) and BOWEN (H. C.).—ENGLISH GRAMMAR EXERCISES. 18mo. 1s.

OLIPHANT (T. L. Kington). — THE OLD AND MIDDLE ENGLISH. Globe 8vo. 9s.
—— THE NEW ENGLISH. 2 vols. Cr. 8vo. 21s.

PEILE (John).—A PRIMER OF PHILOLOGY. 18mo. 1s.

PELLISSIER (E.).—FRENCH ROOTS AND THEIR FAMILIES. Globe 8vo. 6s.

TAYLOR (Isaac).—WORDS AND PLACES. 9th Edit. Maps. Globe 8vo. 6s.
—— ETRUSCAN RESEARCHES. 8vo. 14s.
—— GREEKS AND GOTHS: A Study of the Runes. 8vo. 9s.

WETHERELL (J.).—EXERCISES ON MORRIS'S PRIMER OF ENGLISH GRAMMAR. 18mo. 1s.

YONGE (C. M.).—HISTORY OF CHRISTIAN NAMES. New Edit., revised. Cr. 8vo. 7s. 6d.

PHILOSOPHY.

Ethics and Metaphysics—Logic—Psychology.

Ethics and Metaphysics.

BIRKS (Thomas Rawson).—FIRST PRINCIPLES OF MORAL SCIENCE. Cr. 8vo. 8s. 6d.
—— MODERN UTILITARIANISM: or, The Systems of Paley, Bentham, and Mill Examined and Compared. Cr. 8vo. 6s. 6d.
—— MODERN PHYSICAL FATALISM, AND THE DOCTRINE OF EVOLUTION. Including an Examination of Mr. Herbert Spencer's "First Principles." Cr. 8vo. 6s.

CALDERWOOD (Prof. H.).—A HANDBOOK OF MORAL PHILOSOPHY. Cr. 8vo. 6s.

FISKE (John).—OUTLINES OF COSMIC PHILOSOPHY, BASED ON THE DOCTRINE OF EVOLUTION. 2 vols. 8vo. 25s.

FOWLER (Rev. Thomas). — PROGRESSIVE MORALITY: An Essay in Ethics. Cr. 8vo. 5s.

HARPER (Father Thomas).—THE META-PHYSICS OF THE SCHOOL. In 5 vols.—Vols. I. and II. 8vo. 18s. each.—Vol. III. Part I. 12s.

KANT.—KANT'S CRITICAL PHILOSOPHY FOR ENGLISH READERS. By J. P. MAHAFFY, D.D., and J. H. BERNARD, B.D. 2 vols. Cr. 8vo.—Vol. I. THE KRITIK OF PURE REASON EXPLAINED AND DEFENDED. 7s. 6d.—Vol. II. THE PROLEGOMENA. Translated, with Notes and Appendices. 6s.
—— KRITIK OF JUDGMENT. Translated by J. H. BERNARD, D.D. 8vo. 10s. net.

KANT—MAX MÜLLER. — CRITIQUE OF PURE REASON BY IMMANUEL KANT. Translated by F. MAX MÜLLER. With Introduction by LUDWIG NOIRÉ. 2 vols. 8vo. 16s. each (sold separately).—Vol. I. HISTORICAL INTRODUCTION, by LUDWIG NOIRÉ, etc.—Vol. II. CRITIQUE OF PURE REASON.

MAURICE (F. D.).—MORAL AND META-PHYSICAL PHILOSOPHY. 2 vols. 8vo. 16s.

McCOSH (Rev. Dr. James).—THE METHOD OF THE DIVINE GOVERNMENT, PHYSICAL AND MORAL. 8vo. 10s. 6d.
—— THE SUPERNATURAL IN RELATION TO THE NATURAL. Cr. 8vo. 7s. 6d.
—— INTUITIONS OF THE MIND. 8vo. 10s. 6d.
—— AN EXAMINATION OF MR. J. S. MILL'S PHILOSOPHY. 8vo. 10s. 6d.
—— CHRISTIANITY AND POSITIVISM. Lectures on Natural Theology and Apologetics. Cr. 8vo. 7s. 6d.
—— THE SCOTTISH PHILOSOPHY FROM HUTCHESON TO HAMILTON, BIOGRAPHICAL, EXPOSITORY, CRITICAL. Roy. 8vo. 16s.
—— REALISTIC PHILOSOPHY DEFENDED IN A PHILOSOPHIC SERIES. 2 vols.—Vol. I. EXPOSITORY. Vol. II. HISTORICAL AND CRITICAL. Cr. 8vo. 14s.
—— FIRST AND FUNDAMENTAL TRUTHS. Being a Treatise on Metaphysics. 8vo. 9s.
—— THE PREVAILING TYPES OF PHILOSOPHY: CAN THEY LOGICALLY REACH REALITY? 8vo. 3s. 6d.
—— OUR MORAL NATURE. Cr. 8vo. 2s. 6d.

MASSON (Prof. David).—RECENT BRITISH PHILOSOPHY. 3rd Edit. Cr. 8vo. 6s.

SIDGWICK (Prof. Henry).—THE METHODS OF ETHICS. 4th Edit., revised. 8vo. 14s.
—— A SUPPLEMENT TO THE SECOND EDITION. Containing all the important Additions and Alterations in the Fourth Edition. 8vo. 6s.
—— OUTLINES OF THE HISTORY OF ETHICS FOR ENGLISH READERS. Cr. 8vo. 3s. 6d.

THORNTON (W. T.). — OLD-FASHIONED ETHICS AND COMMON-SENSE METAPHYSICS. 8vo. 10s. 6d.

PHILOSOPHY.
Logic.

BOOLE (George).— THE MATHEMATICAL ANALYSIS OF LOGIC. 8vo. sewed. 5s.

CARROLL (Lewis).—THE GAME OF LOGIC. Cr. 8vo. 3s. net.

JEVONS (W. Stanley).—A PRIMER OF LOGIC. 18mo. 1s.

—— ELEMENTARY LESSONS IN LOGIC, DEDUCTIVE AND INDUCTIVE. 18mo. 3s. 6d.

—— STUDIES IN DEDUCTIVE LOGIC. 2nd Edit. Cr. 8vo. 6s.

—— THE PRINCIPLES OF SCIENCE : Treatise on Logic and Scientific Method. Cr. 8vo. 12s. 6d.

—— PURE LOGIC : and other Minor Works. Edited by R. ADAMSON, M.A., and HARRIET A. JEVONS. 8vo. 10s. 6d.

KEYNES (J. N.).—STUDIES AND EXERCISES IN FORMAL LOGIC. 2nd Edit. Cr. 8vo. 10s. 6d.

McCOSH (Rev. Dr.).—THE LAWS OF DISCURSIVE THOUGHT. A Text-Book of Formal Logic. Cr. 8vo. 5s.

RAY (Prof. P. K.).—A TEXT-BOOK OF DEDUCTIVE LOGIC. 4th Edit. Globe 8vo. 4s. 6d.

VENN (Rev. John).—THE LOGIC OF CHANCE. 2nd Edit. Cr. 8vo. 10s. 6d.

—— SYMBOLIC LOGIC. Cr. 8vo. 10s. 6d.

—— THE PRINCIPLES OF EMPIRICAL OR INDUCTIVE LOGIC. 8vo. 18s.

Psychology.

BALDWIN (Prof. J. M.).—HANDBOOK OF PSYCHOLOGY: Senses and Intellect. 8vo. 12s. 6d.

—— FEELING AND WILL. 8vo. 12s. 6d.

CALDERWOOD (Prof. H.).— THE RELATIONS OF MIND AND BRAIN. 3rd Ed. 8vo. 8s.

CLIFFORD (W. K.).—SEEING AND THINKING. Cr. 8vo. 3s. 6d.

HÖFFDING (Prof. H.).—OUTLINES OF PSYCHOLOGY. Translated by M. E. LOWNDES. Cr. 8vo. 6s.

JAMES (Prof. William).—THE PRINCIPLES OF PSYCHOLOGY. 2 vols. Demy 8vo. 25s. net.

—— TEXT BOOK OF PSYCHOLOGY. Cr. 8vo. 7s. net.

JARDINE (Rev. Robert).—THE ELEMENTS OF THE PSYCHOLOGY OF COGNITION. 3rd Edit. Cr. 8vo. 6s. 6d.

McCOSH (Rev. Dr.).—PSYCHOLOGY. Cr. 8vo. I. THE COGNITIVE POWERS. 6s. 6d.— II. THE MOTIVE POWERS. 6s. 6d.

—— THE EMOTIONS. 8vo. 9s.

MAUDSLEY (Dr. Henry).—THE PHYSIOLOGY OF MIND. Cr. 8vo. 10s. 6d.

—— THE PATHOLOGY OF MIND. 8vo. 18s.

—— BODY AND MIND. Cr. 8vo. 6s. 6d.

MURPHY (J. J.).—HABIT AND INTELLIGENCE. 2nd Edit. Illustrated. 8vo. 16s.

PHOTOGRAPHY.

MELDOLA (Prof. R.).—THE CHEMISTRY OF PHOTOGRAPHY. Cr. 8vo. 6s.

PHYSICS OR NATURAL PHILOSOPHY.
General—Electricity and Magnetism—Heat, Light, and Sound.

General.

ANDREWS (Dr. Thomas): THE SCIENTIFIC PAPERS OF THE LATE. With a Memoir by Profs. TAIT and CRUM BROWN. 8vo. 18s.

DANIELL (A.)—A TEXT-BOOK OF THE PRINCIPLES OF PHYSICS. Illustrated. 2nd Edit. Med. 8vo. 21s.

EVERETT (Prof. J. D.).—THE C. G. S. SYSTEM OF UNITS, WITH TABLES OF PHYSICAL CONSTANTS. New Edit. Globe 8vo. 5s.

FESSENDEN (C.).—ELEMENTS OF PHYSICS. Fcp. 8vo. 3s.

FISHER (Rev. Osmond).—PHYSICS OF THE EARTH'S CRUST 2nd Edit. 8vo. 12s.

GUILLEMIN (Amédée).—THE FORCES OF NATURE. A Popular Introduction to the Study of Physical Phenomena. 455 Woodcuts. Roy. 8vo. 21s.

KELVIN (Lord).—POPULAR LECTURES AND ADDRESSES.—Vol. I. CONSTITUTION OF MATTER. Cr 8vo. 7s. 6d.

KEMPE (A. B.).—HOW TO DRAW A STRAIGHT LINE. Cr 8vo. 1s. 6d.

LODGE (O. J.).—PIONEERS OF SCIENCE. Ext. cr. 8vo. 7s 6d.

LOEWY (B.).—QUESTIONS AND EXAMPLES IN EXPERIMENTAL PHYSICS, SOUND, LIGHT, HEAT, ELECTRICITY, AND MAGNETISM. Fcp. 8vo. 2s.

—— A GRADUATED COURSE OF NATURAL SCIENCE. Part I. Gl. 8vo. 2s.—Part II. 2s. 6d.

MOLLOY (Rev. G.).—GLEANINGS IN SCIENCE : A Series of Popular Lectures on Scientific Subjects. 8vo. 7s. 6d.

STEWART (Prof. Balfour). — A PRIMER OF PHYSICS. Illustrated. 18mo. 1s.

—— LESSONS IN ELEMENTARY PHYSICS. Illustrated. Fcp. 8vo. 4s. 6d.

—— QUESTIONS. By T. H. CORE. 18mo. 2s.

STEWART (Prof. Balfour) and GEE (W. W. Haldane).—LESSONS IN ELEMENTARY PRACTICAL PHYSICS. Illustrated.—GENERAL PHYSICAL PROCESSES. Cr. 8vo. 6s.

TAIT (Prof. P. G.).—LECTURES ON SOME RECENT ADVANCES IN PHYSICAL SCIENCE. 3rd Edit. Cr. 8vo. 9s.

Electricity and Magnetism.

CUMMING (Linnæus).—AN INTRODUCTION TO ELECTRICITY. Cr. 8vo. 8s. 6d.

DAY (R. E.).—ELECTRIC LIGHT ARITHMETIC. 18mo. 2s.

GRAY (Prof. Andrew).—THE THEORY AND PRACTICE OF ABSOLUTE MEASUREMENTS IN ELECTRICITY AND MAGNETISM. 2 vols. Cr. 8vo. Vol. I. 12s. 6d.

—— ABSOLUTE MEASUREMENTS IN ELECTRICITY AND MAGNETISM. Fcp. 8vo. 5s. 6d.

GUILLEMIN (A.).—ELECTRICITY AND MAGNETISM. A Popular Treatise. Translated and Edited by Prof. SILVANUS P. THOMPSON. Super Roy. 8vo. 31s. 6d.

HEAVISIDE (O.) — ELECTRICAL PAPERS. 2 vols. 8vo. 30*s.* net.

KELVIN (Lord). — PAPERS ON ELECTRO-STATICS AND MAGNETISM. 8vo. 18*s.*

LODGE (Prof. Oliver).—MODERN VIEWS OF ELECTRICITY. Illust. Cr. 8vo. 6*s.* 6*d.*

MENDENHALL (T. C.).—A CENTURY OF ELECTRICITY. Cr. 8vo. 4*s.* 6*d.*

STEWART (Prof. Balfour) and GEE (W. W. Haldane).—LESSONS IN ELEMENTARY PRAC-TICAL PHYSICS. Cr. 8vo. Illustrated.—ELEC-TRICITY AND MAGNETISM. 7*s.* 6*d.*
—— PRACTICAL PHYSICS FOR SCHOOLS. Gl. 8vo.—ELECTRICITY AND MAGNETISM. 2*s.* 6*d.*

THOMPSON (Prof. Silvanus P.). — ELE-MENTARY LESSONS IN ELECTRICITY AND MAGNETISM. Illustrated. Fcp. 8vo. 4*s.* 6*d.*

TURNER (H. H.).—EXAMPLES ON HEAT AND ELECTRICITY. Cr. 8vo. 2*s.* 6*d.*

Heat, Light, and Sound.

AIRY (Sir G. B.).—ON SOUND AND ATMO-SPHERIC VIBRATIONS. Cr. 8vo. 9*s.*

CARNOT—THURSTON.—REFLECTIONS ON THE MOTIVE POWER OF HEAT, AND ON MACHINES FITTED TO DEVELOP THAT POWER. From the French of N. L. S. CAR-NOT. Edited by R. H. THURSTON, LL.D. Cr. 8vo. 7*s.* 6*d.*

JOHNSON (Amy).—SUNSHINE. Illustrated. Cr. 8vo. 6*s.*

JONES (Prof. D. E.).—HEAT, LIGHT, AND SOUND. Globe 8vo. 2*s.* 6*d.*
—— LESSONS IN HEAT AND LIGHT. Globe 8vo. 3*s.* 6*d.*

MAYER (Prof. A. M.).—SOUND. A Series of Simple Experiments. Illustr. Cr. 8vo. 3*s.*6*d.*

MAYER (Prof. A. M.) and BARNARD (C.).—LIGHT. A Series of Simple Experiments. Illustrated. Cr. 8vo. 2*s.* 6*d.*

PARKINSON (S.).—A TREATISE ON OPTICS. 4th Edit., revised. Cr. 8vo. 10*s.* 6*d.*

PEABODY (Prof. C. H.).—THERMODYNAMICS OF THE STEAM ENGINE AND OTHER HEAT-ENGINES. 8vo. 21*s.*

PERRY (Prof. J.).—STEAM: An Elementary Treatise. 18mo. 4*s.* 6*d.*

PRESTON (T.).—THE THEORY OF LIGHT. Illustrated. 8vo. 15*s.* net.
—— THE THEORY OF HEAT. 8vo.

RAYLEIGH (Lord).—THEORY OF SOUND. 8vo. Vol. I. 12*s.* 6*d.*—Vol. II. 12*s.* 6*d.*

SHANN (G.).—AN ELEMENTARY TREATISE ON HEAT IN RELATION TO STEAM AND THE STEAM-ENGINE. Illustr. Cr. 8vo. 4*s.* 6*d.*

SPOTTISWOODE (W.).—POLARISATION OF LIGHT. Illustrated. Cr. 8vo. 3*s.* 6*d.*

STEWART (Prof. Balfour) and GEE (W. W. Haldane).—LESSONS IN ELEMENTARY PRAC-TICAL PHYSICS. Cr. 8vo. Illustrated.—OPTICS, HEAT, AND SOUND.
—— PRACTICAL PHYSICS FOR SCHOOLS. Gl. 8vo.—HEAT, LIGHT, AND SOUND.

STOKES (Sir George G.).—ON LIGHT. The Burnett Lectures. Cr. 8vo. 7*s.* 6*d.*

STONE (W. H.).—ELEMENTARY LESSONS ON SOUND. Illustrated. Fcp. 8vo. 3*s.* 6*d.*

TAIT (Prof. P. G.).—HEAT. With Illustra-tions. Cr. 8vo. 6*s.*

TAYLOR (Sedley).—SOUND AND MUSIC. 2nd Edit. Ext. cr. 8vo. 8*s.* 6*d.*

TURNER (H. H.). (*See* ELECTRICITY.)

WRIGHT (Lewis).—LIGHT. A Course of Experimental Optics. Illust. Cr. 8vo. 7*s.* 6*d.*

PHYSIOGRAPHY and METEOROLOGY.

ARATUS.—THE SKIES AND WEATHER FORE-CASTS OF ARATUS. Translated by E. POSTE, M.A. Cr. 8vo. 3*s.* 6*d.*

BLANFORD (H. F.).—THE RUDIMENTS OF PHYSICAL GEOGRAPHY FOR THE USE OF INDIAN SCHOOLS. Illustr. Cr. 8vo. 2*s.* 6*d.*
—— A PRACTICAL GUIDE TO THE CLIMATES AND WEATHER OF INDIA, CEYLON AND BURMAH, AND THE STORMS OF INDIAN SEAS. 8vo. 12*s.* 6*d.*

FERREL (Prof. W.).—A POPULAR TREATISE ON THE WINDS. 8vo. 18*s.*

FISHER (Rev. Osmond).—PHYSICS OF THE EARTH'S CRUST. 2nd Edit. 8vo. 12*s.*

GALTON (Francis).—METEOROGRAPHICA; or, Methods of Mapping the Weather. 4to. 9*s.*

GEIKIE (Sir Archibald).—A PRIMER OF PHY-SICAL GEOGRAPHY. Illustrated. 18mo. 1*s.*
—— ELEMENTARY LESSONS IN PHYSICAL GEOGRAPHY. Illustrated. Fcp. 8vo. 4*s.* 6*d.*
—— QUESTIONS ON THE SAME. 1*s.* 6*d.*

HUXLEY (Prof. T. H.).—PHYSIOGRAPHY. Illustrated. Cr. 8vo. 6*s.*

LOCKYER (J. Norman).—OUTLINES OF PHY-SIOGRAPHY: THE MOVEMENTS OF THE EARTH. Illustrated. Cr. 8vo, swd. 1*s.* 6*d.*

MELDOLA (Prof. R.) and WHITE (Wm.).—REPORT ON THE EAST ANGLIAN EARTH-QUAKE OF APRIL 22ND, 1884. 8vo. 3*s.* 6*d.*

PHYSIOLOGY.

FEARNLEY (W.).—A MANUAL OF ELEMEN-TARY PRACTICAL HISTOLOGY. Cr. 8vo. 7*s.* 6*d.*

FOSTER (Prof. Michael).—A TEXT-BOOK OF PHYSIOLOGY. Illustrated. 5th Edit. 8vo.—Part I. Book I. BLOOD: THE TISSUES OF MOVEMENT, THE VASCULAR MECHANISM. 10*s.* 6*d.*—Part II. Book II. THE TISSUES OF CHEMICAL ACTION, WITH THEIR RESPECTIVE MECHANISMS: NUTRITION. 10*s.* 6*d.*—Part III. Book III. THE CENTRAL NERVOUS SYSTEM. 7*s.* 6*d.*—Part IV. Book III. THE SENSES, AND SOME SPECIAL MUSCULAR MECHANISMS.—BOOK IV. THE TISSUES AND MECHANISMS OF REPRODUCTION. 10*s.* 6*d.*—Appendix, by A. S. LEA. 7*s.* 6*d.*
—— A PRIMER OF PHYSIOLOGY. 18mo. 1*s.*

FOSTER (Prof. M.) and LANGLEY (J. N.).—A COURSE OF ELEMENTARY PRACTICAL PHYSIOLOGY AND HISTOLOGY. Cr. 8vo. 7*s.* 6*d.*

GAMGEE (Arthur).—A TEXT-BOOK OF THE PHYSIOLOGICAL CHEMISTRY OF THE ANIMAL BODY. Vol. I. 8vo. 18*s.* Vol. II.

PHYSIOLOGY—*continued.*

HUMPHRY (Prof. Sir G. M.).—THE HUMAN FOOT AND THE HUMAN HAND. Illustrated. Fcp. 8vo. 4s. 6d.

HUXLEY (Prof. Thos. H.).—LESSONS IN ELEMENTARY PHYSIOLOGY. Fcp. 8vo. 4s. 6d.
—— QUESTIONS. By T. ALCOCK. 18mo. 1s.6d.

MIVART (St. George).—LESSONS IN ELEMENTARY ANATOMY. Fcp. 8vo. 6s. 6d.

PETTIGREW (J. Bell).—THE PHYSIOLOGY OF THE CIRCULATION IN PLANTS IN THE LOWER ANIMALS AND IN MAN. 8vo. 12s.

SEILER (Dr. Carl).—MICRO-PHOTOGRAPHS IN HISTOLOGY, NORMAL AND PATHOLOGICAL. 4to. 31s. 6d.

POETRY. (*See under* LITERATURE, p. 14.)

POLITICAL ECONOMY.

BASTABLE (Prof. C. F.).—PUBLIC FINANCE. 12s. 6d. net.

BÖHM-BAWERK (Prof.).—CAPITAL AND INTEREST. Trans. by W SMART. 8vo. 12s.net.
—— THE POSITIVE THEORY OF CAPITAL. By the same Translator. 12s. net.

BOISSEVAIN (G. M.).—THE MONETARY QUESTION 8vo, sewed. 3s. net.

BONAR (James).—MALTHUS AND HIS WORK. 8vo. 12s. 6d.

CAIRNES (J. E.).—SOME LEADING PRINCIPLES OF POLITICAL ECONOMY NEWLY EXPOUNDED. 8vo. 14s.
—— THE CHARACTER AND LOGICAL METHOD OF POLITICAL ECONOMY. Cr. 8vo. 6s.

CANTILLON.—ESSAI SUR LE COMMERCE. 12mo. 7s. net.

CLARKE (C. B.).—SPECULATIONS FROM POLITICAL ECONOMY. Cr. 8vo. 3s. 6d.

DICTIONARY OF POLITICAL ECONOMY, A. By various Writers. Ed. R. H. I. PALGRAVE. 3s.6d. net. (Part I. July, 1891.)

ECONOMIC JOURNAL, THE. — THE JOURNAL OF THE BRITISH ECONOMIC ASSOCIATION. Edit. by Prof. F. Y. EDGEWORTH. Published Quarterly. 8vo. 5s. (Part I. April, 1891.) Vol. I. 21s. [Cloth Covers for binding Volumes, 1s. 6d. each.]

ECONOMICS: THE QUARTERLY JOURNAL OF. Vol. II. Parts II. III. IV. 2s.6d. each. —Vol. III. 4 parts. 2s. 6d. each.—Vol. IV 4 parts. 2s.6d. each.—Vol. V, 4 parts. 2s.6d. each.—Vol. VI. 4 parts. 2s 6d. each.

FAWCETT (Henry).—MANUAL OF POLITICAL ECONOMY. 7th Edit. Cr. 8vo. 12s.
—— AN EXPLANATORY DIGEST OF THE ABOVE. By C. A. WATERS. Cr. 8vo. 2s. 6d.
—— FREE TRADE AND PROTECTION. 6th Edit. Cr. 8vo. 3s. 6d.

FAWCETT (Mrs. H.).—POLITICAL ECONOMY FOR BEGINNERS, WITH QUESTIONS. 7th Edit. 18mo. 2s. 6d.

FIRST LESSONS IN BUSINESS MATTERS. By A BANKER'S DAUGHTER. 2nd Edit. 18mo. 1s.

GILMAN (N. P.). — PROFIT-SHARING BETWEEN EMPLOYER AND EMPLOYEE. Cr. 8vo. 7s. 6d.

GOSCHEN (Rt. Hon. George J.).—REPORTS AND SPEECHES ON LOCAL TAXATION. 8vo. 5s.

GUIDE TO THE UNPROTECTED: In EVERY-DAY MATTERS RELATING TO PROPERTY AND INCOME. Ext. fcp. 8vo. 3s. 6d.

GUNTON (George).—WEALTH AND PROGRESS. Cr. 8vo. 6s.

HORTON (Hon. S. Dana).—THE SILVER POUND AND ENGLAND'S MONETARY POLICY SINCE THE RESTORATION. 8vo. 14s.

HOWELL (George).—THE CONFLICTS OF CAPITAL AND LABOUR. Cr. 8vo. 7s. 6d.

JEVONS (W. Stanley).—A PRIMER OF POLITICAL ECONOMY. 18mo. 1s.
—— THE THEORY OF POLITICAL ECONOMY. 3rd Ed. 8vo. 10s. 6d.
—— INVESTIGATIONS IN CURRENCY AND FINANCE. Edit. by H. S. FOXWELL. 8vo. 21s

KEYNES (J. N.).—THE SCOPE AND METHOD OF POLITICAL ECONOMY. Cr. 8vo. 7s. net.

MACDONELL (John).—THE LAND QUESTION. 8vo. 10s. 6d.

MARSHALL (Prof. Alfred).—PRINCIPLES OF ECONOMICS. 2 vols. 8vo. Vol. I. 12s.6d. net.
—— ELEMENTS OF ECONOMICS OF INDUSTRY. Crown 8vo. 3s. 6d.

MARTIN (Frederick). — THE HISTORY OF LLOYD'S, AND OF MARINE INSURANCE IN GREAT BRITAIN. 8vo. 14s.

PRICE (L. L. F. R.).—INDUSTRIAL PEACE: ITS ADVANTAGES, METHODS, AND DIFFICULTIES. Med. 8vo. 6s.

SIDGWICK (Prof. Henry).—THE PRINCIPLES OF POLITICAL ECONOMY. 2nd Edit. 8vo. 16s.

SMART (W.).—AN INTRODUCTION TO THE THEORY OF VALUE. Cr. 8vo. 3s. net.

THOMPSON (H. M.).—THE THEORY OF WAGES AND ITS APPLICATION TO THE EIGHT HOURS QUESTION. Cr. 8vo. 3s. 6d.

WALKER (Francis A.).—FIRST LESSONS IN POLITICAL ECONOMY. Cr. 8vo. 5s.
—— A BRIEF TEXT-BOOK OF POLITICAL ECONOMY. Cr. 8vo. 6s. 6d.
—— POLITICAL ECONOMY. 8vo. 12s. 6d.
—— THE WAGES QUESTION. Ext. cr. 8vo. 8s. 6d. net.
—— MONEY. New Edit. Ext.cr.8vo. 8s.6d.net.
—— MONEY IN ITS RELATION TO TRADE AND INDUSTRY. Cr. 8vo. 7s. 6d.
—— LAND AND ITS RENT. Fcp. 8vo. 3s. 6d.

WALLACE (A. R.).—BAD TIMES: An Essay. Cr. 8vo. 2s. 6d.

WICKSTEED (Ph. H.).—THE ALPHABET OF ECONOMIC SCIENCE.—I. ELEMENTS OF THE THEORY OF VALUE OR WORTH. Gl.8vo. 2s.6d.

POLITICS.

(*See also* HISTORY, p. 10.)

ADAMS (Sir F. O.) and **CUNNINGHAM** (C.).—THE SWISS CONFEDERATION. 8vo. 14s.

BAKER (Sir Samuel W.).—THE EGYPTIAN QUESTION. 8vo, sewed. 2s.

BATH (Marquis of).—OBSERVATIONS ON BULGARIAN AFFAIRS. Cr. 8vo. 3s. 6d.

BRIGHT (John).—SPEECHES ON QUESTIONS OF PUBLIC POLICY. Edit. by J. E. THOROLD ROGERS. With Portrait. 2 vols. 8vo. 25s. —*Popular Edition.* Ext. fcp. 8vo. 3s. 6d. —— PUBLIC ADDRESSES. Edited by J. E. T. ROGERS. 8vo. 14s.

BRYCE (Jas., M.P.).—THE AMERICAN COMMONWEALTH. 2 vols. Ext. cr. 8vo. 25s.

BUCKLAND (Anna).—OUR NATIONAL INSTITUTIONS. 18mo. 1s.

BURKE (Edmund).—LETTERS, TRACTS, AND SPEECHES ON IRISH AFFAIRS. Edited by MATTHEW ARNOLD, with Preface. Cr. 8vo. 6s. —— REFLECTIONS ON THE FRENCH REVOLUTION. Ed. by F. G. SELBY. Globe 8vo. 5s.

CAIRNES (J. E.).—POLITICAL ESSAYS. 8vo. 10s. 6d. —— THE SLAVE POWER. 8vo. 10s. 6d.

COBDEN (Richard).—SPEECHES ON QUESTIONS OF PUBLIC POLICY. Ed. by J. BRIGHT and J. E. THOROLD ROGERS. Gl. 8vo. 3s. 6d.

DICEY (Prof. A. V.).—LETTERS ON UNIONIST DELUSIONS. Cr. 8vo. 2s. 6d.

DILKE (Rt. Hon. Sir Charles W.). — GREATER BRITAIN. 9th Edit. Cr. 8vo. 6s. —— PROBLEMS OF GREATER BRITAIN. Maps. 3rd Edit. Ext. cr. 8vo. 12s. 6d.

DONISTHORPE (Wordsworth). — INDIVIDUALISM : A System of Politics. 8vo. 14s.

DUFF(Rt. Hon. Sir M. E. Grant).—MISCELLANIES, POLITICAL AND LITERARY. 8vo. 10s. 6d.

ENGLISH CITIZEN, THE.—His Rights and Responsibilities. Ed. by HENRY CRAIK, C.B. New Edit. Monthly Volumes from Oct. 1892. Cr. 8vo. 2s. 6d. each.

CENTRAL GOVERNMENT. By H. D. TRAILL.

THE ELECTORATE AND THE LEGISLATURE. By SPENCER WALPOLE.

THE LAND LAWS. By Sir F. POLLOCK, Bart. 2nd Edit.

THE PUNISHMENT AND PREVENTION OF CRIME. By Col. Sir EDMUND DU CANE.

LOCAL GOVERNMENT. By M. D. CHALMERS.

COLONIES AND DEPENDENCIES : Part I. INDIA. By J. S. COTTON, M.A.—II. THE COLONIES. By E. J. PAYNE.

THE STATE IN ITS RELATION TO EDUCATION. By HENRY CRAIK, C.B.

THE STATE AND THE CHURCH. By Hon. ARTHUR ELLIOTT, M.P.

THE STATE IN ITS RELATION TO TRADE. By Sir T. H. FARRER, Bart.

THE POOR LAW. By the Rev. T. W. FOWLE.

THE STATE IN RELATION TO LABOUR. By W. STANLEY JEVONS.

JUSTICE AND POLICE. By F. W. MAITLAND.

THE NATIONAL DEFENCES. By Colonel MAURICE, R.A. [*In the Press.*

FOREIGN RELATIONS. By S. WALPOLE.

THE NATIONAL BUDGET; NATIONAL DEBT; TAXES AND RATES. By A. J. WILSON.

FAWCETT (Henry).—SPEECHES ON SOME CURRENT POLITICAL QUESTIONS. 8vo. 10s. 6d. —— FREE TRADE AND PROTECTION. 6th Edit. Cr. 8vo. 3s. 6d.

FAWCETT (Henry and Mrs. H.).—ESSAYS AND LECTURES ON POLITICAL AND SOCIAL SUBJECTS. 8vo. 10s. 6d.

FISKE (John).—AMERICAN POLITICAL IDEAS VIEWED FROM THE STAND-POINT OF UNIVERSAL HISTORY. Cr. 8vo. 4s. —— CIVIL GOVERNMENT IN THE UNITED STATES CONSIDERED WITH SOME REFERENCE TO ITS ORIGIN. Cr. 8vo. 6s. 6d.

FREEMAN (Prof. E. A.).—DISESTABLISHMENT AND DISENDOWMENT. WHAT ARE THEY? 4th Edit. Cr. 8vo. 1s. —— COMPARATIVE POLITICS and THE UNITY OF HISTORY. 8vo. 14s. —— THE GROWTH OF THE ENGLISH CONSTITUTION. 5th Edit. Cr. 8vo. 5s.

HARWOOD (George).—DISESTABLISHMENT : or, a Defence of the Principle of a National Church. 8vo. 12s. —— THE COMING DEMOCRACY. Cr. 8vo. 6s.

HILL (Florence D.).—CHILDREN OF THE STATE. Ed. by FANNY FOWKE. Cr. 8vo. 6s.

HILL (Octavia).—OUR COMMON LAND, AND OTHER ESSAYS. Ext. fcp. 8vo. 3s. 6d.

HOLLAND (Prof. T. E.).—THE TREATY RELATIONS OF RUSSIA AND TURKEY, FROM 1774 TO 1853. Cr. 8vo. 2s.

JENKS (Prof. Edward).—THE GOVERNMENT OF VICTORIA (AUSTRALIA). 8vo. 14s.

JEPHSON (H.).—THE PLATFORM: ITS RISE AND PROGRESS. 2 vols. 8vo. 21s.

LOWELL (J. R.). (*See* COLLECTED WORKS.)

LUBBOCK (Sir J.). (*See* COLLECTED WORKS.)

MACDONELL (John).—THE LAND QUESTION. 8vo. 10s. 6d.

PALGRAVE (Reginald F. D.).—THE HOUSE OF COMMONS: Illustrations of its History and Practice. Cr. 8vo. 2s. 6d.

PALGRAVE (W. Gifford). — ESSAYS ON EASTERN QUESTIONS. 8vo. 10s. 6d.

PARKIN (G. R.).—IMPERIAL FEDERATION. Cr. 8vo. 4s. 6d.

POLLOCK (Sir F., Bart.).—INTRODUCTION TO THE HISTORY OF THE SCIENCE OF POLITICS. Cr. 8vo. 2s. 6d. —— LEADING CASES DONE INTO ENGLISH. Crown 8vo. 3s. 6d.

PRACTICAL POLITICS. 8vo. 6s.

ROGERS (Prof. J. E. T.).—COBDEN AND POLITICAL OPINION. 8vo. 10s. 6d.

ROUTLEDGE (Jas.).—POPULAR PROGRESS IN ENGLAND. 8vo. 16s.

RUSSELL (Sir Charles).—NEW VIEWS ON IRELAND. Cr. 8vo. 2s. 6d. —— THE PARNELL COMMISSION : THE OPENING SPEECH FOR THE DEFENCE. 8vo. 10s. 6d. —*Popular Edition.* Sewed. 2s.

SIDGWICK (Prof. Henry).—THE ELEMENTS OF POLITICS. 8vo. 14s. net.

POLITICS.

SMITH (Goldwin).—CANADA AND THE CANADIAN QUESTION. 8vo. 8s. net.

STATESMAN'S YEAR-BOOK, THE. (See below under STATISTICS.)

STATHAM (R.).—BLACKS, BOERS, AND BRITISH. Cr. 8vo. 6s.

THORNTON (W. T.).—A PLEA FOR PEASANT PROPRIETORS. New Edit. Cr. 8vo. 7s. 6d.
—— INDIAN PUBLIC WORKS, AND COGNATE INDIAN TOPICS. Cr. 8vo. 8s. 6d.

TRENCH (Capt. F.).—THE RUSSO-INDIAN QUESTION. Cr. 8vo. ~s. 6d.

WALLACE (Sir Donald M.).—EGYPT AND THE EGYPTIAN QUESTION. 8vo. 14s.

PSYCHOLOGY.

(*See under* PHILOSOPHY, p. 28.)

SCULPTURE. (*See* ART.)

SOCIAL ECONOMY.

BOOTH (C.).—A PICTURE OF PAUPERISM. Cr. 8vo. 5s.—Cheap Edit. 8vo. Swd., 6d.
—— LIFE AND LABOUR OF THE PEOPLE OF LONDON. 4 vols. Cr. 8vo. 5s. 6d. each.—Maps to illustrate the above. 5s.

FAWCETT (H. and Mrs. H.). (*See* POLITICS.)

HILL (Octavia).—HOMES OF THE LONDON POOR. Cr. 8vo, sewed. 1s.

HUXLEY (Prof. T. H.).—SOCIAL DISEASES AND WORSE REMEDIES: Letters to the "Times." Cr. 8vo. sewed. 1s. net.

JEVONS (W. Stanley).—METHODS OF SOCIAL REFORM. 8vo. 10s. 6d.

STANLEY (Hon. Maude). — CLUBS FOR WORKING GIRLS. Cr. 8vo. 3s. 6d.

SOUND. (*See under* PHYSICS, p. 29.)

SPORT.

BAKER (Sir Samuel W.).—WILD BEASTS AND THEIR WAYS: REMINISCENCES OF EUROPE, ASIA, AFRICA, AMERICA, FROM 1845–88. Illustrated. Ext. cr. 8vo. 12s. 6d.

CHASSERESSE (D.).—SPORTING SKETCHES. Illustrated. Cr. 8vo. 3s. 6d.

EDWARDS-MOSS (Sir J. E., Bart). — A SEASON IN SUTHERLAND. Cr. 8vo. 1s. 6d.

STATISTICS.

STATESMAN'S YEAR-BOOK, THE. Statistical and Historical Annual of the States of the World for the Year 1892. Revised after Official Returns. Ed. by J SCOTT KELTIE. Cr. 8vo. 10s. 6d.

SURGERY. (*See* MEDICINE.)

SWIMMING.

LEAHY (Sergeant).—THE ART OF SWIMMING IN THE ETON STYLE. Cr. 8vo. 2s.

THEOLOGY.

The Bible—History of the Christian Church—The Church of England—Devotional Books—The Fathers—Hymnology—Sermons, Lectures, Addresses, and Theological Essays.

The Bible.

History of the Bible—
THE ENGLISH BIBLE; An External and Critical History of the various English Translations of Scripture. By Prof. JOHN EADIE. 2 vols. 8vo. 28s.
THE BIBLE IN THE CHURCH. By Right Rev. Bp. WESTCOTT. 10th edit. 18mo. 4s. 6d.

Biblical History—
BIBLE LESSONS. By Rev. E. A. ABBOTT. Cr. 8vo. 4s. 6d.
SIDE-LIGHTS UPON BIBLE HISTORY. By Mrs. SYDNEY BUXTON. Cr. 8vo 5s.
STORIES FROM THE BIBLE. By Rev. A. J. CHURCH. Illust. Cr. 8vo. 2 parts. 3s. 6d. each.
BIBLE READINGS SELECTED FROM THE PENTATEUCH AND THE BOOK OF JOSHUA. By Rev. J. A. CROSS. Gl. 8vo. 2s. 6d.
THE CHILDREN'S TREASURY OF BIBLE STORIES. By Mrs. H. GASKOIN. 18mo. 1s. each.—Part I. Old Testament; II. New Testament; III. The Apostles.
A CLASS-BOOK OF OLD TESTAMENT HISTORY. By Rev. Dr. MACLEAR. 18mo. 4s. 6d.
A CLASS-BOOK OF NEW TESTAMENT HISTORY By the same. 18mo. 5s. 6d.
A SHILLING BOOK OF OLD TESTAMENT HISTORY. By the same. 18mo. 1s.
A SHILLING BOOK OF NEW TESTAMENT HISTORY. By the same. 18mo. 1s.

The Old Testament—
SCRIPTURE READINGS FOR SCHOOLS AND FAMILIES. By C. M. YONGE. Globe 8vo. 1s. 6d. each; also with comments, 3s. 6d. each. — GENESIS TO DEUTERONOMY.—JOSHUA TO SOLOMON.—KINGS AND THE PROPHETS.—THE GOSPEL TIMES.—APOSTOLIC TIMES.
THE PATRIARCHS AND LAWGIVERS OF THE OLD TESTAMENT. By F. D. MAURICE. Cr. 8vo. 3s. 6d.
THE PROPHETS AND KINGS OF THE OLD TESTAMENT. By same. Cr. 8vo. 3s. 6d.
THE CANON OF THE OLD TESTAMENT. By Prof. H. E. RYLE. Cr. 8vo. 6s.

The Pentateuch—
AN HISTORICO-CRITICAL INQUIRY INTO THE ORIGIN AND COMPOSITION OF THE HEXATEUCH (PENTATEUCH AND BOOK OF JOSHUA). By Prof. A. KUENEN. Trans. by P. H. WICKSTEED, M.A. 8vo. 14s.

The Psalms—
THE PSALMS CHRONOLOGICALLY ARRANGED. By FOUR FRIENDS. Cr. 8vo. 5s. net.
GOLDEN TREASURY PSALTER. Student's Edition of the above. 18mo. 3s. 6d.
THE PSALMS. With Introduction and Notes. By A. C. JENNINGS, M.A., and W. H. LOWE, M.A. 2 vols. Cr. 8vo. 10s. 6d. each.
INTRODUCTION TO THE STUDY AND USE OF THE PSALMS. By Rev. J. F. THRUPP. 2nd Edit. 2 vols. 8vo. 21s.

Isaiah—
ISAIAH XL.—LXVI. With the Shorter Prophecies allied to it. Edited by MATTHEW ARNOLD. Cr. 8vo. 5s.

Isaiah—

ISAIAH OF JERUSALEM. In the Authorised English Version, with Introduction and Notes. By MATTHEW ARNOLD. Cr. 8vo. 4s. 6d.

A BIBLE-READING FOR SCHOOLS. The Great Prophecy of Israel's Restoration (Isaiah xl.—lxvi.). Arranged and Edited for Young Learners. By the same. 18mo. 1s.

COMMENTARY ON THE BOOK OF ISAIAH: Critical, Historical, and Prophetical; including a Revised English Translation. By T. R. BIRKS. 2nd Edit. 8vo. 12s. 6d.

THE BOOK OF ISAIAH CHRONOLOGICALLY ARRANGED. By T. K. CHEYNE. Cr. 8vo. 7s. 6d.

Zechariah—

THE HEBREW STUDENT'S COMMENTARY ON ZECHARIAH, Hebrew and LXX. By W. H. LOWE, M.A. 8vo. 10s. 6d.

The New Testament—

THE NEW TESTAMENT. Essay on the Right Estimation of MS. Evidence in the Text of the New Testament. By T. R. BIRKS. Cr. 8vo. 3s. 6d.

THE MESSAGES OF THE BOOKS. Discourses and Notes on the Books of the New Testament. By Archd. FARRAR. 8vo. 14s.

THE CLASSICAL ELEMENT IN THE NEW TESTAMENT. Considered as a Proof of its Genuineness, with an Appendix on the Oldest Authorities used in the Formation of the Canon. By C. H. HOOLE. 8vo. 10s. 6d.

ON A FRESH REVISION OF THE ENGLISH NEW TESTAMENT. With an Appendix on the last Petition of the Lord's Prayer. By Bishop LIGHTFOOT. Cr. 8vo. 7s. 6d.

THE UNITY OF THE NEW TESTAMENT. By F. D. MAURICE. 2 vols. Cr. 8vo. 12s.

A COMPANION TO THE GREEK TESTAMENT AND THE ENGLISH VERSION. By PHILIP SCHAFF, D.D. Cr. 8vo. 12s.

A GENERAL SURVEY OF THE HISTORY OF THE CANON OF THE NEW TESTAMENT DURING THE FIRST FOUR CENTURIES. By Bishop WESTCOTT. Cr. 8vo. 10s. 6d.

THE NEW TESTAMENT IN THE ORIGINAL GREEK. The Text revised by Bishop WESTCOTT, D.D., and Prof. F. J. A. HORT, D.D. 2 vols. Cr. 8vo. 10s. 6d. each.—Vol. I. Text.—Vol. II. Introduction and Appendix.

SCHOOL EDITION OF THE ABOVE. 18mo. 4s. 6d.; 18mo, roan, 5s. 6d.; morocco, gilt edges, 6s. 6d.

The Gospels—

THE COMMON TRADITION OF THE SYNOPTIC GOSPELS. In the Text of the Revised Version. By Rev. E. A. ABBOTT and W. G. RUSHBROOKE. Cr. 8vo. 3s. 6d.

SYNOPTICON: An Exposition of the Common Matter of the Synoptic Gospels. By W. G. RUSHBROOKE. Printed in Colours. In Six Parts, and Appendix. 4to.—Part I. 3s. 6d. —Parts II. and III. 7s.—Parts IV. V. and VI., with Indices, 10s. 6d.—Appendices, 10s. 6d.—Complete in 1 vol. 35s.

INTRODUCTION TO THE STUDY OF THE FOUR GOSPELS. By Bp. WESTCOTT. Cr. 8vo. 10s. 6d.

THE COMPOSITION OF THE FOUR GOSPELS. By Rev. ARTHUR WRIGHT. Cr. 8vo. 5s.

Gospel of St. Matthew—

THE GREEK TEXT, with Introduction and Notes by Rev. A. SLOMAN. Fcp. 8vo. 2s. 6d.

CHOICE NOTES ON ST. MATTHEW. Drawn from Old and New Sources. Cr. 8vo. 4s. 6d. (St. Matthew and St. Mark in 1 vol. 9s.)

Gospel of St. Mark—

SCHOOL READINGS IN THE GREEK TESTAMENT. Being the Outlines of the Life of our Lord as given by St. Mark, with additions from the Text of the other Evangelists. Edited, with Notes and Vocabulary, by Rev. A. CALVERT, M.A. Fcp. 8vo. 2s. 6d.

CHOICE NOTES ON ST. MARK. Drawn from Old and New Sources. Cr. 8vo. 4s. 6d. (St. Matthew and St. Mark in 1 vol. 9s.)

Gospel of St. Luke—

GREEK TEXT, with Introduction and Notes by Rev. J. BOND, M.A. Fcp. 8vo. 2s. 6d.

CHOICE NOTES ON ST. LUKE. Drawn from Old and New Sources. Cr. 8vo. 4s. 6d.

THE GOSPEL OF THE KINGDOM OF HEAVEN. A Course of Lectures on the Gospel of St. Luke. By F. D. MAURICE. Cr. 8vo. 6s.

Gospel of St. John—

THE GOSPEL OF ST. JOHN. By F. D. MAURICE. 8th Ed. Cr. 8vo. 6s.

CHOICE NOTES ON ST. JOHN. Drawn from Old and New Sources. Cr. 8vo. 4s. 6d.

The Acts of the Apostles—

GREEK TEXT, with Notes by T. E. PAGE, M.A. Fcp. 8vo. 3s. 6d.

THE CHURCH OF THE FIRST DAYS: THE CHURCH OF JERUSALEM, THE CHURCH OF THE GENTILES, THE CHURCH OF THE WORLD. Lectures on the Acts of the Apostles. By Very Rev. C. J VAUGHAN. Cr. 8vo. 10s. 6d.

The Epistles of St. Paul—

THE EPISTLE TO THE ROMANS. The Greek Text, with English Notes. By the Very Rev. C. J. VAUGHAN. 7th Edit. Cr. 8vo. 7s. 6d.

THE EPISTLES TO THE CORINTHIANS. Greek Text, with Commentary. By Rev. W. KAY. 9s.

The EPISTLE TO THE GALATIANS. A Revised Text, with Introduction, Notes, and Dissertations. By Bishop LIGHTFOOT. 10th Edit. 8vo. 12s.

THE EPISTLE TO THE PHILIPPIANS. A Revised Text, with Introduction, Notes, and Dissertations. By the same. 8vo. 12s.

THE EPISTLE TO THE PHILIPPIANS. With Translation, Paraphrase, and Notes for English Readers. By the Very Rev. C. J. VAUGHAN. Cr. 8vo. 5s.

THE EPISTLES TO THE COLOSSIANS AND TO PHILEMON. A Revised Text, with Introductions, etc. By Bishop LIGHTFOOT. 9th Edit. 8vo. 12s.

THE EPISTLES TO THE EPHESIANS, THE COLOSSIANS, AND PHILEMON. With Introduction and Notes. By Rev. J. Ll. DAVIES. 2nd Edit. 8vo. 7s. 6d.

THE FIRST EPISTLE TO THE THESSALONIANS. By Very Rev. C. J. VAUGHAN. 8vo, sewed. 1s. 6d.

THE EPISTLES TO THE THESSALONIANS. Commentary on the Greek Text. By Prof. JOHN EADIE. 8vo. 12s.

THEOLOGY.

The Bible—*continued.*

The Epistle of St. James—
THE GREEK TEXT, with Introduction and Notes. By Rev. JOSEPH MAYOR. 8vo. 14s.

The Epistles of St. John—
THE EPISTLES OF ST. JOHN. By F. D. MAURICE. 4th Edit. Cr. 8vo. 6s.
— The Greek Text, with Notes, by Bishop WESTCOTT. 3rd Edit. 8vo. 12s. 6d.

The Epistle to the Hebrews.—
GREEK AND ENGLISH. Edited by Rev. FREDERIC RENDALL. Cr. 8vo. 6s.
ENGLISH TEXT, with Commentary. By the same. Cr. 8vo. 7s. 6d.
THE GREEK TEXT, with Notes, by Very Rev. C. J. VAUGHAN. Cr. 8vo. 7s. 6d.
THE GREEK TEXT, with Notes and Essays, by Bishop WESTCOTT. 8vo. 14s.

Revelation—
LECTURES ON THE APOCALYPSE. By F. D. MAURICE. 2nd Edit. Cr. 8vo. 6s.
THE REVELATION OF ST. JOHN. By Rev. Prof. W. MILLIGAN. Cr. 8vo. 7s. 6d.
LECTURES ON THE APOCALYPSE. By the same. Crown 8vo. 5s.
LECTURES ON THE REVELATION OF ST. JOHN. By Very Rev. C. J. VAUGHAN. 5th Edit. Cr. 8vo. 10s. 6d.

THE BIBLE WORD-BOOK. By W. ALDIS WRIGHT. 2nd Edit. Cr. 8vo. 7s. 6d.

History of the Christian Church.

CHURCH (Dean).—THE OXFORD MOVEMENT, 1833—45. Gl. 8vo. 5s.

CUNNINGHAM (Rev. John).—THE GROWTH OF THE CHURCH IN ITS ORGANISATION AND INSTITUTIONS. 8vo. 9s.

CUNNINGHAM (Rev. William). — THE CHURCHES OF ASIA: A Methodical Sketch of the Second Century. Cr. 8vo. 6s.

DALE (A. W. W.).—THE SYNOD OF ELVIRA, AND CHRISTIAN LIFE IN THE FOURTH CENTURY. Cr. 8vo. 10s. 6d.

HARDWICK (Archdeacon).—A HISTORY OF THE CHRISTIAN CHURCH: MIDDLE AGE Edited by Bp. STUBBS. Cr. 8vo. 10s. 6d.

—— A HISTORY OF THE CHRISTIAN CHURCH DURING THE REFORMATION. 9th Edit., revised by Bishop STUBBS. Cr. 8vo. 10s. 6d.

HORT (Dr. F. J. A.).—TWO DISSERTATIONS. I. ON ΜΟΝΟΓΕΝΗΣ ΘΕΟΣ IN SCRIPTURE AND TRADITION. II. ON THE "CONSTANTINOPOLITAN" Creed and other EASTERN CREEDS OF THE FOURTH CENTURY. 8vo. 7s. 6d

KILLEN (W. D.).—ECCLESIASTICAL HISTORY OF IRELAND, FROM THE EARLIEST DATE TO THE PRESENT TIME. 2 vols. 8vo. 25s.

SIMPSON (Rev. W.).—AN EPITOME OF THE HISTORY OF THE CHRISTIAN CHURCH. 7th Edit. Fcp. 8vo. 3s. 6d.

VAUGHAN (Very Rev. C. J.).—THE CHURCH OF THE FIRST DAYS: THE CHURCH OF JERUSALEM, THE CHURCH OF THE GENTILES, THE CHURCH OF THE WORLD. Cr. 8vo. 10s. 6d.

WARD (W.).—WILLIAM GEORGE WARD AND THE OXFORD MOVEMENT. 8vo. 14s.

The Church of England.

Catechism of—
A CLASS-BOOK OF THE CATECHISM OF THE CHURCH OF ENGLAND. By Rev. Canon MACLEAR. 18mo. 1s. 6d.
A FIRST CLASS-BOOK OF THE CATECHISM OF THE CHURCH OF ENGLAND. By the same. 18mo. 6d.
THE ORDER OF CONFIRMATION. With Prayers and Devotions. By the same. 32mo. 6d.

Collects—
COLLECTS OF THE CHURCH OF ENGLAND. With a Coloured Floral Design to each Collect. Cr. 8vo. 12s.

Disestablishment—
DISESTABLISHMENT AND DISENDOWMENT. WHAT ARE THEY? By Prof. E. A. FREEMAN. 4th Edit. Cr. 8vo. 1s.
DISESTABLISHMENT; or, A Defence of the Principle of a National Church. By GEO. HARWOOD. 8vo. 12s.
A DEFENCE OF THE CHURCH OF ENGLAND AGAINST DISESTABLISHMENT. By ROUNDELL, EARL OF SELBORNE. Cr. 8vo. 2s. 6d.
ANCIENT FACTS AND FICTIONS CONCERNING CHURCHES AND TITHES. By the same. 2nd Edit. Cr. 8vo. 7s. 6d.

Dissent in its Relation to—
DISSENT IN ITS RELATION TO THE CHURCH OF ENGLAND. By Rev. G. H. CURTEIS. Bampton Lectures for 1871. Cr. 8vo. 7s. 6d.

Holy Communion—
THE COMMUNION SERVICE FROM THE BOOK OF COMMON PRAYER. With Select Readings from the Writings of the Rev. F. D. MAURICE. Edited by Bishop COLENSO. 6th Edit. 16mo. 2s. 6d.
BEFORE THE TABLE: An Inquiry, Historical and Theological, into the Meaning of the Consecration Rubric in the Communion Service of the Church of England. By Very Rev. J. S. HOWSON. 8vo. 7s. 6d.
FIRST COMMUNION. With Prayers and Devotions for the newly Confirmed. By Rev. Canon MACLEAR. 32mo. 6d.
A MANUAL OF INSTRUCTION FOR CONFIRMATION AND FIRST COMMUNION. With Prayers and Devotions. By the same. 32mo. 2s.

Liturgy—
AN INTRODUCTION TO THE CREEDS. By Rev. Canon MACLEAR. 18mo. 3s. 6d.
AN INTRODUCTION TO THE THIRTY-NINE ARTICLES. By same. 18mo. [*In the Press.*]
A HISTORY OF THE BOOK OF COMMON PRAYER. By Rev. F. PROCTER. 18th Edit. Cr. 8vo. 10s. 6d.
AN ELEMENTARY INTRODUCTION TO THE BOOK OF COMMON PRAYER. By Rev. F. PROCTER and Rev. Canon MACLEAR. 18mo. 2s. 6d.

Liturgy—

TWELVE DISCOURSES ON SUBJECTS CONNECTED WITH THE LITURGY AND WORSHIP OF THE CHURCH OF ENGLAND. By Very Rev. C. J. VAUGHAN. Fcp. 8vo. 6s.

A COMPANION TO THE LECTIONARY. By Rev. W BENHAM, B.D. Cr. 8vo. 4s. 6d.

JUDGMENT IN THE CASE OF READ AND OTHERS v. THE LORD BISHOP OF LINCOLN. Nov. 21, 1890. By his Grace the ARCHBISHOP OF CANTERBURY. 8vo. 1s. 6d. net.

Devotional Books.

EASTLAKE (Lady).—FELLOWSHIP: LETTERS ADDRESSED TO MY SISTER-MOURNERS. Cr. 8vo. 2s. 6d.

IMITATIO CHRISTI. Libri IV. Printed in Borders after Holbein, Dürer, and other old Masters, containing Dances of Death, Acts of Mercy, Emblems, etc. Cr.8vo. 7s.6d.

KINGSLEY (Charles).—OUT OF THE DEEP: WORDS FOR THE SORROWFUL. From the Writings of CHARLES KINGSLEY. Ext. fcp. 8vo. 3s. 6d.

—— DAILY THOUGHTS. Selected from the Writings of CHARLES KINGSLEY. By HIS WIFE. Cr. 8vo. 6s.

—— FROM DEATH TO LIFE. Fragments of Teaching to a Village Congregation. Edit. by HIS WIFE. Fcp. 8vo. 2s. 6d.

MACLEAR (Rev. Canon).—A MANUAL OF INSTRUCTION FOR CONFIRMATION AND FIRST COMMUNION, WITH PRAYERS AND DEVOTIONS. 32mo. 2s.

—— THE HOUR OF SORROW; or, The Office for the Burial of the Dead. 32mo. 2s.

MAURICE (F. D.).—LESSONS OF HOPE. Readings from the Works of F. D. MAURICE. Selected by Rev. J. LL. DAVIES, M.A. Cr. 8vo. 5s.

RAYS OF SUNLIGHT FOR DARK DAYS. With a Preface by Very Rev. C. J. VAUGHAN D.D. New Edition. 18mo. 3s. 6d.

SERVICE (Rev. J.).—PRAYERS FOR PUBLIC WORSHIP. Cr. 8vo. 4s. 6d.

THE WORSHIP OF GOD, AND FELLOWSHIP AMONG MEN. By Prof. MAURICE and others. Fcp. 8vo. 3s. 6d.

WELBY-GREGORY (Hon. Lady).—LINKS AND CLUES. 2nd Edit. Cr. 8vo. 6s.

WESTCOTT (Rt. Rev. Bishop).—THOUGHTS ON REVELATION AND LIFE. Selections from the Writings of Bishop WESTCOTT. Edited by Rev S. PHILLIPS. Cr. 8vo. 6s.

WILBRAHAM (Francis M.).—IN THE SERE AND YELLOW LEAF: THOUGHTS AND RECOLLECTIONS FOR OLD AND YOUNG. Globe 8vo. 3s. 6d.

The Fathers.

DONALDSON (Prof. James).—THE APOSTOLIC FATHERS. A Critical Account of their Genuine Writings, and of their Doctrines. 2nd Edit. Cr. 8vo. 7s. 6d.

Works of the Greek and Latin Fathers:

THE APOSTOLIC FATHERS. Revised Texts, with Introductions, Notes, Dissertations, and Translations. By Bishop LIGHTFOOT.—Part I. ST. CLEMENT OF ROME. 2 vols. 8vo. 32s.—Part II. ST. IGNATIUS TO ST POLYCARP. 3 vols. 2nd Edit. 8vo. 48s.

THE APOSTOLIC FATHERS. Abridged Edit. With Short Introductions, Greek Text, and English Translation. By same. 8vo. 16s.

THE EPISTLE OF ST. BARNABAS. Its Date and Authorship. With Greek Text, Latin Version, Translation and Commentary. By Rev. W. CUNNINGHAM. Cr 8vo. 7s. 6d.

Hymnology.

BROOKE (S. A.).—CHRISTIAN HYMNS. Gl. 8vo. 2s.6d. net.--CHRISTIAN HYMNS AND SERVICE BOOK OF BEDFORD CHAPEL, BLOOMSBURY. Gl. 8vo. 3s. 6d. net.—SERVICE BOOK. Gl. 8vo. 1s. net.

PALGRAVE (Prof. F. T.). — ORIGINAL HYMNS. 3rd Edit. 18mo. 1s. 6d.

SELBORNE (Roundell, Earl of).—THE BOOK OF PRAISE. 18mo. 2s. 6d. net.

—— A HYMNAL. Chiefly from "The Book of Praise."—A. Royal 32mo, limp. 6d.—B. 18mo, larger type. 1s.—C. Fine paper. 1s.6d. —With Music, Selected, Harmonised, and Composed by JOHN HULLAH. 18mo. 3s.6d.

WOODS (Miss M. A.).—HYMNS FOR SCHOOL WORSHIP. 18mo. 1s. 6d.

Sermons, Lectures, Addresses, and Theological Essays.

ABBOT (F. E.).—SCIENTIFIC THEISM. Cr. 8vo. 7s.6d.

—— THE WAY OUT OF AGNOSTICISM ; or, The Philosophy of Free Religion. Cr. 8vo. 4s. 6d.

ABBOTT (Rev. E. A.).—CAMBRIDGE SERMONS. 8vo. 6s.

—— OXFORD SERMONS. 8vo. 7s. 6d.

—— PHILOMYTHUS. A discussion of Cardinal Newman's Essay on Ecclesiastical Miracles. Cr. 8vo. 3s. 6d.

—— NEWMANIANISM. Cr. 8vo. 1s. net.

AINGER (Canon).—SERMONS PREACHED IN THE TEMPLE CHURCH. Ext. fcp. 8vo. 6s.

ALEXANDER (W., Bishop of Derry and Raphoe).—THE LEADING IDEAS OF THE GOSPELS. New Edit. Cr. 8vo. 6s.

BAINES (Rev. Edward).—SERMONS. Preface and Memoir by Bishop BARRY. Cr. 8vo. 6s.

BATHER (Archdeacon).—ON SOME MINISTERIAL DUTIES, CATECHISING, PREACHING, Etc. Edited, with a Preface, by Very Rev. C. J. VAUGHAN, D.D. Fcp. 8vo. 4s. 6d.

BERNARD (Canon). —THE CENTRAL TEACHING OF CHRIST. Cr. 8vo. 7s. 6d.

BETHUNE-BAKER (J. F.).—THE INFLUENCE OF CHRISTIANITY ON WAR. 8vo. 5s.

—— THE STERNNESS OF CHRIST'S TEACHING, AND ITS RELATION TO THE LAW OF FORGIVENESS. Cr. 8vo. 2s. 6d.

BINNIE (Rev. W.).—SERMONS. Cr. 8vo. 6s.

THEOLOGY.

Sermons, Lectures, Addresses, and Theological Essays—*continued*.

BIRKS (Thomas Rawson).—THE DIFFICULTIES OF BELIEF IN CONNECTION WITH THE CREATION AND THE FALL, REDEMPTION, AND JUDGMENT. 2nd Edit. Cr. 8vo. 5s.
—— JUSTIFICATION AND IMPUTED RIGHTEOUSNESS. A Review. Cr. 8vo. 6s.
—— SUPERNATURAL REVELATION; or, First Principles of Moral Theology. 8vo. 8s.

BROOKE (S. A.).—SHORT SERMONS. Crown 8vo. 6s.

BROOKS (Bishop Phillips).—THE CANDLE OF THE LORD: and other Sermons. Cr. 8vo. 6s.
—— SERMONS PREACHED IN ENGLISH CHURCHES. Cr. 8vo. 6s.
—— TWENTY SERMONS. Cr. 8vo. 6s.
—— TOLERANCE. Cr. 8vo. 2s. 6d.
—— THE LIGHT OF THE WORLD. Cr.8vo. 3s.6d.

BRUNTON (T. Lauder).—THE BIBLE AND SCIENCE. Illustrated. Cr. 8vo. 10s. 6d.

BUTLER (Archer).—SERMONS, DOCTRINAL AND PRACTICAL. 11th Edit. 8vo. 8s.
—— SECOND SERIES OF SERMONS. 8vo. 7s.
—— LETTERS ON ROMANISM. 8vo. 10s. 6d.

BUTLER (Rev. Geo.).—SERMONS PREACHED IN CHELTENHAM COLL. CHAPEL. 8vo. 7s. 6d.

CAMPBELL (Dr. John M'Leod).—THE NATURE OF THE ATONEMENT. Cr. 8vo. 6s.
—— REMINISCENCES AND REFLECTIONS. Edited by his Son, DONALD CAMPBELL, M.A. Cr. 8vo. 7s. 6d.
—— THOUGHTS ON REVELATION. Cr. 8vo. 5s.
—— RESPONSIBILITY FOR THE GIFT OF ETERNAL LIFE. Compiled from Sermons preached 1829—31. Cr. 8vo. 5s.

CANTERBURY (Edward White, Archbishop of).—BOY-LIFE: ITS TRIAL, ITS STRENGTH, ITS FULNESS. Sundays in Wellington College, 1859—73. Cr. 8vo. 6s.
—— THE SEVEN GIFTS. Primary Visitation Address. Cr. 8vo. 6s.
—— CHRIST AND HIS TIMES. Second Visitation Address. Cr. 8vo. 6s.
—— A PASTORAL LETTER TO THE DIOCESE OF CANTERBURY, 1890. 8vo, sewed. 1d.

CARPENTER (W. Boyd, Bishop of Ripon).—TRUTH IN TALE. Addresses, chiefly to Children. Cr. 8vo. 4s. 6d.
—— THE PERMANENT ELEMENTS OF RELIGION. 2nd Edit. Cr. 8vo. 6s.

CAZENOVE (J. Gibson).—CONCERNING THE BEING AND ATTRIBUTES OF GOD. 8vo. 5s.

CHURCH (Dean).—HUMAN LIFE AND ITS CONDITIONS. Cr. 8vo. 6s.
—— THE GIFTS OF CIVILISATION: and other Sermons and Letters. Cr. 8vo. 7s. 6d.
—— DISCIPLINE OF THE CHRISTIAN CHARACTER; and other Sermons. Cr. 8vo. 4s. 6d.
—— ADVENT SERMONS, 1885. Cr. 8vo. 4s. 6d.
—— VILLAGE SERMONS. Cr. 8vo. 6s.
—— CATHEDRAL AND UNIVERSITY SERMONS. Cr. 8vo. 6s.

CLERGYMAN'S SELF-EXAMINATION CONCERNING THE APOSTLES' CREED. Ext. fcp. 8vo. 1s. 6d.

CONGREVE (Rev. John).—HIGH HOPES AND PLEADINGS FOR A REASONABLE FAITH, NOBLER THOUGHTS, AND LARGER CHARITY. Cr. 8vo. 5s.

COOKE (Josiah P., jun.).—RELIGION AND CHEMISTRY. Cr. 8vo. 7s. 6d.

COTTON (Bishop).—SERMONS PREACHED TO ENGLISH CONGREGATIONS IN INDIA. Cr. 8vo. 7s. 6d.

CUNNINGHAM (Rev. W.).—CHRISTIAN CIVILISATION, WITH SPECIAL REFERENCE TO INDIA. Cr. 8vo. 5s.

CURTEIS (Rev. G. H.).—THE SCIENTIFIC OBSTACLES TO CHRISTIAN BELIEF. The Boyle Lectures, 1884. Cr. 8vo. 6s.

DAVIES (Rev. J. Llewelyn).—THE GOSPEL AND MODERN LIFE. Ext. fcp. 8vo. 6s.
—— SOCIAL QUESTIONS FROM THE POINT OF VIEW OF CHRISTIAN THEOLOGY. Cr.8vo. 6s.
—— WARNINGS AGAINST SUPERSTITION. Ext. fcp. 8vo. 2s. 6d.
—— THE CHRISTIAN CALLING. Ext.fp.8vo. 6s.
—— ORDER AND GROWTH AS INVOLVED IN THE SPIRITUAL CONSTITUTION OF HUMAN SOCIETY. Cr. 8vo. 3s. 6d.
—— BAPTISM, CONFIRMATION, AND THE LORD'S SUPPER. Addresses. 18mo. 1s.

DIGGLE (Rev. J. W.).—GODLINESS AND MANLINESS. Cr. 8vo. 6s.

DRUMMOND (Prof. Jas.).—INTRODUCTION TO THE STUDY OF THEOLOGY. Cr. 8vo. 5s.

DU BOSE (W. P.).—THE SOTERIOLOGY OF THE NEW TESTAMENT. By W. P. DU BOSE. Cr. 8vo. 7s. 6d.

ECCE HOMO: A SURVEY OF THE LIFE AND WORK OF JESUS CHRIST. Globe 8vo. 6s.

ELLERTON (Rev. John).—THE HOLIEST MANHOOD, AND ITS LESSONS FOR BUSY LIVES. Cr. 8vo. 6s.

FAITH AND CONDUCT: AN ESSAY ON VERIFIABLE RELIGION. Cr. 8vo. 7s. 6d.

FARRAR (Ven. Archdeacon).—WORKS. *Uniform Edition.* Cr. 8vo. 3s. 6d. each. Monthly from December, 1891.
SEEKERS AFTER GOD.
ETERNAL HOPE. Westminster Abbey Sermons.
THE FALL OF MAN: and other Sermons.
THE WITNESS OF HISTORY TO CHRIST. Hulsean Lectures, 1870.
THE SILENCE AND VOICES OF GOD. Sermons.
IN THE DAYS OF THY YOUTH. Marlborough College Sermons.
SAINTLY WORKERS. Five Lenten Lectures.
EPHPHATHA; or, The Amelioration of the Mercy and Judgment. [World.
SERMONS AND ADDRESSES DELIVERED IN AMERICA.
—— THE HISTORY OF INTERPRETATION. Bampton Lectures, 1885. 8vo. 16s.

FISKE (John).—MAN'S DESTINY VIEWED IN THE LIGHT OF HIS ORIGIN. Cr. 8vo. 3s. 6d.

FORBES (Rev. Granville).—THE VOICE OF GOD IN THE PSALMS. Cr. 8vo. 6s. 6d.

FOWLE (Rev. T. W.).—A NEW ANALOGY BETWEEN REVEALED RELIGION AND THE COURSE AND CONSTITUTION OF NATURE. Cr. 8vo. 6s.

FRASER (Bishop).—SERMONS. Edited by JOHN W. DIGGLE. 2 vols. Cr. 8vo. 6s. each.

HAMILTON (John).—ON TRUTH AND ERROR. Cr. 8vo. 5s.
—— ARTHUR'S SEAT; or, The Church of the Banned. Cr. 8vo. 6s.
—— ABOVE AND AROUND: Thoughts on God and Man. 12mo. 2s. 6d.

HARDWICK (Archdeacon).—CHRIST AND OTHER MASTERS. 6th Edit. Cr. 8vo. 10s. 6d.

HARE (Julius Charles).—THE MISSION OF THE COMFORTER. New Edition. Edited by Dean PLUMPTRE. Cr. 8vo. 7s. 6d.
—— THE VICTORY OF FAITH. Edited by Dean PLUMPTRE. With Notices by Prof. MAURICE and Dean STANLEY. Cr. 8vo. 6s. 6d.

HARPER (Father Thomas).—THE META-PHYSICS OF THE SCHOOL. Vols I. and II. 8vo. 18s. each.—Vol. III. Part I. 12s.

HARRIS (Rev. G. C.).—SERMONS. With a Memoir by C. M. YONGE. Ext. fcp. 8vo. 6s.

HUTTON (R. H.). (See p. 22.)

ILLINGWORTH (Rev. J. R.).—SERMONS PREACHED IN A COLLEGE CHAPEL. Cr. 8vo. 5s.

JACOB (Rev. J. A.).—BUILDING IN SILENCE: and other Sermons. Ext. fcp. 8vo. 6s.

JAMES (Rev. Herbert). — THE COUNTRY CLERGYMAN AND HIS WORK. Cr. 8vo. 6s.

JEANS (Rev. G. E.).—HAILEYBURY CHAPEL: and other Sermons. Fcp. 8vo. 3s. 6d.

JELLETT (Rev. Dr.).—THE ELDER SON: and other Sermons. Cr. 8vo. 6s.
—— THE EFFICACY OF PRAYER. Cr. 8vo. 5s.

KELLOGG (Rev. S. H.).—THE LIGHT OF ASIA AND THE LIGHT OF THE WORLD. Cr. 8vo. 7s. 6d.
—— GENESIS AND GROWTH OF RELIGION. Cr. 8vo. 6s.

KINGSLEY (Charles). (See COLLECTED WORKS, p. 22.)

KIRKPATRICK (Prof.).—THE DIVINE LI-BRARY OF THE OLD TESTAMENT. Cr. 8vo. 3s. net.
—— DOCTRINE OF THE PROPHETS. Cr. 8vo. 6s.

KYNASTON (Rev. Herbert, D.D.).—CHEL-TENHAM COLLEGE SERMONS. Cr. 8vo. 6s.

LEGGE (A. O.).—THE GROWTH OF THE TEM-PORAL POWER OF THE PAPACY. Cr. 8vo. 8s. 6d.

LIGHTFOOT (Bishop).—LEADERS IN THE NORTHERN CHURCH: Sermons. Cr. 8vo. 6s.
—— ORDINATION ADDRESSES AND COUNSELS TO CLERGY. Cr. 8vo. 6s.
—— CAMBRIDGE SERMONS. Cr. 8vo. 6s.
—— SERMONS PREACHED IN ST. PAUL'S CATHEDRAL. Cr. 8vo. 6s.
—— SERMONS ON SPECIAL OCCASIONS. 8vo. 6s.
—— A CHARGE DELIVERED TO THE CLERGY OF THE DIOCESE OF DURHAM, 1886. 8vo. 2s.
—— ESSAYS ON THE WORK ENTITLED "SU-PERNATURAL RELIGION." 8vo. 10s. 6d.
—— ON A FRESH REVISION OF THE ENGLISH NEW TESTAMENT. Cr. 8vo. 7s. 6d.
—— DISSERTATIONS ON THE APOSTOLIC AGE. 8vo. 14s.

MACLAREN (Rev. A.).—SERMONS PREACHED AT MANCHESTER. 11th Ed. Fcp. 8vo. 4s. 6d.
—— SECOND SERIES. 7th Ed. Fcp. 8vo. 4s. 6d.
—— THIRD SERIES. 6th Ed. Fcp. 8vo. 4s. 6d.
—— WEEK-DAY EVENING ADDRESSES. 4th Edit. Fcp. 8vo. 2s. 6d.
—— THE SECRET OF POWER: and other Ser-mons. Fcp. 8vo. 4s. 6d.

MACMILLAN (Rev. Hugh).—BIBLE TEACH-INGS IN NATURE. 15th Edit. Globe 8vo. 6s.
—— THE TRUE VINE; or, The Analogies of our Lord's Allegory. 5th Edit. Gl. 8vo. 6s.
—— THE MINISTRY OF NATURE. 8th Edit. Globe 8vo. 6s.
—— THE SABBATH OF THE FIELDS. 6th Edit. Globe 8vo. 6s.
—— THE MARRIAGE IN CANA. Globe 8vo. 6s.
—— TWO WORLDS ARE OURS. Gl. 8vo. 6s.
—— THE OLIVE LEAF. Globe 8vo. 6s.
—— THE GATE BEAUTIFUL: and other Bible Teachings for the Young. Cr. 8vo. 3s. 6d.

MAHAFFY (Prof. J. P.).—THE DECAY OF MODERN PREACHING. Cr. 8vo. 3s. 6d.

MATURIN (Rev. W.).—THE BLESSEDNESS OF THE DEAD IN CHRIST. Cr. 8vo. 7s. 6d.

MAURICE (Frederick Denison).—THE KING-DOM OF CHRIST. 3rd Ed. 2 vols. Cr. 8vo. 12s.
—— EXPOSITORY SERMONS ON THE PRAYER-BOOK, AND THE LORD'S PRAYER. Cr. 8vo. 6s.
—— SERMONS PREACHED IN COUNTRY CHURCHES. 2nd Edit. Cr. 8vo. 6s.
—— THE CONSCIENCE: Lectures on Casuistry. 3rd Edit. Cr. 8vo. 4s. 6d.
—— DIALOGUES ON FAMILY WORSHIP. Cr. 8vo. 4s. 6d.
—— THE DOCTRINE OF SACRIFICE DEDUCED FROM THE SCRIPTURES. 2nd Edit. Cr. 8vo. 6s.
—— THE RELIGIONS OF THE WORLD. 6th Edit. Cr. 8vo. 4s. 6d.
—— ON THE SABBATH DAY; THE CHARACTER OF THE WARRIOR; AND ON THE INTERPRE-TATION OF HISTORY. Fcp. 8vo. 2s. 6d.
—— LEARNING AND WORKING. Cr. 8vo. 4s. 6d.
—— THE LORD'S PRAYER, THE CREED, AND THE COMMANDMENTS. 18mo. 1s.
—— SERMONS PREACHED IN LINCOLN'S INN CHAPEL. 6 vols. Cr. 8vo. 3s. 6d. each.
—— COLLECTED WORKS. Monthly Volumes from Oct. 1892. Cr. 8vo. 3s. 6d. each.
CHRISTMAS DAY AND OTHER SERMONS.
THEOLOGICAL ESSAYS.
PROPHETS AND KINGS.
PATRIARCHS AND LAWGIVERS.
THE GOSPEL OF THE KINGDOM OF HEAVEN.
GOSPEL OF ST. JOHN.
EPISTLE OF ST. JOHN
LECTURES ON THE APOCALYPSE.
FRIENDSHIP OF BOOKS.
SOCIAL MORALITY.
PRAYER BOOK AND LORD'S PRAYER.
THE DOCTRINE OF SACRIFICE.

MILLIGAN (Rev. Prof. W.).—THE RESUR-RECTION OF OUR LORD. 2nd Edit. Cr. 8vo. 5s.
—— THE ASCENSION AND HEAVENLY PRIEST-HOOD OF OUR LORD. Cr. 8vo. 7s. 6d.

MOORHOUSE (J., Bishop of Manchester).—JACOB: Three Sermons. Ext. fcp. 8vo. 3s. 6d.
—— THE TEACHING OF CHRIST: its Condi-tions, Secret, and Results. Cr. 8vo. 3s. net.

MYLNE (L. G., Bishop of Bombay).—SERMONS PREACHED IN ST. THOMAS'S CATHEDRAL, BOMBAY. Cr. 8vo. 6s.

THEOLOGY.
Sermons, Lectures, Addresses, and Theological Essays—continued.

NATURAL RELIGION. By the Author of "Ecce Homo." 3rd Edit. Globe 8vo. 6s.

PATTISON (Mark).—SERMONS. Cr. 8vo. 6s.

PAUL OF TARSUS. 8vo. 10s. 6d.

PHILOCHRISTUS: MEMOIRS OF A DISCIPLE OF THE LORD. 3rd. Edit. 8vo. 12s.

PLUMPTRE (Dean).—MOVEMENTS IN RELIGIOUS THOUGHT. Fcp. 8vo. 3s. 6d.

POTTER (R.).—THE RELATION OF ETHICS TO RELIGION. Cr. 8vo. 2s. 6d.

REASONABLE FAITH: A SHORT ESSAY By "Three Friends." Cr. 8vo. 1s.

REICHEL (C. P., Bishop of Meath).—THE LORD'S PRAYER. Cr. 8vo. 7s. 6d.
—— CATHEDRAL AND UNIVERSITY SERMONS. Cr. 8vo. 6s.

RENDALL (Rev. F.).—THE THEOLOGY OF THE HEBREW CHRISTIANS. Cr. 8vo. 5s.

REYNOLDS (H. R.).—NOTES OF THE CHRISTIAN LIFE. Cr. 8vo. 7s. 6d.

ROBINSON (Prebendary H. G.).—MAN IN THE IMAGE OF GOD: and other Sermons. Cr. 8vo. 7s. 6d.

RUSSELL (Dean).—THE LIGHT THAT LIGHTETH EVERY MAN: Sermons. With an Introduction by Dean PLUMPTRE, D.D. Cr. 8vo. 6s.

RYLE (Rev. Prof. H.)—THE EARLY NARRATIVES OF GENESIS. Cr. 8vo. 3s. net.

SALMON (Rev. George, D.D.).—NON-MIRACULOUS CHRISTIANITY: and other Sermons. 2nd Edit. Cr. 8vo. 6s.
—— GNOSTICISM AND AGNOSTICISM: and other Sermons. Cr. 8vo. 7s. 6d.

SANDFORD (Rt. Rev. C. W., Bishop of Gibraltar).—COUNSEL TO ENGLISH CHURCHMEN ABROAD. Cr. 8vo. 6s.

SCOTCH SERMONS, 1880. By Principal CAIRD and others. 3rd Edit. 8vo. 10s. 6d

SERVICE (Rev. J.).—SERMONS. Cr. 8vo. 6s

SHIRLEY (W. N.).—ELIJAH: Four University Sermons. Fcp. 8vo. 2s. 6d.

SMITH (Rev. Travers).—MAN'S KNOWLEDGE OF MAN AND OF GOD. Cr. 8vo. 6s.

SMITH (W. Saumarez).—THE BLOOD OF THE NEW COVENANT: An Essay. Cr. 8vo. 2s. 6d

STANLEY (Dean).—THE NATIONAL THANKSGIVING. Sermons Preached in Westminster Abbey. 2nd Edit. Cr. 8vo. 2s. 6d.
—— ADDRESSES AND SERMONS delivered in America, 1878. Cr. 8vo. 6s.

STEWART (Prof. Balfour) and TAIT (Prof. P. G.).—THE UNSEEN UNIVERSE, OR PHYSICAL SPECULATIONS ON A FUTURE STATE. 15th Edit. Cr. 8vo. 6s.
—— PARADOXICAL PHILOSOPHY. A Sequel to the above. Cr. 8vo. 7s. 6d.

STUBBS (Rev. C. W.).—FOR CHRIST AND CITY. Sermons and Addresses. Cr. 8vo. 6s.

TAIT (Archbp.).—THE PRESENT CONDITION OF THE CHURCH OF ENGLAND. Primary Visitation Charge. 3rd Edit. 8vo. 3s. 6d
—— DUTIES OF THE CHURCH OF ENGLAND. Second Visitation Addresses. 8vo. 4s. 6d
—— THE CHURCH OF THE FUTURE. Quadrennial Visitation Charges. Cr. 8vo. 3s. 6d.

TAYLOR (Isaac).—THE RESTORATION OF BELIEF. Cr. 8vo. 8s. 6d.

TEMPLE (Frederick, Bishop of London)—SERMONS PREACHED IN THE CHAPEL OF RUGBY SCHOOL. SECOND SERIES. Ext. fcp. 8vo. 6s.
—— THIRD SERIES. 4th Edit. Ext. fcp. 8vo. 6s.
—— THE RELATIONS BETWEEN RELIGION AND SCIENCE. Bampton Lectures, 1884. 7th and Cheaper Edition. Cr. 8vo. 6s.

TRENCH (Archbishop). — THE HULSEAN LECTURES FOR 1845—6. 8vo. 7s. 6d.

TULLOCH (Principal).—THE CHRIST OF THE GOSPELS AND THE CHRIST OF MODERN CRITICISM. Ext. fcp. 8vo. 4s. 6d.

VAUGHAN (C. J., Dean of Landaff).—MEMORIALS OF HARROW SUNDAYS. 8vo. 10s. 6d.
—— EPIPHANY, LENT, AND EASTER. 8vo. 10s. 6d.
—— HEROES OF FAITH. 2nd Edit. Cr. 8vo. 6s
—— LIFE'S WORK AND GOD'S DISCIPLINE. Ext. fcp. 8vo. 2s. 6d.
—— THE WHOLESOME WORDS OF JESUS CHRIST. 2nd Edit. Fcp. 8vo. 3s. 6d.
—— FOES OF FAITH. 2nd Edit. Fcp. 8vo. 3s. 6d.
—— CHRIST SATISFYING THE INSTINCTS OF HUMANITY. 2nd Edit. Ext. fcp. 8vo. 3s. 6d.
—— COUNSELS FOR YOUNG STUDENTS. Fcp. 8vo. 2s. 6d.
—— THE TWO GREAT TEMPTATIONS. 2nd Edit. Fcp. 8vo. 3s. 6d.
—— ADDRESSES FOR YOUNG CLERGYMEN. Ext. fcp. 8vo. 4s. 6d.
—— "MY SON, GIVE ME THINE HEART." Ext. fcp. 8vo. 5s.
—— REST AWHILE. Addresses to Toilers in the Ministry. Ext. fcp. 8vo. 5s.
—— TEMPLE SERMONS. Cr. 8vo. 10s. 6d.
—— AUTHORISED OR REVISED? Sermons. Cr. 8vo. 7s. 6d.
—— LESSONS OF THE CROSS AND PASSION; WORDS FROM THE CROSS; THE REIGN OF SIN; THE LORD'S PRAYER. Four Courses of Lent Lectures. Cr. 8vo. 10s. 6d.
—— UNIVERSITY SERMONS, NEW AND OLD. Cr. 8vo. 10s. 6d.
—— THE PRAYERS OF JESUS CHRIST. Globe 8vo. 3s. 6d.
—— DONCASTER SERMONS; LESSONS OF LIFE AND GODLINESS; WORDS FROM THE GOSPELS. Cr. 8vo. 10s. 6d.
—— NOTES FOR LECTURES ON CONFIRMATION. 14th Edit. Fcp. 8vo. 1s. 6d.

VAUGHAN (Rev. D. J.).—THE PRESENT TRIAL OF FAITH. Cr. 8vo. 9s.

VAUGHAN (Rev. E. T.)—SOME REASONS OF OUR CHRISTIAN HOPE. Hulsean Lectures for 1875. Cr. 8vo. 6s. 6d.

VAUGHAN (Rev. Robert).—STONES FROM THE QUARRY. Sermons. Cr. 8vo. 5s.

VENN (Rev. John).—ON SOME CHARACTERISTICS OF BELIEF, SCIENTIFIC, AND RELIGIOUS. Hulsean Lectures, 1869. 8vo. 6s. 6d.

WARINGTON (G.).—THE WEEK OF CREATION. Cr. 8vo. 4s. 6d.

WELLDON (Rev. J. E. C.).—THE SPIRITUAL LIFE: and other Sermons. Cr. 8vo. 6s.

WESTCOTT (Rt. Rev. B. F., Bishop of Durham).—ON THE RELIGIOUS OFFICE OF THE UNIVERSITIES. Sermons. Cr. 8vo. 4s. 6d.
—— GIFTS FOR MINISTRY. Addresses to Candidates for Ordination. Cr. 8vo. 1s. 6d.
—— THE VICTORY OF THE CROSS. Sermons Preached in 1888. Cr. 8vo. 3s. 6d.
—— FROM STRENGTH TO STRENGTH. Three Sermons (In Memoriam J. B. D.). Cr. 8vo. 2s.
—— THE REVELATION OF THE RISEN LORD. 4th Edit. Cr. 8vo. 6s.
—— THE HISTORIC FAITH. Cr. 8vo. 6s.
—— THE GOSPEL OF THE RESURRECTION. 6th Edit. Cr. 8vo. 6s.
—— THE REVELATION OF THE FATHER. Cr. 8vo. 6s.
—— CHRISTUS CONSUMMATOR. Cr. 8vo. 6s.
—— SOME THOUGHTS FROM THE ORDINAL. Cr. 8vo. 1s. 6d.
—— SOCIAL ASPECTS OF CHRISTIANITY. Cr. 8vo. 6s.
—— THE GOSPEL OF LIFE. Cr. 8vo. 6s.
—— ESSAYS IN THE HISTORY OF RELIGIOUS THOUGHT IN THE WEST. Globe 8vo. 6s.

WICKHAM (Rev. E. C.).—WELLINGTON COLLEGE SERMONS. Cr. 8vo. 6s.

WILKINS (Prof. A. S.).—THE LIGHT OF THE WORLD: An Essay. 2nd Ed. Cr. 8vo. 3s. 6d.

WILSON (J. M., Archdeacon of Manchester). —SERMONS PREACHED IN CLIFTON COLLEGE CHAPEL. 2nd Series, 1888—90. Cr. 8vo. 6s.
—— ESSAYS AND ADDRESSES. Cr. 8vo. 4s. 6d.
—— SOME CONTRIBUTIONS TO THE RELIGIOUS THOUGHT OF OUR TIME. Cr. 8vo. 6s.

WOOD (Rev. E. G.).—THE REGAL POWER OF THE CHURCH. 8vo. 4s. 6d.

THERAPEUTICS. (See MEDICINE, p. 24.)

TRANSLATIONS.

From the Greek—From the Italian—From the Latin—Into Latin and Greek Verse.

From the Greek.

AESCHYLUS.—THE SUPPLICES. With Translation, by T. G. TUCKER, Litt.D. 8vo. 10s. 6d.
—— THE SEVEN AGAINST THEBES. With Translation, by A. W. VERRALL, Litt. D. 8vo. 7s. 6d.
—— EUMENIDES. With Verse Translation, by BERNARD DRAKE, M.A. 8vo. 5s.

ARATUS. (See PHYSIOGRAPHY, p. 29.)

ARISTOPHANES.—THE BIRDS. Trans. into English Verse, by B. H. KENNEDY. 8vo. 6s.

ARISTOTLE ON FALLACIES; OR, THE SOPHISTICI ELENCHI. With Translation, by E. POSTE M.A. 8vo. 8s. 6d.

ARISTOTLE.—THE FIRST BOOK OF THE METAPHYSICS OF ARISTOTLE. By a Cambridge Graduate. 8vo. 5s.
—— THE POLITICS. By J. E. C. WELLDON, M.A. 10s. 6d.
—— THE RHETORIC. By same. Cr. 8vo. 7s. 6d.
—— THE NICOMACHEAN ETHICS. By same. Cr. 8vo. 7s. 6d.
—— ON THE CONSTITUTION OF ATHENS. By E. POSTE. 2nd Edit. Cr. 8vo. 3s. 6d.

BION. (See THEOCRITUS.)

HERODOTUS.—THE HISTORY. By G. C. MACAULAY, M.A. 2 vols. Cr. 8vo. 18s.

HOMER.—THE ODYSSEY DONE INTO ENGLISH PROSE, by S. H. BUTCHER, M.A., and A. LANG, M.A. Cr. 8vo. 6s.
—— THE ODYSSEY. Books I.—XII. Transl. into English Verse by EARL OF CARNARVON. Cr. 8vo. 7s. 6d.
—— THE ILIAD DONE INTO ENGLISH PROSE, by ANDREW LANG, WALTER LEAF, and ERNEST MYERS. Cr. 8vo. 12s. 6d.

MELEAGER.—FIFTY POEMS. Translated into English Verse by WALTER HEADLAM. Fcp. 4to. 7s. 6d.

MOSCHUS. (See THEOCRITUS).

PINDAR.—THE EXTANT ODES. By ERNEST MYERS. Cr. 8vo. 5s.

PLATO.—TIMÆUS. With Translation, by R. D. ARCHER-HIND, M.A. 8vo. 16s. (See also GOLDEN TREASURY SERIES, p. 20.)

POLYBIUS.—THE HISTORIES. By E. S. SHUCKBURGH. Cr. 8vo. 24s.

SOPHOCLES.—ŒDIPUS THE KING. Translated into English Verse by E. D. A. MORSHEAD, M.A. Fcp. 8vo. 3s. 6d.

THEOCRITUS, BION, AND MOSCHUS. By A. LANG, M.A. 18mo. 2s. 6d. net.—Large Paper Edition. 8vo. 9s.

XENOPHON.—THE COMPLETE WORKS. By H. G. DAKYNS, M.A. Cr. 8vo.—Vols. I. and II. 10s. 6d. each.

From the Italian.

DANTE.—THE PURGATORY. With Transl. and Notes, by A. J. BUTLER. Cr. 8vo. 12s. 6d.
—— THE PARADISE. By the same. 2nd Edit. Cr. 8vo. 12s. 6d.
—— THE HELL. By the same. Cr. 8vo. 12s. 6d.
—— DE MONARCHIA. By F. J. CHURCH. 8vo. 4s. 6d.
—— THE DIVINE COMEDY. By C. E. NORTON. I. HELL. II. PURGATORY. III. PARADISE. Cr. 8vo. 6s. each.
—— NEW LIFE OF DANTE. Transl. by C. E. NORTON. 5s.
—— THE PURGATORY. Transl. by C. L. SHADWELL. Ext. cr. 8vo. 10s. net.

From the Latin.

CICERO.—THE LIFE AND LETTERS OF MARCUS TULLIUS CICERO. By the Rev. G. E. JEANS, M.A. 2nd Edit. Cr. 8vo. 10s. 6d.
—— THE ACADEMICS. By J. S. REID. 8vo. 5s. 6d.

HORACE: THE WORKS OF. By J. LONSDALE, M.A., and S. LEE, M.A. Gl. 8vo. 3s. 6d.
—— THE ODES IN A METRICAL PARAPHRASE. By R. M. HOVENDEN, B.A. Ext. fcp. 8vo. 4s. 6d.
—— LIFE AND CHARACTER AN EPITOME OF his Satires and Epistles. By R. M. HOVENDEN, B.A. Ext. fcp. 8vo. 4s. 6d.
—— WORD FOR WORD FROM HORACE: The Odes Literally Versified. By W. T. THORNTON, C.B. Cr. 8vo. 7s. 6d.

JUVENAL.—THIRTEEN SATIRES. By ALEX. LEEPER, LL.D. New Ed. Cr. 8vo. 3s. 6d.

TRANSLATIONS—continued.

LIVY.—Books XXI.—XXV. The Second Punic War. By A. J. Church, M.A., and W. J Brodribb, M.A. Cr. 8vo. 7s. 6d.

MARCUS AURELIUS ANTONINUS.—Book IV. of the Meditations. With Translation and Commentary, by H. Crossley, M.A. 8vo. 6s.

SALLUST.—The Conspiracy of Catiline and the Jugurthine War. By A. W. Pollard. Cr. 8vo. 6s.—Catiline. 3s.

TACITUS, The Works of. By A. J. Church, M.A., and W. J. Brodribb, M.A. The History. 4th Edit. Cr. 8vo. 6s. The Agricola and Germania. With the Dialogue on Oratory. Cr. 8vo. 4s. 6d. The Annals. 5th Edit. Cr. 8vo. 7s. 6d.

VIRGIL: The Works of. By J. Lonsdale, M.A., and S. Lee, M.A. Globe 8vo. 3s. 6d.—The Æneid. By J. W. Mackail, M.A. Cr. 8vo. 7s. 6d.

Into Latin and Greek Verse.

CHURCH (Rev. A. J.).—Latin Version of Selections from Tennyson. By Prof. Conington, Prof. Seeley, Dr. Hessey, T. E. Kebbel, &c. Edited by A. J. Church, M.A. Ext. fcp. 8vo. 6s.

GEDDES (Prof. W. D.).—Flosculi Graeci Boreales. Cr. 8vo. 6s.

KYNASTON (Herbert D.D.).—Exemplaria Cheltoniensia. Ext. fcp. 8vo. 5s.

VOYAGES AND TRAVELS.

(See also History, p. 10; Sport, p. 32.)

APPLETON (T. G.).—A Nile Journal. Illustrated by Eugene Benson. Cr. 8vo. 6s.

"BACCHANTE." The Cruise of H.M.S. "Bacchante," 1879—1882. Compiled from the Private Journals, Letters and Note-books of Prince Albert Victor and Prince George of Wales. By the Rev. Canon Dalton. 2 vols. Med. 8vo. 52s. 6d.

BAKER (Sir Samuel W.).—Ismailia. A Narrative of the Expedition to Central Africa for the Suppression of the Slave Trade, organised by Ismail, Khedive of Egypt. Cr. 8vo. 6s.—The Nile Tributaries of Abyssinia, and the Sword Hunters of the Hamran Arabs. Cr. 8vo. 6s.—The Albert N'yanza Great Basin of the Nile and Exploration of the Nile Sources. Cr. 8vo. 6s.—Cyprus as I saw it in 1879. 8vo. 12s. 6d.

BARKER (Lady).—A Year's Housekeeping in South Africa. Illustr. Cr. 8vo. 3s. 6d.—Station Life in New Zealand. Cr. 8vo. 3s. 6d.—Letters to Guy. Cr. 8vo. 5s.

BOUGHTON (G. H.) and ABBEY (E. A.).—Sketching Rambles in Holland. With Illustrations. Fcp. 4to. 21s.

BRYCE (James, M.P.).—Transcaucasia and Ararat. 3rd Edit. Cr. 8vo. 9s.

CAMERON (V. L.).—Our Future Highway to India. 2 vols. Cr. 8vo. 21s.

CAMPBELL (J. F.).—My Circular Notes. Cr. 8vo. 6s.

CARLES(W. R.).—Life in Corea. 8vo. 12s. 6d.

CAUCASUS: Notes on the. By "Wanderer." 8vo. 9s.

CRAIK (Mrs.).—An Unknown Country. Illustr. by F. Noel Paton. Roy. 8vo. 12s. 6d.—An Unsentimental Journey through Cornwall. Illustrated. 4to. 12s. 6d.

DILKE (Sir Charles). (See pp. 25, 11.)

DUFF (Right Hon. Sir M. E. Grant).—Notes of an Indian Journey. 8vo. 10s. 6d

FORBES (Archibald).—Souvenirs of some Continents. Cr. 8vo. 6s.—Barracks, Bivouacs, and Battles. Cr. 8vo. 7s. 6d

FULLERTON (W. M.).—In Cairo. Fcp. 8vo. 3s. 6d.

GONE TO TEXAS: Letters from our Boys. Ed. by Thos. Hughes. Cr. 8vo. 4s. 6d.

GORDON (Lady Duff).—Last Letters from Egypt, to which are added Letters from the Cape. 2nd Edit. Cr. 8vo. 9s.

GREEN (W. S.).—Among the Selkirk Glaciers. Cr. 8vo. 7s. 6d.

HOOKER (Sir Joseph D.) and BALL (J.).—Journal of a Tour in Marocco and the Great Atlas. 8vo. 21s.

HÜBNER (Baron von).—A Ramble Round the World. Cr. 8vo. 6s.

HUGHES (Thos.).—Rugby, Tennessee. Cr. 8vo. 4s. 6d.

KALM.—Account of his Visit to England. Trans. by J. Lucas. Illus. 8vo. 12s. net.

KINGSLEY (Charles).—At Last: A Christmas in the West Indies. Cr. 8vo. 3s. 6d.

KINGSLEY (Henry).—Tales of Old Travel. Cr. 8vo. 3s. 6d.

KIPLING (J. L.).—Beast and Man in India. Illustrated. Ext. cr. 8vo. 7s. 6d.

MACMILLAN (Rev. Hugh).—Holidays on High Lands. Globe 8vo. 6s.

MAHAFFY (Prof. J. P.).—Rambles and Studies in Greece. Illust. Cr. 8vo. 10s. 6d.

MAHAFFY (Prof. J. P.) and ROGERS (J. E.).—Sketches from a Tour through Holland and Germany. Illustrated by J. E. Rogers. Ext. cr. 8vo. 10s. 6d.

MURRAY (E. C. Grenville).—Round about France. Cr. 8vo. 7s. 6d.

NORDENSKIÖLD.—Voyage of the "Vega" round Asia and Europe. By Baron A. E. Von Nordenskiöld. Trans. by Alex. Leslie. 400 Illustrations, Maps, etc. 2 vols. 8vo. 45s.—Popular Edit. Cr. 8vo. 6s.

OLIPHANT (Mrs.). (See History, p. 11.)

OLIVER (Capt. S. P.).—Madagascar: An Historical and Descriptive Account of the Island. 2 vols. Med. 8vo. 52s. 6d.

PALGRAVE (W. Gifford).—A Narrative of a Year's Journey through Central and Eastern Arabia, 1862-63. Cr. 8vo. 6s.—Dutch Guiana. 8vo. 9s.—Ulysses; or, Scenes and Studies in many Lands. 8vo. 12s. 6d.

PERSIA, EASTERN. An Account of the Journeys of the Persian Boundary Commission, 1870-71-72. 2 vols. 8vo. 42s.

PIKE (W.)—The Barren Ground of Northern Canada. 8vo. 10s. 6d.

ST. JOHNSTON (A.).—Camping among Cannibals. Cr. 8vo. 4s. 6d.

SANDYS (J. E.).—An Easter Vacation in Greece. Cr. 8vo. 3s. 6d.

SMITH (G.)—A Trip to England. 18mo. 3s.

STRANGFORD (Viscountess).—Egyptian Sepulchres and Syrian Shrines. New Edition. Cr. 8vo. 7s. 6d.

TAVERNIER (Baron): Travels in India of Jean Baptiste Tavernier. Transl. by V. Ball, LL.D. 2 vols. 8vo. 42s.

TRISTRAM. (See Illustrated Books.)

TURNER (Rev. G.). (See Anthropology.)

WALLACE (A. R.). (See Natural History.)

WATERTON (Charles).—Wanderings in South America, the North-West of the United States, and the Antilles. Edited by Rev. J. G. Wood. Illustr. Cr. 8vo. 6s.—People's Edition. 4to. 6d.

WATSON (R. Spence).—A Visit to Wazan, the Sacred City of Morocco. 8vo. 10s.6d.

YOUNG, Books for the.

(See also Biblical History, p. 32.)

ÆSOP—CALDECOTT.—Some of Æsop's Fables, with Modern Instances, shown in Designs by Randolph Caldecott. 4to. 5s.

ARIOSTO.—Paladin and Saracen. Stories from Ariosto. By H. C. Hollway-Cal-throp. Illustrated. Cr. 8vo. 6s.

ATKINSON (Rev. J. C.).—The Last of the Giant Killers. Globe 8vo. 3s. 6d.
—— Walks, Talks, Travels, and Exploits of two Schoolboys. Cr. 8vo. 3s. 6d.
—— Playhours and Half-Holidays, or Further Experiences of two School-boys. Cr. 8vo. 3s. 6d.
—— Scenes in Fairyland. Cr. 8vo. 4s. 6d.

AWDRY (Frances).—The Story of a Fellow Soldier. (A Life of Bishop Patteson for the Young.) Globe 8vo. 2s. 6d.

BAKER (Sir S. W.).—True Tales for my Grandsons. Illustrated. Cr. 8vo. 3s. 6d.
—— Cast up by the Sea : or, The Adventures of Ned Gray. Illus Cr. 8vo. 6s.

BUMBLEBEE BOGO'S BUDGET. By a Retired Judge. Illust Cr. 8vo. 2s. 6d.

CARROLL (Lewis).—Alice's Adventures in Wonderland. With 42 Illustrations by Tenniel. Cr. 8vo. 6s. net.
People's Edition. With all the original Illustrations. Cr. 8vo. 2s. 6d. net.
A German Translation of the same. Cr. 8vo. 6s. net. -A French Translation of the same. Cr. 8vo. 6s. net. An Italian Translation of the same. Cr. 8vo. 6s. net.
—— Alice's Adventures Under-ground. Being a Fascimile of the Original MS. Book, afterwards developed into "Alice's Adventures in Wonderland." With 27 Illustrations by the Author. Cr. 8vo. 4s net.

CARROLL (Lewis).—Through the Looking-Glass and what Alice Found There. With 50 Illustrations by Tenniel. Cr. 8vo. 6s. net.
People's Edition. With all the original Illustrations. Cr. 8vo. 2s. 6d. net.
People's Edition of "Alice's Adventures in Wonderland," and "Through the Looking-Glass." 1 vol. Cr. 8vo. 4s. 6d. net.
—— Rhyme and Reason? With 65 Illustrations by Arthur B. Frost, and 9 by Henry Holiday. Cr. 8vo. 6s. net.
—— A Tangled Tale. With 6 Illustrations by Arthur B. Frost. Cr. 8vo. 4s. 6d. net.
—— Sylvie and Bruno. With 46 Illustrations by Harry Furniss. Cr. 8vo. 7s.6d. net.
—— The Nursery "Alice." Twenty Coloured Enlargements from Tenniel's Illustrations to "Alice's Adventures in Wonderland," with Text adapted to Nursery Readers. 4to. 4s. net.—People's Edition. 4to. 2s. net.
—— The Hunting of the Snark, An Agony in Eight Fits. With 9 Illustrations by Henry Holiday. Cr. 8vo. 4s. 6d. net.

CLIFFORD (Mrs.W.K.).—Anyhow Stories. With Illustrations by Dorothy Tennant Cr. 8vo. 1s. 6d. ; paper covers, 1s.

CORBETT (Julian).—For God and Gold. Cr. 8vo. 6s.

CRAIK (Mrs.).—Alice Learmont : A Fairy Tale. Illustrated. Globe 8vo. 4s. 6d.
—— The Adventures of a Brownie. Illustrated by Mrs. Allingham. Gl. 8vo. 4s. 6d.
—— The Little Lame Prince and his Travelling Cloak. Illustrated by J. McL. Ralston. Cr. 8vo. 4s. 6d.
—— Our Year : A Child's Book in Prose and Verse. Illustrated. Gl. 8vo. 2s. 6d.
—— Little Sunshine's Holiday. Globe 8vo. 2s. 6d.
—— The Fairy Book : The Best Popular Fairy Stories. 18mo. 2s. 6d. net.
—— Children's Poetry. Ex. fcp. 8vo. 4s. 6d.
—— Songs of our Youth. Small 4to. 6s.

DE MORGAN (Mary).—The Necklace of Princess Fiorimonde, and other Stories. Illustrated by Walter Crane. Ext. fcp. 8vo. 3s. 6d.—Large Paper Ed., with Illustrations on India Paper. 100 copies printed.

FOWLER (W. W.). (See Natural History.)

GREENWOOD (Jessy E.).—The Moon Maiden : and other Stories. Cr. 8vo. 3s. 6d.

GRIMM'S FAIRY TALES. Translated by Lucy Crane, and Illustrated by Walter Crane. Cr. 8vo. 6s.

KEARY (A. and E.).—The Heroes of Asgard. Tales from Scandinavian Mythology. Globe 8vo. 2s. 6d.

KEARY (E.).—The Magic Valley. Illustr. by "E.V.B." Globe 8vo. 4s. 6d.

KINGSLEY (Charles).—The Heroes ; or, Greek Fairy Tales for my Children. Cr. 8vo. 3s. 6d.—Presentation Ed., gilt edges. 7s.6d.
Madam How and Lady Why ; or, First Lessons in Earth-Lore. Cr. 8vo. 3s. 6d.
The Water-Babies : A Fairy Tale for a Land Baby. Cr. 8vo. 3s. 6d.—New Edit. Illus. by L. Sambourne. Fcp. 4to. 12s. 6d.

BOOKS FOR THE YOUNG—*continued.*

MACLAREN (Arch.).—THE FAIRY FAMILY. A Series of Ballads and Metrical Tales. Cr. 8vo. 5s.

MACMILLAN (Hugh). (*See* p. 37.)

MADAME TABBY'S ESTABLISHMENT. By KARI. Illust. by L. WAIN. Cr. 8vo. 4s. 6d.

MAGUIRE (J. F.).—YOUNG PRINCE MARIGOLD. Illustrated. Globe 8vo. 4s. 6d.

MARTIN (Frances).—THE POET'S HOUR. Poetry selected for Children. 18mo. 2s. 6d.
—— SPRING-TIME WITH THE POETS. 18mo. 3s. 6d.

MAZINI (Linda).—IN THE GOLDEN SHELL. With Illustrations. Globe 8vo. 4s. 6d.

MOLESWORTH (Mrs.).—WORKS. Illust. by WALTER CRANE. Globe 8vo. 2s. 6d. each.
"CARROTS," JUST A LITTLE BOY.
A CHRISTMAS CHILD.
CHRISTMAS-TREE LAND.
THE CUCKOO CLOCK.
FOUR WINDS FARM.
GRANDMOTHER DEAR.
HERR BABY.
LITTLE MISS PEGGY.
THE RECTORY CHILDREN.
ROSY.
THE TAPESTRY ROOM.
TELL ME A STORY.
TWO LITTLE WAIFS.
"US": An Old-Fashioned Story.
CHILDREN OF THE CASTLE.
—— A CHRISTMAS POSY. Illustrated by WALTER CRANE. Cr. 8vo. 4s. 6d.
—— SUMMER STORIES. Cr. 8vo. 4s. 6d.
—— FOUR GHOST STORIES. Cr. 8vo. 6s.
—— NURSE HEATHERDALE'S STORY. Illust. by LESLIE BROOKE. Cr. 8vo. 4s. 6d.
—— THE GIRLS AND I. Illust. by L. BROOKE. Cr. 8vo. 4s. 6d.

"MRS. JERNINGHAM'S JOURNAL" (Author of).—THE RUNAWAY. Gl. 8vo. 2s. 6d.

OLIPHANT (Mrs.). — AGNES HOPETOUN'S SCHOOLS AND HOLIDAYS. Illust. Gl. 8vo. 2s. 6d.

PALGRAVE (Francis Turner).—THE FIVE DAYS' ENTERTAINMENTS AT WENTWORTH GRANGE. Small 4to. 6s.
—— THE CHILDREN'S TREASURY OF LYRICAL POETRY. 18mo. 2s. 6d.—Or in 2 parts, 1s. each.

PATMORE (C.).—THE CHILDREN'S GARLAND FROM THE BEST POETS. 18mo. 2s. 6d. net.

ROSSETTI (Christina). — SPEAKING LIKENESSES. Illust. by A. HUGHES. Cr. 8vo. 4s. 6d.

RUTH AND HER FRIENDS: A STORY FOR GIRLS. Illustrated. Globe 8vo. 2s. 6d.

ST. JOHNSTON (A.). — CAMPING AMONG CANNIBALS. Cr. 8vo. 4s. 6d.
—— CHARLIE ASGARDE: THE STORY OF A FRIENDSHIP. Illustrated by HUGH THOMSON. Cr. 8vo. 6s.

"ST. OLAVE'S" (Author of). Illustrated. Globe 8vo.
WHEN I WAS A LITTLE GIRL. 2s. 6d.
NINE YEARS OLD. 2s. 6d.
WHEN PAPA COMES HOME. 4s. 6d.
PANSIE'S FLOUR BIN. 4s. 6d.

STEWART (Aubrey).—THE TALE OF TROY. Done into English. Globe 8vo. 2s. 6d.

TENNYSON (Hon. Hallam).—JACK AND THE BEAN-STALK. English Hexameters. Illust. by R. CALDECOTT. Fcp. 4to. 3s. 6d.

"WANDERING WILLIE" (Author of).— CONRAD THE SQUIRREL. Globe 8vo. 2s. 6d.

WARD (Mrs. T. Humphry).—MILLY AND OLLY With Illustrations by Mrs. ALMA TADEMA. Globe 8vo. 2s. 6d.

WEBSTER (Augusta).—DAFFODIL AND THE CROÄXAXICANS. Cr. 8vo. 6s.

WILLOUGHBY (F.).—FAIRY GUARDIANS. Illustr. by TOWNLEY GREEN. Cr. 8vo. 5s.

WOODS (M. A.). (*See* COLLECTIONS, p. 17.)

YONGE (Charlotte M.).—THE PRINCE AND THE PAGE. Cr. 8vo. 2s. 6d.
—— A BOOK OF GOLDEN DEEDS. 18mo. 2s. 6d. net. Globe 8vo. 2s.—*Abridged Edition.* 1s.
—— LANCES OF LYNWOOD. Cr. 8vo. 2s. 6d.
—— P'S AND Q'S; and LITTLE LUCY'S WONDERFUL GLOBE. Illustrated. Cr. 8vo. 3s. 6d.
—— A STOREHOUSE OF STORIES. 2 vols. Globe 8vo. 2s. 6d. each.
—— THE POPULATION OF AN OLD PEAR TREE; or, Stories of Insect Life. From E. VAN BRUYSSEL. Illustr. Gl. 8vo. 2s. 6d.

ZOOLOGY.

Comparative Anatomy—Practical Zoology—Entomology—Ornithology.

(*See also* BIOLOGY; NATURAL HISTORY; PHYSIOLOGY.)

Comparative Anatomy.

FLOWER (Prof. W. H.).—AN INTRODUCTION TO THE OSTEOLOGY OF THE MAMMALIA. Illustrated. 3rd Edit., revised with the assistance of HANS GADOW, Ph.D. Cr. 8vo. 10s. 6d.

HUMPHRY (Prof. Sir G. M.).—OBSERVATIONS IN MYOLOGY. 8vo. 6s.

LANG (Prof. Arnold).—TEXT-BOOK OF COMPARATIVE ANATOMY. Transl. by H. M. and M. BERNARD. Preface by Prof. E. HAECKEL. Illustr. 2 vols. 8vo. Part I. 17s. net.

PARKER (T. Jeffery).—A COURSE OF INSTRUCTION IN ZOOTOMY (VERTEBRATA). Illustrated. Cr. 8vo. 8s 6d.

PETTIGREW (J. Bell).—THE PHYSIOLOGY OF THE CIRCULATION OF PLANTS, IN THE LOWER ANIMALS, AND IN MAN. 8vo. 12s.

SHUFELDT (R. W.).—THE MYOLOGY OF THE RAVEN (*Corvus corax Sinuatus*). A Guide to the Study of the Muscular System in Birds. Illustrated. 8vo. 13s. net.

WIEDERSHEIM (Prof. R.).—ELEMENTS OF THE COMPARATIVE ANATOMY OF VERTEBRATES. Adapted by W. NEWTON PARKER. With Additions. Illustrated. 8vo. 12s. 6d.

Practical Zoology.

HOWES (Prof. G. B.).—AN ATLAS OF PRACTICAL ELEMENTARY BIOLOGY. With a Preface by Prof. HUXLEY. 4to. 14s.

HUXLEY (T. H.) and MARTIN (H. N.).—A COURSE OF PRACTICAL INSTRUCTION IN ELEMENTARY BIOLOGY. Revised and extended by Prof. G. B. HOWES and D. H. SCOTT, Ph.D. Cr. 8vo. 10s. 6d.

THOMSON (Sir C. Wyville).—THE VOYAGE OF THE "CHALLENGER": THE ATLANTIC. With Illustrations, Coloured Maps, Charts, etc. 2 vols. 8vo. 45s.

THOMSON (Sir C. Wyville).—THE DEPTHS OF THE SEA. An Account of the Results of the Dredging Cruises of H.M.SS. "Lightning" and "Porcupine," 1868-69-70. With Illustrations, Maps, and Plans. 8vo. 31s. 6d.

Entomology.

BUCKTON (G. B.).—MONOGRAPH OF THE BRITISH CICADÆ, OR TETTIGIDÆ. 2 vols. 33s. 6d. each net; or in 8 Parts. 8s. each net.

LUBBOCK (Sir John).—THE ORIGIN AND METAMORPHOSES OF INSECTS. Illustrated. Cr. 8vo. 3s. 6d.

SCUDDER (S. H.).—FOSSIL INSECTS OF NORTH AMERICA. Map and Plates. 2 vols. 4to. 90s. net.

Ornithology.

COUES (Elliott).—KEY TO NORTH AMERICAN BIRDS. Illustrated. 8vo. 2l. 2s.

—— HANDBOOK OF FIELD AND GENERAL ORNITHOLOGY. Illustrated. 8vo. 10s. net.

FOWLER (W. W.). (See NATURAL HISTORY.)

WHITE (Gilbert). (See NATURAL HISTORY.)

INDEX.

MACMILLAN AND CO., LONDON.

J. PALMER, PRINTER, ALEXANDRA STREET, CAMBRIDGE.

B 75/1/93